One Last Waltz

by

Peter Scholes

Dedicated to Jessica

I hope I am lucky enough to remember all the good memories we have made together when I'm older and wiser.

For Dora and Leonard. RIP

CONTENTS

Prologue

"And when you're dancing and laughing and finally living, hear my voice in your head and think of me kindly."

The Smiths, Rubber Ring, 1986.

Prologue

When God comes calling

Frank could be a tactless so-and-so, but he did make me giggle.

He always had that cheeky grin on his face – always up to mischief, and usually at the expense of someone else.

In this case it was poor old Alfie. But Alfie was in no position to retaliate.

"Another one for the meat wagon!" Frank chortled as the men in black suits wheeled the trolley by. "Can I have his dressing gown and slippers, Ang?"

The 'meat wagon' as Frank called it, was a rather crude name for the hearse.

Sadly, Alfie had been our fourth that month. He followed Lillian, Enid and Helena.

We all knew it was coming. He was ninety-seven years old and looked a lot older.

How he had managed to survive for so long was a miracle in itself. He smoked and he drank. He gambled and he womanised. He was rude, cantankerous and obnoxious. He didn't seem to have any friends, and his family had long since deserted him when they realised there were so many better things to do than be verbally abused for an hour or two on a Sunday.

"He won't be much of a loss", Frank chipped in again.

"The miserable bugger was a right mood hoover. A fun sponge! Having a conversation with him was like socialising with the Grim Reaper."

Again, I scalded him for his insensitivity, but this only encouraged him to carry on, even when the undertakers moved the coffin along the corridor, past the conservatory and towards the front door.

"If I ever get like that, you have my permission to put a bullet in my head."

I told him it would be my pleasure and to keep his voice down.

"I bet there won't be anyone there at the crematorium either", he went on. "He had four wives, six children, a few grandchildren and even a great grandchild. After a few weeks in here, not one of them bothered to visit again. He was about as popular with his own family as he was with us. But it didn't seem to bother him. Not a jot!"

Frank's rantings had attracted an audience. Three or four of the other residents turned in their chairs to face him, and Doreen appeared at the door on her Zimmer frame.

"He was a devil with the ladies by all accounts. Look at me, Ang. I was a handsome man in my day. I had my fair share of admirers I can tell you, but I was always the gentleman."

I looked at him with mock shock. He just winked back at me.

"Alfie had a face like a bulldog sucking on a lemon. Fat as butter too. I don't know what he had, but it wasn't looks or money that's for sure."

A couple of the old ladies gave a knowing chuckle and let Frank rant on.

"Still, his welcome departure has freed up a room and a chair at the dining table. And the smell of tobacco and sweat won't be as bad now - especially in the summer months. Check his room for my liquorice toffees, Ang. I am sure it was him who nicked them from me last week. I wouldn't care, he didn't even have any teeth!"

I stood up to go. He didn't need any more encouragement. I was nearly at the end of my shift and I didn't want to get into a tit-for-tat argument with Frank. I told him to behave himself and walked away, waving to the residents as I made my way to the staff room near the exit door.

"Before you go, love, check for those toffees!" Frank laughed.

I looked back and gave him another disapproving look.

He was a character old Frank. I really liked him.

Anyway, it wasn't Alfie who had pinched his liquorice toffees – it was me. I bloody love them.

1

A Home from Home

We have forty-eight residents currently residing at The Acorns. We are a residential home for the elderly. A care home. A convalescent facility. A retirement hospital. Assisted living or rest home. An old folk's home.

There are other names for us too. God's waiting room or Hearse House to name but two. Whatever people choose to call us, we know that we are likely to be the last place our residents will ever call home before they expire. For most, this finality is met with resignation or humour, not depression or sadness. They can't change what's to come. Life comes and life goes.

Some consider old age a blessing. They have lived. They have survived what life has thrown at them. Their wrinkles and failing senses prove that. Yes, life has aged them, but it hasn't beaten them. When the Grim Reaper finally does come a calling, they can look him in the eye and tell him they have had their time.

No dying young for our residents. No life cut short through accidental tragedy or illness.

Time. The only thing to overtake them – to smother them – is time.

"If death didn't exist, some bugger would invent it!" Frank once said to me.

Despite the constant conveyor belt of coffins and funeral directors, The Acorns was a happy and fun place to work. We appreciated time.

We cherished it. We knew how important it was, and as a result, we did what we could to create a loving, caring and jovial atmosphere in the home – despite Frank.

The Acorns is located just outside the small market town of Brampton in the north east of Cumbria. A beautiful double-fronted stone-built mansion house dating back to the 1800s. It offers spacious accommodation over three principal floors and a private garden to the rear. At full capacity, we can accommodate sixty-three people.

All the catering is delivered in-house by our very own chef, Neil Tweddle. Neil has worked at the home for almost twenty years, and is nearly as old as some of the paying customers. His reputation for delicious home-cooked fayre is legendary, and this is a huge bonus for The Acorns when trying to compete for custom up against some of the more 'affordable' competitors.

This is just one of the many reasons the facility has such a great reputation, and a waiting list as long as your arm.

The home is fully equipped with all modern amenities to help cater for the needs of its residents, but we offer so much more to make the day-to-day experience fulfilling and enjoyable. We have an allotment for our green-fingered fans, a pet corner for the animal lovers, a TV and music room, and even a hot tub adjoining our spacious conservatory leading out into the gardens.

We have regular visitors and guests to entertain. A magician comes along on the last Friday of the month. We have bingo and art classes, singers and acts, and even a karaoke night each month. You are never too old to step up to the mic!

If I am sounding like a saleswoman reading the page of a brochure, I apologise. I am just so incredibly proud of this place, the people in it, and the service we provide.

It isn't cheap. None of these homes are. Any long-term guests will soon see their hard-earned savings disappear in a matter of months. The families - often begrudgingly - help out where they can, but more often than not, the taxpayer ends up footing the extortionate bill.

Little of the money filters down for staff wages. Many of us remain on, or just above, minimum wage. It is a vocation not a career and yet, here we are – here I am – sixteen years after first stepping through that door.
Back then, I was so wet behind the ears. A seventeen-year-old with no qualifications who didn't know an arsehole from an ear hole, and yet I've loved every second of it – even back then.

And yes, here I am now. One of the more experienced ones. A Senior Health Care Worker. For senior, read older. The wages still aren't great, but you can live off them. Just.

I am still waiting for the right man to come and sweep me off my feet, but I am hardly likely to find him at work, as I spend so much time here. I am sure he will come along when the time is right. What does fate have in store for me? Que sera sera, whatever will be will be.

As with the residents, The Acorns has been a second home to me all these years. I only live down the road in Brampton with my parents, but I spend more time here than there. For such a low paid job, the staff turnover is surprisingly low. We have a great team who really love the work along with the people we care for. We have four cleaners, a site manager, two junior health care workers, five established health care workers (of which I am one), two students on placement, two supervisors and three managers who rotate shifts to ensure a senior member of staff is always on site at any time of day.

We call upon agency staff from time to time but the core remains constant. We know all the residents and their families and they know us. We love them and they love us – most of the time.

Thankfully, we rarely see the leaders of this trust. This is our home, not theirs.

And yet, in the summer of 2022, we took a huge gamble. We nearly jeopardised it all.

But it was worth it. God knows it was worth it.

2

She Sells Her Spells Not on the Sea Shore

A re-run of Dallas from 1986 was on the television, but nobody was really watching it. People were more interested in watching Edith put on her tights.

Edith was eighty-seven years old, arthritic in almost every limb and about as agile and flexible as the concrete animal statues in each corner of the garden. Despite her ailments and disabilities, she was incredibly headstrong, and always refused help unless it was a last resort. Something as simple as putting on a pair of tights was a monumental task for Edith, and yet it was never one that phased her.

She had a knack you see. She would position the garment on the end of her walking stick and carefully place it on the end of one of her big toes. With a litter picker in her other hand, she would then proceed to pull the tight – is that the right term for one half of the pair? – over the rest of her gnarled foot. She would refuse any offer of help at any stage. If it took her half an hour, she would persist. Determined to the last. She wouldn't be beaten.
Sometimes it would slip on without fuss, other times it would hang limply off her toe, refusing to go on. She would stare at it like one would stare down at a puppy who had just cocked its leg up on your handbag or ripped up your slippers.

The rest of us would look on, waiting for her next move. J.R and Bobby Ewing would be arguing in silence on the television screen as Edith again reached for her litter picker and the reluctant pair of tights. The toes were a challenge, but the heel was the real trouble maker. It was like trying to guide a stick around a u-bend. It just didn't want to go, but this was a battle of wills and Edith had years of experience. The tights had no chance.

The tension in the room would build and build as she neared the knee. By the time she had them on and collapsed back into her chair only to see a silent Sue Ellen storm out of an office on screen, the room was in raptures. We would clap and cheer as she tossed the litter picker across the room in mock anger.

"The fuckers won't beat me!" she would call out and we would howl with laughter.

Within minutes of the fight, she would be fast asleep - wrinkled nylon just about covering each frail and skinny leg.

The TV was often on, but it was more of a distraction than a tool to entertain. These hardened souls were from a generation before the box. It would capture their attention from time to time if there was a good film on or something about the war, but it was by no means a necessity. Most of them wouldn't have noticed if it wasn't even there!

They were just so good at creating their own entertainment. They could converse and communicate without the need to reach out for a metaphorical crutch. A real crutch maybe, but not a metaphorical one.

I could be sitting drinking a cup of tea in the Sunshine Room when all of a sudden one of them would burst into song. It didn't ever seem to shock the others when it happened. More often than not, they would all join in!

And then the room would fall silent again like it had never happened. I would chuckle, and they would all turn to look at me as if I was going bonkers!

They made me feel like a child a lot of the time. At thirty-three years old I was hardly a juvenile, but in their eyes I was merely a young slip of a girl with no idea of the real world.

I played along, but in many ways they were right. I had grown up in Brampton, and lived there all my life. My parents were from Brampton and their parents too. Most of my family lived within twenty miles of the town and, aside from an occasional holiday on the Costa-Del-Crime, I was very much a home bird.

Don't get me wrong, I had plans to travel. I had plans to live. I just hadn't gotten around to it. The more I talked to them all, the more I wanted to.

"What's stopping you then, lass?" Frank would mock.

"Money. Time. Someone to go with," I'd whine.

"Nonsense. If you wanted it badly enough, you would do it!" he continued.

He was right too. I was the block. It was me making up excuse after excuse. I needed to start living a little.

"When I was your age I had travelled halfway around the world for King and Country!" he would say.

Betty would jump to my defence.

"When you were her age, you also had a wife and three kids. You only went abroad because you were in the Navy and you had to. If it hadn't been for HMS Sodoff you would have been stuck in a terraced house knee deep in nappies, so don't give that poor lass such grief."

She would turn to me and smile. So would Frank. He was only teasing, but he was right.

"You never mention the war, Frank!" I would respond. "Do tell us one day."

"Bugger off!" He would laugh, and Betty would too.

The inappropriately named 'Sunshine Room' was one of the lounge areas filled with comfy chairs of all shapes and sizes. Everyone seemed to have their favourite and slunk into them at various times of the day. The room was on the south side of the building and the windows overlooked two tall weeping willow trees which blocked out what little light there was. There was a log fire in the room and numerous heaters to ensure the place was always toasty and warm.

The Keith Chegwin Lounge (don't ask!) was a more spacious, well-lit area near the conservatory. This room was more popular in the summer months.

"It could freeze the bollocks off a statue in there!" Frank would say when asked why more people didn't use the room in the winter.

We would keep it clean and tidy should anyone wish to use it, but it was the Sunshine Room that drew the crowds when it was cold out. There would always be a presence in there, but it was the evenings, after tea, when it would really fill up. As a staff, we would take turns sitting in with them. And what a laugh it could be. Even when they were arguing they would make me laugh. They could be so cutting with their comments, and yet nobody ever took it to heart. It was never nasty.
It was as though they knew at the back of their minds that it didn't really matter. There was no time for tension, for stress, for nastiness or grudges. Time was precious. Time mattered. People mattered.

I could - and often did - listen to them talk all night or at least until the last one dozed off in their chair mid conversation. There were no taboo subjects either, and everyone and everything was fair game.

I could be bowled over by their knowledge and then tickled by their innocence in the next breath.

Wednesday evenings were particularly popular. Sally visited on a Wednesday. She was a volunteer from a local charity. In a previous life she had been a primary school teacher, but had become disillusioned by the profession like so many others, and left school to work on a supermarket checkout.

I am not sure what she was like at packing groceries, but she was wasted as a till girl. I could imagine her being a fabulous teacher. She had such a soothing, calming voice and made everyone feel so special in her company. She would stay for two or three hours, working the crowd and lighting up the room with her smile and infectious laugh. And if that wasn't enough, she had another quite extraordinary talent. She could tell a story.

Each week she would arrive with a big, cardboard box. She wouldn't tell the staff what she had brought along with her. It was just as much a surprise for us as it was for the residents. The contents would be based on conversations from the previous week. She would always focus on one individual. That night would be their night. She would have a story just for them. Personal to them. This didn't mean the rest of us were excluded – far from it – but she would have someone in mind and the rest of us would listen excitedly.

This one occasion was for Agnes.

Agnes was one of the oldest residents at ninety-three years old and she was really starting to wane. She was a quiet lady and rarely joined in the conversations instead preferring to listen.

The previous week I noticed Sally was talking with her, holding her hand.

Agnes' senses were fading. She wore hearing aids in both ears and her sight was all but lost.

Sally placed the box in the corner of the room near the bookshelves and set about mingling. She made sure she had spent some time with everyone before retrieving her box and kneeling in front of Agnes.

We all knew this was the cue for one of her stories, and a hush descended over the room as people shuffled in their chairs to get a clear view.

Sally reached up and held on to her hands to reassure her.

"Can you remember when we talked last week, Agnes?" she said, smiling and looking up into the eyes of the oldest of old women in the room. Agnes nodded and smiled down at her. It was lovely to see them like this.

"My story is for you tonight. Just for you."

Sally retrieved the box and placed it on the floor in front of her. Everyone watched on in silence, straining to see what was inside.

She began.

"It was a fine day as the train rattled along at its own pace. It stopped at every village, didn't it? No rush though. It was all part of the fun. Mum had the sandwiches, and dad held the flask. They sat opposite each other on the table of four leaving the two window seats for their young girls. The first sight of the coast was a magical one. The blue sea stretched out into the distance – as far as you could see – and the bright, hazy sunshine overhead illuminated the towns and beaches. It was like a hundred picture postcards rolled into one, and everybody soaked in the views and enjoyed every second. And then, finally, the train slowed one last time. It had reached its destination."

Sally looked up again at Agnes. She had broken into the biggest of smiles. "Tenby," she whispered.

Sally held her hand again and squeezed a little.

"Tenby," she said.

The rest of us had no idea what this meant, but we were all transfixed. It clearly meant a lot to Agnes.

Sally continued.

"The Bed and Breakfast wasn't great, was it? Dad wasn't happy, was he? He complained to the landlady and moved you all to something a little more suitable. He wasn't for paying, was he? They weren't very happy either, were they? But he wasn't bothered. Nothing but the best for his three girls. You found somewhere though, didn't you?"

Agnes nodded.

Sally reached into the box and handed something to her. It was too small and too far away for us to see what it was, but Agnes knew straight away and she beamed again.

"The Mermaid!" she said, softly. "What a lovely place it was. So close to the beach. Just perfect. We were so lucky."

She held onto the little object in her hand. I could just make out the tail.

"And what a wonderful week you had didn't you? The best."

As Sally spoke, she reached into her box again and pulled out a washing up bowl. She carried on talking about delicious, fried breakfasts, the sound of seagulls and dad's snoring. As she talked, I noticed her taking off the slippers Agnes was wearing and she carefully lifted her feet and placed them in the bowl. If she noticed she didn't seem to mind. She allowed herself to be guided.

"And those crabs!" Sally winced. "Pincers sharp enough to take your fingers off!"

Agnes giggled and nodded.

Sally took two large flasks from the box and a Tupperware container. She took the lid off the container and began to pour the contents gently over her legs and into the bowl. It was sand. Fine, white sand.

"Just like Tenby beach," she said to her.

Agnes felt the sand fall over her feet, gathering between her toes. Her eyes closed as she enjoyed the sensation. She pushed her feet down into the bowl and into the sand.

"You were never a swimmer, Agnes, but you loved to paddle with your sister, didn't you?"

We watched in amazement as Sally unscrewed the lids on the flasks and began to pour water on top of the sand and into the bowl making Agnes jump a little.

"Cold, isn't it? Just like the sea. You were not expecting it then, just like now."

The two ladies giggled as the initial shock subsided and the sensation of standing at the water's edge took over the senses and the imagination once again.

Sally reached into the box one more time and pulled out a little bag. She dropped the contents into the bowl and asked Agnes to search with her feet.

"What have you found?" she giggled.

"Shells!"

Agnes clapped her hands together and beamed. I remember looking over at Frank. He was in tears.

Sally reached down into the bowl and picked out one of the shells. She washed the sand off with the last of the water in the flask and handed it to her.

"It's beautiful," Agnes said.

"Like you," said Sally. "Just like you."

Agnes started crying then. But these were happy tears not sad tears.

"My Malcolm. That is what he said to me. You remembered."

"Hold that shell." Sally continued. "Like I would like to hold you."

"That's what he said too! And he did." Agnes whispered again. "That day and nearly every day going forward for the next fifty-five years or so. Thank you, Sally. Thank you so much."

Later that evening, I found out the back story. The previous week, Agnes had talked to Sally about her husband and when, where and how they first met.

It was on a beach in Tenby, Wales.

She had stayed there with her parents and sister. Their last family holiday before she reached adulthood.
She had been seventeen back then, and she could remember it all like it was yesterday. Sally brought back the magic.
She had taken her back to that most treasured time.

She had made her feel young again, and all through a few kind words, a washing up bowl, a handful of sand and a few shells.

3

Family matters

At The Acorns we were quite flexible when it came to visitors and visiting times. We had our guidelines and recommendations, but we rarely objected to a visitor if the resident was happy to receive them.

As a staff, we got to know a lot of the friends and family members. Most were absolutely delightful, many of whom gave up their own time and expertise to help spruce up the place at no charge. We have had painters and decorators, gardeners and even a chimney sweep give up their time for free for us! We work on quite a tight budget. Every little bit helps and is greatly appreciated.

Most of the old folk are there to either ease the burden on their family or because they have no family left to burden. As I mentioned before, the overall cost for residency is astronomical, and most families have to make some serious decisions with regard to any possible inheritance or financial windfall they may have banked on.

Unless families are willing to sacrifice their own time and severely compromise their own living arrangements to accommodate their dear relatives, they have to accept the reality that there won't be much left in the pot when they pass away.

Most of them reluctantly accept this, and realise that the money they thought would allow them to retire early would instead be swallowed up by the care home and the government.

Of course, it isn't always the families who make the choice.

Some of the residents have chosen not to move in with their offspring much to the chagrin of their little darlings who were willing to put up with them at their home for a couple of years in return for a lump of cash when they croaked. Some would rather have the audacity to live in semi-luxury with those of a similar age and outlook. In some cases, they would rather live anywhere than move in with their family, and it is these rejected family members who cause us the most grief if, or when, they even bother to visit.

Rita is one such resident. A plump, head-strong woman in her late 70s. She receives a visit from her son, Colin, and his wife, every couple of weeks. She doesn't really want to see him, and he doesn't really want to see her. He is there under duress of his wife who is still clinging on to the hope that there will be something left in the purse when Rita's time is up which, I can predict with some confidence, isn't going to be any time soon.

After losing her husband to cancer and before moving into The Acorns, she sold her house in Scotby for over £350,000. Along with savings, she had a nest egg of over half a million pounds. And, as she told me without any sentiment of remorse or regret, "If that grasping little bastard and his make-up-on-a-mop wife ever see a penny of it, I will have failed in my duty as a mother. He needs to learn to stand up to her and stand on his own two feet."

Rita told me all about her son with about as much maternal affection as a wild prairie dog getting ready to eat her own young shortly after giving birth.

"It has always been take, take, take with our Colin. We gave him pocket money – it was never enough. We bought him a scooter; he wanted a bike. We took him to Spain on holiday, he wanted to go to Disneyland. I don't know where he got this greedy streak from. Neither Ted nor I spoiled him, but he was just never satisfied with what he had."

I loved listening to Rita. She just opened up and let it all come out. No airs and graces.

"And then he met *her*," she went on. "She was one of those air hostesses. You know the kind – all tits and teeth. As transparent as that bloody window over there. You could tell the first day he brought her over to the house. He was infatuated of course. His first serious girlfriend. She was no more into him as he hoped to be inside her, but there you go. Lust is blind. She had her grubby little paws on everything – vases, furniture, tools in the garage. 'This can't have been cheap' or 'doesn't this look lovely, Colin? You can imagine how much it cost.' It was like she was adding it all up in her head as she walked around our house. He followed her like a bloody lap dog."

Rita would sit up in her chair and adjust her wig before continuing.

"She would spend half the week three miles up in the air handing out crisps and nuts, but it was our Colin's nuts she had a hold of when she was on the ground, I can tell you. He had a decent enough job, even back then. Sales in computers or something like that. Enough to buy a nice semi-detached in Belle Vue, but she could see the bigger picture, and when Ted got the cancer, it was like a eureka moment for her. When she wasn't in the air she was around our house playing the dutiful daughter in law."

I suggested she go easy on Colin. Surely the wife was the problem.

"Oh, I know she was the one wearing the trousers, my dear, but he was hardly the picture of innocence himself. He was always on my shoulder asking about our insurance or savings accounts. He wanted to know the funeral arrangement for Ted six months before he even died! He dropped hints about when I should sell up and asked me what colour I would like the walls painted in the spare room. There was more chance of me moving in with Doctor Harold Shipman than my own son, and I told him so."

Mischievously, I asked how he reacted.

"Like the petulant little child he is. He stormed off, before storming back to have another go. Then he realised what he was storming away from and stormed back with his tail between his legs and a sob story about how much he wanted to care for me. When I dismissed that, she came around for round two. It was like bad cop, bad cop. They couldn't have been more obvious if they had just pinned me to the ground, pinched my bank card and tortured me until I gave them my PIN number. But I wasn't for backing down!"

She was all fire and fury, but I couldn't help laugh as she told me the story. She didn't mind.

"That's when I thought it best to start looking for a place to go and to get my house in order so to speak. I had visions of the two of them spiking my tea or pushing me in front of a bus. I had to act fast. Before Ted was even cold in the ground, I had my solicitor sort out all the paperwork on the house and the accounts. The money would be spent on my future accommodation in a home and any spare at the end was to go to some animal charity. I didn't have any grandchildren to leave it to."

I asked her how he took the news.

"Like you would expect. The two of them didn't speak to me for three months. It was the best three months of my life. It couldn't last forever though. They still came crawling back, hoping I would change my mind. That's why they still come here now every couple of weeks. Hoping I'll soften. I haven't though, and I won't. The only thing they will get out of me is a cup of tea and a slice of cake."

I felt a pang of guilt for Colin and wondered if she did too.

"Nope!" she said without hesitation. "And she will leave him for a better model when she realises the best she can hope for is that semi-detached in Belle Vue. She is still young and tarty enough to snare another victim. Just watch this space."

And with that, she gave me a wink and pulled out her knitting from underneath her backside.

"When they come again, will you make the tea and cut the cake, my dear. Don't let them make it. God knows what poison she has in her bag. I'll be dead by morning. I plan to be around for a good few years yet."

Thursday evenings tended to be the busiest time of the week for visitors. We would always put on a bit of a spread in the 'Chegwin' suite. Folk never turn down free food. We would have half a dozen grandchildren running around the garden, totally oblivious as to why they were there in the first place. Sons and daughters would gather around making small talk with their elderly parents. Clockwatching. Always clockwatching. I would wander around the room collecting the empty cups and plates, listening in to the conversations.

"Are you sure you have everything you need Dad?"

"Did you watch that wildlife programme about whales?"

"You will never guess who has bought a new four-wheel drive!"

"I've brought you some of that toffee you like. You know the one? The one I like too."

"Samantha got a certificate at school this week for swimming twenty-five metres."

"Can you remember Bob from the newsagents? Lovely man. Died last week."

"How are the piles, mam? Are you using the cream I sent you?"

"Philip had a win on the lottery. £10 on a scratch card."

"Remember Brian from my class at school. He is gay now. Came out last week."

"There are new traffic lights outside our house. It's chaotic now!"

"Half the pubs are closed now. It's all changed since your day."

"Where have you left your teeth Dad? You are forever leaving them lying around."

"We are only going to Greece this year for ten days. Money is tight."

Life. Or aspects of it.

I would look at our residents as they sat there being talked to. I didn't see the same level of enthusiasm or excitement on their faces as they had when Sally walked in the other night. They didn't look mesmerised or enthralled. They just sat and listened. Some even tried to force a smile.

When the clock chimed for 9:00 p.m. to signal the end of the visiting time, there was a mad rush to put on coats, wave goodbyes, and get to the car park to beat the bottleneck of traffic at the gate to get back on the road and home.

When the last one walked out and the door closed behind them, we all breathed a collective sigh of relief knowing that was it for another week or so.

Well, nearly all of us.

"Thank fuck for that!" shouted Frank causing a ripple of laughter around the room.

Family matters (but only in small doses).

4

A Moment in Time

In the sixteen years I have been employed by The Acorns, I worked out from the records that I have cared for nearly two hundred and fifty old people. That works out at around a fifteen-person turnover each year. It sounds so horrible when phrased in that way, and also quite shocking, but that is the reality of the job.

On occasion, a person will move to a different facility or hospital. One or two have even moved back in with family members, but in the main, they end their days here and leave in a wooden box.

Some have been known to stay here up to ten years, others a matter of days or weeks. Working here has taught me never to be too complacent or to take people for granted. One day they are there and the next they might be gone.

This scared me early on. I was wary of getting too close or attached, but then I slowly learnt that this was the wrong approach. I *had* to throw myself into the job wholeheartedly leaving nothing behind. The residents deserve nothing less. People spend their lives chasing material or monetary gains. They work towards unrealistic goals and dreams. They compete and fight with others to be top dog, and at the end of it all what does it really matter? I think we only learn the real value of human life when we reach old age, and the reality dawns on us that life's path is coming to an end. It is then that we reflect and pause to think and contemplate. It is then that we really start to appreciate others around us and how they are feeling. We can empathise more, tolerate more and understand more. We will all take grievances and grudges to the grave, but one thing I

25

have learned watching old people interact, is a willingness to accept and appreciate. To enjoy and to love.

Only last Monday, I sat out in the garden with Ralph and Stan. It was a lovely, sunny day and the two men were perched on a bench near the fountain just watching the world go by.

I was basically on wheelchair and toilet watch. Should either or both require the toilet, I was there ready to whisk them away to avoid unnecessary accidents. I needn't have worried. They were both perfectly content and in no rush to go anywhere.

Ralph and Stan arrived at The Acorns at roughly the same time and struck up a friendship almost straight away. They were both in their eighties, they had both lived in the area all their lives and they both loved their football and cricket. Enough in common to keep the conversation flowing without a pause. What laughs they had too. They would spark off each other and start giggling and snorting at the slightest thing. I'd often be running around looking for their inhalers when they couldn't catch their breath for laughing.

Despite their shared interests, the two men could not have come from more different backgrounds. Ralph was brought up in a two up-two down terrace on Morton Street in Carlisle. A gloomy stretch of small houses almost hidden by factories, chimneys and warehouses. Blackened by soot and lost in the shadows, their family home was as basic as they come. No central heating, no double-glazing and no inside toilet - not until much, much later anyway. He was one of eight children scrabbling and scraping to get by, get fed and get a job. His own father's meagre wage was not enough to support an ever-growing family, and he confessed to me that his parents relied on charity handouts throughout his early years.

Ralph left home to join the army in 1950 at the age of sixteen. He said it was his only real option, but still the best decision he ever made. On returning to the city ten years later, he worked as a carpet fitter, then as a joiner. He worked hard all his life to be independent and self-sufficient, and this dream became a reality when he started his own business making picture frames from a small studio apartment in Denton Holme.

When age crept up on him, he sold the business to help pay for The Acorns. That was two years ago.

Stan, on the other hand, came from money. His parents were both solicitors and they lived in a delightful cottage on the banks of the River Eden near Wetheral. Stan performed well in his eleven-plus, and a place in the grammar school was secured. Further education was both expected and wanted, and he left the city to study engineering at Edinburgh University.

He too ran his own business, and managed to retire at only fifty-five years old. The desire to keep busy saw him take up roles as a magistrate, a local city councillor and a scout leader. He lost his wife five years ago, and their two children had long since fled the nest to live abroad. He found the house too cumbersome to maintain, and the thought of rattling around on his own under its thatched roof (and three acres of garden) just wasn't going to suffice. The 'For Sale' sign was soon put up and a place in The Acorns secured. And here they both are now. Side by side, enjoying the sunshine and sharing what they have in common rather than dwelling on what they haven't.

I'd just been to the kitchen to bring them a glass of lemonade and a plate of biscuits, and when I returned, they were discussing jam. The giggles had already started.

"I love the ones with the full strawberries in. The ones that are hard to spread on toast." Ralph was saying. "You know the kind? Not the smooth stuff. The kind with big chunks of fruit in. I could eat it on its own with a spoon!"

"Oh no, that is not for me," Stan laughed. "Give me the smooth and seedless any day of the week. I can't be doing with that lumpy stuff."

The two of them stopped to sip their lemonade and take a bite out of a custard cream. Stan started tittering to himself.

"What's got into you?" Ralph asked, suppressing a smile.

"Our Susan used to make her own, you know." By this time, he was already starting to giggle.

The infectiousness tickled Ralph too, and he started laughing which then set me off.

"It is her fault I can't abide the chunky stuff. She used to watch those programmes on the TV and thought she was Delia Smith. She would set off out into the garden with a carrier bag, and return with a stack of fruit and a look of determination on her face. The trouble though, she was in that much of a bloody rush to get it made, she would forget the basics."

By this time, Ralph and I were egging him on, but he could barely talk for laughing.

"What did she do?" Ralph asked.

"Well, she didn't bloody wash it or sieve it for a start. She would mush the stuff, add the pectin and sugar and stick it on to boil. She would have a handful of jars and lids at the ready for when it cooled down."

"What kind was it?" Ralph interrupted, wiping his eyes.

"Fruit. What kind of fruit, God only knows? She would throw the lot in – raspberries, strawberries, blackberries. Anything she could lay her hands on in the garden. I wouldn't be surprised if there wasn't a carrot and an onion in there!"

By this time, we were doubled over.

"She would leave it to cool then go do the dishes. A woman on a mission. She filled about seventeen jars of the stuff by the time she emptied the pan. Jars of all sizes. 'Some for the neighbours,' she said. I didn't dare speak. You don't, do you? You just let them get on with it." Stan wiped his eyes again and looked up at us both. His cheeks were bright red and he had biscuit crumbs stuck all around his mouth. He let out an involuntary snort, and that set us off again.

"Did you have to eat it?" Ralph asked.

"Of course I bloody did. I was the tester. The things you do for love. She handed a jar over with a teaspoon and half a scone. She stood there, arms folded, waiting for the verdict. I took a spoonful..."

He couldn't take it anymore. He leaned forward and howled, his face wet from crying, his whole body shaking and bobbing up and down. He tried to get his words out, but couldn't.

Ralph and I followed suit. We were both crying and laughing uncontrollably. The kind of laugh everyone needs now and again. The kind that renders you paralysed and looking ridiculous. The kind of laugh that you remember.

Eventually, Stan managed to speak but only intermittently before collapsing into another fit of laughter.

"She was livid..." he went on. "I tried. God knows I tried." Again, he doubled up. We were all exhausted by this point.
"I remember her storming out of the room in tears. Oh my God." At this point I seriously thought he was having a heart attack such was his inability to get his words out.

"What happened to you then you daft bugger?" chipped in Ralph, trying to get to the end of the story before we rang for an ambulance. Death by laughter!

"I broke three teeth, swallowed a wasp and nearly choked on a pebble."

The three of us, and a few others walking through the garden were in bits.

"And the thing is," he went on, "She blamed me! She didn't speak to me for days after."

He took a sip of lemonade and looked at us both through watery eyes.

"So, my good friend, you can stick your lumpy jam with seeds and pieces of fruit where the sun doesn't shine. If it ain't smooth, I ain't eating it!"

If they didn't need the toilet before that conversation, they did after. I did too.

That afternoon reminded me why it was so important not to hold back. To be there. To be involved. A minute in a day. A recollection. A smile. Whatever it is and no matter how small. I learned not to be afraid of their lack of time. I learned to enjoy the time they had left.

Preserve them.

5

Out With the Old...

Death. It will come to us all.

When did I first think about death? When did I first consider it as a part of life? As a child, death wasn't even on the radar. It wasn't a thought. It wasn't even a thing. Life and death were not on the same page.

As children, we are selfish. We live. Others provide. We enjoy. We think of ourselves.

Yes, we need our family and friends, but we take them all for granted. They are there. They will always be there. They are a part of my life, and as such, they won't be going anywhere or so we think as children. It is innocent naivety, but also a nice headspace in which to reside.

Death, to me, first came in the form of murder. I inflicted death. I was the killer. Of ants. Of insects. Of flowers. God's creatures they may well be, but if they had the audacity to crawl on my arm or frighten me in the garden, woe betide them. They would be duly squashed or dismembered without a hint of guilt or regret. Ants, spiders, woodlice – they all came a cropper. And yet, even as a toddler I had a sense of hierarchy. I would happily stand on an ant or squash a fly, but there was an inbuilt barometer holding me back from harming anything bigger than my fingernail. Even as a young child, I would never dream of harming a bird or a cat or a dog. Perhaps it was the notion that such animals are kept as pets, and are there to be loved and cherished. They show distress. They show pain. The same pain we feel. Perhaps, subconsciously, I could empathise with any suffering. Dogs and cats show happiness. We know if they are

31

content. We know when they are struggling or hurt or ill. We can't say the same about an ant. And yet, as we grow older, we learn that all life should be valued. Every beast – whether human or otherwise – has been granted life and we realise this life is precious. Unique. Something that, once lost, will never return. A finality.

We might not shed a tear over the death of a small fly, but it still registers with us that a life lost is a loss. As we grow older and develop relationships and bonds with animals or fellow human beings, we begin to understand this loss. We also start to appreciate the impact we have on others and we slowly start to appreciate them. It is only when we lose something do we truly appreciate its value.

A toy. A teddy. Moving house. Changing schools.
We are burdened by memories and attachments. Inanimate objects and treasures matter a great deal to us. More than they probably should. And yet they offer security – a comfort.

At the age of five, my teddy meant more to me than my parents. Pets have been more valued family members than uncles, aunts, cousins and grandparents. When my Cocker Spaniel, Fleck, died when I was only fourteen, I was heartbroken. Had I been presented with the choice of choosing between Fleck and my Uncle Dave, I would have happily sent Dave to the crematorium if it meant my little fluffy baby could have lived another day.

When growing up, death didn't really mean a thing to me until my grandma passed away. I was sixteen years old, and she was seventy-one. I would visit her two or three times a week with my mam. We only ever stayed half an hour or so each time. Mam always had to 'get back' to do non-existent jobs.

Grandma was a funny lady.

With Mam, she used to moan and whinge but when the two of

us were on our own she would change altogether. She was fun and bubbly. I think I brought out the child in her. She would want to play games and chat. She would ask all about my day, and be genuinely interested in what I had to say, and what I had been up to. I loved her stories and silly jokes. I loved looking through her old jewellery boxes and books. There was nothing of any value in there, but the mystery of a life lived fascinated me even then. She loved the fact that I was interested in her too.

Mam loved her to bits but she never seemed to have the time for her that I did.

I had the time.

Grandma died of a heart attack.

A neighbour found her slumped in her favourite chair. The TV was on and a cold cup of tea sat untouched on the side table to her left.
Her death came as a shock to my parents. She had shown no sign of any distress beforehand. I remember my dad answering the phone and falling silent. He signalled to me to fetch my mother. I remember her bursting into tears when she took the receiver from my dad. I had never seen my mother cry like that before. She covered her face and tried to hide her pain from me – protecting me. I remember just staring at her.

Dad invited me into another room, and we sat side by side. He reached out to hold my hand, but I didn't take it. It wasn't cool. Even in this state of depression, I maintained my teenage aloofness. I regret it now. Dad was just trying to help.

I just wanted to know why mam was crying. Isn't it strange the little things you remember? He told me that Grandma had passed away.

We both sat in silence for a few minutes before I burst into tears and ran to my room. I couldn't understand it. I didn't want to understand it.

By then I knew what death was. Or at least I thought I did. I knew people died – usually when they were old and ill. And yet it was still an alien concept to me until Grandma passed away. Grandma was the first. The first that really mattered. The first death that really hit home to me. And I couldn't cope with it.

Deaths are like buses. You wait sixteen years for one, then a few come at once.

Grandma passed away in the March. Fleck a month later. Aunt Philippa died of cancer at the start of the summer. Uncle Brian followed after quite a nasty pile up on the M6 motorway, and Aunt Sue (who was just a neighbour, not an auntie) committed suicide when her husband, Uncle Bob (not my real uncle) left her for another man.

Out of all these deaths, only Grandma and Fleck really mattered to me, but death had reared its ugly head with a vengeance.

From then on, I started to pay more attention. I started to appreciate those around me just that little bit more.

When my cousin Harry developed a lump on his testicle and had to be taken into hospital for emergency treatment. I was inconsolable. In my mind, at the tender age of thirty-six, he was as good as dead. I mourned him when he was taken in for surgery with the intention of removing the lump. My grief was a little premature. He survived and the operation was 100% successful. He currently lives in Australia with his Thai bride who is twenty years younger than him.

A realisation that he needed to make the most of the time he had left once the lump was removed. His parents disapproved of the relationship of course, but Harry didn't care.   He still had the bollock to go ahead with it!

But there it was again – death. Hovering like a fart in an elevator. Waiting to strike.

And then I got the job at The Acorns. My experience of death before then was merely a taster for what was to come.

By seventeen, I was a novice.

By nineteen, I was a expert.

By twenty, death was just an occupational hazard.

At first, I was shocked. After six months I was beginning to harden to it. After a year, I was almost apathetic. I was young and I was stupid. I was doing a job and not enjoying a vocation. I was cynical and stupid. Naïve and callous. I didn't have the emotional attachments. I didn't allow myself to. I was on minimum wage doing the minimum amount of work. Reminiscing now, I cannot believe how I behaved back then. I wasted the first two years being selfish and greedy. I did not appreciate what – or who – was in front of me.

That is until I met Judi Mortimer and her mother, Pat. That was the turning point. That was the moment I really understood the value of life and death.

Pat arrived at home the day after my twenty-first birthday. The family had moved up to Cumbria from Lancashire a few years before, and they had all lived together in a converted farmhouse near the airport. It soon became apparent that Pat needed twenty-four-hour care, and it was with a heavy heart that they all agreed a nearby care home would be the better option for her. The farmhouse was lovely, but totally ill-equipped for an old lady with mobility issues.

They settled on The Acorns after a couple of visits and a look at the other places in the area. It wasn't far from home and Pat seemed to be happy.

I remember the day she moved in. Judi's husband, Louis, was in charge of cases and boxes. It was his job to be the pack horse and her job to unpack for her mother.

There was a real bond between the two ladies. They often fussed over each other without saying a word. Judi would straighten her mother's skirt when she sat down.

Pat would hold her daughter's hand or stroke her hair while they talked or looked out of the window. It was lovely to see. They never argued or snapped at each other. It was as though that would have been a waste of energy. They didn't always agree and they were not shy in voicing an opinion, but it never resulted in raised voices or upset. They merely agreed to disagree, and moved on to what was important such as instructing Louis to go and get the kettle on or which programme to watch together on the television.

Judi was a regular visitor to The Acorns. She would volunteer to help if we were taking some of the residents out for the day or muck in when the garden needed weeding. I think she just wanted to be close to her mother.

One Monday morning when I arrived to start my shift, I was told to check on the residents on the second floor. This was normal. A head around the door to ask if they needed anything, and to check they were alright was good enough.

When I arrived at number 15, Pat's room, the door was closed. I knocked two or three times, but there was no response. It was only about 9:00 a.m. and I just thought she must still be asleep. I carried on with my rounds and after half an hour or so, I was back in the staff room chatting to the others and passing the time of day. The supervisor at that time, Debbie, asked if everyone was alright. I mentioned that there was no answer from Pat's room. She asked if I had looked in. I hadn't. She asked if I had tried again after checking on the others. I hadn't.

She scalded me and briskly scuttled out the door towards the stairs, indicating that I should follow and be quick about it. At the same time, Judi walked through the front door and heard Debbie calling out to another staff member that she needed to "Check Pat is ok. A no responder!"

I caught Judi's eye as we passed, and the colour seemed to drain from her face. Without saying a word, she followed us up the stairs towards room fifteen.

Debbie knocked. No answer. She called Pat's name. No answer. In a fit of panic, Judi pushed between the two of us and tugged at the handle, but it was locked from the inside. She called out for her mother. No response. She started to cry. She was shaking and her voice trembled as she called out again. No response. Debbie bent down to look through the keyhole. "I can't see through. She must have put the key in the door and forgot to take it out."

"We must get in there. NOW!"

It was the first time I had heard Judi shout and I was quite taken aback.

Nothing was said, but we were all thinking the same thing. Death.

The emotional attachment – the need – between mother and daughter had never been more apparent to me than in that moment. All Judi wanted, all she needed, was her mother. A heavy wooden door acted as a barrier between them. She didn't have the strength to break it down. She felt totally helpless and slumped against the wall and slid down until she was curled up into a ball, her arms wrapped around her legs and her head buried between her knees. Debbie sent a message to fetch Keith, the Site Manager. I just stood there watching. Hovering. The enormity of the situation hit me and I burst into tears. Judi looked up at me and reached out a hand. I held it and she pulled me towards her down to where she was sitting.

Side by side, we cuddled and cried.

As we sat there, a million thoughts went through my mind. How would I cope if I was to lose one or both of my parents? Am I doing enough for them? Do they need me? Am I as good a daughter as Judi?

By the time Keith arrived with his tool box, we must have been sitting in that position for ten minutes or more lost in our own thoughts.

He managed to unscrew the handle and loosen the lock enough for us to enter. The curtains were closed and the room was in darkness. Pat lay still on the bed, head to one side. Her arms were crossed over her chest. She looked ever so peaceful. Ever so calm.

Debbie was the first to walk in, and Judi and I followed, hand in hand.

We stood there a moment or two before Debbie broke the silence.

"Let me open the curtains. We need some light in here." We didn't argue, we both just stared at the lifeless body on the bed.

"I need to call Louis," Judi said softly.

Debbie looked at another nurse, and she understood what she needed to do.

She walked over to the bay window and held a curtain in each hand before pulling them aside sharply to let the light flood into the room.

All of a sudden, Pat sat bolt upright in the bed and the three of us screamed and nearly jumped out of our skin.

"What on earth!" shrieked Pat, reaching up and grabbing at her ears.

I can't speak for Judi and Debbie, but my heart was beating like crazy and I thought I was going to pass out.

Finding her voice, Judi wailed, "Mum. Are you alright? We thought you were dead". Emotion hit her, and tears began streaming down her cheeks once again. She ran to the bed and knelt down, wrapping her arms around Pat's waist.

Instinctively, Pat started stroking her hair.

"Are you alright, Pat?" Debbie said, composing herself. "The door was locked. We were terribly worried about you when you didn't answer this morning."

"I had these earbud things stuck in. I couldn't hear a thing. Frank gave them to me yesterday. I've been listening to Glen Miller."

"The door?" said Debbie.

"I was taking my underwear off. I didn't want any Tom, Dick or Harry walking in. I must have forgotten to unlock it!"

This seemed to lighten the mood and suck life back into the room. We were all still crying. We were all still in shock, but the most important thing was Pat. She was still with us. She was still with Judi and Judi was still with her mum. That's when it really struck me. Just how important life is, and just what we mean to each other.

I have never taken life for granted since. Not once. It means too much.

All the commotion had startled a few of the other residents who were now shuffling around trying to see what all the fuss was about.

After a few minutes, Frank poked his head around the door. He noticed his ear phones on the bedside table.

"Great aren't they Pat? You feel like you are in a world of your own when you have those in. Dead to the world!"

Pat smiled and nodded back to him. He walked on but then a second or two later, he reappeared at the doorway.

"Oh, by the way, Debbie. We have a stiff in Room 22. Josephine. I thought she would be next. She hasn't looked right for a while!"

And with that, he carried on down the corridor, whistling to himself without a care.

One of the other nurses was the next to appear at the door. It was the one Debbie had met in the corridor only a few minutes earlier.

"Louis is on the way" she said, out of breath after running up the stairs. "I told him about Pat. He said he is on his way and will be here as fast as he can!"

"What about me?" asked Pat.

Out of sheer relief, Judi, Debbie and I burst out Laughing. Laughing and crying at the same time. Poor Josephine.

6

In the Midst of Life

There was always a quick turnaround when a resident departed The Acorns.

As mentioned earlier, we have a waiting list of people keen to secure a place in the home thanks to the excellent reputation we have built up over the years.
A reputation of outstanding care and customer service. The fact of the matter is, although we see these elderly residents and their families as friends, they are first and foremost, our customers. They pay an awful lot of money for the services we provide and we need to ensure we spend their money wisely. We like to go the extra mile.

We aren't the most expensive in the area, and we aren't the cheapest either, but we are the best, and I am not just biased. We have worked hard to create a culture here, not just a facility. There is a homely atmosphere. A caring atmosphere. One where people feel safe and secure. Our staff team are caring, friendly and supportive as well as experienced. We are inclusive and fair. We are understanding and helpful. We aren't a dominant force.

We want the residents to lead, and to say what they want. Nothing is forced on them. Everything from the activities and entertainments, to the menus and the décor, we want The Acorns to represent their personalities, and we want them to put their individual stamp on the place. We offer support and help, but know when to leave be.

No two people are the same and should never be treated as such.

The only thing 'uniform' in The Acorns is how the staff dress.

The residents know and appreciate this. We are there when they need us, and in the periphery when they don't.

We are a home away from home in every sense of the word. A new place that they can call home.

Josephine hadn't been with us for very long. Three months at the most. We didn't really get the chance to get to know her or her family. Her medical history was fine. She did not have any underlying conditions causing the doctors any concern, and she was certainly loved and cherished in the family unit. She was eighty-three when she passed away. No pain, no fuss – just natural causes.

I never liked that phrase – natural causes. I always associated it with natural disasters, I don't know why. Josephine died of natural causes, they said. Was she sucked up inside a tornado or engulfed by a Tsunami? Was she shaken by an earthquake or blown away in a typhoon?
No. She simply stopped breathing. Her body had had enough and given up.

Her family were naturally upset, but we had never really got to know them like we got to know most of the others. It was all very perfunctory. A nice old lady, a nice family, a sad end and a respectful funeral.

Josephine made me think about death in general. People are dying all over the place. Their deaths don't affect me. Maybe because I don't know them. Yes, it is sad, yes, it is awful to see other people suffering, and yes, it is yet another reminder that our own mortality hangs by a thread, but life and death go on regardless.
It struck me that it was unlikely that I would even remember

Josephine in five years' time, and then that upset me. I'm so silly, I know.

I really hoped her life mattered to a lot of people. Nice people deserve that at least.

That got me thinking about legacies. How long are we remembered for? We aren't all like J.F.K or John Lennon. But how long will generations to come remember them? The famous ones. Will we still be talking about Elvis or Martin Luther King in five hundred years time? I hope so. King Henry VIII still holds our attention. Hitler will too no doubt.

Does it pay to be bad – to be evil? How many good folk do we remember from five hundred years ago? We remember inventors, scientists and great thinkers, but do we remember those who spend their lives giving rather than creating? Will we remember the charity workers and volunteers above the serial killers and gangsters? I think I already know the answer to that.

Glamour and infamy seem to trump good and right.

I often wonder what my own legacy will be. Will I leave a mark in life? Will I be remembered?

And then there is the question of faith!

As a non-believer, I have often been fascinated by those with a faith in a higher power. Throughout my time at The Acorns, we have welcomed people of every denomination and faith. Not one person has ever tried to convert me or win me over. Faith is very much a private thing. Especially in old age. It is often said that people turn to religion late in life as an insurance for what might come after their day, but not in my experience. Faith isn't something you can suddenly adopt with any sincerity unless you truly believe. It isn't something you can bank on to see you through the other side. It is a heartfelt belief that there is something beyond the grave. Beyond the corpse. A spiritual world that I am unable to comprehend or understand.

Over the years, we have enjoyed every kind of festival or celebration here. As well as Christmas and Easter, we have celebrated Diwali, Ramadan and Hanukkah. We've partied wearing every kind of traditional dress, and we have greeted each other in every known language under the sun. We have enjoyed the food of every culture and country. We have been united in every faith and every nation important to our residents.

We haven't suffered as a consequence. Quite the contrary – we have been enriched and emboldened by the experience. We have been educated in life. It hasn't hurt us or brainwashed us. It has helped form us into better people.

Another thing I have noticed throughout my time here – old people are the most welcoming, accepting and tolerant. Whoever has arrived through our doors has been greeted with warmth, affection and understanding. Life is too short.

The old folk may not always be PC, but most are past caring about things like that. They don't mean to offend and if they do so, they don't dwell on it. They have bigger things to worry about. Things like staying alive. They haven't got time to keep up with the new, politically correct terminology or the many abbreviations used these days to avoid offending.

They can cope with BBC or ITV, and one or two could even tell you what LOL stands for but start talking about LGBTQIA+, and they will be wondering why you are performing an eye test on them.

Society, now, is told not to label people – to let them be who they choose to be. To identify as what they wish to be. That confuses me. If you identify as something, then that is what you are isn't it? That is your invisible label.

These feelings - these wants and desires, this demand to be accepted is evidence of a developing society. An evolving society. These supposed new identities or feelings are just more visible now. Tolerated. Accepted. More 'out there'. They are nothing new.

There is nothing wrong with that. I try not to judge. I try to be accepting and open minded and, for the most part, I think I am. I can't quite get my head around why some people want to 'identify' as a monkey or a lamp post, but each to their own. They aren't hurting anyone.

Old people – or the older generation – often bear the brunt of perceived stereotyping and prejudice which, in my experience, is very unfair. I am not sure of the actual figures, but I would imagine hate crime, racism and homophobia is largely committed by a much younger demographic than the age group I cherish and support. They haven't got the anger and hatred in them that we see spouted on social media or in the tabloid press.

The residents in The Acorns have lived and loved. Most have been brought up through hard times or difficult conditions. Most haven't been blessed with wealth or privilege. They grew up in communities where people looked out for one another. They lived their lives based on their shared morals and values. Maybe I am just being sentimental and protective, but this place has always been a place of love and acceptance not of hate and discrimination.

That's not to say they can't be wholly un-PC and discriminatory – most of the time totally unwittingly.

TV time on a Saturday night is quite possibly my favourite night of the week.

The Sir Jimmy Glass Suite, where the television is located, is rarely full during the week. One or two people will stop and watch the daytime drivel if they have nothing better to do, but half the time the TV is either background noise or it is switched off altogether. Except on a Saturday evening. For whatever reason, after the evening meal, the room slowly fills up until every armchair and sofa is taken.

It is always BBC1. Always. No one argues. No one complains. It is as though it is the only channel available! We invested in Satellite TV a while back, but ended up cancelling the subscription as nobody ever watched anything on there other than BBC1.

"You see, there are no adverts, pet", Gillian once told me.

I tried to explain that there are no adverts on BBC2 either, but that didn't seem to wash. If I dared suggest a good film on a commercial channel I would be shot down in flames or sent away with a flea in my ear.

"What do I want with life insurance at my age?"

"What a waste of money!"

"£70 for a shirt and they call that a bargain! I would want the whole shop for that amount."

"Who the hell would want one of those? It would cut off your circulation!"

The daytime adverts on the commercial channels also put them off. Funeral arrangements, solicitors offering deals on wills, financial advice on what to do after you pass on and adverts for stair lifts, incontinence pads and hearing aids. Constant reminders of the end of their time. Targeted ads.

No, BBC1 it was and that was final.

On Saturday night television, there was something for everyone. Game shows, chat shows, variety performances, news, weather and the football highlights. If any of them were still awake after all that, they might get to see a film. Usually, "One of those action films with him from that thing on, you know! The one with the bald fella and the woman with the legs."

I would look at them all nodding as if it was all very obvious what they were talking about.

"Is that queer one on tonight?" Joyce would say.

"Aye, he is. He has some good guests on tonight. That singer from America. The black woman with the gold tooth. I like her. And that explorer. The one who drank his own pee in the desert."

They would all nod in agreement. No more explanation needed.

"I like him" Enid would say to Joyce. "Always full of beans. Always happy when talking to his guests. His fella must have such a good laugh with him. He has such a jolly face. If he wasn't one of them, I wouldn't turn him away!"

They would all giggle and nod.

"He is Irish, isn't he?" another would join in. "Gift of the gab. The American one won't have a clue what he is on about."

"I wouldn't drink my own piss." Frank said, taking up his usual seat at the front. "It is bad enough having to sit in it!"

This would cause a ripple of laughter around the room then a "Shhhhh" as the chatty Irishman introduced his first guest.

Throughout the show, there would be a few heckles. People thinking aloud or asking rhetorical questions.

"That fruit on the table can't be real. He had the same grapes last week."

"Look how pointy his shoes are! They can't be comfortable."

"My breasts used to stand up like hers. Mind you, that was sixty years ago!"

"Why doesn't he move up a bit on that sofa? The black lass is hanging on by one arse cheek."

They would watch game shows, willing the contestants to win a life changing amount of money. They genuinely cared. They wanted everyone to go home happy as they shouted out encouragement or correct answers in the vain hope they could hear. Hoping to help and make a difference from the Sir Jimmy Glass Suite in Brampton.

"It's Canberra you dozy bugger! Not Sydney! Ah, he has lost that £3,000 now."

"Go on, spin the wheel a bit harder. Put a bit of effort into it."

"If she knows that, I'm a monkey's uncle. I bet she hasn't been out of Wolverhampton, never mind studied the tribes of the Amazon Rainforest."

They would cheer and clap when somebody won a prize – which was never a big prize on the BBC. No commercial money to splash around. They would share in the happiness of the winners and commiserate with the losers. They wanted the best for the people on the screen regardless of colour, class or creed.

By the time the news came on at 10:00 p.m., one or two would have dozed off. Those who remained continued with the commentary.

"Poor souls. Look at them, bless them. You can't tell me there isn't enough money in the world to feed and clothe everyone. It is a bloody shame. A disgrace."

"He should be sent to prison and they should throw away the key."

"Can't cope with the money she is on? She can still churn out a new kid every nine months and pay for a smartphone. Smokes like a chimney too."

"That Prime Minister has more lives than a litter of cats!"

Then the weather. They would watch it intently. Rain. More rain. Snow. Strong winds. That is Northern England for ten months of the year. Occasionally, the forecaster would happily inform us that a heatwave was on the way.

"It'll be too hot."

"You won't catch me out in that."

"I won't sleep if it is like that."

I would just sit and chuckle. The weatherman couldn't win!

The men tried to stay awake for Match of the Day. A few women too, but mainly the men. Most of them supported Carlisle United – the big local team – but men and football go hand in hand. They would watch a group of dogs pushing a ball about if there was a goal post at either end. Maybe this will be the girls too in years to come. That would be nice.

Some of them would have a second favourite team, but most would cheer on the underdog.

They would have all tried hard to avoid seeing the result during the day, thus making the highlights even more exciting.
There would be cheers for Watford, Bournemouth, Norwich and

Southampton and boos for Arsenal, Spurs, Liverpool, Chelsea or Manchester United.

"They make the game far more complicated than it needs to be!"

"Tactics? It is all about players not tactics."

"He will be for the chop next."

"That referee couldn't keep up with me!"

"That winger couldn't cross his legs."

"That keeper couldn't catch a cold."

"Why do they have to spit all the time? They must be covered in each other's phlegm with the amount of rolling about they do!"

"What a bloody goal that was, Ken. Just like yours against the Rose and Crown in '67."

Expert commentators and pundits were given short shrift. Modern day players were soft or greedy. "They don't care like they used to."

After the football, as the clock approached midnight, most of the remaining watchers would retire to their beds. One or two would remain for the film, and one or two more would hang in there and catch the opening credits. It would be rare for any of them to make it to the end let alone the sex scene.

If they fell asleep, they were covered up and made comfortable. A member of staff would always be on hand to help no matter the time of day.
The days went by at the pace of the residents, not the staff.

Saturday night was fun because it was slightly different.

It wasn't the norm. TV was just another discussion point. If it was taken away, it wouldn't be missed for long. They would have made their own entertainment. The residents didn't need to be entertained. They made their own. Their own experiences, their own memories, their own lives made them entertaining.

From the outside, we were simply viewed as an old folk's home. A rest home. A place of rest – of last rest.

From the inside, the place was full of life. Of lives. A micro-community of humour, acceptance, tolerance, friendship, care, spirit, experience, will, wisdom and love. An almost perfect world within a world.

But will we learn from them before they pass on?

They might not be remembered in ten years' time. Just another Grandparent or old timer dead and gone. Each one a footnote in human history. They deserve more than that.

I cherish those Saturday nights. I treasure them. And every other night I spend in their company.

I'm on little more than minimum wage, and I live with my parents, but these people make me feel so rich and special and wanted.

They pass their life on to me and to others who are prepared to look for it.

Is there a better gift than that?

7

Fagin

Anyone who has watched the film or read the book, The Shawshank Redemption, will be familiar with the character, Red.

Red is an old lag in the Shawshank Prison. An institutionalised prisoner of many years standing who is known, within this community of crooks, as the man who can 'get anything you want' – for a price! When friend and fellow inmate, Andy Dufresne, asks him for a Rock Hammer, he comes up trumps. Even when he asks him to bring in a poster of Rita Hayworth, Red comes good.

What made me think of that? Well, in The Acorns, we have our very own *'Red'*.

Peter Brockbank has lived in the home with us for nearly five years. He came to us with a colourful past having spent as much time inside as out! A loveable rogue and a likeable character, Peter is our very own Mr. Fixit. Our very own, 'Red'.

He would often moan that he had more freedom in Wakefield Prison than he does at The Acorns. To a certain extent, he has a point. With health and safety regulations and red tape covering our backsides at every turn, freedom does seem a little limited for some of the residents – especially those who have lived their life on the move.

"You need to have a risk assessment just to go out and have a fag here!" Peter would complain. "Set meal times, wardens on patrol, security doors and room checks every day. Her Majesty's Prison, Brampton!"

Frank told him the room checks were just to make sure he was still alive, but Peter wouldn't have it.

"Cell checks. That's what they are. I went for a pee the other day and when I got back to the room, they had my mattress turned over looking for drugs."

I explained that the cleaners were just changing the sheets, but he just smiled at me and nodded as if what I had just told him was a complete lie and he knew best.

Frank asked him if they had found any.

"No way mate. I keep them in my sock drawer."

Peter didn't have a large family, but he had no shortage of friends and visitors. There would be at least half a dozen of them each week. They would never stay long, but they were regular. Without sounding overly judgemental, some of them didn't look like the most trustworthy of souls, but they were always polite with the staff and the other residents so we had no cause for complaint. What we didn't know at the time was that our very own 'Red' was using them to bring in contraband from the outside world. Peter was the man in The Acorns who could 'get things'.

We didn't purposefully try to limit the residents from their little luxuries and needs, but unless a family brought gifts in for their elderly relatives, our own inmates didn't have the means to go out and get it for themselves, and it was not in our job description to do that for them either even though we did. The home provided the basics. Most of the time, if they wanted any more, they had to source it themselves.

They had a maximum weekly allowance of £10 (paid for by their families). With this money, they could buy toiletries such as shaving foam, deodorant, razors or their own choice of soap. Peter used to whine that using the soap we provided was like "rubbing a wire brush on your face."

A member of staff would take the money for the weekly order, and nip down to the nearest supermarket to buy the necessaries.

We were not allowed to take requests for cigarettes or vapes. We couldn't use the money to buy alcohol or any kind of implement likely to cause harm to themselves or others. We had to play it safe and follow policy.

And that's where Peter came in...

The other residents gave him the nickname, Fagin – the wily old thief from the famous Charles Dickens classic novel, Oliver Twist. It was a nickname Peter rather liked.

Thieving was just one of a string of offences that he had been arrested and charged with in the dim and distant past, so the comparison was an accurate one. He would stress, however, that he only ever stole from those who had too much – whatever 'too much' meant – or those who 'deserved it'.

After a while, we found that the weekly toiletries order was becoming less and less and the residents were only buying essentials not luxuries.

When we finally got the bottom as to why, we found the money was not going into the supermarket tills, rather into the pockets of Peter.

When I confronted him about it, he simply said, "They get more for their money with me. Cost price so to speak, and they can set their sights a little higher than a quilted bog roll and a spray of anti-perspirant."

It was then the penny dropped with me. Peter's visitors were more like a set of delivery boys – mules – than close friends. Old pals from inside, or young men who had their fingers in more pies than Little Jack Horner!

At first, I was a little angry with him. I felt he was taking advantage of the others for his own selfish gain, and also for from bringing undesirables in to the home, possibly putting others at risk.

It was Frank who set me straight and put my mind at ease.

"Don't be so bloody daft, Ang. It was us who approached Fagin, not the other way around. You wouldn't believe what he can get his hands on for a tenner. I'd rather go to the Peter Brockbank supermarket than any other. Talk about value for money."
I asked him what he meant.
"See this watch I'm wearing. You can get the exact same one in the jewellery shop in town for £150. Well, if they have a spare one now. Fagin – well, one of his mates – got me it for just £20. Two week's savings here and I have a timepiece worth more than everything else I own in total."

"He stole it for you?" I asked.

"What are you – a grass?!" he laughed. "He would do the same for you. All the staff. He has already sorted out the kitchen staff with a few things."

"Like what?" I said, totally aghast.

"A new blender, a cracking microwave, a new hob and that chest freezer in the garage."

"That was from Fagin?" I said.

"Well, they didn't come free of course, but he got all of that for less than a fifth of the price in the shops. They were chuffed and it saved a few quid in their budget. Everyone is a winner."

"But it's stealing" I said, weakly.

"They make enough profit. They won't miss a few appliances and we all benefit. He is very careful. He uses the right people. Covers his tracks."

"Disgusting" I said.

"What would you like him to get for you?" Frank asked.

"Nothing!" I said forcefully. "It's immoral and wrong."

That was a year ago. I have since had a Louis Vuitton bag, Gucci perfume, Pandora bracelets and a new android tablet all for a fraction of the price of the stuff in the shops. I do feel guilty, but I wouldn't be without the Vuitton bag!

Peter was in his mid-seventies and still fairly sprightly for his age. He was a natural entertainer, and the other residents – and staff – all enjoyed listening to his prison stories, even if we suspected one or two were a little embellished. He shared cells with so many different characters and personalities over the years. Young men who had lost their way, old cons like himself who couldn't resist the temptation put in their way. Violent offenders, one off offenders and gang leaders too. He admitted the first time inside was the hardest. Not knowing what to do or who to trust. Watching your back – and your backside – every second of every day. It was easier to serve your time in some prisons compared to others, but the routines were pretty much the same.

The biggest killer, he said, was boredom. Yes, they had games, TVs and exercise, but they are just time fillers in a long day stuck within the same four walls. You had plenty of time on your hands to reflect and plan, whether that be another crime when you got out or a meaningful attempt to put it all behind you and start afresh. Sadly, for too many of them, the first option was more appealing. Being a career criminal was not an easy life, but they could not resist the buzz or the adrenalin rush of doing something you shouldn't. Reward or remand. Prize and pleasure or prison. They all knew they would be caught in the end, and yet it was worth it somehow. Once a con always a con.

So that was that. Peter could not shake off habits of old even when he moved into The Acorns – and the residents loved him for it.

One Saturday night in mid-winter, in the Sir Jimmy Glass Suite, the ones who had stayed up late to watch Match of the Day were arguing over football yet again. I loved listening to the banter from the side lines. They were all experts. They all had an opinion on who was the best player and why. It had been ten years or more since most of them had stepped foot inside a football ground, but that didn't stop them squabbling over everything from substitutes to sending offs. On this particular evening, there were a few ladies in the room and between games, the focus and conversation turned to the varying degrees of sex appeal radiating from the pundits.

"I like that Gary Lineker," said Joyce. "He has a lovely smile. Remember those shorts he used to wear when he was playing for England back in the day? They were so tight; I'm surprised he could run in them. Such lovely thighs too."

"You are joking, aren't you?" chipped in Susan. "He has a nose like a bulb and his ears are like two satellite dishes. He does nothing for me."

"I liked Ian Wright. And he looks even better now he has shaved all his hair off." crooned Mavis.

"Get away with you. He is all bling. That gold tooth. Bloody horrible. And that laugh he has! It would drive me up the wall" Jean grumbled. "I much prefer Shearer. Northern lad. You know where you are with northern lads. None of that arrogance and flash of the southerners."

"Boring bugger if you ask me" chipped in Frank. "An hour in his company and you would be in a coma."

"What do you know, Frank Williams? He is better looking than you ever were and he comes across as a pure gentleman. I would date him."

"Well, he wouldn't date you" Frank snapped back, "You have more hair on your upper lip than he has on his head. He wouldn't go for an old granny like you. You will have to make do with Rooney!"

This sent a ripple of laughter around the room.

"I will tell you who I liked when I was younger," said Eleanor. "Stanley Bowles. He was only a skinny little scrap of a lad when he played for Carlisle, but I loved him. We were about the same age. I met him in a pub one evening. A few of us girls were out for a drink, and we sat down on the table next to him. He was on his own, reading a newspaper. The Racing Post probably. I was the only football fan amongst us and I recognised him straight away. I was shy and when he caught me looking, I'm sure I turned crimson. He put the paper down and shuffled over to chat to me. That big, cheeky smile of his! My heart melted. He was such a charmer and what a player he was too. He asked me out and we went on a couple of dates. It was never anything more serious than that, but we stayed friends for a while. When he moved to London, Queens Park Rangers became my second team because of Stan. He was brilliant at Carlisle, but he was just starting then. He became a legend after that. One of the best."

This delve back into the past prompted a great deal of head nodding and appreciative sounds of approval.

"The seventies was a good decade for football," Bob added. "Some real characters. Hard as nails most of them. The games were played on cabbage patches back then, but some players just glided over those bogs and swamps like they were golf greens. Stanley Bowles was one of them. Worthington and Currie. Osgood, Summerbee, George. So many stars, and all a joy to watch. Characters. Masters of their craft. Not like the cardboard, cloned cut outs of today's game, too scared to say anything controversial in case they lose their shampoo advert."

More head nods. Then Peter spoke up.

"I got to know Stan Bowles well when he lived up here. We ended up as good pals."

"Away with you," said Frank. "You didn't know him at all."

"I bloody did. Still do" Peter replied, rummaging around in his pocket at the same time. He pulled out his wallet and took out an old photograph. He showed it to me first and I passed it around the others. It was a picture of Peter and Bowles, raising a pint together.

"He was – is – a good mate. We had some good laughs together I can tell you. I often used to go to London to see him. He liked his women did our Stan. He liked gambling too. We were alike. Life in the fast lane."

"The fast lane didn't do you much good, did it? Always getting done for speeding or something. Probably in a stolen car too" Frank giggled.

This caused another titter around the room.

The next set of match highlights were showing on the television, but the conversation was more interesting than what was on the screen.

"He is suffering now with Alzheimer's, bless him. The memories come and go, but what a legend he was back then. I'd love to have my old friend back."

This caused the room to fall silent as they all reflected on what had passed and what might have been.

Eleanor was the first to speak.

"I'd love to meet him again. To see him."

More silence. Then Peter spoke.

"I'll get him for you."

The postman is a welcome figure at The Acorns. For years our regular postie has been a Scottish gentleman, Graeme Cochrane. I think he looks forward to coming to The Acorns as much as the residents love to see him. Letters matter. Not emails or texts – letters.

And they are letters too. Not bills, flyers or adverts. This is one of the benefits of living in a home. The junk is filtered and disposed of.

There is something extra special about receiving a handwritten letter. The knowledge that someone has taken the time to write – to put pen to paper just for you. Knowing they have had to go out to buy a stamp and post it. To send a letter to someone is still special. It means more than a two-minute type and the click of a button.

And so, when Graeme whistles his way down the drive at 10:30 a.m. each morning, a wave of excitement spreads across the Keith Chegwin Lounge and up the stairs into all the rooms.

They don't all get a letter every day, of course, but that is what makes it even more special when one does receive one. Graeme would usually bring half a dozen each day, and the lucky recipients would eagerly open the envelopes and take out the folded paper within as though it were written on gold-leafed parchment. It would be read and read again. Treasured. Kept in a drawer to be pored over when the sentimentality struck. They usually brought good news or news just to enjoy no matter how trivial. Postcards and pictures. Anecdotes and jokes. Occasionally there would be invites to birthday parties or weddings or other family occasions requiring the recipient to attend. Graeme knew the importance of his daily visits to The Acorns. He knew what the post meant. Another window to the outside world. Life on a piece of paper. They mattered.

One freezing morning in early January a couple of years ago, Graeme arrived to deliver the mail as usual, but this time he had an extra package. A long cylindrical shape tucked under his arm. It was addressed to Eleanor. Graeme liked the drama of hand delivering each letter rather than just pass the bundle to a member of staff. However busy he may have been, he always found the time for that personal touch.

Most of the residents were finishing off their breakfasts in the lounge when Graeme walked in that day. He saved the package under his arm until last.

"Here you go love," he said to Eleanor. "This one is for you."

The shape and size of the package drew curious glances from the others. Sheila handed her a pair of scissors to cut off the sticky tape at each end.

"What is it?" Edna called out.

"Give me a bloody chance will you!" Eleanor shouted back.

Eventually, she managed to open one end and slowly pull out

61

the contents. It was held together by three elastic bands. One at each end and one in the middle of the scroll. She placed it on the table and let the scissors do their job once again. When the third and final rubber band was clipped, the whole thing burst open and spread across the table.   It was at least five feet long and three feet wide. Eleanor stood up to look down. Others had gathered around too. It was a poster.

A poster of Stan Bowles, decked in full QPR kit, ball at his feet in mid flow. In the background, the opposition looked on – helpless. Stan the Man at his finest.

"Rita Hayworth" shouted a voice from across the room. It was Peter. "I told you I would get him for you."

Everyone turned to look in his direction. Except for Eleanor. She was already halfway across the room. When she reached him, she wrapped her arms around him and thanked him profusely. It was a lovely moment and everyone started to clap and cheer.

"Get off me woman," Peter laughed. "He said he was going to sign it. Has he?"

Someone at the table confirmed that he had. In the bottom right-hand corner, there was a signature and a note. "To Eleanor. I hope this is how you remember me. I wish I could remember you. Love Stan."

"I have something else to show you too," Peter said. He took out his mobile phone – he was one of the few in The Acorns who had, and knew how to use, a Smart Phone. Eleanor sat beside him on the sofa and waited for him to find what he was looking for.

It was a short video clip. It was Stan Bowles.

"Eleanor, I hope this finds you well. I'm well. As well as I can be. Time is catching up on me now. Old age and all that. You can't stop time. I wish you all the very best. I enjoyed my time up north. It toughened me up. Made a man of me. Anyway, I will leave you now before I say something I might forget." He smiled and waved at the camera. "Tell my old mate Peter, I love him and miss him. Take care sweetheart. Thanks for caring."

Peter clicked the stop button and popped the phone back in his pocket. He had a tear in his eye but a smile on his face.

"That one is from me. That one is free."

Peter continued to make money. Goods and services continued to arrive and every dodgy character within twenty miles came to visit the home to see him at one point or another.

The poster of Stan continued to hang on Eleanor's bedroom wall until she passed away a couple of years later. A treasured possession worth more than any watch, perfume or Louis Vuitton bag.

8

Lockdown

I have often been asked why I do this job. What do I get out of it? What is my reward? The pay is rubbish, the hours are long, and where is the job satisfaction in wiping bottoms and cleaning false teeth?

From the outside, I can understand the scepticism, and I can accept the mockery, but for many of us, this is not a job – more of a vocation. We do this for the love of it. For the love of the people in our care.

Our job may be all those things mentioned above, but to me and many like me, it is an absolute joy to be surrounded by so much life and experience. Of course, there are aspects of the job you don't enjoy, but these are far outweighed by the many positives. The residents are a second family to me and my colleagues. I have about twenty-five Grandads and twenty-five Grandmas. They bring out the child in me. I'm a grown woman now with lumps and bumps, spots and sores, fillings and scars, and even the odd grey hair. But when I'm in their company, I'm a teenager again. A child. I feel innocent and humble. I look up to them, and I respect them all.

Dignity is so important to them. They don't want to be helped to dress or cleaned-up if they have had an accident. They want to be as independent as possible. We learn that there is a time to laugh and joke, and other times just to do the work. We don't dwell on those moments. We don't fuss or complain. We get the job done, and don't mention it again. They appreciate that. They trust us, and I love them for it.

As staff, we all know about Maslow's Hierarchy of Needs. It is part of the training. It concerns the theory of psychology explaining human motivation based on different levels of need.

First there is the physiology. The basics we need to survive – air, water, food, clothing, shelter. Then we move to safety needs – health, a job, security. Love and belonging follow that. A sense of worth. A family. Love and care.

Then comes esteem. People have a craving to be respected and desired. They want to be recognised for their work and achievements. They want to enjoy their freedom.

These are the four steps and, at The Acorns, we do our best to satisfy all of those needs. Some are harder to achieve than others, but we try. If we tick those boxes to the best of our ability, we know we are doing enough to provide a happy and stable environment for our residents.

At the top of Maslow's hierarchy is Self-Actualization. The goal of striving to be the best you can be. Some may argue that our residents have had their time. They have achieved all they are going to achieve. That makes me so cross. It would make them cross too if they knew. They still harbour dreams and ambitions. Even from their armchairs or wheelchairs. They write, they sing, they invent and they share knowledge. The Acorns is a hive of activity and creative thinking. Alive and kicking. Full of life.

And then Covid came along.

In late 2019, news bulletins informed us of a mystery virus originating from a city in China most of us had never heard of before – despite having a population comparable to London. The origins of the virus were unknown. Theories ranged from unclean markets and uncooked meat to hidden laboratories and men in white coats. At the time it didn't affect us. It was on the other side of the world.

It would affect us soon enough though. It would come to Britain, and every other corner of the globe.

It knocked on the door of The Acorns too, and once inside it tried to destroy everything we had built and every person we cared for.

This was no time for self-actualization. This was no time for dreams or ambitions. Survival was all that mattered and, by God, we had a job on our hands.

When our Prime Minister soberly announced that the country was to go into lockdown on 23rd March 2020, we didn't really understand its significance or what it would mean to The Acorns. What did lockdown mean to us?

"We are locked in here most of the time anyway," Edith chuckled.

"Another prison," muttered Peter.

"At least we will be able to get to know each other a little better," added Frank, sarcastically.

The reality was far worse than expected. Initially, it was all a novelty. Nobody suffered. Communal areas were altered to observe the two-metre distancing rule. Cleaning and sanitising became even more important and more regular than usual. Visitations were restricted, then stopped altogether to ensure the residents were protected as much as possible.

For us staff, we had to ensure our clothes and uniforms were washed and changed every day. Twice a day. Three times even!

We had to shower before, during and after work to maintain the highest possible levels of cleanliness. Some meals were prepared externally and delivered in sealed units.

"This is like the stuff those astronauts eat," Frank scoffed as he peeled off the plastic wrapper to reveal something that resembled a spaghetti bolognaise.

Novelty turned to boredom and boredom turned to panic and stress. Family members couldn't visit their elderly relatives. Phone calls and photographs were poor substitutes for hugs and cuddles. Some family members would come to the door, demanding to see their mother or father. We couldn't let them in. There were tears on both sides of the wall and windows. It was for their own safety, but try telling that to a lady in her nineties who has to watch her son sob his heart out for his mother sitting only inches away from him or try telling that to a daughter who needs one of her dads reassuring cuddles to get her through the day.

The weeks turned to months, and the worst was yet to come. The death toll rose each day and the news reported little else other than the virus and its catastrophic effects on people the world over.

And then it hit us!

It was 25th May 2020.

Sam was found lying on the floor one morning, struggling to catch his breath. We called for the emergency services and, thankfully, an ambulance arrived within half an hour. He was taken to the hospital in Carlisle and it was confirmed that evening that he did indeed have the virus. Despite all our best efforts, Covid had entered The Acorns.

It was then that the real battle began.

Residents were confined to their rooms. Staff were allocated certain areas to avoid cross contamination. This meant we had our own 'bubbles' and we couldn't mix with the others. There was a terrific amount of stress and uncertainty. It really was a matter of life and death.

Staff were tested regularly, and so were the residents. That is until we ran out of tests. Not only tests – masks, gloves, sanitiser and aprons. We were using torn up uniforms to cover our faces. Make-shift aprons or gloves made out of carrier bags. To say it wasn't ideal would be an understatement. The NHS had none to give us so we turned to local businesses and shops for help. They were fantastic and brought us all they could. We might not have been allowed to let people inside, but the community certainly let us know they were there for us.

As restrictions eased elsewhere, cases inside the home started to rise. Four more residents were taken to the hospital as emergencies.

We found out that Sam had passed away, and would be buried alone. There would be no family in attendance. No friends. He wouldn't be the last.

We lost three more that summer. The summer from hell. Doris, Belle and Simon. All taken too early. Lovely people lost. More would follow in time.

Others caught it and recovered. Others are still recovering now. The effects of the lockdown took its toll on all the residents. On all of us.

When restrictions were lifted following the first round of vaccination injections, we were allowed to hold a socially distanced vigil in the grounds of the home. It was a sombre affair as you can imagine. Four saplings were planted in the garden that summer. One for each life lost.

2020 was a horrible year, 2021 was little better, but as restrictions slowly began to lift, and more and more people were given their vaccinations and boosters, some normality returned to the home.

The lounges were open again.

People could mingle and mix. Chef Neil was back, and the food was good again.

But the most important thing – the thing that mattered more than anything else in the world – was the reuniting of families and friends.

To stand at the side and see the embraces, the kisses and the happy tears broke my heart. The 'survivors' had their loved ones back. These were treasured moments and the hugs were tight but tender, with people desperately trying make up for all the time lost.

I tested positive in June of 2021. I lost my sense of smell and taste for over two weeks. I had the symptoms of a bad cold, but other than that, I was fine.

When I returned to work, negative and refreshed a fortnight later, I was greeted like royalty by the residents. They had missed me and I had missed them.

So much.

We all vowed never to take each other for granted again. We, once again, promised to make the most of the time we had left.

We could look to the stars again. We could dream. We had our lives back and we were ready to live them.

Maslow would have been very proud of us.

But we would definitely save the parties for when it was safe and legal. That was only right.

9

Memories

Covid 19 had taken its toll on us all and we were extra vigilant and careful for a long time after the restrictions were fully lifted. Every one of us had been affected one way or another. We had all lost someone close or knew someone who had.

Most of us, at one stage or another, had caught the virus, and suffered to varying degrees. We read in the newspapers that some folk were sceptical, citing conspiracy theories or elaborate hoaxes. I don't think anyone within The Acorns doubted the authenticity of the pandemic regardless of its origins.

The elderly were particularly susceptible. It was another stark reminder of the frailty of life. Death was always around the corner, waiting to pounce.

Throughout it all, a fighting spirit remained - and no shortage of dark humour too.

"I read that ticket sales for the latest Batman film are down 50%," said Frank to the others in the Les Dawson Conservatory. "They don't trust him. Or anything to do with bats. Spiderman is all the rage now."

The audience groaned.

"And they are having to cancel cricket matches left, right and centre as no one will go near the batsman."

More groans.

"Well, have you got any better ones?" Frank chortled.

"It is not compulsory to wear a mask anymore" chipped in Edith, "but I wish you still had yours on, you ugly bugger!"

The room burst out laughing and Frank chuckled along with them.

"It's been a while since we had a good laugh together, hasn't it?" said Ralph.

"Too bloody long. I can barely remember the times before the virus," Mavis added, thoughtfully.

"You can't remember what you had for breakfast, never mind before Covid!" Frank sniggered.

"Oh, go boil your head, you sarcastic old fool" she replied.

It was all in jest. Never any malice.

The banter was interrupted by a few new faces at the door. We all turned to look. Vera was showing a prospective new guest around. She was flanked by two younger ladies whom I presumed were her daughter and granddaughter.

"These people," Vera said, pointing around the room, "Would be your new friends and neighbours should you wish to join us here at The Acorns. They may not look an exciting bunch, but they are a lovely crowd."

"Charming!" shouted Frank in mock disgust.

The lady in the middle nodded at us all and smiled. She looked terrified. I noticed the younger lady give her hand a reassuring squeeze before Vera led them out of the room to continue the tour of the building.

"What do you make of that one then?" asked Frank.

"Handsome lady. We need more of them," said Stan.

I looked through the glass panels in the door. Vera was leading them up the stairs, pointing in every direction. I noticed the ladies both still had hold of her hands as they slowly ascended. They were not for letting go.

Later that evening, I was sitting in the staff room with Vera, drinking coffee and demolishing a packet of chocolate biscuits. I asked her about the group she was showing around earlier in the day. She told me that the old lady was called Dora. She knew little more about her than that. Dora had been living with her daughter since her husband passed away a couple of years earlier. Vera said she was very quiet and terribly nervous. Shy, but polite too.

Vera said her daughter asked so many questions that, at first, she thought she was the controlling type, but it turned out there were genuine reasons for her concerns. Over the last few months, the family had become more and more concerned about Dora's general state of mind. They would find her sitting out in the garden in the middle of the night or just standing staring at the walls in a kind of trance, almost like she was lost in a daydream. Most of the time she was fine, but these odd occasions had troubled them. Doctors visited the house to examine her and carry out various tests and their conclusions confirmed what the family had suspected. Dora was in the early stages of Dementia. The news, whilst not a total shock, had rocked the family. According to her daughter, she had always been the backbone of the family. Quiet, but strong, reliable and dependable. They admitted she hadn't been the same since her husband's death, and this confirmation of the onset of such a debilitating illness was another hammer blow to an already fragile family.

Vera explained that the family had tried to cope. They wanted their mam and grandma to stay at home, but she was determined not to become a burden to them all. She had her own savings and security. She chose the home, not them. She had shopped around and decided on The Acorns.

I thought about my own parents. What would they choose to do under the same circumstances? Dad often joked about mam losing her marbles, but this was nothing more than a bit of fun when she forgot something or took too long to get ready.

It must have been incredibly hard for the family to come to terms with something so tragic.

To see the illness slowly penetrate their loved one – slowly stealing her memories. What is worse – a quick death or a slow decline? There is no right or wrong answer, I suppose. You just don't know until you are at the heart of it.

To exist in the present is hard enough. The future, if we are lucky, is something to look forward to. The past is something to reflect on with fondness. Again, time is relative to the individual concerned.

I have been fortunate, with a few bumps along the road, to have enjoyed my past and present. I am positive for the future too. But times can change. Without warning, our comfort blankets can be whipped away from us, and the very fragility of life comes back to the forefront of our minds.

That night, I worried for our potential new resident. I knew little to nothing about her, and yet I was already fretting about what I could do to help her – to make her comfortable and secure in our home. It was silly, I know, but I couldn't help it.

She was a still a stranger to me then.

We didn't even know if she would be joining us on a permanent basis, but I worried nonetheless.

The next day, I sat out in the garden with Ralph and Stan. It was a lovely day and the garden was looking beautiful. Dandelion seeds danced through the air in front of us looking for a place to settle. Bees bobbed from flower to flower hoping to catch any pollen left behind, and the pathways and beds teemed with insects going about their business.

It was Ralph who noticed first. "What's wrong with you love?" he asked, poking my leg gently with his stick.

"Nothing. I'm good" I replied unconvincingly.

"You aren't your usual bubbly self," he said. "I can tell something is up. You might be our carer, but we are your carers too you know."

I offered him a weak smile, but he wasn't going to give up that easily.

"I might be a man – and we are noted for our lack of sensitivity and understanding as a sex – but when something is so obviously out of place, we get there in the end. I know you, young lady, now what's up?"

I started crying. I felt stupid later on, but right there and then, I started crying like a little girl in front of the two old men.

When I had finished blubbing, I told them about the lady who had been shown around the home the other day. I told them about my conversation with Vera, and what she had told me about her condition. I told them that I could not stop thinking about it and it troubled me.

Stan reached over and held my hand. The three of us sat in silence for a while watching the wildlife and the beauty in front of us.

"You know what?" Stan said, smiling at me, "Losing my mind was always my greatest fear. When you reach this age, memories are all you have got and, by God, I treasure mine. My wife, my family, my friends – so many happy times. I seem to remember everything that is important to me. The bad

74

memories – the things that upset me – are shoved away now. I haven't forgotten them. They are still there in the back of my mind, but I don't think about them unless I choose to. And now, I choose not to. As daft as it sounds, you learn that with age. As a youngster, you dwell on stuff too much. You think about things too much. You keep dredging up the times that hurt the most – lost love, arguments with friends, grief and loss. All things that can rip you to pieces if you let it. With age, you learn to live with it. Death is more frequent, failing health more prevalent. Your mind has too much to deal with, so – to sound like some bloody office executive – you compartmentalise. You choose what to remember and what to leave behind. My wife's death was the hardest thing I have ever had to deal with. But now I can enjoy the memories we had. I revel in the good times and block out the bad – and there were some bad times too! They don't matter now though. The rows and arguments, the days without talking, the tears. I don't think of those times. I choose to leave those locked away. The holidays, the family gatherings, the laughs we had, the intimate moments. They matter. That is what I remember. Do you understand where I am coming from?"

I nodded.

"This lady coming to us will still have all her memories. They will come and go. They might be locked away in a dark room at the very back of her mind, but they will be there. The illness is a cruel one. A horrible one for the family who think they are no more than a distant memory, but I don't believe that is the case. There will be flickers of recognition. Those good memories – and a few bad – will come to the fore, and the mind will work again. We must care for her, but not feel sorry for her. We must all give her the support she needs. Those moments of clarity might be few and far between, but when they arrive, we must be ready to savour them – to cherish them. Am I making sense?"

I nodded again.

"My own mother suffered from Dementia in later life. It was never really understood then, and I don't think it is truly understood now, but even with my own limited experience, one thing I do know is this – when she showed a moment of understanding, a moment of recognition and love towards myself and the others – it meant the world to me. My mam was back."

Stan squeezed my hand and smiled. These old buggers certainly knew how to counsel. Life skills over qualifications.

"And we will look after her. Whatever it takes" he said. Ralph nodded in agreement.

"I can't remember what I had for tea yesterday. I can't remember where I left my cap, and I can't remember the names of half my teachers at school. I do remember the score of nearly every Carlisle United match I have watched – including the attendances and scorers – since I started going over sixty years ago. What does that say about me?"

"That you are a bloody idiot," laughed Stan.

"Maybe so, but it always amazes me just how the mind works. We remember what we want to remember. What is important to us. What matters. This illness, this disease. It is so cruel. But, from what you have told us, she is surrounded by good people and she has lived a good life – so far. She isn't beaten by it.

She is fighting it and while there is a fight, there is that hope. We faced Covid and we will face whatever comes our way. We are a team, aren't we?"

I nodded again, but this time I was smiling too.

We were a team – and a bloody good one at that.

From that moment on, I couldn't wait for Dora to arrive, and be our next welcome resident in The Acorns.

10

Compositions for the Young and Old

Friday 16th July 2021 was manic day. Another one of those risk assessments from hell, but always one worth doing. The choir from Brampton Primary School were scheduled to visit The Acorns to perform a selection of summer songs for the residents.

At the same time, a few children from the Year 6 class were visiting to carry out some interviews, and talk with the old people about what life was like when they were the same age as them. Apparently, they had been studying the local area and one of the teachers had come up with the bright idea of encouraging them to talk with the old folk at The Acorns, and encourage them to open up about their own lives too. I shuddered at the thought.

The idea of some innocent little boy or girl interviewing Frank about what he got up to when he was a child didn't bear thinking about, but Vera thought it was a great idea and booked them in.

Even with ongoing Covid restrictions it was possible if we used the garden and open spaces.

When old and young meet you never really know what to expect. It could be beautiful; it could be a disaster. You can plan and risk assess all you like, but when the day arrives, you just have to cross your fingers and hope for the best.

We suggested the singers visit in the morning before lunch, and the others to come later in the afternoon to chat to a select few of our residents.
We would have to hand-pick who we felt would do a good job,

and I was sure the teachers would be doing the same at their end.

To be fair, visits from the school children were always appreciated and supported. Some of the old people had grandchildren in the school, and they were very keen to see their little ones perform.

There was a buzz around the breakfast tables as they discussed the children's impending performance. We had popped a few flyers on the tables, given to us by the school. On one side there was a picture of the choir and on the other, a list of songs they planned to perform.

They were to start with a couple of hymns (Morning Has Broken and All Things Bright and Beautiful) before bursting into their own rendition of 'Walking on Sunshine' by Katrina and the Waves. All the songs had a summer theme and, with the sun beating down outside, they couldn't have scheduled it better.

The chairs were ordered in the Keith Chegwin Suite to form a semi-circle around the cork floor which would act as a temporary stage for the singers.

The children were due to arrive at 10:00 a.m. for a 10:30 a.m. start, and after the last of the breakfast plates were cleared away, the residents wandered through to claim their seats and a coveted place on the front row.

Everyone sat and chatted as we waited for the arrival of the little ones.

Just before ten, we heard the pitter-patter of dozens of feet approaching along the gravel pathway outside. High-pitched voices, giggles and chatter filled the air, and we could hear the teachers telling them to settle down as they approached the front door.

Vera opened the door before they had a chance to ring the bell and welcomed them all inside. There must have been about twenty children – all shapes and sizes.

The youngest ones were just the tots from the reception class. They were holding hands with the older boys and girls. It was nice to see more boys than usual, there must have been seven or eight.

Their teacher, Mrs. Hill, hushed them before leading them all through to stand in front of their eager audience. She positioned the smallest at the front and the tall ones behind them until the group were almost symmetrical and ready to begin.

It was clear she commanded respect from each and every one of them as they stood to attention, acting on every word she uttered. She was accompanied by Mr. Bowler, who was clearly just there to make up the numbers and get out of school for a morning. He paid little attention to the choir and took up a seat on the back row beside Ralph and me.

I asked him if he would like a coffee and he jumped at the chance. Ralph asked him if he needed something stronger, and he jumped at the chance of that too. I explained that we didn't have a licensed bar in the home, but when Ralph pulled out a hip flask, he was more than happy to take a swig before his hot drink arrived.

Mrs. Hill jostled and jiggled, fussed and flapped until she was happy with everyone's position before standing to the side, indicating that they were good to go.

Vera stood in front of the choir and introduced them to their audience. They gave the children an enthusiastic round of applause, and a few whistles which made them giggle. I am sure that helped take away a few nerves.

The two from the reception class at the front bravely started off on their own before the others joined in. They looked terrified at first but, by mid song, they were in their element. By the time they got to the chorus of 'All Things Bright and Beautiful', most of the old folk were joining in, clapping along and tapping their sticks and slippers along with the beat. Mrs. Hill was beaming. Everything was going to plan.

'Summer Holiday' by Cliff Richard came next before 'Cruel Summer' by Bananarama.

The children took a well-earned break halfway through for orange juice and biscuits, and Mr. Bowler carried on chatting and drinking 'coffee' with Ralph.

I congratulated the children on their performance so far. They were ever so polite and respectful. A real credit to the school. I mentioned this to Mrs. Hill, who in turn said she would pass it on to the head. "They are a good lot to be fair. There were others who wanted to come, but we left the idiots back in class. They may be able to sing, but I didn't want them spoiling it for the others." I nodded in agreement and looked around to see what Frank was doing. We didn't need our own idiots starting to play up!

The second half was as good as the first, and when they finished with a rousing rendition of 'Summer Nights' from the Grease soundtrack, most of the audience were up dancing.

It could not have gone any better. The children were given a huge round of applause at the end and three big cheers. A couple of the ladies even asked the choir members for their autographs which had them jumping up and down with excitement. It was lovely.

"That's my job done for the day," laughed Mrs. Hill. "It is junior sports day this afternoon, and I am taking a back seat. He is in charge of that" she said nodding to her half-cut counterpart still sat talking to Ralph.

I asked her who was coming over in the afternoon.

"Oh, that lot? You have a handful of Year 6's. Smart arses.
The head insisted we send up those we wouldn't normally
choose to send. She thinks it will do them good to talk to the
older folk, but be on your guard. Don't let them take the piss.
They have the potential to be a bit cheeky and inappropriate if
they think they can get away with it. I hope not. You have a
lovely crowd here. It would be a shame if they tarnished the
reputation of the school, but we have to trust them to do right.
We have to give them a chance."

And with that, we shook hands and wished each other well.

I made a mental note to change the running order for the
afternoon. I decided to bring Frank and Peter off the
substitute's bench. It sounded like we would need to fight fire
with fire.

A couple of staff members cleared up the Keith Chegwin Suite
as the children made their way back to school. The residents all
wandered off to their rooms or into the garden to relax. It was a
glorious day, and everyone was in a good mood after the lovely
performance.

Vera toddled off to do some paperwork in the office, and asked
me to greet the afternoons visitors and make them welcome.

Frank was sitting out in the garden with Beatrice. I walked out
to sit with them both and asked Peter if he would join us as
well.

I'd initially asked Clarence if he would like to take part in the
interviews, but he was fast asleep under the pagoda which gave
me the excuse I needed to change the team line up.

Beatrice had already agreed to be interviewed. She was a wise

old head and knew how to deal with difficult children having been a teacher herself when she was a lot younger.
I needed at least one or two more, and when I lost Clarence to the land of nod, I decided to bring in the big guns.

"Why me?" asked Peter, quite honestly. "With my history, I am hardly the best role model. I can't tell them much about building go-karts or climbing trees, but I can give them a crash course in lock picking."

Frank was equally sceptical. "I haven't the patience for this kind of thing. And I will be brutally honest with my answers. Is that really what you want?"

Stupidly, I just told them to relax and be themselves. They both laughed and agreed.

This was either going to be a really fun afternoon or a bloody nightmare.

The children and the staff arrived shortly after 2:00 p.m.

Miss Wright was the teacher in charge and she was accompanied by Miss Clayton, one of the ladies who worked in the office.

"We were short staffed today," Miss Wright explained. "It's the sports day, and to be honest, it was hard to get anyone who wanted to spend an afternoon with these little buggers. I hope they behave for you and the old dears. If at any time you want them out, just say. They are on their final of final warnings. If they insult anyone, swear, break wind or belch, just say the word and they will be out the door and on the way to a suspension before you can say Oliver Twist." She gave me a wink and a smile, but I knew she meant it. Straight to the point. I liked that.

I was about to say the same to her about our crowd, but she was already distracted by one of the boys dangling an energy drink over the fish tank.

Her number two, Miss Clayton had a worried expression on her face. I asked if she was alright.

"Watch them like a hawk. Don't leave anything lying around – they will have it! I should be in the office listening to the radio, eating biscuits and playing card games on the computer. This isn't what I signed up for."

Miss Wright came back over to us with half a bottle of the energy drink and a red-faced pre-pubescent boy.

"This is Dwayne. He is one of the nice boys we invited here to ask a few polite questions to the gentlemen and ladies who reside here."

She tossed the bottle into a nearby bin. "I hope the fish don't mind a sugar rush."

Miss Clayton ushered the other three over.

"Joining Dwayne will be Crystal, and the twins, Pacific and Atlantic," she said. "Pacific is the girl by the way. Atlantic the boy. Sister and brother – the sister was the bigger of the two. God knows what the parents were thinking! We won't take up too much of your time. It is for a project they are doing on how society has changed."

"For the worse" chipped in Miss Wright.

I led them all through to the garden. The children followed looking disinterested and bored. They were clearly there under duress – the staff were too.

I'd asked Peter, Frank and Beatrice to sit on separate benches, all spread out across the lawn so they could each have some privacy. Miss Wright (Shauna) and Miss Clayton (Jo) said they would supervise from the side lines.

I had no idea how this was going to pan out, but I felt strangely excited by it all. Two very different worlds were about to collide.

Dwayne went to sit with Peter. Crystal with Beatrice and 'Ocean's Eleven-year-olds' with Frank. I wandered between all three to eavesdrop on the conversations. They didn't disappoint.

Dwayne asked Peter how old he was. Peter reluctantly told him. "You look older," Dwayne shot back with a smug smile on his face.

I moved on.

Crystal asked Beatrice what she used to do when she was able to get about. Beatrice told her, causing her to snort and curse. Shauna was about to step in until she noticed me shaking my head. She stood back again and let nature take its course.

Ten yards further on, the seas were already choppy.

"Your dad wasted a couple of sperm with you two, didn't he?" Frank laughed. "What kind of a question is that?"

I don't know what it was they had asked him, but they had no idea what he meant with his reply.

"Let me ask you a question," he went on. "If you were born and bred in Brampton, why do you talk like you have just stepped out of the Bronx?"

More blank expressions.

"And yes, you might be right. I am a grumpy old bastard, but you are obese and ignorant. If this is you at eleven, what the hell are you going to be like when you reach twenty? I was going to say, wait until you are my age, but you won't get that far. Your hearts will be giving up before you have a chance to shed your spots."

Shauna and Jo stood there, mouths open, suppressing a laugh.

Beatrice was on form too. "If you grew up when I grew up, and had the audacity to speak that way to an adult, you would get six of the best off your teacher and then another six off your parents. What business is it of yours since I last had sex?"

I was cringing. This was a bad idea. A very bad idea.

Dwayne, on the other hand, was engrossed in a conversation with Peter. It was only when I got a bit closer did I realise why.

"...and that is the best way to pick a padlock. Forget what you see in the films. A hair clip will do the trick."

I bit my lip and looked over at Shauna and Jo. They were loving it.

Peter continued teaching Dwayne the art of doing wrong.

"I know people. If your dad wants weed, I know just the man to get the good stuff very cheap. Forget the main dealers – shop local."

Dwayne was writing it all down.

Crystal looked well and truly roasted and Atlantic and Pacific were shedding salty tears.

Shauna put her teacher head back on and suggested they take their leave and return to school. It was a lesson they wouldn't forget.

When they had gone, I went back into the garden.

"I enjoyed that," said Frank.

"Me too," said Peter.

"It was nice to bring back the old teacher in me," laughed Beatrice.

My little plan had backfired on me. What was I thinking of? I wandered back inside with my tail between my legs. I didn't dare tell Vera. She would go crazy. I promised myself I would call the school the following Monday and apologise on behalf of the residents. I needn't have worried.

Before the end of the school day, I received a telephone call from Miss Wright.

"That was the best ever! They have never been so subdued and apologetic. Whatever those old guys said and done was enough to put the wind up them. They promised to write a letter of apology to Frank, Peter and Beatrice, and the head would like to thank you for being so accommodating and supportive of the school. Can you pass on the message?"

I thanked her so much and promised I would.

"The choir wants to come again next year. We will worry about the Q&A session nearer the time." I knew she was smiling down the phone. I was too.

I hung up and made my way back out to the garden. Frank and Peter were playing cards.

"Here she comes," said Frank. "What have we done now? Are we staying in at breaktime?"

I leaned over and kissed them both on the top of their heads. "You make me feel young. Do you know that?" I walked away with a huge smile on my face.

Old Folk (1) v (0) Young.

11

The Explorer

Dora joined us at the end of July 2021. It was the 30th actually. I remember that because it was the day after her 85th birthday. The family wanted to spend her birthday with her before she moved into The Acorns.

The car pulled up not long after the breakfast dishes had been cleared away. We watched through the window as Dora and her daughter and granddaughter climbed out.

I was on duty with Shirley – a dumpy little Scottish woman with curly, blonde hair. She had worked with us for around five years, but only for one day a week to, "get her out the house".

Her husband owned a popular garden centre near Gretna. She didn't need the wage, but she did enjoy the social side and the gossip, and I could totally understand that.

Considering our residents rarely ventured out of the grounds, they seemed to have their finger on the pulse. If it was happening outside, they knew all about it inside before any of the staff did. There were no secrets either, and when they started a sentence with "Don't tell anybody..." you knew they meant, "Tell whoever you like."

They knew before journalists found out. They knew before the TV and the Radio broadcasts. Burglaries, Royal visits, football club signings, shop openings, accidents, road closures, fires, scandals – you name it. This collection of old heads seemed to have more hotlines and spies than the secret services!
They would have had the codes cracked for the Enigma machine within half an hour if someone had left it lying in the Keith Chegwin Suite on a quiet Wednesday.

Needless to say, before Dora Eleanor Dewsnap had even entered her new home, the residents already had some knowledge of her past.

"Her husband was a copper before he died," Alice said.

"That's all we need," moaned Peter.

"My sister, Philippa, lived down the street from them a few years back. Apparently, she used to answer the phones and clean the police houses. She used to look after the police dogs too. You know the kind – Alsatians. The kind that would take your hand off if you so much as looked at them."

"I've been chased by a few of them over the years. They can bite and they can run, but they can't climb trees. They haven't taught them to do that yet, thank God," Peter mused.

"They will one day, just you watch!" laughed Doreen.

"I wouldn't be surprised," Pete replied, "But I bet they couldn't climb a tree with a VHS video recorder in one hand and half a dozen cassette tapes up their jumper!"

"She is only a little one, isn't she?" continued Doreen as Shirley greeted the family, and welcomed them into the building.

"She is, bless her. Loved though. Look how that granddaughter clings to her. So protective of her, isn't she?" Alice said in a whisper so loud it could have been heard in the attic.

I shot them a stare, and they realised it was time to shut up for a few minutes.

I walked over and introduced myself to Dora and her family. It was only when I stood beside her that I realised just how small and frail she was.

"Happy belated birthday, Dora, and welcome to The Acorns. I'm Angie."

She looked up to me and gave me that nervous smile.

"Hello Angie. Thank you. It is lovely to be here. I do hope I don't become a burden to you. I will do my best to make your lives as easy as possible."

Her voice was soft and gentle, but clear and kind too. The kind of voice that could persuade someone not to toss themselves off a bridge. The kind of voice that would calm a Alsatian after it had chased Peter Brockbank up a tree.

"You will be no trouble at all, Dora, don't you worry about that" I said, reassuringly. "I see you have brought along your daughter and granddaughter to carry your cases. Lovely."

She turned and looked around at them as if not realising she even had an entourage, before returning her gaze to me.

"They insisted they came. I am sorry. If there are house rules on guests, I can ask them to go back to the car?"

I told her it wasn't a problem. The more the merrier.

Dora's new room was on the first floor, and we used the lift to go up. Some children who were visiting other elderly relatives bounded up the stairs, and were there to meet us as the doors slowly slid open. I noticed she was holding her daughter's hand again. Or maybe it was the other way round.

I led them all down the corridor. It was another lovely day outside and the sunshine burst through the windows, lighting up the burgundy carpet.
I realised I was only in stockinged feet as I could feel the warmth toasting my toes as we walked along.

Shirley had already gone ahead to open the door and windows to let some air in. Dora's room was to be number 18. It was a nice room with a view of the back garden and the rolling hills heading towards Greenhead. She walked over towards the window as her daughter and granddaughter explored the room.

She stood and gazed out for what seemed like an age before turning back to face us.

"He would have liked it here," she said. "I think I will like it here too. He would have liked me to be here."

Dora stayed in her new room with Joanne, her granddaughter. One staff member went back to the car to bring in her other personal belongings while I took her daughter, Amanda, back downstairs to the office to sort out some of the paperwork. I could tell she was reluctant to leave her mother even then.

She looked exhausted, bless her. I made her a coffee and we indulged in some small talk before the nitty gritty.

"I love her so much," Amanda said, trying to put on a brave face. "She means the world to me. More so since we lost dad a couple of years ago. And now there is the condition to deal with too – Dementia. Alzheimer's. I can't bear to think about how bad it might get. She has always had such a sharp mind. It was always dad who forgot things. She was his walking diary."

I asked her to tell me more about how the condition was affecting Dora.

"She isn't going to get any better. Only worse. At the moment, it isn't a huge issue. She is able to function and, as long as we keep a close eye on her, she seems fine. Little things really – she would leave a light on or a tap running. Sometimes she will just, sort of, faze out...lose her train of thought. She will stop talking midway through a conversation and totally forget what it was she was talking about. We don't dwell on it. We don't want her to feel embarrassed or anything, so we would just start talking about something else. It isn't that regular either. Most of the time she would be normal. That is what is so sad...so... frustrating."

I asked her if there was anything else we needed to know at this stage. The doctors' reports had arrived, and I had read through them, but they lacked detail. They talked about the condition, not the person.

"She will wander," Amanda said, looking down into her coffee cup. "That worries me. Especially here – especially when we aren't with her to keep an eye on her. We take turns at home – in shifts, if you like. Sometimes she will just get up out of her chair and walk. She doesn't get far, and someone has always been there to guide her back, but it frightens me. What if she was to get out of the grounds? She wouldn't know where she was. Anything could happen."

Her eyes filled up. I passed her a tissue and rested my hand on hers.

"That won't happen, " I whispered to her. "We have a great team here. This is why these conversations are so important. Reports and policies help, of course they do, but we value the human touch here. Your mam will be well-cared for by each and every one of us. She will soon get to know us and we will get to know her. We will be like an extended family for her. She will be safe and happy here, trust me."

She did trust me. She squeezed my hand and wiped her eyes.

We made our way back to Room 18. Out of the window, we could see the children running around in the garden. The adults were sitting watching them with half a dozen of the residents. Dora's granddaughter – Joanne – was with them.

"Why is she there? Where's mam?"

Amanda started to walk faster down the corridor until she

reached number 18. The door was open, the unpacked cases lay on the floor. The window was wide open and Dora's handbag sat on the pillow.

Amanda started to panic. "Oh God, where is she?"

She rushed to the window to look out and down. No sign of her. She could see people on the lawn chatting to other visitors.

"Oh God" she repeated and rushed out the room calling out for her mother.

I padded after her in my stockinged feet. I was starting to worry then.

Amanda ran through the Keith Chegwin Suite, looking, searching, and panicking.

No sign of Dora.

"I knew this would happen. Oh God, please let her be alright."

And then she looked into the Jimmy Glass TV room, and the worry on her face lifted only to be replaced with a huge smile of relief.

There was Dora, sitting around a little table with Alice and Doreen. They were playing cards and chuckling away together.

"Full house!" Alice called out. "That's five pence you owe me, the pair of you. Another hand?"

Dora and Doreen nodded and pushed a coin each across the table to Alice.

"Are you alright, mam?" Amanda called out to her mother, her voice beginning to crack with the emotion of it all.

"I'm on top of the world, my love. I'm having a great time, despite being fifteen pence down!"

Dora turned back to the game and Amanda turned to me.

"I know I have to let her go. I am so sorry. What must you think of me?"

"What must I think of you?" I said. "I think you love and you care. That's all that matters to me."

I held her hand again and we both watched the ladies play their game, lost in their own world.

Our new resident was only tiny, but she would go on to leave a huge impression on us all.

Me in particular.

12

Place Value

Apart from the odd excursion, The Acorns was our world – mine as well as the residents. I wasn't particularly well travelled, and I would spend most of my week within the confines of the complex. For those actually living here, their travelling and exploring days were a thing of the past. Occasionally, they would go somewhere with their families, such as a special birthday meal or a wedding, but generally they would be confined to the home.

We tried to bring the outside world to them through guests and live entertainment. We offered taster sessions for food from around the world. We had the library loan bus, and celebrate special days from other countries. The residents had a keen interest in current affairs - locally, nationally and internationally, but their world was inside the four walls of the home.

There were some regrets. A few of the residents wished they had ventured further afield or travelled to different places to try different cultures.

For many, the done thing was to marry young – to start a family and build a home. There was even a degree of envy at 'the youngsters of today' who 'had everything on a plate'.

"There were no overseas holidays for us" I'd hear them say. "No mobile phone or internet. No fast cars or fast trains in our day. If you wanted to go to the beach, you would have to plan weeks in advance – and save for it too."

But for all the whinging observations, few, if any of them, would give up what they had for what the new generation have today.

They were delighted that a mobile phone hadn't interrupted their youth.

"We talked. We actually had conversations, and we got to know one another – we knew how each other ticked. We understood facial expressions – not those emojicons or whatever it is they use today. We weren't shut away in our rooms for hours on end staring at a screen. We mingled. We merged. We quizzed. We probed. We laughed. We shared life."

As a member of the so-called younger generation living and working with the old, I can see and appreciate the best of both. I can see the benefits of advanced technology, and how it has made the world a smaller and more accessible place, but I also see the dangers – the isolation, the addiction, the spy in the sky.

I try to avoid using my phone in the home, but it isn't easy. I'm drawn to it at break times and lunchtimes. I use it to solve an argument or find information. Any excuse. And yet I see the harm it does – to society and to how we interact, or no longer interact, as one.

There is certainly an innocence amongst the old. Technology is moving apace, leaving all of us behind – not least those who had no intention of trying to keep up with it in the first place.

The television baffles them too. When they were young, they were lucky to have one in the house – sometimes even the street! And those that did only had the benefit of one or two channels, not the hundreds we have to choose from today but, as Frank often puts it, "It's just five hundred channels of shite!"

He would go on with his familiar rant while flicking through the channels with the remote control. "Twenty channels of sports that no one has ever watched. Repeats, repeats, repeats. Twenty channels of films no one has heard of or wants to watch. Twenty channels of people gardening, another twenty of some idiotic family looking to buy a house they can't afford. Twenty channels of music no one wants to listen to. Twenty channels of comedies from the 70s that were crap when they were on the first time around. Twenty channels of war documentaries, twenty channels of celebrity documentaries. Twenty channels of travel programmes showing cruises no one can afford. Twenty channels of God-botherers from the Bible belt in America, all trying to save your soul if you put your credit cards details in, and pay your weight in dollars. And twenty channels of children's programmes without one kid getting into a fight, climbing a tree, or daring to do anything un-PC in case they offend some bugger who hasn't been offended for the last twenty seconds."

Frank would keep flicking through the channels, ranting, until someone told him that unless he turned it off, they would stick the controls where the sun didn't shine.

If mobile phones and televisions didn't do it for them, then what did? Conversations of course. Debates and stories – many of them I had heard a hundred times before, but I never tired of them.

I loved listening to them reminisce, especially when they talked about the places they had visited and the things they got up to when they were there. How some of their relationships started never mind lasted, beggared belief.

Once, I was being teased about my attitude towards relationships.

I had the nerve to suggest love and romance were the cornerstones of a good relationship.

"In an ideal world," laughed Yvonne. "Tolerance and patience and a little forgiveness will get you as far as any love and romance."

She went on to describe one of her most memorable – and

testing – dates.

"On one of our first dates, he arranged to meet me in the town to go for a meal. I was terrified. I didn't know what to wear, how to behave, what to talk about. It took me ages to get ready to go out – I must have changed outfits half a dozen times. All day I was a bag of nerves. Eventually, I plucked up the courage and agreed to meet at a designated place and time. No mobile phones then – you just had to stand and wait and hope your date would turn up.

Anyway, I waited and waited and waited some more. No show. I was distraught. Humiliated even. The start of our romance cut short before it had a chance to blossom."

I cursed him on her behalf. "Sod him" I told her. "At least you got to meet and marry John. You were together for over sixty years!"

"It was John I was bloody waiting for!" she shouted. "The bugger had only got on the supporter's bus for the football match away at Ipswich! He had forgotten all about the date. Someone in the pub had a spare ticket and asked him to go so off he went!"

"And you gave him another chance?" I asked.

"I am ashamed to say I did," she laughed. "They got beat. I must have felt sorry for him or something. More fool me. I bloody hate Ipswich."

"And I hate Swansea City for the same reason" chipped in Hilda. "My fella was meant to take me dancing. I stood outside the venue like some street corner hooker, waiting for him to appear only for one of his mates to pass by and tell me he had gone to Swansea on the train for the night match. He didn't get back for three days. And then he had the audacity to ask me to go out again the following weekend"

"And did you?" I asked her in astonishment.

"Like Yvonne, I bloody did. Maybe if we had had mobile phones and Netflix back then I would have told him where to go. I bloody hate Swansea!"

We all giggled like little schoolgirls. Both women went on to marry their tormentors.

There were plenty of places they didn't like, but plenty they did like too – and many were just a stone's throw from their current home.

"You know where I love?" said Jimmy, folding up his paper. "Where the river Caldew joins the Eden. I used to sit there all day as a boy watching the fishermen. From what I can remember, they didn't seem to catch much. I am not even sure they tried to. They, like me, just enjoyed the peace and tranquillity of the place. I'd sometimes take off my shoes and socks on a warm day and bathe my feet in the water. I'd take something to eat and drink – maybe a book too. It was my place. My little pocket of peace. I used to go there when I was a bit down sometimes. I'd stay there until I was all right with the world before going back home. The river helped wash away any worries. I'd never leave the place upset. It would always make me feel good about the world. Brilliant therapy."

It was lovely to listen to Jim talk. He had such a quiet, soothing voice. I often thought he would have made a narrator for audio books or something. I'd certainly pay to listen to him.

"Do you have a special place?" I asked the others gathered around the coffee table.

"Oh, I have many pet," Lucy started. "Strangely enough – and I don't want to come across as morbid here – I love the cemetery. The big one off Dalston Road. It is just so beautiful at any time of year. I know I might end up in it soon, but that doesn't trouble me. We lived on Richardson Street just around the corner. I would walk the dogs around there most days before going on the way to the riverside walk. You would meet the same people day in and day out and they became friends. I used to read the headstones. Hundreds of them dating back hundreds of years. All those people, all those lives. All the families, all the people they loved and loved them back in return. Some people think cemeteries are scary or depressing places, but not to me. They house the dead, but they tell a story of life."

No one spoke for a few seconds as though a period of dignified silence was expected at that point.

"You know where I loved?" said Edna. "My kitchen!"

This caused a ripple of laughter around the room with the obvious question – "Why?"

"It was my space. My place. I loved to cook and bake and prepare. I could get lost in there listening to the wireless and doing my own thing. I know it is stereotypical and boring, but it really was my place. Bob would never come in for fear of me asking him to do the dishes or peel some potatoes. The boys wouldn't show face for the same reason. They left well alone which was fine by me. My home in our home so to speak. My special place."

The last to speak was Dora. She had sat in silence all this time drinking in the conversation, and we were all quite shocked when we heard her little voice speak up.

"My special place was the kennels. The kennels at the police station. I used to look after all the police dogs and, while they didn't belong to us, they were part of our family too. They were all shapes and sizes. All breeds. We could have as many as eight or nine in at any one time, and I adored them all. Some of them were loud and angry looking, but not with me. I seemed to have a knack with them. They seemed to feel sorry for me because I was so small and slim. We had a sofa in there, and I used to unlock the kennels and go back and sit in the middle. Before I knew it, half a dozen of them would be snuggled up beside me. A big ball of fur surrounding me. They kept you warm in the winter, that's for sure. John would be out on his shifts and come back to find me fast asleep in the middle of this pack of wolves. He would click his fingers, and they would toddle off back to their cages without any fuss, and then we would go home together. It was so lovely. So magical. I would do anything to have those days again." She blinked and started to cry.

Hilda reached over and held her hand. "You have the memories, Dora. They are yours to keep."

Again, the room fell into a dignified silence again until Frank burst through the door.

"If anyone wants to watch TV, that holiday programme is on. I can't turn it over. The batteries must be dead! It's that one where they go abroad and show you how the other half live – A Place in the Sun."

"We have just been discussing a place in the sun," said Jimmy, smiling. "Our place in the sun. And it is better than money can buy, I am sure these ladies would agree."

They all nodded.

Frank tossed the TV remote control to me.

"Batteries" he said again, looking around at the others with a confused look on his face.

"Where is your place, Frank?" asked Jimmy.

"Wherever she puts me" he said, looking at me and smiling.

I looked down at the controls. The failed technology. There was no place for it here.

13

The Charabanc Trip

Every summer, thanks to the fundraising efforts of the local Round Table, we are able to take the residents out for the day. A bit like a school trip only for old people.

Due to Covid, the 2020 and 2021 trips had to be shelved, so when we announced that the 2022 outing would go ahead as planned, you could hear whoops and shouts from all around the home.

It wasn't obligatory and, if any of the residents didn't want to or couldn't go, a skeleton staff would remain on site to look after them. I made sure I was never one of them. I loved these trips out and we always managed to fill the bus.

This year, we decided to go to a university in Scotland! Why a university I hear you shout? Why not Blackpool or Manchester or Liverpool or The Lake District? And if you are going to go to Scotland, why not enjoy the Lochs and mountains, the festivals or the distilleries?

When I say 'we' decided to go ` to university, I meant 'them'. The residents. They chose the destination, the home merely supplied the transport and brought along the picnic.

So why a university?

Well, it all started one Saturday night – TV night.

By 8 o'clock, every seat and sofa was taken in anticipation of what was about to come on screen. Apart from Match of the Day, Strictly Come Dancing was the show they all wanted to watch.

As the celebrities trotted and twirled, glided and glowed under the studio lights, every twist and turn was analysed by a panel of judges – and the fifty odd critical spectators under the roof of The Acorns.

"She is out of step" cackled Frank.

"Give her a break for goodness sake. She was reading the news last week," Sheila retaliated in her defence. "She has only had three coaching sessions, and he is half her age."

"And half her weight too," laughed Frank, determined to have the last word.

The pair on screen were clearly in the early stages of their partnership and, as such, the panellists cooed with sympathy and took pity on them as the audience applauded their approval. The celebrity and her dance expert then made their way backstage to sit with the other couples under the watchful glare of the cameras. They seemed happy with their efforts, even if Frank was not.

There were six couples in total. This was only the second week of the show and the focus was more on the celebrities' backgrounds and fitness levels rather than the dancing. Tonight, was their first chance to dance in front of the judges and, with nothing at stake, the mood was relaxed. The competition had yet to really start, but Peter was already taking bets on who was going to win.

"Hasn't she got a lovely dress?" Hilda smiled. "Look at the way it sparkles under those lights. She will have had that specially made for her; I shouldn't wonder. They don't sell those in Primark!"

The others nodded and agreed without taking their eyes off the screen for a second.

"Who's the fat fella?" asked Frank. "I recognise the face. Was he on that cooking programme?"

Half a dozen of the others shook their heads and dismissed him.

"One of those reality shows then? What is he famous for? It can't be a sport, surely. Was he a singer?"

The others sat forward and craned their necks to get a better view.

"Didn't he present that quiz show a few years back? The one where you had to beat the experts?" asked Colin.

"Bloody hell, he has put on the beef, hasn't he?"

More nodding. It was funny to watch them all. If only these celebrities could have heard them. They would have been crestfallen.

At the end of the show, the credits rolled and the familiar soundtrack played out across the Sir Jimmy Glass Suite.

As they waited for the news to start, the conversation turned to the past as memories of their own dancing careers were shared.

"Jean and I were poetry in motion on the dance floor. I was better than that Len Goodman who used to be on it. We would glide together, perfectly In sync. I knew exactly what she was going to do and she would know exactly what I was going to do" Frank said.

"You had two left feet" Edith laughed. "I remember you – old wooden horse we used to call you."

The others laughed. Frank did too.

"Everyone loved dancing in those days. It's a dying art now. Maybe this show has helped bring it back in some places. Remember the venues? There was one on every estate. Church halls, sports halls, working men's clubs, hotels. You could be out dancing every night of the week if you wanted to."

"Who is Jean anyway, Frank? That wasn't the wife?" Peter asked mischievously.

"Shut up, the news is starting!" said Frank pointing at the screen.

The rest of them burst out laughing and settled back down for the rest of the night's viewing.

The next day, around the breakfast tables, the talk of dance – and dance halls in the city – continued.

"I used to go up to the Cosmo. Always lively and plenty of single ladies there," said Peter.

"That was more for disco dancing," said Anne. "We are talking about traditional ballroom dancing here. The Crown and Mitre was one of my favourites. No riff raff in there. People used to travel from afar to dance in there."

"The Crown and Mitre was special, wasn't it? I used to go with my friend, Maureen. We would begin the evening with a gin and lime in the hotel bar before the dancing. It would go straight to my head. We used to run to the station to catch the last train. I felt like Cinderella at midnight, dashing up there in my finest frock!" laughed Sarah.

"Speaking as one of the riff raff, I used to avoid that place like the plague," Peter countered.

"I'm no toff, but I used to love performing at the Crown and Mitre," George shouted across from another table. "I was part of the Mayfair Band. I played the saxophone. We had a great group of lads in that band, and we played all over the city. Happy days. One of my favourite places was the Cameo. It was always heaving in there."

"Ah, the Cameo!" Daphne smiled. "Now that was some place. And the County Hotel on the same stretch. Remember the County anyone?"

"Remember it?" Brenda joined in, "I met my husband in The County. We danced the night away in there. We were married for sixty-one years and I still remember those nights as though they were yesterday!"

"What was the name of that place near the old fire station? It looked like the inside of an old RAF hanger?" Frank said before stuffing a whole fried egg into his mouth.

"You are thinking of the NAAFI huts. They were wooden sheds – built for the forces. They looked like nothing from the outside but inside they were quite ornate. It was like The Tardis too. There was a games room, a bar, a lounge and even a cafeteria! And then there was the actual dance floor – the ballroom. I remember the curved roof and cork floor. There was a small stage at one end for the band and little booths down the side for those who preferred to watch. It was a lovely venue" added Maureen.

"I liked The Queens too," said Frank. "Blackfriars Street."

"Bonds on Fisher Street was my favourite," Irene said as she plonked herself down on the only remaining chair around the table nearest to me.

"Yeah. Us girls used to stand in the middle while the boys circled us deciding who to dance with. It was like a cattle market at times. Nobody wanted to be the last picked. You would end up with someone like Frank!" Eileen smirked, raising another laugh at Frank's expense.

"There was the Embassy, the Market Hall, The Gretna, The Co-op – so many!" said Eleanor. "And those are just the ones in and around the city.

Plenty more around the county and, whichever town you visited up and down the country, there would be dozens more like them. Happy days."

"Aye, you're right there," said Joyce. "We used to take the bus down to Blackpool. A proper old charabanc trip. No motorway in those days. What takes two hours now took the best part of a day then! You could get to Australia quicker these days. We used to stop at the top of Shap for a few drinks on the way. The Jungle Café. We were as drunk as Lords by the time we eventually reached Blackpool. I used to think I was a good dancer, but it might just have been the booze talking."

I could have listened to them all day. They all seemed to glow when talking about the past – about their youth. Inside these frail old bodies were young spirits. Forget the wrinkles and the white hair. Ignore the wheelchairs and brittle bones. The passion and enthusiasm for life was still as strong as it ever was.

And it was at this point, just as the staff started to clear the tables the idea for the 2022 trip blossomed.

"Wouldn't it be nice if we could dance again?" said Eleanor. "One last time maybe – one last Waltz."

"Those places are all shut now. Long gone," Peter replied.

"I know that, you daft sod. But people still dance. Somewhere. Ballroom dancing hasn't died a death yet. We haven't sorted our day out yet, have we? Why not go dancing?"

Eleanor looked over at me and I nodded in agreement.

I looked around the room and they were all looking in my direction. Smiling.

"What she means to say," Frank said, wiping bean juice off his chin, "is get on that bloody mobile device of yours, and see where we can all go for a day out dancing!"

They all cheered and clapped at the same time, and I blushed at the unwanted attention from the whole room.

Half an hour later, thanks to the wonderful world of Google, I had found a suitable venue – Glasgow University Ballroom. I emailed them on behalf of the residents and they replied before everyone had shuffled out of the room.

A lady called Eli thought it would be a wonderful idea, and she was happy to help organise a day of dancing for our motley crew. If we provided the transport, they would host us for the day. She went on to say that they would happily provide free instructors, and as much tea and coffee as we could handle.

So that was that. We weren't going to a zoo or a museum or a beach. For The Acorns 2022 trip out, we were going to Scotland to dance.

"I have never passed an exam in my life," laughed Frank. "And here I am going to University. To dance!"

"And you can't dance either" said Edith, still determined to have the last word.

14

Risky Business

Planning a road trip for forty-five elderly people with every medical condition under the sun isn't easy. On top of that, we needed half a dozen staff members, a reliable but cheap coach company, and an absolute mountain of paperwork. Risk assessments, doctor and family approvals, medication records and allergy records.

Then there was everything else we needed to remember on behalf of the residents. Everything from spare glasses and changes of clothing to false teeth and wigs.

On top of all that there were sticks, chairs, Zimmer frames, cushions, inhalers and medicines. This was no normal day out. Teachers think they have it bad with school trips, but they are a doddle compared to a day out with The Acorns lot.

Vera pulled me into the office shortly after the venue was decided to tell me I would be the lead for the day. She smiled and tried to make out it was some kind of honour or privilege, but we both knew the truth. It was a job and a half – one she certainly didn't want the responsibility for! She did say she would be happy to be included as one of the staff members on the day thus taking the easy option.

After consultation with Glasgow University, we agreed a date – Thursday 25th August 2022.

The Acorn Trust agreed to pay up to £350 for transport and travel out of an already tight budget, and an extra £50 for 'supplementary benefits' (drinks and snacks for the journey).

After calling around a few local bus companies, I soon found out that £350 would fall some way short of what was required. It was the summer holidays and coaches were in demand. Most companies had no availability on that date, and those that did were charging almost double our budget. As a staff, we all agreed to chip in to help make up the difference, but we still couldn't stretch to £700 plus. I was starting to panic and considered pulling the plug on the whole thing until my knight in shining armour appeared. Well, more like a knight in jeans and a t-shirt, but you get the point.

I was sitting in the hallway beside the phone looking for other coach companies within fifty miles of the city when in walked Peter. He had been outside sunbathing in the garden, and the top of his bald head glowed pink.

"If I don't put some cream on soon, I am going to fry," he said, chuckling as he toddled by. "What are you up to, Ang? You look as hot and bothered as I do, and you haven't even been outside!"

There was no point in hiding anything from him. He knew me well enough, and he could tell I was upset. I explained the problem and how, if I couldn't find a cheaper coach, we might have to cancel the trip. He put his hand on my shoulder and gave it a little squeeze of reassurance.

"Leave it with me chicken. I will make a couple of phone calls of my own. I know a few folk who might be able to pull a couple strings for me. I will just nip up to my room to moisturise my burning scalp, and I will see what I can do."

He smiled down at me and winked before taking the receiver from my hand and popping it back into the cradle.

"We are not missing this trip; do you hear me? I'll sort it out. You go and get yourself a cup of tea."

And with that, he set off up the staircase, rubbing his head and whistling to himself.

I had no idea who he was planning to call, but at this stage I didn't really care. I just wanted to get the transport sorted so I could get on with the paperwork, and the million and one other tasks.

Twenty minutes later, I heard a knock on the office door, then in walked Peter. He had a blob of white cream on his head, and he had changed into a new white t-shirt and shorts. He looked like a geriatric tennis player.

"Sorted. Coach booked. They will be picking us up at 9:30 a.m. on the 25th and setting off back from Glasgow about 5 p.m., but times are flexible. The driver is a mate. He will work around us."

"How on earth did you sort that so quickly?" I asked him, not really wanting an answer in case it incriminated me.

"Friend of a friend. He is bringing the bus over from the North East. A sixty-seater he said. It has a toilet on it and everything. We will need that with our lot no doubt."

"How much will it cost?" I asked.

"Nothing. Nada. Zip. He owes me a favour or two. He said we could have it for free for the day. He will drive for us too – just keep him topped up with fags and coffee at the services and he will be happy."

"Free!" I yelped like an excited teenager.

"Free as a bird," Peter replied, laughing.

I jumped up and kissed him on the top of his head, forgetting all about the blob of sun cream.

"Steady on love," he chuckled, "I need that!"

I was walking on cloud nine. A free coach and £350 saved. What a result.

"I'll need the registration number of the bus for the paperwork," I told him.

"No, you won't" he said, walking back out towards the garden. "It's best if you don't. Just make one up and hope they don't check it."

And with that, he was gone.

The legality of it all didn't really trouble me at that time. I was buzzing. We had a coach and a driver, and it wasn't going to cost us a penny.

The paperwork took hours and hours to complete, but by the time I had crossed the 't's' and dotted the 'i's', I felt a huge weight lift from my shoulders. The last thing I needed to do was prepare an itinerary for the day and meet with the family and first contacts for the residents.

I sent out a group email and text, and set a date for the meeting on the night of Sunday 31st July. That would give me time to answer any questions and resolve any concerns.

In a way, it was very much like a school trip. The residents were vulnerable without our care and supervision, and to take them out of the familiar and comfortable surroundings of the home was a big deal.

Sure enough, on the night of the meeting, the Keith Chegwin Suite was packed to the rafters with family members as well as the trip goers. I had never spoken in front of such a big audience and I don't mind saying, I was bloody petrified.

In the days leading up to the meeting, Vera teased me.

'Operation Fandango' she called it.

'Just be yourself. You know everyone in the room and they know you. Not a problem!" she said.

It was precisely the fact that they all knew me that made it all the more difficult. I imagined them thinking of questions I couldn't answer – Frank making 'comments' from the back, me sweating and stuttering through it all.

When the night actually arrived, I stood in reception greeting everyone and shaking hands while the other staff found a seat for everyone. We had to borrow a load of chairs from the community centre. The place was heaving by the time we shut the front door. And then Vera – the cow – walked up to the front and hushed the crowd before inviting me to the front. They all cheered and clapped. I was so embarrassed.

I wandered to the front, head down, with all the confidence of a nun in a rugby club locker room which just seemed to make them worse.

Sure enough, Frank was there to whip them up into a frenzy with chants of "Ang, Ang, Ang!"

I looked up and mouthed something rude to him before realising there were a lot of children in the room. I blushed. When they eventually quietened down, I raised my head to speak and couldn't believe just how many people were there – there must have been two hundred! Four hundred eyes all watching me. I glanced over at Vera for support and she nodded and smiled. I turned back to face them and said, "So, are you all ready for Operation Fandango?"

The crowd cheered and laughed, and I felt the knot in my stomach ease and unloosen.

"My job – our job – is to get everyone to Glasgow and back in one piece, in one piece and have a great time in between."

Another cheer from the crowd. I was warming to them.

"We have a bus, we have all the paperwork and permissions, and we have enough supplies to see us through ten trips, never mind one. You have been invited here tonight to share any concerns or worries, and I will do my best to answer them."

One chap put his hand up at the back. Hilda's son.

"Are the instructors all qualified?"

I heard her hiss at him to keep his hand down and shut up. I was just about to answer until she did for me.

"Of course, they are qualified you daft sod. We are going to the Glasgow University Ballroom, not a youth training scheme in Brampton Town Hall!"

Everyone laughed, and her son sat down ashen-faced and suitably chastised.

"Are they aware of any allergies? I think my mother struggles with nuts?" Joan's son asked, meekly.

Again, I was about to answer, but Joan beat me to it.

"I am not allergic to nuts. One bite of a Walnut Whip went down the wrong way in about 1986 and you have been obsessed with bloody nuts ever since. If I want to eat nuts, I'll eat nuts. I am ninety-two years old and a nut hasn't taken me out yet!

More laughter and another embarrassed sixty-year-old child.

I just stood there like a spare part as other banal questions were asked then shot down by the residents without me having to say a word.

Doreen stood up and walked over to me. She raised her hand and the noise subsided as though she were some kind of Demigod.

"We are going on a bus trip to Glasgow. We are going to dance – as well as we can. We all know how to do it, and we all want to give it a go. We are lucky enough to be going to a place full of qualified instructors, on a dancefloor second to none in the area.

They are feeding us, sheltering us and looking after us. We will then get back on the bus – with help if needed – after numerous toilet breaks. Most of us will no doubt sleep on the way back and be a bit stiff the next day, but that is a sacrifice we are all happy to make. We have our medicines, cough sweets, tissues and toilet roll. If we fall asleep and wet ourselves then so be it. If we forget how to dance then so be it. If we choke on a nut and die happy then so be it. If there are any accidents or injuries or worse, then this young lass won't be to blame for any of it. She works her socks off for us and we couldn't be in better hands. Roll on the 25th August and hopefully we don't lose anyone before then, never mind on the day!"

Another spontaneous cheer went up after she had finished speaking and the room was full of happiness and life. I was beaming. Everyone was.

All the work, all the stress, all the form filling and flapping – it was all worth it.

Operation Fandango was going to be a success.

All my worries had disappeared, then I spotted Peter walking up the stairs, and my mind went back to buses and registration numbers.

What a job this is!

15

Histeria and Hermoans

"It is not easy being a woman, you know," my mother would say.

Dad would sit and stare at the television and know better than to interrupt her when she was in 'one of those moods'.

For the most part they are a content and happy couple, but the way to marital bliss is not without its bumps in the road, and they had their fair share of disagreements and rows along the way. They were careful not to show it in front of me, other than the odd flare up which was easily solved with a sulk from my dad, and an apology from my mum – even when it wasn't her fault.

She was always easy to talk to, my mam. Other girls at school complained about their mothers – they weren't close to them. I was. We would talk about anything and everything from shopping and fashion to spots and periods. Never once was I embarrassed to approach her if I had a problem.

Dad was the same in the main, although he would shy away from anything involving the body. "Your mother is the one to ask about that!" he would say if I ever dared to mention bras or sanitary products. I knew it embarrassed him, but I would ask anyway just to get a reaction.

My childhood innocence left me between the age of thirteen and fourteen – sometime in the Spring. I remember sitting in my room listening to music and feeling a terrible pain in my stomach. A constant ache or a cramp like feeling. At first, I had no idea what it was. I thought it was food related or a pulled muscle.

It was only when I went to the toilet and saw red that reality dawned.

I called out for my mam, and she rushed upstairs to see what the fuss was about. Thankfully, Dad was out walking the dog or something.

She sat on the side of the bath and reached out for my hand. "It's started then," she said, smiling down at me.

I just burst into tears – relief, pain, shock – I don't remember why now. It just happened, and I stood and hugged my mother. She hugged me back and whispered in my ear. "Nothing to worry about. You are growing up. Becoming a woman."

After a while, and a shower, we walked to my room and sat on the bed. My mum sat cross legged like a teenager herself, and held my hand again.

She talked through the mechanics of it all – the biology - and what I needed to do when I felt it happening. She explained that it would soon become routine and second nature, but at first it might be sporadic.

"The pain or discomfort will come and go. I would like to say you will get used to it, but I won't lie to you. Don't ever be embarrassed or ashamed though. You just ask me anything you like. This is all perfectly natural, darling. As horrible as it might seem right now, this is what it means to be a woman. This is life."

I did have a lot of questions, and she answered them all.
I asked about what I needed to use and how to use them.
I asked about the mess and the discomfort. I asked about what happens if it starts at school or on the bus or somewhere away from home.

Reassuringly, she talked me through everything, and I felt so much better and more empowered afterwards.

She knew what to say and how to say it to make me feel better.

She was right – the pain didn't get any better. Manageable, but not better. Even now it is a struggle some months, but I manage – you have to.

God only knows how Dad would have handled it had she not been there, but I didn't need to worry about that. She was there, and always has been for me.

Living with two hormonal ladies can't have been an easy ride for Dad. I admit, I could be a grumpy sod at times. A typical teen. He let most of it wash over him, and he learned when to speak and when not to. One daft comment or sarcastic joke could be enough to set me off.

Mam was more in control of her emotions than me, but she still had her moments too. After a while, we all fell into a routine. Dad knew not to cross the line. He could read the signs – even when they weren't bleeding obvious.

He would go for a walk or do something in the garden. He would retire to the bedroom to read or do his crossword. Sometimes one of us would go looking for him just so we could start an argument. He must have suffered – not like us of course – but he must have suffered.

And then - after the teenage years - a new lady blooms.   A working lady – a lady with a purpose. That is when I really clicked with dad. I understood him then. He was witty and funny and kind. He was patient and caring. I learned to love him all over again. I could see in him what my mother did. Not in that way – just in how easy he was to get along with. How easy he was to live with. We spent more time together.

He never put any pressure on me to leave home or move out. I know I should. I want to when the time is right and I can afford to, but he doesn't put any pressure on me though, neither of them do, and I am so grateful to them for that.

And then came the next change. As I reached my mid-twenties, I was at my most confident. I was as confident as I had ever been in my own skin. I was shapely and fit, happy and content. As I was reaching my peak my mother was wrestling with the next stage of womanhood – the menopause. It didn't happen overnight, and it didn't go away quickly either. The physical changes were hard enough for her, but it was the emotional trauma that she really struggled to cope with.

The hot flushes, the headaches, the weariness – they all took their toll. But it was the effect it all had on her wellbeing and mental health that troubled her the most. Spells of anxiety and depression. An inability to see anything positive in the present or the future. A body clock realisation that she was no longer young. That realisation that she could no longer bear children. She questioned her purpose in life – her role in the family.   She thought of herself as a general dogsbody. The more dad reassured her the more she felt patronised or mocked. Dad spent more time in the garden, and the dog must have been the fittest on the estate with the amount of walks he got.

There were good days – good weeks – but it was always hiding just under the surface ready to return.

It troubled me seeing her this way, and also knowing I had it to come in the future. It was during this time that she really snapped at dad. The only time I have ever seen her lose her cool and go for him. It was during an episode of Masterchef. Dad made some quip about puff pastry, and she lost it.

"You don't know the half of it. You don't know what she has had to go through to get to this stage. You sit there judging like some Lord or other, and you know nothing. All you have to worry about is nostril hair and a bald patch! You don't realise how bloody lucky you are. Men! You wouldn't know the difference between puff pastry and Puff the Magic Dragon, you bloody imbecile!"

She then proceeded to throw the remote control at him and storm out the room in tears. We looked at each other in shock. After about five minutes, he got up to walk the dog.

When he returned to the house, I hadn't moved from the sofa. He looked in and smiled at me before making his way upstairs to see my mam. He apologised to her.

The next day, they were all fine.

She discovered HRT later that year, and 'the change' changed for the better soon after that.

It all seems a bit of a blur now. The three of us look back on it and laugh, but it was no laughing matter at the time.

In many ways – most ways - I love being a woman, but we have certainly been given the shorter straw when it comes to biological changes in life.

In The Acorns – in old age – I see equality again. The ladies have overcome these huge transitions in life and, although blighted by the ravages of time, they are in the same boat as the men folk. Stiff backs, hearing aids, bedsores, memory loss and cataracts are not exclusive to men or women. These problems are shared equally. They don't discriminate based on gender.

My upbringing, my own family troubles, seem insignificant compared to others. We were lucky. In the home, I see all sorts come and go. I hear so many stories about families in turmoil or grief. They bring their problems to their elders hoping to unburden themselves. Our residents sit and listen. Old sounding boards.

Alice's family visit every week without fail, and they seem to do nothing but moan and complain about their lot in life. They are so different from my own family, and I always make a mental note to do something nice for my own parents after each one of their visits.

The dad – Alice's son in law – is a lazy, work-shy jelly. He always arrives in his ill-fitting jeans with his huge bum cheeks protruding above the waistline like two hairy white beach balls. His AC-DC or Def Leppard T-shirts fail to cover his overhanging stomach or his many tattoos of naked women and Chinese quotes which, I am sure, have no relevance to his lifestyle.

He makes no secret of the fact that he doesn't want to be there, and he spends most of the time watching TV or making himself a coffee.

Alice's daughter comes to vent. She will moan about money, her job, the house, her clothes, the children. Alice sits and listens. She has no choice. How such a nice old lady can have such a vile family still amazes me. They 'put her' in The Acorns because they couldn't cope with her at home.

Their two children – an angry looking 'boy' in his early twenties, and his teenage sister, sit sullenly in the corner until their mother is ready to leave.

There is never any intimacy between them. They never hug Alice or bend down to kiss her goodbye. But they will be back – at the same time the following week – to moan and groan again. The same routine. The same angry and depressed faces.

I often looked at the young girl and tried to imagine myself at the same age. Was I that teen? Was I that depressed? Was I that much of a burden to my parents? I don't think so. But then I question myself.

After one visit, I went to sit with Alice. We talked about the family and how upset she was by the way they behaved. She apologised for them and I told her never to apologise for the behaviour of others.

"She met him when she was about eighteen" she said. "We never liked him. He was controlling and rude. He would dominate the conversation and take over. My daughter might do all the talking, but it is him who has all the control and power. Horrible man"

I asked her about the children.

"When she fell pregnant with Daniel, we watched her lose even more control. He would boss her around. Tell her what to do and how to behave. He even decided what she should wear and when she should go out. Myself and Bob couldn't do much. She wouldn't listen. Daniel is his own man though. He will be out of that house as soon as he is able to. Once he gets a good job, he will be off. He wants to join the army which might well be the best thing for him."

I poured her a cup of tea.

"Courtenay is the one that troubles me," she went on. "She was sixteen last week. I don't think they made any fuss of her. They are too wrapped up in themselves to notice her. She was such a lovely girl growing up. Such a bright spark – always smiling. You shouldn't have favourites, I know, but she was mine. Look at her now – she hardly says boo to a goose. She never speaks or acknowledges me. I'm an old fossil to her now. I know it is hard being a teen, but I miss her though. Do you know, she used to come and see me every day for a chat before I came in here? Everyday. She would sit on the arm of the chair and just talk and talk. We would eat biscuits and drink juice and put the world to rights while her mother fussed over that fat bastard."

Her unexpected swearing made me chuckle.

"She was such a kind-hearted girl. I loved spending time in her company. I wish I could whisk her away and get the old Courtenay back, but you can't do that can you? They have to live their own lives and when you are young, the last thing you want is an old bird like me interfering. I miss her though."

Again, I thought about my own life and how I was with my own parents and grandparents. I loved them all dearly. I only have my dad's dad left, and he is a little treasure.

A couple of weeks after my chat with Alice she received an unexpected visitor – Courtenay. On her own.

I opened the door and she asked to see her gran. No smile, no please or thank you. I wasn't in the mood for teenage stroppiness, and I told her so. I told her to follow me and she did so, head bowed. Alice was in the conservatory and her face lit up into a big smile when she saw her granddaughter approach. I asked if they wanted anything to drink, then I left them in peace.

Courtenay stayed for the rest of the afternoon, and just before evening meal time, I walked by the conservatory only to see them holding hands. Both smiling and laughing too. It was so nice to see. She left shortly afterwards.

I noticed her walking to the door, waving back at her grandma as she did. She looked like a different girl altogether.

Later that evening, I went to speak with Alice to ask if everything was alright.

"I have my granddaughter back," she said, grinning. "Beneath the black make-up and ripped t-shirt and jeans is my Courtenay."

"What happened? What did you say?" I asked. She looked so happy and it made me happy too.

"When she arrived, I knew something wasn't right. She sat in silence until we were the last two in the conservatory and then she broke down. It all came out. Tears and truth. How miserable she was and how nobody understands her. How she longed for a different life. And then we got to the bottom of it. A boy – a man. Someone she has fallen for. Not reciprocated though.

Well, not beyond a knee-trembler in the park. Not the ideal place for your first time, is it? But where is I suppose?"

Her outlook surprised me and I let out a laugh. She did too.

"She isn't pregnant or anything. Nothing like that. She is just mildly devastated. We have all been there – one of the stepping stones in life I suppose. She is ok though. She just needed to talk to someone. Me."

"What did she say?" I nosily asked.

"She said she got a splinter in her bum!"

Alice smiled at me, then we both grimaced at the very idea.

"She is a mixed-up girl at the moment. Life is a burden for her, but she will get through it. I told her to come and see me anytime she wanted to. That really cheered her up. She is coming again tomorrow. I'm going to teach her to knit."

It was so charming. Two girls – two ladies – at the opposite ends of life, coming together and making each other smile.

"Do you know what she said to me before she left, Ang? She said 'I love you, Grandma. You are my world.' And I said back to her, 'You have always been my world.' And I meant it. Ever since she was born. My little girl."

Courtenay did come back the next day. And she was smiling. And she said 'Good morning' and 'please' and 'thank you'.

She came back the day after that too – and most other days. The two of them would sit in the conservatory and talk and knit and laugh.

And then she got a job. At The Acorns – in the kitchens training to be a chef.

And now she is coming on our trip to Glasgow to support the

residents, and sit with her grandma and be wanted and needed.

Her life is only just beginning and she will get through every problem the world throws at her – thanks to her grandma!

16

The Trip

Thursday 25th August 2022 – Trip Day.

At 9:15 a.m. after breakfast, the residents gathered in the Keith Chegwin Suite once again. There was a buzz of excitement around the place, and they giggled and chattered in little huddles waiting for the coach to arrive.

Peter assured me it would be on time, but I couldn't help staring out of the window every ten seconds, checking my watch and pacing up and down the hall.

As the lead, I felt responsible for everything – even for things I wasn't responsible for!

Sure enough, just before half past nine, the coach turned off the main road and onto the driveway at the front of the home. It was very flash. A double-decker!

It was jet black with a white flash on either side. The windows were tinted, and on the roof was a small white dome.

"That's the satellite dish," Peter informed me.

The coach pulled up beside the fountain at the front. A few of the others noticed its arrival, and made their way to the windows to have a look.

"Bloody hell, we are travelling in style today, Ang!" Frank said. "That must have cost a fortune. Good on you girl."

Peter looked at me and winked.

"So long as it gets us there and back, I will be happy," I replied trying to sound passive, but really, I was as impressed as he was.

The side door of the coach opened and the driver jumped out and stretched - lighting up a cigarette and looking down at his mobile phone.

He looked almost exactly like Danny Devito. He was about five feet tall, fat and squat. I wondered how on earth his feet reached the pedals.

I asked Peter to introduce us, and we both made our way outside to join him.

The two men shook hands and slapped each other on the back, exchanging a bit of small talk before Peter turned back to me to complete the introductions.

"Ang, this is Arnold – like Schwarzenegger. Similarities end with the first name," he quipped.

Arnold offered me his hand. He had a vice-like grip, and I had to pull my own hand free after a second to avoid breaking a finger.

"I will be your driver for the day, madam," he said, trying to sound posh. So long as I get the bus back by 8 a.m. tomorrow morning, everything should be just fine."

"Is it booked out for tomorrow?" I asked.

"Well technically, it is booked out every day. It isn't on hire – it is owned. By Sunderland Football Club. It's the team coach. They think I have taken it for its service today. Like I say, so long as I get it back to the stadium tomorrow morning, they will be none the wiser."

I was gobsmacked and started to panic.

"How are we going to get away with this?" I mumbled to Peter – to the pair of them.

They just laughed and changed the subject.

"It's the top spec model," Arnold went on. "The old dears won't have been on anything like it. Sky TV, coffee and tea making facilities, magazine racks, fridges in a small kitchen unit, wireless connection, heated leather seats, a toilet. There is even a hot tub at the back. I can fill it up if you want?"

Peter just nodded like it was the most natural, normal thing in the world.

"Right," said Arnold. "Let's get this show on the road."

The residents began filing out of The Acorns and started boarding the bus.

"Please don't tell them who it belongs to," I implored them both.

"Don't worry," said Peter, "I am not going to do anything daft like that. Ken is a Newcastle United fan – he wouldn't get on it if he knew it belonged to Sunderland."

Arnold chuckled and made his way back round to the driver's door, flicking the end of his fag onto the lawn.

He clicked on a button in the cab and the side door in the middle of the bus opened. A small flight of stairs led to the upper deck, and the more able made their way to the top. They were all taken aback by the quality of the transportation and, by the time we were all on, seated and ready to go, the excitement had reached fever pitch.

I put all the other stuff we needed in the luggage compartment at the back before joining them all on board.

"Come up and sit on the seat behind me" Arnold shouted. "That's the manager's seat!"

I didn't know where to look! I had to go along with it.

As the coach pulled out again onto the main road, Arnold leaned back and said, "If you open the drawer under your seat, it is full of miniature champagne bottles. Help yourself. I often do. They will notice."

By the time we reached the motorway, everyone was settled and raring to go. Playing cards were spread on the tables, Alice and Courtney had their knitting out, and a few others had already started filling in crosswords and puzzles. They all looked so happy.

I started to relax – just a little.

Before we reached Gretna, the overhead speakers started crackling into life, then Arnold spoke.

"Can you hear me ladies and gentlemen? Am I coming across loud and clear?"

Everyone cheered their approval

He cleared his throat. "Now tell me to bugger off if you like, but I thought a bit of musical accompaniment and entertainment might help get you in the mood for the dancing. What do you say?"

There were one or two grumbles from the men with the crosswords, but the majority cheered and urged him on.

"Let's start with a game. I call it 'I start the song and you lot carry it on. Catchy, eh? Don't worry if you see me turn around now and again. The cruise control is on and this is a long straight stretch."

I looked out of the front window, and I must have had a look of terror on my face.

"Don't worry about it, love. We are safe as houses, and this lot won't care. They learned to drive in death traps with no seat belts or warning lights. Half of them probably didn't even pass a test. Two minutes around the estate with their dad telling them what the pedals are for, and they were considered roadworthy."

Arnold just laughed and took a hold of the microphone, occasionally checking the road from time to time and glancing in his side mirror.

"Here we go – a nice easy one to start with."

He may have looked like Danny Devito, but he had a voice like Dean Martin. The crooning that came out the mouth of this dumpy little doughnut was not what I was expecting at all.

"We'll meet again, don't know where, don't know wheeeen..."

He paused after the first line and forty voices from both the upper and lower deck joined in to continue the Vera Lynn classic. I watched as they swayed from side to side and held hands, lost in the song.

When they finished with 'some sunny day', the clouds parted ahead as if on cue, and the bright blue summer sky welcomed us into Scotland.

Arnold was just warming up.

"Well done ladies and gentlemen. That song was before my time if not yours. This next one is a nod to old blue eyes himself. Frank!"

I looked over at Frank and he straightened his tie and put down his paper. He was getting in the mood, and I am sure he thought of himself as a bit of a local Sinatra.

"Start spreading the news..." sang Arnold, almost kneeling up on his driver's chair to face his audience.

Again, they didn't give him a chance to get onto the second line before joining in. By the time they reached the chorus, half a dozen of them had taken off their seatbelt and were stood up in the aisles, swaying about and dancing in step. I couldn't believe what I was watching. It was a health and safety nightmare and I was meant to be in charge.

A car horn sounded as the bus veered slightly into the middle lane. Arnold had kicked the steering wheel a little and lost control. Nobody seemed to notice. He acknowledged the driver's warning with a two finger salute out the side window. Could this get any worse?

Yes.

He gave them a couple of minutes to draw breath and settle down before introducing song number three.

"Ladies and gentlemen, old farts and fartesses, this is a more recent number. By more recent, you will have all been about sixty when it came out."

They didn't take any offence to his offence – in fact, they were loving it.

"Well, you can tell by the way I use my walk, I'm a woman's man, no time to talk…"

I looked at Frank and he laughed.

To see and hear a bus load of octogenarians bang out 'Stayin Alive' by The Bee Gees was just surreal.

Vera had been sitting upstairs but she came down to see me. She could see straight away how shocked I was – how helpless.

"If I had been in charge, I would look like you too," she said, laughing. "Relax – let them get on with it. They are having the time of their lives up there. It's like a school disco!"

By the time we pulled up at Abington Services about halfway to Glasgow, there were more whoops and cheers with every new song or game. Arnold was clearly enjoying himself as much as they all were. He had a crazy game of 'Simon says' and a set of celebrity impressions which had everyone in stitches. He was brilliant at accents and voices – everyone from John Wayne to Brian Clough. He was an all-round entertainer to go with his rather erratic driving methods.

The coach pulled into Abington at around 10:30 a.m., and Arnold took to the microphone once again.

"Normally for a stop, I would give my travellers ten minutes for a pee and a stretch, but for you lot I better make it half an hour. If you are not back on by eleven, I am leaving without you so don't be late. If anyone is going in the shop, can you pick me up a Mars Bar and a can of something unhealthy? Full fat please – I don't want to waste away!"

He pressed the button to open the door and those who wanted to (or were able to) climbed off and made their way to the main entrance. I counted them off like school children, and asked Vera to keep watch at the door to make sure none of them escaped or went wandering off.

It was a glorious day and I spent a few moments enjoying the breath-taking countryside in every direction. The hills and mountains, the rivers and streams. It was incredible, and the background noise from the motorway traffic seemed nothing more than a quiet hum.

After a few minutes, The Acorns crowd started to make their way back to the bus. They filed out of the building in pairs, chatting away and munching on bags of sweets or bars of chocolate that they had bought from the shop inside. I counted them back on the bus. There were two missing. Typical.

"Edna and Doris are arguing with the manager in the coffee shop," laughed Ken. "You had better go and sort the situation out before there is a riot."

I made my way into the building and, sure enough, there were the two old ladies leaning on the counter, making their point to a stunned, red-faced cashier.

"What's wrong?" I asked, trying to bring calm to the situation.

"He is trying to give us a stick to stir this thing with and I want a spoon!" said Doris.

The staff member looked at me for understanding and support.

"It is to stir the coffee with. They all do it now" I tried to explain to her.

"Sticks are for dogs not people. What can you stir with that anyway? By the time it dissolved the sugar we would be in Glasgow!"

Not to be left out, Edna decided to have a moan too.

"And the cups – plastic rubbish. How are you meant to drink from that without a handle? And look at that flimsy lid – you could get third degree burns if that fell off when you were having a sip."

A queue was starting to develop behind us, and the young lad at the till was clearly struggling.

I decided to be matron and take control.

"Listen you two. Time is marching on. Get yourselves back on the bus and give this poor soul a break. I will carry the coffees, and I will even stir in the sugar for you!"

The two old ladies tutted and complained, but at least they were compliant. The young lad mouthed a 'thank you' as I ushered them away.

By the time we got them back onto the bus, they had calmed down. I popped the cups into the drink holders, and signalled to Arnold that we were good to go. He gave me the thumbs up and pressed the button to close the doors. Before he set off, Peter approached the ladies, holding a blue carrier bag.

"At your service ladies. I was listening to your discussion with Mr. Jobsworth, and I think I have a solution for you."

From of the bag, he pulled out two branded coffee shop cups, two saucers and two teaspoons and placed them on the small table in front of Edna and Doris. He then took off the lids of the plastic coffee cups and proceeded to pour the contents into the cups. Finally, he put his hand into the bag and pulled out two chocolate muffins.

"They wanted £3.50 for a cake!" he said. "Let's just say, these ones didn't cost a penny. I sort of acquired them while you were distracting the chap on the till."

The two old ladies laughed and picked up their pottery, happy that they now had a 'proper' cup.

And this, after all my risk assessments and careful planning!

So far, we had stolen a bus from Sunderland Football Club, risked life and limb with a lunatic of a bus driver, caused a mini riot in a motorway services coffee shop, and stolen crockery and expensive muffins! Whatever next?

I turned to Arnold and told him to get his foot down. He obliged.

We made it to the outskirts of Glasgow not long before midday. The traffic was heavy, but we kept on moving onto the M8 motorway, and soon we could see the many high rises of the city. Not having any tower blocks in Cumbria, it was the first real sign that we were in the big city and a realisation, to me, of how lucky I was to live where I did. Arnold had a rough idea where he was going, but fiddled with his phone to set the Sat Nav, causing more motorists to beep angrily as he veered across the lanes, seemingly oblivious to the chaos he was causing. By the time we pulled up outside the Glasgow University building, I felt older than half the folk on board the bus!

Courtney came rushing down the stairs, buzzing with excitement.

"Are we here? Is this it? So excited. I can't believe it. What a cool trip. Aren't they all brilliant? Grandma can't wait. Do you want me to help them off? I hope I can dance too. Do you think they will mind? So exciting."

It was as though she had never left the house before. Maybe she hadn't. I didn't want to burst her bubble by telling her to calm down, so I just let her carry on.

Arnold opened the side door again and, slowly but surely, the crowd made their way onto the pavement in front of the dark, impressive stone structure that was the University Union building.

At the top of the stairs, beside the entrance, stood an attractive young blonde. She waved over to me and smiled the widest of smiles. How she knew I was in charge is anyone's guess. Maybe the panicked expression on my face gave it away.

I waved back and walked through the crowd to meet her and introduce myself.

Her name was Eli and she was to be our guide for the day. She said she would be part of the dancing team, and if we needed anything, all we had to do was ask. She said she would give us a little tour first, and then go through some demonstrations. "We have a bit of a show planned," she said, "then a break for refreshment. After that, the ball is in their court so to speak. The floor is theirs! We will be on hand to coach and support, but I'm guessing they will know what to do. Age is no obstacle. It will all come flooding back. When they are finished dancing, we will have another break and end the day with a competition. Does that sound good to you?"

It sounded perfect. She was ever so welcoming and happy. From the top of the stairs, she welcomed everyone to the venue and repeated to them what she had just said to me. I looked down on them all by her side. They all looked so contented. She suggested they walk up the ramp to avoid any accidents and follow her through into the main hall.

The room was glorious. The wooden floor seemed soft underfoot, and the dark drapes at either side of the room gave off a homely, warm feel. Six small chandeliers hung from the ceiling, and the pine, panelled walls added that touch of class. At one end was a small, raised stage with a microphone in the middle and numerous instruments positioned behind it. Around the outside were a hundred or so chairs, and in the far-left corner stood two circular tables filled with trays of covered sandwiches, quiches, nibbles and cakes. The place was immaculate.

Eli invited everyone to find a seat. As they all settled in, a tea trolley was wheeled in and the chinks and rattles echoed beautifully off the walls, sounding almost musical.

"Proper cups" said Edna leaning over to Doris. "Proper cups. None of that plastic and stick nonsense here."

While a few willing students served the teas and coffees, Eli introduced the team for the day. She was the Vice President of the University Ballroom team, and to her right was Maddy, the

President. Then there was Tess, the secretary and Daniel, the team captain. Standing near to the door was Bas and his girlfriend Jennifer. We were reassured that Bas, a professional dance teacher, would be on hand during the day to help and support.

They were all giving up their time for free, and when I told everyone, they burst into a spontaneous round of applause which seemed to delight the staff. They all took a bow.

Bas explained that they planned to work on five main ballroom dance styles – the foxtrot, the tango, the quickstep, the waltz and the Viennese waltz. I had no idea what the difference was between any of them. Eli told me I would by the end of the day.

I scanned the hall for any sign of discomfort or upset. Nothing. Every single one of them sat upright, looking eager and excited. They listened intently to everything that the staff told them. You could tell they were keen to get out there but, for many, it had been decades since they last glided around a dance floor. They all absorbed the safety advice and nodded and asked questions when Bas talked about how to move and when to step. Daniel and Jennifer modelled as he talked. I watched the feet of the dancers. Even at a slow pace, they seemed to float above the floor and glide across the room, barely making a sound. It was an art form. I noticed Courtenay. She couldn't keep her eyes off them. She was holding her grandma's hand, totally transfixed by what was happening in front of her.

And then Eli clapped her hands and the room fell silent. It was the cue for more arrivals. Through the same door we came in, a handful of men in suits walked in and greeted the audience of old folk with waves and smiles.

"Your band for the day," she said. "They help us out occasionally when we have a big performance. Usually, we make do with a CD or a music app on the phone, but when they heard you were coming, they wanted to give you the big band experience. Can you give a big hand to 'The Mavericks'?".

This was yet another unexpected surprise and, without any prompting, everyone rose to their feet and clapped and cheered the band as they took up their positions behind the microphone and on to the stage.

Maddy took over as compere while the others found their positions on the dance floor. The students who had served the drinks proceeded to join them. When they were all paired up, Maddy waved to the band to begin, and introduced the foxtrot. I listened to those around me. "Slow, slow, quick, quick. Slow, slow, quick, quick." A simple dance it may be but the experts moved around with speed and agility, avoiding bumping into the other couples moving around the floor. The band played on and kept the rhythm. It looked stunning and I wanted to get up and dance myself.

"Make sure you move in time with each other," Maddy said, "no clumsy feet gentlemen."

"Are you listening, Frank?" Eleanor called over, making the others giggle.

And then, through a smooth transition and a change of music, the dancers started to tango.

The tango was quicker and, again, I was impressed at how the dancers glided around the room with such confidence. Our gang clapped along with the music and young Daniel quickened the pace with Tess, to encouraging roars of approval from the crowd.

Maddy then called for the quickstep. "A bit like a quicker version of the foxtrot with a bit of the Charleston thrown in for good measure," she said, as the dancers changed positions again, almost effortlessly.

I tried to imagine our lot moving like this when they were younger. The twinkle in their eyes suggested to me that they were ever so keen to try it again, despite their ageing limbs.

And then the Waltz and the Viennese Waltz. Maddy explained the difference as the dancers in front of her demonstrated for their transfixed audience.

When the music stopped and the couples turned to face their fans to bow, the room was in uproar. It was like a huge release of energy and excitement. The years seemed to peel away, and in those few seconds of elation, they forgot the aches and pains and faults and flaws and they clapped and cheered, smiled and laughed like there wasn't a care in the world. At that moment, they didn't have a care. In that room, there was just a sea of happiness and it brought a lump to my throat. I was so proud of them. I was proud of myself for helping to make it happen.

And then it was their turn.

They all paired up and, for the first time in a long time, they danced. The band played at a slower pace and the staff moved in and out of the couples, giving pointers and instructions as they moved. Men with women, women with other women and men with men. It didn't matter. Everyone swapped partners every minute so no one could get too comfortable.

"You be the lady," I heard Ken say to Frank when the two paired up. Frank leaned forward and kissed Ken on the cheek.

"Steady on, old boy," he laughed.

Frank allowed himself to be led around the floor.

"Watch and learn, watch and learn," Ken said as he guided Frank over towards the musicians.

I kept a close eye on Dora in case she felt lost or confused, but there was no sign of that. She moved with the agility of a younger woman, smiling throughout. Often, she would have her eyes closed as she danced, just letting her memories take control of her body. She was in heaven.

We stopped to eat around 3 p.m. Everyone was ready for it, and what a lovely spread it was. The students took up their serving role again, and handed out paper plates and plastic knives and forks neatly wrapped in a serviette. There was more than enough for everyone, and the choice of desserts were a joy to behold after the sandwiches. Cheesecakes, chocolate cakes, trifles, pavlovas… it was simply delicious. Eli told me the students provided all the food. They wanted to do something for the old folk. Seriously, they couldn't have done any more.

The rest of the afternoon was a mix of dancing, socialising and singing before Maddy called everyone back together for competition time.

She explained that there would be a number of categories and at the end of the session, Bas would choose the winners. He brought in half a dozen trophies with engraved discs on the front base of each.

"No pressure," said Maddy, "Only join in if you want to. Don't feel you have to, and please, just go at your own pace."

Everybody joined in.

Eleanor won the trophy for the most elegant, Ralph and Ruth for the best couple. Frank for the most dangerous, and Courtenay for the most improved. They were all delighted.

The overall, most accomplished dancer award was given to Dora. When it was presented to her, the cheer could have been heard in Edinburgh. She held it close to her chest with both hands and looked up and smiled. I wondered who or what she was thinking about.

We made our way back onto the coach just after 6:30 p.m. The rush hour traffic was beginning to subside, and the sun was low in the sky giving the city a warm, orange glow. Before leaving the hall, everyone hugged and kissed every single member of staff. I thought we were never going to get out, but it was so lovely and so right. They had helped make the day so incredibly special. A day no one present would ever forget.

When everyone was back on board the coach, and the seatbelts were all fastened and doors all closed, Arnold manoeuvred the bus into the road and we set off for home. The staff kept waving from the steps until the bus was out of sight, despite not being able to see anything through the blacked-out windows.

We didn't stop on the way back. We didn't need to. Everyone was exhausted and asleep before we got as far as Motherwell.

It was around 9:30 p.m. when the coach pulled up outside The Acorns. We helped everyone off and into the warmth of the home.

They were all there. We hadn't left any behind.

One by one, the staff made sure they were safely in their rooms and ready for bed. Each one purred about what a wonderful day it had been. They were all full of thanks and praise for the staff there and the staff here. They couldn't have asked for more.

It was, without a shadow of a doubt, the best trip there had ever been at The Acorns. They would be stiff the next day, but what did that matter?

A couple of days later, Peter told me that Sunderland had lost away at Middlesbrough. That was no big surprise in itself, but Arnold had to try and explain to the team manager why there was a set of false teeth wedged under the arm rest on the bus.

"It must have been kids," he told him. He wasn't far wrong.

17

Let Me Entertain You

The staff at The Acorns prided themselves on the services they provided for the residents. One particular service that always proved popular was the guest speakers we invited in to entertain and educate. Who we invited and when was largely down to the residents themselves.

We set aside some funds to pay for the more high-profile acts or names, but in the main, invited guests were happy enough to talk or act for free.

We would aim for a minimum five or six a year. Everyone would be encouraged to put forward their suggestions and then vote for who or what they would like to see. It was a good system and, once we had a few ideas, we would set about trying to find the best people in the area.

In the last couple of years, we've had a regular magician, a ventriloquist, a local MP, a soul singer, a comedian, an impersonator, a fisherman and the chief of police. Only the impersonator charged for his services, and he was the worst of the lot. Nobody could actually work out who he was trying to be! His 'Tony Blair' sounded more like Kenneth Williams. He won't be coming back.

One lady who did stand out was Maria Hicks – an amateur clairvoyant. She came highly recommended by a friend of a friend of Edna. Ms. Hicks lived with her two cats (Alan and Derek) in Willow Barn Cottage on the fells, near Thirlmere.

Apparently, she had worked most of her life in a bank as an administrator, but had discovered that she had the power to contact the spiritual world after an enlightening holiday at a caravan park in Cleethorpes. Apparently, she was visited by a series of dead relatives throughout the week in the caravan, and they all proceeded to tell her about the future, and what it held for her and the rest of the family.

Imagine *A Christmas Carol* set in a caravan site near Grimsby.

Anyway, despite the scepticism of the staff, the residents – mainly the ladies I should add – lapped it up, and couldn't wait to tap into her spiritual talents.

Before Maria arrived, she had sent a form for each member of the audience to fill in. She wanted to know a little bit about her audience in advance of the show. Questions like 'What are your hobbies and interests?', 'Can you tell me a little about your family?', 'Where did you work?' 'Name your favourite place'.

You couldn't make it up!

Everyone planning to attend – which was nearly everyone – eagerly filled in one of these forms, and handed them back to the office to be returned to Ms. Hicks.

I remember the date of her performance. It was Friday 13th August 2021. Understandably, she wasn't too keen on that date, but agreed to come as she was going to the Bingo the next day in Carlisle, and she planned to make a weekend of it.

On the night in question, everyone gathered in the Keith Chegwin Suite as Maria psyched herself up in one of the staff rooms. There was a lot of excited chatter as we all awaited her arrival onto the small stage. Eventually, she burst through the door at the back of the room, and strode purposefully to the front. Right arm raised as she walked. The crowd of old folk clapped and cheered with gusto. You would have thought The Queen herself had just walked in. She was draped in a purple velvet cloak which trailed on the floor behind her. Around her neck she wore a necklace with a medallion resting on her ample bosom. This was clearly her stage outfit but to me she looked like she had just mugged Dracula and a gangster from downtown Los Angeles!

She sat down on the swivel chair at the front and soaked up the applause. Eventually, she held her hand up to signal for the crowd to hush. "Dim the lights would you, love?" she said to Courtenay as the crowd settled down. Courtney did as she was asked.

"My name is Maria Hicks," she began, "but tonight I am... Mystic Maria – One eye on you, one eye on the future."

It wasn't the catchiest of introductions, but that didn't seem to matter to her audience who were hanging on her every word.

"What is your name, my dear?" she asked, pointing at Joan on the front row.

"Joan," said Joan.

"Ah, the hair stylist!" she replied, causing the crowd to gasp.

"Wasn't that question two on the form they all filled in?"

I whispered to Vera who was standing next to me. She smiled and nodded.

"I can tell you, Joan, you were a very popular hair stylist too. Your customers from beyond the grave tell me they wouldn't have gone to anyone else. Your perms were legendary!"

Joan put her hand over her mouth. She looked genuinely shocked. Those around her patted her on her shoulder, nodded and smiled.

"Was it Sarah who said that?" asked Joan. "She had the most beautiful black hair."

"It was," Maria said, giving her that reassurance she needed. "And not only was she pleased; she still has that perm now. In heaven!"

This was too much for Joan. She jumped to her feet and looked around the room at all her friends, who looked just as shocked and as delighted as she was. Maria just nodded and smiled smugly as the room settled down once again.

She turned her attention to Maureen who was sitting at the end of the second row.

"And what about you, my love? What is your story?"

Maureen proceeded to tell her all about her family, where she lived and what she had done for a living. Mystic Maria listened intently, and then paused dramatically, before speaking again.

"You are going to be a great grandmother soon. A little boy will be born into the family."

"I knew it!" Maureen called out. "Our Kathleen is keen to start a family. She got married last year. Oh my gosh, wait until I tell her. This is incredible."

The other ladies sat, open-mouthed in awe and then the applause started again.

Vera looked at me and raised her eyebrows. "Maureen has six children. Five sons. She has about fifteen grandchildren – twelve of whom are boys. Her granddaughter's husband has more brothers than Snow White has dwarves. If I was a betting woman, I would say the odds of her becoming a great grandmother to another boy are pretty much stacked in her favour. But let's not let logic get in the way – they are loving this!"

They certainly were. The revelations kept coming over the next hour, and each one was lapped up with the same enthusiasm as the first. She told Ken he was good with machinery (he used to be a mechanic). She advised Tom not to use the garden for his own good (he suffered from hay fever – a fact he noted in his questionnaire). She reassured Philippa that her husband was no longer suffering from backache – he died ten years ago!

You couldn't make it up – well, she could.

It was crazy watching and listening from the side lines, but it was a great laugh too.

As the evening came to a close, she turned her attention to Solomon, who was standing, leaning on the mantelpiece.

"I bet you were a handsome man in your youth!" she said, making him blush.

"Well, that's the first thing you have got wrong this evening!" shouted Frank from the other side of the room.

Everyone burst out laughing – even Solomon – which was a fitting end to the evening's entertainment.

Another guest I really enjoyed listening to was Laterha Choate – a singing instructor originally from Ohio but now living in Maryport teaching wannabe pop stars how to hold a note and broaden their vocal range.
Sandra found her online after watching *The Sound of Music* on the TV one afternoon. When we called her, she was more than happy to give up an evening to sing with the old folk.

We had booked her for a slot in April, and I remember it was a beautiful, spring evening. The sun was shining and there wasn't a cloud in the sky. We had all the doors and windows open, and everyone was upbeat and happy.

Laterha arrived just after meal time. She was accompanied by Mike – a tall, strapping, gent with a thick ginger beard and swept back hair. He was clearly there as the pack horse, carrying in a variety of instruments, speakers, microphones, and other pieces of electrical equipment the likes of which I had never seen before.

"I hope you don't mind me bringing all this along" said Laterha, "I have had an idea and I hope they go along with it. I...we...are going to write, sing and record our own song. Do you think they will like that?"

"Like it? They will love it!" I told her.

By the time Mike had set up the equipment, the room had started to fill up. Again, they all bristled with excitement and enthusiasm for what was to come.

Laterha started with some simple breathing exercises, concentrating on posture and pose. They loved that.

"Practice these every day," she told them. "It will do wonders for your movement, lung capacity and energy levels."

I watched them stretch and puff out their chests. They seemed to be having the time of their lives. The men managed the low notes, but let the ladies attempt the high.

"If my balls drop any lower, they will be on the floor," laughed Frank. "If God wants me to be a choir boy again, he can go whistle!"

After the warm up exercises, she moved on to echoing.

"Me then you, me then you. We start off slow and then speed up. Ok everyone?"

They all nodded like little children desperate to please their teacher.

She started with a few "la, la, la's" or "Ooompah do's" before introducing some funny lyrics, pitching high then low, whispering and building to a crescendo, encouraging them to hold a note. They hummed and hissed, growled and gargled. They were loving it.

After these exercises, she sang a few popular upbeat songs with them – 'Help' by The Beatles, Cliff Richard's 'Summer Holiday', 'Happy Talk' by Captain Sensible and 'It's Raining Men' by The Weather Girls. The last one was a request by Doris.

After all that, she sat them all back down and explained that they were going to write and perform a song together. Her trusty husband, Mike, was on hand with the laptop and microphone set to record.

Laterha had assembled a whiteboard and flipchart paper to record some ideas. She told them that they were going to produce their own version of Queen's 'We are the Champions'. This new version was to be called, 'We are The Acorns'. They all had great fun shouting out ideas for lyrics.

I remember it as though it were yesterday, and now I can't get the song out of my head.

Laterha and Mike emailed me a copy of the recording along with the lyrics the next day, and we played it over the speaker system for weeks after their visit for the residents to sing along to.

They even gave themselves a band name – The Wrinklies!

I printed off a copy for you. It makes more sense if you sing it whilst playing the original tune.

This is what they came up with:

WE ARE THE ACORNS

I've paid the fees, time after time,

They've emptied my account, but committed no crime

And dribbles and shakes – I've had a few

I've got piles and varicose veins, but I'll pull through!

(And my family have just sold it, sold it, sold it…so)

We are The Acorns my friend

And we'll keep on fighting to the end

We are The Acorns, we are The Acorns

No time to lose now

Cos we are in The Acorns, to our end!

I've taken my pills and had various falls

I've had pokes and prods and everything that goes with it

But we thank you all.

But it's been no bed of roses

No pleasure cruise

It's been just a challenge to get out of my chair

To go to the loo!

(And my family have just sold it, sold, it, sold it...so)

We are The Acorns my friend

And we'll keep on fighting to the end

We are The Acorns, we are The Acorns

No time to lose now

Cos we are in The Acorns, to our end!

It was just so typical of them. Laterha and Mike were in stitches – we all were. They sang with such enthusiasm, and it sounded great on the recording.

In the main body of the email, to go with the recording and the lyrics, Laterha wrote;

"I came to entertain and left entertained. Can I just say a big thank you to everyone in the home? 'The Acorns' is full of life – and we have had the time of ours! Love L & M."

I pinned it up on the noticeboard near reception.

I read it every time I walk by.

18

Common Senses

Not all the guests invited to visit or speak at The Acorns were artists or performers. A number of people were invited to educate rather than entertain. Some did both.

A lot of the residents were keen to learn – age was no barrier here!

They liked to acquire new skills and absorb new knowledge about nature and the natural world. They wanted to know more about something they had watched on television or read in a book. Their thirst for knowledge seemed to grow the older they became.

There was, however, one subject matter they all shared a common interest in – themselves.

They all wanted to find out what was happening to their bodies - inside and out.

The ageing process is rarely kind. The body starts to deteriorate and fail. We become weaker, slower and more dependent on others. Ultimately, as we battle against these ailments, conditions, illnesses and disabilities, we ask ourselves the age-old question – how long have I got left?

Time. That is what it boils down to. How much you have got, and how are you going to use it.

In all the time I have worked with old people the one thing that never ceases to amaze and surprise me, is their spirit and their absolute resolution to carry on for as long as they can. Giving up isn't an option – at least it isn't here at The Acorns.

Even when death stares them in the face, they want to battle on. That extra day – that extra week, month or year – it matters.

And that is why their guest request list often reached out for professionals and speakers in other fields. Doctors, nurses, opticians, physios. We have even had shout-outs for aromatherapists, hypnotists and spiritualists. Surprisingly (or unsurprisingly depending on how you look at it), we rarely see requests for the clergy or other religious leaders. I suspect this is because we see enough of them already.

Men and women of the cloth are regular visitors to The Acorns whether it be for funerals or last rites or simply to come and check on their aged parishioners who are no longer able to attend on a Sunday.

They are still considered to be fully paid-up members of the local flocks after years of dedicated service. I also think the priests and vicars enjoy their company as much as the other way round.

We had two more 'acts' booked in during the April of 2022 and then one in December.

The two 'Spring Chicks' as we called them were Mrs. Zoe Clarke (granddaughter of Beatrice), and Kathy Kalauhi who we found via a few dodgy internet searches.

Both were memorable and inspirational speakers, and they brought out that fighting spirit I mentioned earlier. Both had stood up to the many obstacles and challenges life had thrown at them. It was amazing to listen to their stories.

Beatrice was very proud of her family. A real doting mother and grandmother. Her bedroom walls were adorned with framed photos of her nearest and dearest, and she relished their visits to the home – none more so than Zoe.

Zoe was born with cerebral palsy, and the condition had

worsened over the years. Naturally, the family were all very concerned and adjusted their own lives to support and care for her. As a child, she required a lot of one-to-one care and no one – doctors included – were quite sure how the condition would manifest itself as she aged. One thing they all agreed on was that it would have a detrimental effect on her opportunities in life, and impact on her relationships.

However, Beatrice was determined to do all she could to help her granddaughter face these challenges head on, and instill a confidence and self-belief which in turn would help her overcome these obstacles in her way.

Mrs. Clarke's invitation to speak came as a direct result of a conversation over breakfast between Ralph and Stan. I say conversation, it was more of a point scoring discussion about which one of them had the worst case of arthritis.

"I could hardly get a wink of sleep last night" Stan was telling him. The pain in my arm was excruciating. Peter said he could get me something for it, but I am too old to be taking drugs now. I just have to live with it."

"In your arm you say?" Ralph said, mockingly, "I am bloody riddled with it. Neck, shoulders..."

"Knees and toes, knees and toes" laughed Stan, interrupting him.

"You wouldn't be so jovial if you had it!" Ralph snapped back.

The two of them went on sniping at each other.

"I couldn't get out of bed"

"I couldn't get my slippers on"

"I can barely hold my knife and fork these days"

"My hand is more like a claw."

Beatrice was sitting on the table next to them, and she looked over at me and raised her eyebrows in mock exasperation.

"You don't know you are born, you two. You are both relatively fit and healthy for your age, and don't go about pretending you are not. The pair of you were out playing badminton on the grass yesterday. Hopping and jumping around like a pair of teenagers. That is why you are stiff today – it has got bugger all to do with arthritis."

The two of them looked sheepish and bowed their heads like naughty school boys. They had been caught out.

The discussion moved on to real disabilities rather than imagined ones, and Beatrice talked about her granddaughter, Zoe.

By the end of their chat, the two men were enthused enough to beckon me over and ask if I wouldn't mind asking the girl to come and talk about her condition at the home.

I asked Beatrice what she thought.

"I'll give her a call later on and see if she is keen. It is a big ask for her."

Later that evening, Beatrice sought me out to tell me she had spoken to Zoe. She said she would be happy to come in and talk to the residents one evening.

We agreed on the 6th April.

It was to her credit that she was willing to come in and stand up in front of fifty strangers and speak about her condition, but also gratifying that the residents were so keen to hear her speak. They were just so eager to listen and learn.

On the evening in question, Beatrice had insisted on paying for a caterer to bring in fish finger butties for everyone, and others chipped in for drinks and desserts. Everyone was in good spirits, and when Zoe arrived, she was greeted with a big cheer and an invitation to 'tuck in'.

I think that helped relax her a little before being introduced to the pack.

She was incredibly nervous at first, and I thought we had made a mistake by asking too much of her. She stood in silence at the front, leaning on the microphone, looking down intently. We could hear her breathing heavily, and at one point I thought she was going to faint. I glanced over to Beatrice who had her hands clasped together as though she were praying, hoping Zoe would come good – and boy did she!

Slowly, she straightened up and looked up at all these old faces willing her on.

Smiling, she said, "Now you know what it feels like when your families are waiting for you to get up."

Beatrice instinctively clapped her hands and others followed. I relaxed too.

She started by telling us a little bit about herself – her family and her home. She talked about the way her house has been adapted to help. Little things – ramps, handles, alarm cords etc. Not too dissimilar to the home we were in.

"They do try to make little adjustments to make my life a little easier," she said, "but the hardest part is the pain. It is almost constant and no pain killers seem to numb it."

I looked over at Stan and Ralph. They were watching intently.

"I have felt like giving up. I will be honest with you, at times I didn't think I had the strength to make it. I wasn't even sure I wanted to make it. This is the first time I have actually said that out loud."

I looked again at Beatrice. The expression on her face had changed. This was news to her too.

"The only thing driving me on was my family. My children, my husband, my parents and..."

She broke off for a second before looking down to the front row.

"....my nan."

The room fell silent again. Beatrice was in tears. She wasn't the only one. This was an incredibly intimate family moment and we were all part of it.

Beatrice stood up and slowly made her way up the steps and onto the small stage.

She reached the microphone and opened her arms wide. Zoe fell into them and the two ladies held onto each other tightly. There wasn't a sound in the room for at least thirty seconds. It was a moment I will never forget.

Then someone clapped. Then another and another. Within seconds, everyone in the room was up and on their feet, clapping. It was such a lovely, touching moment.

Eventually, Beatrice made her way back to her seat, and the others followed her lead.

Zoe composed herself and grabbed hold of the microphone again.

"I didn't know what to expect when I agreed to come tonight, but it wasn't that!"

Everyone chuckled and clapped again.

"What I wanted to do tonight was inspire you, like my nan inspires me. Everyone needs someone to believe in them. Nan believes in me – she always has. When they said I wouldn't be able to work, she made me apply for jobs. When they said I would need full time care, she told me to look after myself and be more independent. When they said I wouldn't be able to have children, she told me she wanted to be a grandma. She wouldn't let me rest on my laurels. She wouldn't let me feel sorry for myself. 'Wasted time is a waste of life' she used to say. And by God, she was right. She made me laugh, and she gave me so many happy memories growing up. The way she used to walk downstairs backwards because she thought it was safer. The way she used to fall asleep at any given moment, and her glasses would fall off her face. The way she could never dip a biscuit in her tea without it falling into her cup. The times I would ask if I could stay over and she said she would have to consult her diary – she never even owned a diary!

She was so proud of me and I was in awe of her. When I gave birth to my first child and she came over to the hospital to see me, she just held my hand and said, 'that's ma girl'.

If I can pass any message on to you, my elders and betters, it is this - YOU matter. You are needed and wanted more than you could possibly know. Every single one of you are perfect as you are. More important than any of you realise."

When she finished speaking, there was another standing ovation.

At the end of the evening, some residents hung around to chat to Zoe and ask her a few questions. She stood side by side with her nan, holding hands with her.

Ralph and Stan wandered past me on the way to the staircase.

"Are you still in pain?" I asked them.

"Can't feel a thing!" Stan replied.

"Me either" said Ralph, looking back over his shoulder towards Zoe. "Me either."

The second of the April visits couldn't have been much more different than the first.

As well as general aches and pains, the residents would often discuss the other downsides of old age. These included everything from hair loss to incontinence, piles or pills used. In the young, these would often be classed as taboo subjects, but not here in the home. Here, the old folk liked to compare notes and they would openly discuss their faults and failings without a care of who might be listening in or what they thought.

The effects of the Covid virus had only added to the list of ailments they were suffering from. A lack of taste and smell to go along with deteriorating eyesight and hearing.

One morning a few of them were talking about their senses and which of the five were the most important.

"Sight, definitely," said Frank. "I couldn't do without my eyes."

"I'd rather not have to look at you," laughed Joan, "But I suppose I am the same. To lose my eyesight would be just terrible. There is so much beauty to see in this world. I never tire of looking out in the garden. It is constantly changing. All those vibrant colours. Beautiful."

The others nodded and agreed. I did too. Sight was considered number one sense by all present.

"When I had my cataracts removed a few years back, I promised myself I would never take my eyesight for granted again," said

Harold. "Before the operation, everything was just a blur. There had been a steady decline in my eyesight for two or three years, and when I eventually got the date through for the op, I could barely see my hand in front of my face. It was terrifying, I can tell you. They aren't perfect now, but I can see well with glasses."

It turned out Harold wasn't the only one who had had the dreaded cataracts. At least five others in the room shared their story.

"So that's decided then," Frank announced. "Which sense is the second most important?"

This wasn't as straightforward.

"I nominate hearing" he went on.

"Nah" said Alan. "I could have given up on hearing a long time ago if I could keep the others. There hasn't been one thing of interest my wife said in thirty-five years of marriage. Deafness would have been a blessing!"

"What about music, laughter and singing?" Hilda said. "I can't imagine not being able to hear what is going on around me. Oh no, hearing has to be up at the top for me."

"I'd put touch above hearing," shouted Joe from across the room. "What's the first thing you do when you see something? You touch it. You want the surprise of what it feels like – rough, smooth, soft, warm, and cold. It is an underestimated sensation. I knew a fella once who couldn't feel the cold or heat. It could be freezing outside and he wouldn't know. He would walk around with a t-shirt on in the middle of winter. We all thought he was as hard as nails. Died of hyperthermia."

The others nodded like it was just one of those things.

"Let's have a vote on it then," said Frank. "Who votes for

hearing for second place?"

Hearing got fourteen votes.

"And who votes for touch?"

Touch got twelve votes.

"Close but no cigar for touch. So that is eyesight number one. Hearing in second and touch in third. Which sense is going to get the wooden spoon – smell or taste?"

"These two are closely linked," said Doreen. "If you lose one you tend to lose the other. Look at Covid or when you get a bad cold!"

"For the purpose of this competition, you will have to separate them," laughed Frank. "Nose or tongue? That is the question."

"If I am forced to choose," said Doreen, "I would go for taste. I love my food."

"Nose for me," said Wilf. "It is a close-run thing though. Why is it that if something is nice, we say we like that smell, but if it is bad, we say it stinks?"

"No time for semantics now Wilf," Frank scolded. "This is a serious competition. Smell or taste? Which one will come in fourth or which will pick up the wooden spoon in the senses challenge?"

After much deliberation, smell pipped taste to fourth place.

"Sight, hearing, touch, smell and taste. In that order," announced Frank.

It was one of those discussions we often had over a meal or in downtime. A conversation that meant nothing, but got everyone thinking. A conversation where everyone's opinion was heard and listened to. The result wouldn't change anything, but it prompted interaction, passion and viewpoint. The result wasn't important – it was how they got there that mattered.

It was following this discussion that prompted the search for the other April guest – our second Spring Chick.

They wanted to find out more about their senses – how they are linked and how much we depend on them. It was a bit of a wide-ranging topic, but after a good internet search I thought I had found just the one.

There was a lady in County Durham. An exiled American called Kathy Kalauhi, who had her own business – 'Common Senses'.

It was a busy website with many services on offer. Her tagline at the top was ANALYSE, MOTIVATE, SUCCEED.

Kathy offered counselling sessions for those suffering from trauma or loss. She also provided yoga sessions, meditation, massage and art classes. She even had a degree in psychology! Was there no end to this woman's talents?

On her introduction page, she sold herself as a guru for feelings, a doctor of love and a woman of empathy. Her interests were music and dancing, cooking and baking, climbing and skiing, reading and writing, walking and pet care and...men.

Unashamedly, on her website, she admitted to being on her fifth husband and stated that, if he didn't cut the mustard, she would be on the lookout for a sixth.

She described herself as determined, chatty, focused and generous.

She also listed her own personal battles in life – in particular, overcoming cancer and living with a serious visual impairment!

This, and another section, caught my eye. She revealed yet another string to her bow – after dinner speaking. There was no mention of price, so I fired off an email to her and thought nothing more about it for a couple of days until I received a reply.

In my email, I told her where I worked and what we were looking for. I explained that our budget was limited and apologised in advance if we were wasting her time.

Her reply was forthright and honest.

Ang,

Thank you for your email. It sounds like you have a bunch of old folks there needing an injection of life. Normally my fee for an evening gig would start at £500, depending on which service you required, and then, factoring in travel costs, the overall invoice would be in the region of £750, but you are in luck. I am coming over to Carlisle in April for a race meeting and staying over the Friday and Saturday night. If you can do Friday 22nd, count me in.

As it is for the olds, I will do this one gratis on one condition – they agree to let me film the session for my website. What do you say?

Kathy

It wasn't the reply I expected, but I couldn't look a gift horse in the mouth! Before I replied, I ran it by the crowd over breakfast the next day.

"She sounds as mad as a box of frogs," said Ralph.

"Nothing to lose. Go for it," said Mabel.

"Sounds like a good laugh to me. We might get a few tips from her for the racing on the Saturday. Get her in," agreed Frank.

After getting their approval, I replied to Kathy and accepted. I penned the date on the calendar and awaited her reply.

It came later that day.

Ang,

Thank you for the reply. I shall be there for 7 p.m. I shall be bringing my friend, Monica, to assist me. For the session, I would be obliged if you could position the seats in a large circle facing the middle and clear the floor space. I will bring along any other resources we might require for the different activities.

Looking forward to meeting you all.

Kathy

As simple as that. I just remember thinking – activities? Resources? What is she planning? It wasn't what I – or the residents – were expecting, but it was yet another memorable night at The Acorns.

The 22nd of April was miserable weather wise. It poured down continuously, and we were all stuck in for the day. The lawn resembled a swimming pool, and large puddles covered the patios outside.

The forecast for the next day was for more of the same, and we were all worried the horse racing would be postponed thereby causing our guest speaker to cancel. We needn't have worried.

At 6:00 p.m. there was a knock at the front door and Vera answered it. She ushered in the two ladies who were huddled under their coats trying to fend off the torrential rain outside.

"England in the Spring!" the smaller woman called out as she dumped her bag on the floor. "I came over here for the green and pleasant lands you hear so much about, but all you get is rain, rain and more rain."

It was hard to disagree with her, but there was something in the tone of her voice that suggested this wasn't a moan, more an amusement.

Vera took their coats and led them through to the staff room to warm up. I joined them.

Kathy introduced herself and then her friend and assistant, Monica.

It turned out that she had lived in England for over ten years, but her New York State accent hadn't softened.

I apologised again for the weather. Kathy just dismissed it with a wave of her hand.

"You have pubs around here, don't you? There is always a back-up if the horses aren't running. The hotel was booked anyway. We don't let a little thing like the weather put us off. We couldn't let our audience down now, could we?"

I sat with Vera and our guests while other staff members set up the Keith Chegwin Suite for the 'talk'. They chatted about anything and everything apart from what they had planned for the evening. I told them about the senses discussion that prompted me to email.

"Perfect, perfect," Kathy said. "Let's see what they think after tonight. They might just change the order."

I had no idea what she meant or what she had planned, but it sounded fun.

Monica passed her the coffee cup, and I noticed how she made sure Kathy had a good grip of the handle before she let go. It was only then I remembered she was visually impaired.

I asked her how she coped.

"Well, I'm worse than the bionic man and better than Stevie Wonder," she laughed. "I can't say it is easy, but you learn to live with it. I will be talking about it this evening amongst other things. Is there anything I need to know about the crowd?"

I assured her that they were all looking forward to it – whatever 'it' was.

By 7:00 p.m. they were all seated in their big circle in the Keith Chegwin Suite. At the conservatory end of the room, one seat had been left empty with a RESERVED sign left on it. Opposite, at the other side of the circle, another seat had been left empty in the same way. I presumed one was for Kathy and the other, Monica.

I stood with Vera outside the circle and waited for the show to begin.

The two ladies entered the room and made their way to their seats. The party gave them a round of applause to begin, and they lapped it up.

"Thank you, thank you," said Kathy. "A sound I never tire of. It is lovely to meet you all, and I hope we are all going to have some fun this evening. You will see that I like a lot of audience participation so I hope you aren't the shy types"

It was then I noticed a large bag under her seat. She bent down and pulled it into the circle between her legs.

"I believe you were talking about your senses recently? Well, this evening we are going to play a few games to help sharpen those senses, and help you appreciate not only what you have got, but how you can make the most of what you haven't got."

She was a small lady, but such a dominant character. Full of confidence and vigour. I remember wishing I was a bit more like that.

She unzipped her bag and pulled out a blindfold.

"Blindfolds are brilliant things. Whoever invented them deserved a sticker. They are used everywhere from the school room to the bedroom."

Betty coughed and blushed at the same time.

"They can be used to help us relax or to heighten tension. They test our senses. They don't just reduce visibility; they require our brains to find solutions – to use other senses in the absence of the one they disable. Let me explain. Our brains are problem solvers. They like to find solutions. If our body is denied one thing, our brain will seek an alternative for the good of the body. If I use this blindfold to take away one sense, our brain tells us to rely on another."

"What you can hear?" asked Ralph.

"Exactly, young man. And not just what you can hear – every sense comes into play. Now I need a volunteer. As you asked the question, would you like to join me in the middle of the circle?"

Ralph jumped to his feet and wandered over to cries and cheers from the others. Kathy tied the blindfold around his head and made sure he couldn't see a thing before continuing.

"One of the first things he will notice is how much he relies on his eyesight for balance. See how he opens his stance and widens his arms for support. Instinctively, his brain is searching for solutions. He knows where he is he knows that there are no dangers nearby, yet his brain knows his body is not functioning as it should."

It was fascinating to watch as she talked.

She reached into her bag and brought out two small fishing rods. At the end of one was a small mouse. She shook it and a bell rang. On the other rod was a tightly packed ball. She explained that the ball gave out a strong lavender scent.

Ralph stood facing her, wobbling slightly from side to side, with his arms stretched out. He looked like he was trying to balance on a tightrope.

"What I want you to do, young man, is find the bell and the smell. She held a rod in each hand and positioned them about two feet either side of his head. She bobbed them up and down, moving them slowly forwards and backwards. We were all enthralled. His hands moved up and around searching for the two moving objects.

"Which one stands out, young man? Which one are you drawn to?"

"The smell," Ralph replied. It is overpowering. I can hear the bell. I know it is to my right, but I am drawn to the smell."

"Do you know?" she said, "I have carried out this experiment dozens of times and most people choose certain smells over sound in the first instance. Powerful aromas are known to trigger all sorts of emotions such as lust, hunger or revulsion. And yet it is not practical to use smell as an aid for visual impairment, so we tend to use bells, whistles, clickers and beepers."

She took off Ralph's blindfold and invited him to sit down again.

In her bag, she had a whole host of aids to show us. She was like a travelling saleswoman, and by the end of the session, Vera had an order list for her.

She explained how each one worked and how they helped make her life easier and safer. I was amazed at just how much was out there and just how much they could help the residents be more independent.

She explained her own visual impairment. Apparently, her condition was incredibly rare, and not something glasses or contact lenses would correct.

Her brother suffered from it too, which suggested it was genetic. The condition had worsened as she aged which must have been frightening. I looked around the room at those who had mentioned cataract operations, and those wearing glasses or patches. They were leaning in, keen to hear every word and piece of advice.

She talked about large print and audio books. In her bag she showed them specially designed gadgets used to help her thread a needle so she could sew. There were guides for kitchen knives to help you cut and chop vegetables safely. She had cooking pots and pans with lockable lids and small holes in the side so you could drain boiling water without risk of burning. Vera ordered five of those. Four for the home and one for herself.

She talked about self-help apps for their phones or iPads. There was an app that would scan and recognise currency, and another that used a sat nav mapping system to describe any obstacles in the road or on the pavement. A talking thermometer, a talking blood pressure monitor, a device to turn the heating system up or down through voice recognition. A voice activated remote control, and a walking stick which vibrates when it senses uneven ground. It was amazing.

Kathy and Monica demonstrated each one and they were incredibly patient, answering every question or concern. By the end of the demonstration, we all felt so empowered.

I looked at my watch – it was 9:30 p.m. She had been talking for over two hours, but it felt like ten minutes.

"We thought," she said, "That we would finish with a couple of games. Who is up for it?"

Every single one of them called out "ME!" with their hands up like excited little school children.

She asked them all to stand up as Monica rearranged the chairs to make two long lines against the wall.

She brought out a football, four cones and a handful of blindfolds. The health and safety warning bells flashed inside my head again. I looked over at Vera and she was just laughing.

"This ball has a bell inside. We are going to test your listening skills with a game of blind football."

For the next thirty minutes I experienced every emotion. I was terrified someone would fall and hurt themselves, but at the same time, I was in stitches as they walked around kicking thin air or bumped into chairs whilst wandering around aimlessly. They loved it. The game ended nil-nil and I think the ball was only kicked three times throughout the match. Anyone who wanted to play played. They were having the time of their lives.

Monica led the last game. She went along the rows of seats and gave everyone a number – one or two. She handed out the blindfolds to all the number ones.

"For our last game we are going to explore, what I consider, an underrated sense. The sense of touch. In a moment, I want all of you number ones to put on your blindfolds. I then want you number twos to walk around the room in silence and stand in front of a number one. The number ones then have twenty seconds to touch the face and head of the person in front of them and try and work out who it is."

"Face only, Frank," I remember Vera shouting out.

Vera and I watched from the side-lines as the game played out, and what a scream it was. They were useless at it. Half of them couldn't distinguish between men and women let alone guess who the person was in front of them. It was a great way to end the evening. It was nearly half past ten by the time Kathy finished up.

"I hope this evening was useful for you all. I don't know what you will take from it, but if you have enjoyed it, that is good enough for me. We talked a lot about the five senses tonight - but there is a sixth sense that, I think, is more important than the others. I am not talking about the supernatural here. I am talking about how you feel inside. How you feel inside dictates your mood, how you behave towards others, and how you live your life. It is what makes you the person you are. Tonight, I have enjoyed the company of fifty or so wonderful people with such a zest and a passion for life."

I looked around the room again. Everyone was smiling or laughing together. Another super night's entertainment at The Acorns.

Kathy and Zoe left a lasting impression on everyone – myself included, but there was one more guest that year.

Do I regret inviting him to speak? I was unsure at first.

And yet, despite the consequences, it was the best thing I ever did.

19

Doctor Who?

We booked Doctor Alasdair Deakin to come to The Acorns to speak at the start of December 2022. Friday the 2nd it was. There was nothing special about the date. Just another Friday, but it was the start of everything to come.

We did not approach Doctor Deakin, he approached us – well, his agency did.

H.I.M (Helping, Inspiring, Motivating) were based in London, but were reaching out to the suburbs with their array of 'associates and experts'. They offered *'inspirational speakers with words for every body and every mind'*. They had contacted large local businesses, councils, schools and health trusts via emails and flyers.

I thought nothing of it – we get these kinds of things through all the time – but I just happened to be in the office when they called.

Doctor Deakin introduced himself and explained who he was working for. He asked if he could make an appointment to speak with the on-site manager of the home with a view to arranging a talk with the residents.

I was on shift with Vera the following week, and we arranged for him to visit on Monday 24th October at 6:00 p.m. when the residents would be eating their evening meal.

I didn't think any more about it until he arrived that evening.

Young Sammy answered the door to him and I watched through the office window as he made his way into the reception area. He wasn't what I imagined him to be – shorter and scruffier.

He was wearing an old quilted jacket and his jeans were torn at the knees. He looked like the supervisor of a building site, and more likely to pull out a tool box than a first aid kit. I have seen enough doctors to know they don't fit the dream-boat image of pristine, flowing white coats and chiselled jaws with strong arms ready to scoop you up and save you from whatever misfortune has come your way.

Maybe that was just my own twisted fantasy, but Doctor Deakin was so far removed from that image. Even with his coat on, I could tell he wasn't in the best of shapes, and his face was more 'sand-blasted' than weathered.

He clapped his hands together and said something to Sammy. She turned and pointed to the office, making me jump. They caught me staring.

He raised a hand in acknowledgement and purposefully strode towards me. Vera was watching something on Netflix on her iPad, and I urged her to turn it off and look professional before our visitor arrived. Reluctantly, she pressed pause and threw it into the draw beside her desk.

I opened the office door and invited him in. He greeted me with a wide smile and a firm handshake – so firm I thought he was going to break my little finger. He then reached over the table to Vera to give her the same treatment. She winced just before he let go.

"It is a bugger to find this place," he said. "I've been to a golf course and a stately home before I found you. I almost gave up."

From the look on Vera's face, I could tell she wished he had.

Whatever Doctor Deakin lacked, it wasn't confidence, but he wasn't arrogant either. He immediately struck me as someone who was very comfortable in his own skin. His attitude was very much, 'Like me or loathe me, this is what I am' and straight away, I felt comfortable in his company.

Despite his ruggedness, Vera soon seemed to take a shine to him too. He sat down in the chair opposite her before being invited to do so, and slouched back in the seat.

"So" he said, "What can I do for you?"

I remember looking over at Vera and the two of us laughed. "I thought you might tell us that!" said Vera. "All we know is that you are a doctor and you work for some flashy agency in London. Question. May I ask, what are you a doctor of, why aren't you still doctoring, and what have you got to offer the residents of an old folk's home? Oh, and what do you charge for your services? Because I will tell you for nothing, we aren't in a position to pay you the fees quoted on that website!"

"That's more than one question," said Doctor Deakin, chuckling away to himself. "Let me answer each one in turn. Hopefully that will put your mind at ease. Firstly, I will tell you a little about myself. I am a specialist in the elderly – a geriatrician. I am also a neurologist. I study disorders to the brain and the nervous system – particularly in the old. Dementia and Parkinson's. I am sure some of your residents and their families are sufferers of such terrible illnesses." He stopped and reached over to grab a biscuit from the table. With his mouth half full, he continued.

"So, what can I bring to you? Well, over twenty years of experience in the field with a whole host of strategies you can use to help treat and support those in need. Nice biscuit by the way. As for money, I will cost you the grand total of bugger all. Nowt.

Apparently, your own Trust's managers had been so taken by the email from H.I.M, they were keen to channel some of their own budget to fund some of my wages. H.I.M, in a bid to promote their brand across the nation, are happy to pay the rest. This means that I will be getting paid more to chat to your old dears for a few sessions than I would get in three months on the job in a ward. It was a no brainer – and I know brains!"
I asked him if he would like a coffee or tea.
"In the absence of anything stronger, I will be very grateful for a black coffee – three sugars please."

By the time I came back to the office with his drink, he was sitting on the other side of the table beside Vera watching Netflix on the iPad.

"Thanks love – just what this doctor ordered," he said, looking up with a big smile on his face. Anyone would have thought he had worked with us for years such was his relaxed manner.

"Shall I leave you to it?" I asked, hands on hips.

Vera barely looked up from the screen. "Thanks Ang love. Alasdair said he would start his talks in December. They are paying him for six sessions. Can you find some time in the diary? Any evenings will do, he said. He doesn't have anything else on."

I toddled off to do as I was told, leaving them watching, whatever it was they were watching, in the office.

I flicked through the pages of the calendar looking for suitable dates, all the time thinking about our residents, and who he might be able to help and support. Two in particular stood out in my mind. Leonard and Dora.

Leonard had been with us for nearly three years and, sadly, his mind was failing fast. To see the decline first hand was both saddening and frightening.

Dora was new to us, but the signs of her Dementia were already showing as predicted.

If Doctor Deakin could help them – and any of the others – in his short time with us, surely it was worth a try.

At the end of the day, it wasn't going to cost us a penny. What could possibly go wrong?

20

Trust Us

Towards the end of 2022, there was speculation going around that The Acorns faced an uncertain future. The board of directors in charge of the Trust were rumoured to be considering a link up with two other homes in the region to 'maximise efficiency and streamline operations' for 'increased profitability' whatever that meant.

We didn't really pay much attention to these corporate emails. They tended to fall into the junk box anyway, but as the year went on, there was increased talk of visits, inspections and walkthroughs by senior leaders and directors. From what we could gather, they intended to merge three homes into two sites - The Acorns was one of those under consideration.

We were told not to worry - these were simply paper audits and a chance for the suits to get to know their 'customers' and staff.

Unsurprisingly, as the dates of the first visit grew closer, rumours of closures, wage reductions and even job losses caused a degree of panic amongst the staff.

The residents were none the wiser at this stage, and nobody wanted to trouble them over something we knew so little about ourselves. It didn't prevent fear or dread growing.

In all the time I had worked there, the board of directors had NEVER visited the home. They made no effort to communicate with staff or the residents. The onsite managers were expected to compile quarterly reports comprising breakdowns of staff turnover, wages paid, hours worked and holidays taken. They also wanted to know how the budget was spent along with projections for the following financial year. The accounts were included in these reports and, although as a facility we watched every penny, the profits each year had been considerable for the owners and stakeholders. This was probably the main reason they kept off our backs.

But now, for whatever reason, they were showing more of an interest.

They obviously wanted to see which of their three operations was the least effective. They wanted to know how they could incorporate one into the other two. They wanted to share resources and staff, and be 'dynamic and proactive in a competitive field'.

In our sector - which was supposed to be all about care - there was no mention of customers as people. Their corporate overview of progress didn't take into account feelings and needs, nor did it recognise the good work of the staff and the relationships they had built up with the residents and their families year on year.

No, this was about money - pure and simple.

We received an email to say the first visit was to be on Friday 4th November 2022 – the night before Bonfire Night. Two appointed advisors would be visiting The Acorns at 2 p.m.

For this visit, we were told they would simply be 'observing daily routines' and we were to go about our business as usual. We were advised to answer any questions openly and honestly without fear of reproach. Yeah, right!

It said the advisors would expect to be accompanied around the home by a manager, but not led or guided. They were to have full access to the home itself, the grounds and the gardens.

Worryingly, and unsurprisingly, the last couple of lines of the email caused the most concern.

It said, *'Feedback will be given to the directors then disseminated to the managers and staff. Should further individual feedback be required, arrangements will be made for one-to-one meetings with the advisors.*

The whole email was purposefully vague - designed to scare.

Vera called me into the office after we had all read the email, and I knew she had the same sense of dread that I did.

"Guess who is on the management rota for the 4th November? Me!"

We talked about what they might do and what they would want to see, but all we could really do was speculate. We knew how capable we were. We knew just how amazing The Acorns was as a facility. We knew the residents were getting the best possible service - we would do anything for them. We knew they loved us too, but we also felt that all of that was going to be irrelevant if a decision had already been made, as we suspected it might have been.

Would they see that? Would they appreciate us like the residents do?

All we could do was our best. We all just had to operate as normal, then surely, they would see how good a job we were doing.

Surely?

Even so, we were convinced there was another agenda.

After Doctor Deakin's visit, I kept a closer eye on Leonard and Dora. He asked me to note down any signs of behaviour linked to Dementia or memory loss. I spoke with Niki, Leonard's daughter, and asked her to look out for any signs of deterioration, stress or mood changes. She knew him better than anyone, and was delighted to know he was going to get extra help and support from a specialist in the field.

Dora's daughter and granddaughter felt the same. They too said they would write down any changes in her condition, and said they would be happy to talk with the doctor before his planned visit.

Dora had been with us a few months by this point, and I was getting to know her and her little mannerisms quite well. She would often 'lose time', in that she would fall silent and go into a sort of daze, just looking up at the ceiling or straight ahead into nothingness. Sometimes she would wander the halls and corridors, and had to be guided back to her room. How long she would lose time for would vary. It could last five or ten minutes or sometimes an hour or two. She would forget what we had talked about or what she had been doing. She was so quiet and unassuming that it was often hard to gauge how she was feeling after an incident, but I suspect she felt frustrated, stressed and even a little scared. She would sometimes retire to her room and cry, but she tried to hide it from staff or fellow residents.

There was always a staff member on hand to follow her or sit with her to make sure she didn't come to any harm.

Leonard was very different to Dora. He had been a tall, strong man in his younger years. He had worked as a club bouncer as well as spells in the forces. He had huge, strong, shovel-like hands, and even in his eighties he had the strength of a much younger man.

Leonard's lapses were more frequent than Dora's, and he too would become frustrated and angry with himself - never towards others though.

He knew his mind was failing and he hated the fact that he sometimes couldn't remember events from his past. He could be in the middle of telling a story, and then lose his train of thought. He would forget what he had just been talking about or the names of his close friends and family. Even photographs wouldn't help jog his memory. He would stare at the once familiar faces like they were perfect strangers. He knew he should recognise the people in the photos, but he often couldn't name them or remember how they were related to him.

The others were acutely aware of his problem, and they tried ever so hard to help him. They would write him notes or repeat what he had been talking about. There was no teasing or laughing. They cared for him and feared his condition.
They knew it could just as easily be them.

There was one incident around that time that made us all chuckle - Leonard included.

He had been telling us a tale about his time in the Navy when he lost track of what he was saying and fell silent. Stan grabbed hold of his newspaper and started writing notes and reminders of the conversation around the edges.

An hour or two later I was walking through the lounge.

They were all playing cards, apart from Leonard who was reading his paper - upside down! I thought he was just lost in his own world so I chose not to say anything to him, but he stopped me in my tracks.

"I'm alright, Ang," he said, smiling. "I'm trying to read that dozy buggers writing!"

Ralph wagged a disapproving finger in the air without taking his eye off his cards.

"It is like trying to read Arabic," he went on. "that said, I have managed to work out four down on the crossword. A ten-letter word beginning with 'I' and ending in 'E'. The clue is 'a person who can't read or write. Illiterate!"

"I don't know why I bother trying to help!" Ralph shouted as the rest burst out laughing.

Leonard chuckled away to himself.

"Next time I fall into one of my comas, can you get Wilf to scribe?"

Even in adversity, they never lost their sense of humour.

We carried on as normal for the next few days, but all the time this 'visit' was playing on my mind. We were a great team, and we all promised to help and support each other through it all. When the day itself arrived, we were all on pins.

I was sitting in the Keith Chegwin lounge doing a jigsaw with Maureen and Alice when our guests arrived. I say guests - they were not invited nor welcome.

Vera met them at the door and led them through to the office. I watched them look around as they walked. I couldn't help but feel nervous and paranoid.

They were in the office for what seemed like an age. They had their backs to me, but I could see Vera nodding and talking. There were no smiles.

"That's a corner piece," said Alice. "Are you going to put it down to help us get started? You look like you are away with the fairies, love. Are you alright?"

I tried to get back to the activity, but the ladies could tell my mind was elsewhere.

"What's up, chicken?" asked Maureen. "Is it something to do with those two women who have just come in?" She didn't miss a trick.

"They have just come to look around. From the council." I lied.

"Pay them no mind, Ang. Whatever it is they want, just you remember - they are no better than you, and they know a lot less than you, I'd wager. Stick with us, love. We will protect you." I wanted to feel reassured. I wanted them to protect me, but it was difficult as I couldn't say it out loud that the people in power often dictate but can't do it themselves.

After a few more minutes, the two women stood up and allowed Vera to lead them out of the office. She looked broken and sullen.

One woman - the one in charge - had a clipboard and a notepad tucked under her arm. The other stood just behind her with her arms folded, like a lapdog. The one with the clipboard set off walking and her lapdog followed leaving Vera to trail behind them. They walked out of sight and down the corridor towards the kitchens.

I carried on with the jigsaw. It was a thousand piece one - a picture of Buckingham Palace in the summer. The flower beds and trees in the foreground looked incredibly detailed, and I remember thinking that it was going to take us days to complete.

About half an hour later, I heard voices behind us, and I didn't need to turn around to know who was approaching.

The three of them walked forward and stood beside our table.

"Research says jigsaws are good therapy," I heard the one in charge say. She was a small, dumpy woman dressed in a baggy, black suit. Her black, wavy hair had streaks of grey giving her the appearance of a round Cruella De Vil. Her sidekick was slim and serious looking. No smiles from her. No warmth. Side by side, they looked like the number ten.

I watched as she made notes on her pad.

"And your name is?" she said rudely without looking up.

"Angie Tomlinson," I replied, trying to make eye contact.

She smiled a false smile and mumbled something to the skinny one who tried, but struggled, to smile back. It was more of a grimace really. I didn't think she was capable of smiling.

"I'd like to do a jigsaw in my spare time?" she said, still making notes.

"Me too." said the skinny one. "*In my spare time.*"

They nodded a 'goodbye' and walked on. Vera followed, shaking her head to me as she passed. She looked exhausted and pale. I felt a knot develop in my stomach - the kind you get when you haven't done anything wrong, but feel like you must have.

I felt like crying. Alice must have sensed it.

"Whatever that is and whoever they are, you are worth a hundred of them. Forget them."

But I couldn't forget them. I had a feeling that they were not going to go away.

Later in the evening, Vera and I sat in the office drinking coffee, and working our way through a plateful of chocolate biscuits.

"It was awful," she said. "Just awful. They seemed to hate everything and everyone - me in particular. They said so much without speaking. Tuts and 'eye rolling' all the way round. They would be whispering and sharing private jokes when I was talking to them. So rude. I wasn't party to what she was writing down, but I know it won't be good – even though we are. I'm expecting the worst."

"I really felt for you." I said, trying to reassure her and failing miserably.

"It was horrible from start to finish. One thing I do know is this - they do not care about the residents or the staff. This is purely and simply about money and ego. Let's just hope the other two places are worse on paper than we are. After all, it is all about what they write down, not what is actually happening."

The two of us sat in silence for a minute or so before Vera spoke.

"Things weren't going well before they met Frank."

Despite the tension and depressive mood, I couldn't help but smile when I heard his name mentioned. Vera smiled too.

"Oh God, what did he do? What did he say?" I asked.

"Never trust a woman with a clipboard!"

"He didn't?!" I gasped.

"He bloody did!" she replied, laughing. "Not only that, but he was standing at the doorway to his bedroom in only his boxer shorts, cleaning his teeth, when they walked by."

I tried to fight the image from my mind. "What did she say?"

"She didn't say anything. She just looked at him in disgust, jotted something down, and walked on. I dread to think what she wrote about him on that pad of hers!"

Vera picked up another biscuit and dunked it in her coffee. We stared at our mugs in silence again.

"She told me to expect an email in the next couple of days," Vera sighed - her voice starting to break. "She forced a smile when she said it, and I knew then it was going to be bad news."

Instinctively, I got up, walked around the table and gave her a huge hug. We both cried.

If I knew then what I know now, I would have shoved that clipboard up her arse. Sideways! It is certainly big enough. The arse that is, not the clipboard."

It felt like gallows humour, but it did make me giggle.

21

Out of Your Mind

The email did arrive a couple of days later as promised. Vera read it out to us in the staff room while the residents were enjoying their breakfast.

It wasn't a long one, but it confirmed our fears and worries. They would be back, and the next time it would be a lot more formal and intrusive.

The email talked of rotas, timetables, work management, time management and better practice. It mentioned a review of job descriptions and staff organization which may well lead to a restructure. Vague phrases were thrown in such as 'at the start of this journey',' accountability for all aspects' and 'taking responsibility for your own actions and for the good of the home'.

It suggested The Acorns needed modernisation. A rigorous overhaul to meet the Trust's expectations and philosophy of the level of care needed to give our 'customers' the comfortable living experience they deserve. Just words really!

It said, on the advisors' next visit, they would outline their views for the way forward.

It also said they will meet with each staff member for vital one to one meetings.

When Vera finished reading, she slumped back into her chair.

"There you are! It is the insinuation that we are not currently providing an 'experience they deserve' that gets me. Patronising bitch!"

The only positive was that this process was not due to begin until the new year. We could at least enjoy Christmas without them breathing down our necks. Before then, we would have Doctor Deakin. Alasdair.

We received another email from him confirming that he would be arriving at 7:00 p.m. on Friday 2nd December 2022. That was something to look forward to. His email was addressed to Vera, and he even ended it with a few kisses after his name. I thought it was weird, but Vera thought it was quite sweet. Romantic even. Something was clearly developing there.

By the end of November, my notes on Dora and Leonard were considerable. I had also added anything their relatives had given me, and I was able to build up quite a behavioural portfolio to give to Doctor Deakin.

It would appear that there were no set times or patterns for these lapses or memory loss. They could happen at any time of day, and for any length of time regardless of where they were, or whose company they were in.

Since I had started taking notes, I noticed their mannerisms and facial expressions all the more.

Dora tended to hug herself. She would fold her arms or wrap them around her torso. It was like a self defence mechanism. Almost like she knew it was happening but couldn't comprehend how or why.

Leonard, on the other hand, would sit down and slowly rock back and forward. He would tense up and would look for something to hold - a cup, a book, the arm of the chair.
In the absence of anything to hold, he would curl his fingers to form a fist and frown. He would never lash out. I just got the impression it was his way of protecting himself - like Dora.

Dora would occasionally wander while Leonard would remain in the same place. She didn't have a preferred place, but she would always go where there were no other people. She sought a quiet place. Once there, she would just stand still and look around, lost in her own world. Neither were in any noticeable pain or discomfort.

Coming out of their little trances they would be disoriented and scared. Dora would reach out for someone to give her reassurance. Leonard would shake and gasp for breath.

The frequency of these lapses were erratic, but I sensed a slight decline in both their conditions over these few weeks of more intense monitoring. The saddest thing was, it was only going to get worse and we all knew it.

I was really looking forward to Doctor Deakin's visit and yet, at the same time, I had the fear of what was around the corner in the new year. I tried to shut it out of my mind, but all the time, it was there, torturing me.

I hoped the doctor could maybe offer me some advice on how to relax.

And then there was Frank. There was always Frank. He could always be relied upon to lighten the mood (or cause an argument). He could make you feel special even when he was insulting you.

"I'm thinking of going on a diet. Would you like to join me?" he said as he walked into the Keith Chegwin Suite with his newspaper folded up and tucked under one armpit.

I fell straight into his trap as usual.

"You don't need to go on a diet," I replied. "There is hardly an ounce of fat on you."

"Maybe you are right. Maybe you are right. But they say it is easier if you team up with someone who needs to. It helps to motivate you they say."

"But you don't need to go on a diet," I repeated. And then it clicked. "Are you trying to suggest I need to lose weight?"

"Not my place to say, Ang, but if that arse keeps growing you will struggle to get through the front door."

The cheeky sod. I wasn't fat - maybe a few pounds overweight - but he enjoyed provoking me, and I couldn't help but argue back. I think he got a bit of a kick from it, but I couldn't get angry. There was no malice in him.

"You shouldn't be looking at my arse anyway," I told him. "You were a happily married man!"

"I was a married man. I wouldn't go so far as to say happy. And anyway, she shuffled off this mortal coil ten years ago. A man has needs. If you shaved a few pounds off that arse of yours, I might consider dating you!"

That cheeky smile lit up his face again and it made me blush. The others in the room just carried on with what they were doing. They were used to this kind of banter between us.

"And what makes you think I would want an old man like you?" I snapped back.

"Experience, love. Experience. I'm like a Rolls Royce Silver Shadow."

"You are like a clapped-out old banger!" shouted Mavis, barely looking up from her knitting. "You wouldn't pass an MOT!".

Frank lapped up the attention. Even when he was being insulted, he revelled in it.

"Nothing wrong with my engine love. The bodywork may need patching up a little, but I still go like a dream."

"A nightmare you mean. That girl has the world at her feet. She could have any man she wanted - not an old fossil like you!"

Mavis winked at me.

Frank took his newspaper out from under his arm and unfolded it, smiling.

"Her loss," he chuckled.

He had done it again. Within two minutes he had taken my mind off all the negative things buzzing around in my head. I imagined that woman's face when she was confronted by him in his boxer shorts. It made me laugh.

On the way out of the lounge, I glanced in the mirror and Frank caught me looking.

"See for yourself," he giggled. "It's massive!"
I stuck two fingers up in his direction and carried on walking.I decided I needed to go on a diet.

Friday 2nd December was a miserable day. Cold, dark, wet and blustery. The kind of day where you just want to stay inside and wrap up warm in front of a nice fire.

The gas and electricity bills had shot up over the past few months, and we were really feeling the pinch. Heating was one thing you cannot scrimp on in an old folk's home, but the bills had almost tripled in the space of two months. That was something for the management to worry about though, not us minions.

Doctor Deakin arrived around 6:00 p.m. Again, he looked bedraggled and sopping wet through. His umbrella had turned itself inside out in the wind, and he tossed it to the side and jumped up and down to get the worst of the rain off his coat and trousers.

He just didn't look - or act - like a doctor at all. He took off his coat and hung it on the pegs near the front door. His jeans were covered in dark wet patches and his black, woollen sweater looked heavy and stretched with the weight of the rain.

Vera walked over to greet him and couldn't stop herself from laughing. He laughed too. She called over to Peter and asked him to "Go and get one of those Armani tracksuits you keep under your bed."

Peter looked up and down at the doctor.

"A large will do him I reckon. Give me five minutes." And off he toddled.

By 7:00 p.m. we were all set to start. The doctor did not want the room set up in any particular way. He was happy to just stand at the front of the Sir Jimmy Glass Suite and let everyone settle down in their own comfy chair. It was all very informal.

The only thing he asked for was a flip chart and a few coloured marker pens which we had an abundance of for some reason.

He stood at the front in his borrowed, bottle green tracksuit, and waited patiently for everyone to find their places and settle down. Despite being dressed like a giant cucumber, he looked incredibly relaxed, greeting each and every member of the audience like he had known them for years. He even high-fived Doris and Joan before they sat down near the front.

I had no idea what he was going to do or say. It was all quite mysterious.

I looked around for Dora and Leonard. They were both in. Dora had found a space in the far corner, and Leonard was about half way back sitting between Norman and Stan.

"Good evening, everyone" he began. "I apologise for my appearance. I don't usually come to work dressed like a cactus, but blame your Cumbrian weather."

Although his accent was distinctly Scottish, he did not have the same harsh tones as the Glaswegians we had met on our trip. He sounded politer - posher.

He told us a little about himself and his background. He grew up in Aberdeen and the family moved to Glasgow when he was a young teen. His first degree was in Hospitality and, for a few years, he worked in hotels and restaurants around England and abroad before realising it was not for him. He retrained as a junior doctor in London before undertaking further qualifications in neurology, specialising in on-going disorders such as Parkinson's disease and Dementia. He had chosen to focus on geriatric medicine and treatments, and worked in specialist wards in and around London. With over fifteen years' experience he was, and is, considered to be an expert in this field.

Even if he did look like a cucumber!

"I have six sessions with you all. I am being paid well for these six sessions so feel free to use me as you wish." He winked and smiled at Vera, who shook her head and blushed again.

"I will also be on hand to meet with you all individually should you want to ask any personal or private questions. I might not have all the answers, but I will do my best to put your minds at ease.

We are going to start off with a little discussion before talking about memories. I want you to start by having a little chat with those around you, and I will jot down your responses on this whiteboard here. There are no right or wrong answers. Just tell me what you think.

My question, to start us off is this; What things do you forget to do in day-to-day life? You have five minutes. Go!"

They didn't need a second invitation to start talking, and within a few seconds the room was buzzing with conversation. Doctor Deakin took a sip of his coffee and stood by the fire.

"Don't get too close to the fire in that tracksuit!" Beatrice warned him. "They are just cheap copies that Peter bought off some rogue in the town. He has about twenty under his bed. Keep away from that fire or you will go up in flames before you can say polyester!" The doctor took her advice on board, and moved away to stand beside Vera.

After a few minutes, he returned to the front and hushed the crowd.

"Right, what have we got?" He patiently worked his way around the room, jotting each suggestion down on the board.

- Not turning the oven off.
- Forgetting to take the shopping list out with you.
- Leaving the light on in another room when you go to bed.
- Not being able to remember someone's name.
- Forgetting the name of a familiar actor on television.
- Missing appointments.
- Forgetting how to spell something.
- Forgetting why you had walked upstairs or gone out into the garden.
- Forgetting birthdays (particularly the wife's)
- Getting people and places mixed up when telling a story.
- Forgetting names of old school friends even when you recognise their face.
- Starting a conversation then forgetting what you were talking about

The list went on and on. With each idea, people across the room nodded in agreement, understanding exactly where that person was coming from.

When the flip chart page was full, Doctor Deakin put the lid back on the pen, and popped it on the tray below.

"I hate it when people leave the top off a pen. My little bugbear. We will come on to those later. Bugbears can be a help as well as a hindrance, trust me. Little things that stick in your mind. We all have them."

He read through the list again before turning back to face his audience.

"Quite a list we have here isn't it? It makes you wonder how we manage to function! And do you know what? Every single one of the things we have listed here could have been said by anyone - no matter how old they were.

Our memories are unique to us. Your brain is different to everyone else's brain and that is what makes my speciality so interesting.

You see, memory is all about neurons. Nerve cells. These nerve cells work with each other - they talk to each other, if you like. And the more they talk, the more active and stronger they become. Let me put it into context."

He looked down at Mavis.

"If this lovely lady and I chatted to each other every day, the bond between the two of us would grow. She would become more and more important to me, and my brain. However, if I was to just say hello to her, and never see her again, the chances are I would forget her. She would not be important to me - no offence. My neuron would have only connected with her neuron for a split second. Not enough to make a strong enough link to form a bond worth remembering. The same principle applies to most of the things we forget on a daily basis. Those neuron links in our brains aren't strong enough to be considered important. Let's look at the list."

He turned back to cast his eye over their suggestions.

"Forgetting to turn the light off when going to bed. Perfectly natural. The body has other priorities. It is thinking of getting into bed and going to sleep. It couldn't give a toss about turning a light off at that particular moment. We do some things through habit more than anything else.

That said, if you were the kind of person who was obsessed with saving money or if you perhaps suffered from OCD or autism, turning the light off would be a priority - the neurons at work here might have stronger bonds because of your condition or habit."

He wandered over to have another drink of coffee, making sure he kept well away from the fireplace.

"How these neurons link, and how strong they are, affect your short-, and long-term memory. I couldn't tell you what I had for lunch on Monday, but I could tell you the starting line-up for the Scotland team who beat England two one at Wembley in 1977. Why? Because it is more important to me than that meal a few days ago. So, if a memory is important to you the bond between those neurons is so strong, and the links that create that memory don't fade. In fact, if anything, these bonds strengthen because it is something I think of quite often. It is a bit like learning your times tables at school. The more they are repeated, the stronger those connections become. Learning by rote. By no means a perfect method, but they haven't come up with a better alternative yet. The more they are repeated, the more likely you will remember them."

Cue Frank.

"If that's the case, why is it that after thirty-five years of constant nagging by the wife, I still couldn't remember a single bloody thing she said to me?" he laughed.

"Simple," said Doctor Deakin. "You had no interest in anything she was saying to you. Your neurons were not actively forming and strong connections were not made. For thirty-five years, you managed to ignore your wife and put your neurons to work elsewhere." Frank seemed suitably impressed by the explanation.

"Sounds about right to me!" he said. "Good old neurons."

"Just out of interest," Doctor Deakin asked him, "What is it you *were* thinking of for thirty-five years?"

"Divorce," laughed Frank

We stopped for short toilet break - I think it was just an excuse for Vera to have ten minutes with the doctor.

When he resumed, he talked a little more about how memories are formed.

"Neurons fascinate me." he began. "The complexity of the links between brain cells is, if you pardon the expression, mind blowing. Every activity you do or any experience you have triggers a reaction in the brain. The reaction and link between one neuron and another. If neurons are left idle they become weaker. The opposite is true too. The strength of the connections between neurons is known as synapses. If the links between neurons are used regularly, they will get stronger. If neurons lay idle and don't connect, they will weaken - they may even die off. This is all linked to memory - both long and short term. There is an area of the brain - the hippocampus - directly linked to memory formation, that can even generate new neurons thus helping the adult brain form new connections and ultimately strengthen the ability to retain knowledge and improve memory."

I am able to recite this because I recorded exactly what he was saying using an app on my phone. My own memory isn't great. I am the kind of person who needs to write everything down. He went on.

"Ultimately, the stronger the links between neurons the more likely you will be able to remember, and draw on, experiences from your past. Sleep is important too. Think of your brain as a computer. When you rest, you are giving your brain a chance to reboot or update itself. Everything you have seen or heard or tasted or smelt or felt will be computed and stored. The greater the significance to you, the stronger the links. The more you experience the more neuron links you will have. And to help service your brain and keep it in tip top condition, you need to make sure you sleep well and stay active. But that is enough science for one day," he chuckled. "Let's end today's session with a fun game. A memory game."

The object of the game was to pretend you were an item of food. Everyone had to say their name and the food they were. Everyone had to listen to everyone else state their name and their choice, then one person had to repeat what they had heard. Doctor Deakin said you would get one point for each correct answer. He admitted he was useless at the game, but he would go first to show how it was done.

"My name is Alasdair and I am a cucumber." He pointed to Mavis. "This is Mavis and she is a loaf of bread." He kept on going. "This is Vera, she is a cauliflower. This is Tony and he is an egg."

He managed to get eight right before failing to remember that Albert was a cabbage.

Next Brenda had a go, then Eleanor. Both managed to score eleven points before a wrong answer. Keith scored a credible fourteen and Alice sixteen.

Dora put her hand up and, through all the noise and laughter, Doctor Deakin managed to pick her out of the crowd. I didn't have my notepad with me, but I was fascinated to see how she got on. She scored an incredible twenty-seven! How, with her condition, was she able to remember so many? That would be one of my questions for Doctor Deakin.

The last to have a go was Beatrice. She started well, mainly repeating the same names the others had used. Her synapses and neurons were making and strengthening links as she talked. She got up to twenty-one before picking out Frank.

"I can't remember what he is!" she said, looking up at the ceiling for inspiration.

"An arsehole!" shouted Mavis.

The room exploded with laughter and cheers yet again.

It had been another great night.

22

Attention and Retention

Doctor Deakin - or Alasdair as he now insisted we call him - was booked in for his second talk on the 16th December. He was also booked in on 25th December as Vera's guest for Christmas dinner. The two of them weren't officially dating, but love (or lust) was definitely in the air.

He told me, for this second session, he was planning to talk about the memory process before addressing the debilitating conditions of Dementia and Alzheimer's disease. I'd already given him copies of my notes and he said he planned to use the third session (and Christmas day) getting to know the individuals. He stressed that, although there were many people suffering from Dementia, no two cases were ever the same. Any help and support plan had to be tailored to the individual.

Although he has been working for the agency for a few weeks, we were his first old folks' home which was quite surprising seeing as though the elderly were his speciality. He said most of his talks had been with NHS Trust management teams and other nondescript corporate groups.

"You take the money and run," he told me. "Half of them aren't even listening, and the other half think they know more than I do. I only have to see a briefcase or a suit and I come out in a cold sweat. This is different though. I love being surrounded by people who genuinely want to learn. People with a sense of fun and an appreciation of life. But I also want to do what I can to help those who are suffering from these horrific illnesses."

The feedback from the residents had been good too. He was

called 'a gentleman', 'a lovely bloke' and 'good fun'. They liked his sense of humour and his compassion, and they were all looking forward to his next visit.

When I told him what they had said, he couldn't stop grinning. "And Vera is also very pleased you are coming back," I said, cheekily.
He flushed and coughed, and his smile seemed to widen all the more.

Before his second visit, we received another email from the advisors. It was a timetable for their visit in January. There were time slots to speak with the managers, monitor aspects of the home and meet with individual staff members. They had used our initials rather than our full names. All very impersonal. Mine was there - AT 4:45 p.m. The last one of the day.

Again, a wave of nausea swept over me and a feeling of dread. I felt sorry for Vera too. She was marked down to be with them most of the day. We were sat together at break time the day the email arrived.

"How can we enjoy Christmas with this looming over us?" I said.

"We just have to do our best," she replied. "Remember who we are here for - the good people out there, not these administrators."

She was right, of course she was, but it was these senior leaders who could be controlling our futures. I just wanted it, and them, to go away.

"They call it progress. Progress my arse!" she laughed. But what else could she do?

The talk around the dinner table was all about Alasdair. Not about his skills as a doctor or what he had said during his talk - more his suitability as a partner for Vera.

If he thought he was being discreet, he underestimated the detective skills of our geriatric clientele.

"How old do you think he is?" said Beatrice. "I would guess about fifty-five."

"No, a bit younger I reckon," pondered Alice.

"He must have had a bloody hard paper round," Beatrice laughed.

"She deserves a nice fella. The last one was a right idiot. What was his name again?"

"Womble," said Derek, joining in.

A number of others chipped in too.

"That's right. He was a litter picker wasn't he?"

"Yeah. Little fella. Hairy ears."

"You would never see him without that luminous jacket on. I think he must have slept in it."

"You would have to ask our Vera that!"

"He was rude as well. Very dismissive."

"Receding hairline too. You can never trust a man with a receding hairline."

"And he smoked. He used to sneak out the back for a fag. He would flick the dead ends all over the lawn."

"He never flattered her or bought her anything nice. He only used to come in here to warm up."

"What the hell did she see in that weird little man?"

I listened to them pull Womble to bits. They were like vultures descending on a carcass.

"Yes, she deserves a nice one. Doctor Deakin seems like a lovely man."

"Yes, he has a nice manner about him. He will treat her right."

"A good sense of humour too."

"And a lovely smile. Did you notice his smile, Alice?"

"They got on ever so well. He makes her laugh."

"They will make a lovely couple. This one is going to last."

"And he will be bloody loaded," Frank called out as he walked into the room.

The rest of them nodded in agreement. A couple of minutes later, Vera walked in and the conversation immediately changed without a hint of panic or fluster. They were all so good at that. Years of practice.

Alasdair's next visit on the 16th followed a similar pattern to his first. A mini lecture followed by a couple of games. His focus this time was on the different types of memory we have, and how we retain information that is useful or important to us.

As the residents shuffled in and made their way to their favourite chairs, Alasdair handed out chocolates and cakes. If he was crawling to them to gain their affection it was definitely working. You would have thought he was handing out ten-pound notes such was the delight on their faces.

"He is a keeper this one," Doreen whispered to Vera as she walked by. Vera turned pink and gave me a hard stare as if to say, "What have you been saying?"

When they were all settled, Alasdair began. I set my phone to record again.

"Last time I was here, we talked about how memories are formed. Today, I want to talk about how they are retained. This might help give you some self-help tips for improving your own memory.

Information is perceived by your senses, and this makes it into your sensory memory. This is happening all the time. You touch something soft - that goes into your sensory memory. Whatever you smell, taste, see or hear goes into your sensory memory. Thousands a day. Your mind couldn't possibly retain it all, and it doesn't. It stores what it thinks is important. Something you might wish to retain. Let me give you an example. You might smell a hundred smells a day, but that lovely roast beef you had earlier meant far more to you than the others. And then you tasted it too. So many thoughts. Synapsis happened. Connections are made - remember like I said last time? The stronger the connection the more likely it is you retain this in your memory bank.

Consider another example. You are driving down the street and see dozens of cars. You recognise their colours and process these as a thought, but they are fleeting. They come and go. Your sensory memory takes them on board then discards them just as easily. If you spotted a yellow Lamborghini, that would stand out. Synapsis would create stronger links through your neurons than, say, a silver Ford. Something unusual, striking or different stands out.

When detectives question witnesses at a crime scene, they try to tap into memory retention; 'Can you remember what he was wearing? What time was this? Can you remember what his face was like?' Unless something stood out or appeared odd, the minor details are so often forgotten. This isn't a problem or a fault with your memory - we are all like that. We retain what we need and we let the insignificant information disappear."

"Like the good times with the wife?" asked Frank, mischievously.

"Beast!" scalded Alice. "Ignore him, love. Go on."

Alasdair lost his train of thought for a second, and I caught Frank's eye and gave him a disapproving look. He just tittered to himself.

"Think of your sensory memory as a holding bay. If it doesn't need to be retained, it gets rid. If it does, it transfers the information to another part of your brain. Connections and links are constantly being formed as your brain goes to work. Now, you might have heard people talking about short-term and long-term memory. How can you remember something from sixty years ago, but you can't remember what you had for breakfast? It is a little more complicated than that. You might remember some teachers from school, but not all of them? Why is that?

Again, it comes down to the links between neurons, and the more neurons that are linked together around an experience, the stronger the memory.

I remember my PE teacher very well. I didn't particularly like him, and he didn't seem to like me, but it wasn't just his name or his position. I linked the lessons to him. I linked the smells of the fields and the changing rooms to him. The fear of being towel whipped in the showers or having to ask for spare shorts from the second-hand box when I had forgotten to bring my own. My friends told stories about him and his lessons. We shared stories and experiences. Every one of these tales would have formed a connection between neurons until hundreds were connecting to ensure a strong memory is stored. I remember my Geography teacher's name, but very little else about her. The links weren't strong, and unless I talk about her or revisit those times with friends, the links will weaken even further until, eventually, they will disappear altogether and are archived in the brain vaults never to be seen again. Your brain can store an incredible amount of information. Have a chat with your friends now, and think about your own school days - you are going even further back than me. What do you remember?"

Again, excited chatter filled the air as they all turned to face their neighbours to reminisce. I purposefully sat quite near to Dora's group.

"I can't say I remember too much about primary school other than how bloody cold it was inside that Victorian building. I seem to remember those massive iron radiators that were never switched on - even in the winter," Doreen said.

"There was a flight of stairs leading up to the headteacher's office," Sheila said. "We used to call them the 'Stairs of Pain' because if you were ever sent up there it was only ever for bad things, never good."

"The boys had one yard and we had another. The only thing that separated us was a small wall, but no one dared cross it. I didn't get to speak to any boys until I was eleven. Alien species!" laughed Betty.

"They still are, love!" said Eleanor.

Dora looked on and smiled, but she didn't join in the conversation. She was happy to listen. I wondered if she had memories of her own, or if they were as alien to her as the boys were to Betty during her primary school days.

Predictably, the men were talking about sports. They could recall results, goal scorers, sport days, competitions etc. as though it were yesterday. The fact that they were talking about events from seventy or eighty years ago made it all the more impressive.

Alasdair clapped his hands and brought us all together again. You could tell from their smiles that they had all enjoyed their trip down memory lane.

"For that exercise, you have all been accessing your long-term memory. Your childhood memories, building relationships, learning how to make or do something. Something as simple as riding a bike or learning to knit. These are all stored in your long-term memory, and we draw on them all the time without thinking about it. If you taught me something, you would draw on your long-term memory. If you were to walk a familiar route around the town, you are drawing on your long-term memory. Your short-term memory works differently.

Some research suggests that information in your short-term memory is likely to be stored for between fifteen and thirty seconds, and will hold about seven pieces of information.   The information is then either lost or transferred to long term memory. Again, every individual is different, but it is an interesting concept. There are thought to be variations between the ages and the sexes, but it gives you an idea as to how, and where, this information is stored."

I thought about myself. Dad calls me a scatterbrain. It makes sense though. If I am being bombarded with a hundred rules and instructions, I can only process a handful at any one time. He doesn't have the same problem. He just has to think about which channel to watch or which book to read now that he has retired. Roll on retirement.

Alasdair continued...

"You also have your working memory. This is a mix of short and long. It allows you to focus on what you are doing at any given time, but it draws on past experience and training. For example, when you get your evening meal, you use your knife and fork quite naturally to help you eat. At some point, many years ago, you were trained to use these tools. Now it is second nature. The connections are so strong it becomes automatic. Have a think about other examples of daily routines you take for granted. It's as easy as riding a bike!"

Alasdair laughed at his own little joke - presumably one he has regurgitated every time he has stood in front of an audience talking about the brain.

"Then there is explicit memory. Information that we consciously store and recollect, like a person's name or age. Implicit memory is information we subconsciously retain and use such as when we make our way to the toilet, in the dark, in the middle of the night. There are many more types of memory, and it is true to say that we cannot say with certainty exactly how the brain works to retain information, but the more research we carry out, the more we are able to understand and use this information to help those who need it. And I will come on to that next."

Alasdair took a sip of coffee.

"Before I go on, I think this would be a good time to have a comfort break. You have all been sitting here a while. I know brains, but I also know bladders!" They all chuckled and nodded.

"Fifteen minutes wee break starting now!"

More than half the audience got up out of their seats and made their way towards the toilets.

"Get out my way," laughed George as he shuffled towards the door. "They used to tell us men to tie a knot in it. It is hard enough to find it half the time, never mind tie a knot in it!"

"Don't make me laugh," Olive groaned. "The muscles aren't there to hold it in!" No shame or embarrassment. They talked about their bodily functions with the same flippancy as if they were discussing the weather.

By the time they returned to their seats, suitably refreshed with empty bladders, Alasdair was ready to continue.

"The next thing I am going to talk about is Dementia. I hope what we have talked about so far has been useful to you, and I hope this next part will help link the theory with reality. As a neurologist, Dementia both intrigues and frightens me in equal measure. It is my enemy. An enemy to us all!

Firstly, I want to explain to you what it is, and how it affects our brains. I then want to give you strategies to help and support going forward.

Dementia is something that affects us all, I am sure. We will either know someone who has suffered or someone who is suffering. We might even be suffering ourselves to varying degrees. Ultimately, we cannot beat it - at least not yet.

We can delay the effects and use medication to help, but I am sad to say, the illness has the upper hand at the moment.
So, what is Dementia? How does it manifest itself?

Dementia isn't a disease as such - it is the general term we use to describe the impaired ability to remember, think or make decisions that interfere with our ability to carry out everyday tasks or activities. Alzheimer's disease is the most common type of Dementia. It is most commonly associated with the elderly, but not exclusively. I should stress that some memory loss is a normal part of the ageing process. Just because you can't remember where you have left your car keys does not mean you are suffering from Dementia. With age comes weakness and deterioration. It will happen to us all - we cannot turn back the clock. And as we age, we begin to fail. That's the natural process and order of things. I'm nearly fifty, fat and unfit. At the moment, I am not suffering from Dementia and yet, nine times out of ten, I walk out the house with my flies down and forget to lock the front door. Read into that as you will. If I am like this at fifty - what will I be like at seventy-five, if I am lucky to get that far?

As we age, some memory loss is natural in a fit and healthy person, but if a person is diagnosed as suffering from Dementia, or a particular disease like Alzheimer's, escalation of the condition will be considerable.

I do not wish to scare you, but I do think it is important to be aware of how this disease manifests itself, and what we can do to help each other - at least in the short term."

I kept an eye on Dora and Leonard. They were both watching attentively. Indeed, they all were.

"When trying to diagnose Dementia, there are many signs to look out for. It's not all about memory loss. People may develop a shorter attention span or an inability to complete simple tasks or puzzles. They may experience a change in vision or struggle to communicate with others. They may struggle to complete tasks independently, or get lost in an area they are familiar with. These things are indicators.

Dementia sufferers may start to develop some or all of these traits along with memory loss. Early diagnosis is difficult as, unless a person's patterns of behaviours are markedly different over a short period of time, we are unlikely to notice. We might just put these faults down to old age or one-offs. The sooner a pattern of behaviour is identified, the sooner we can diagnose and take action to help the individual. My own father had Dementia. We didn't notice for over a year. He displayed many of the triggers I mentioned, but they didn't seem out of the ordinary. That was just him. He was like that most of the time. A bit daft, a bit off the wall. Forgetful and dizzy. But we must be vigilant. We must try and diagnose as swiftly as possible if we are to put an efficient care plan in place to help the sufferer."

Again, I thought about Dora and Leonard. When were they first diagnosed? And if it was only recently, when did the symptoms start to show? I would need to ask their families.

"Like I said, Alzheimer's is the most common type of condition and accounts for approximately three quarters of all Dementia cases. Early symptoms include short- and long-term memory loss. People may repeat what they have said or forget a conversation from minutes earlier. As the illness progresses, a person may struggle with walking and talking, and general mobility. Sadly, it is also hereditary. If a close relative has suffered, this increases the chance of the next generation developing the disease.

Strokes, diabetes, high blood pressure or high cholesterol can cause Vascular Dementia. This effects around ten percent of Dementia sufferers. Many of these cases could be avoided if people looked after themselves a bit better. We drink too much, we smoke, we don't exercise enough. We are inviting danger - myself included!"

Alasdair patted his protruding stomach apologetically.

"Although many of the symptoms are the same, it is vital we, as doctors, identify the root causes and type. Lewy Body Dementia, will also cause memory loss, but the body is targeted in different ways. A sufferer may shake or tremble a lot. Sleep patterns will be erratic and they may hallucinate or stare blankly into space for long periods.

Fronto-temporal Dementia leads to changes in personality, because of the part of the brain it affects.
People with Fronto-temporal Dementia may embarrass themselves by behaving out of character or by using inappropriate and insulting language. Speech problems may develop. They may slur or struggle to form their words.

It is also common for people - especially those over eighty - to suffer from more than one of these conditions thus making it very hard to diagnose, as many of the symptoms are similar.

Think back to our first chat. Think of all the things we listed on that flip chart paper. How many of those were short term memory lapses? Thoughts your mind discards as unimportant. Thoughts that are not worth keeping in the long term. Think about how many were forgotten because they didn't really matter to you or because your mind was clogged with more pressing issues. Just because we forget, doesn't mean we are suffering from Dementia. Over the next couple of weeks, I will use our time together to get to know each and every one of you. I'd love to chat to you, and get to know you a little better. I should be able to give you tips on how to stay on top of your thoughts and stay in control of your behaviour and actions whether you are suffering from changes to the brain or simply because you are all just old wrinklies!"

Alasdair looked over to Vera, and she gave him a reassuring smile.

"I hope I have been of some help so far. I know I go on a bit, but if it helps you understand a little about what is going on in your mind, then I will have been of some use. From now on, I will be trying to help you with practical solutions. No more theory."

"Can I ask a question, Doctor Alasdair? Can I say something?" said Alice

"Of course you can," he replied, ready to impart some more knowledge.

"There were a couple of women being shown around The Acorns the other day. On the way around, they bumped into Frank. He was walking down the corridor in just his boxer shorts. He shocked them, he embarrassed Vera, and he made a right tit of himself! Does that mean he is suffering from Fronto-temporal Dementia or is he just a dickhead?"

The whole room burst out laughing - Alasdair too. After quite a serious discussion, it was just what everyone needed to lighten the mood again.

"I forgot all about that!" Vera said, wiping tears of laughter from her eyes.

I had forgotten all about it too, but now they were back. Back at the forefront of my mind, and that knot in the stomach returned.

23

The Tree of Us

On the third of December, we received a string of visitors to The Acorns. Postman Graeme was the first to knock. He arrived just after breakfast, and brought in the usual mountain of letters. Vera and I sorted through the pile, discarding the junk mail and taking the brown envelopes to the office while Graeme handed out the personal letters to the residents as per usual. The good people of Brampton must wonder why their own mail never arrives until late morning. Graeme must spend an hour a day here walking around, delivering letters and chatting to the residents. We don't mind and he loves it. It has become a daily routine.

After Graeme came a man called Spud. I'm guessing that wasn't his real name, but it was all I was going to get. Spud brought in three large cardboard boxes and stacked them on top of each other in the reception area. Then he asked, "Where do you want the tree?"

"What tree?" I replied.

"The Christmas tree," he said matter-of-factly. I shouted for Vera and she poked her head around the office door.

"Hiya Spud," she said, smiling. "Just leave it outside the front door for now if you don't mind. My brother said they would come and put it up this afternoon. What's in the boxes?"

"Decorations and lights," shouted Spud. "Good ones too. Got them from Newcastle."

"Oh smashing," said Vera. "Which shop?"

"Direct from the council. Grainger Street I think."

"How much do we owe you?" asked Vera, not really registering what he had just said.

"Nothing at all, love. Just ask Peter to hold back some of that good weed for me. I'll catch up with him before Christmas." And with that, he turned, waved and made his way back out the door.

"Grainger Street? Peter?" I stood with my hands on my hips giving Vera my coldest of cold stares.

"He said he knew someone who could sort us out with a tree. I didn't ask questions," she answered, sheepishly.

"So now The Acorns residential care home will have the best Christmas decorations this side of..."

"Newcastle!" said Peter, as he walked down the stairs towards us. "I'm sure they won't miss the lights from one city centre street."

"And the tree?" I asked, incredulously.

"Morpeth, I think. They always have a good one, but they never tie it down, Spud said.   It was asking to be taken."

"One of these days you are going to get us all in big tr..."

Before I could finish my sentence, the doorbell rang again. Peter just smiled and walked on to see what was in the cardboard boxes. I went to answer the door. It was Doctor Deakin - Alasdair.

In each hand, he was holding a large basket full to the brim with treats - chocolates, cakes, sweets - and tucked under his arm was a huge bouquet of flowers.

"The contents of the baskets are to be shared with all the

residents. A big thank you to them from me for being so welcoming."

"And the flowers," I said. "Are they for the staff?"

He blushed. "One in particular. Is she in?"

"She is in. And she is very lucky she isn't inside!" I said, looking over at Peter.

Alasdair had no idea what I was going on about, but he stood patiently at the door as I shouted through for Vera again. She poked her head around the door and started smiling when she spotted the good doctor.

"He has something for you," I said.

"And not just the flowers!" laughed Peter.

I gave him another one of my looks and he took the hint to bugger off out of it.

Vera invited him Alasdair in and took the flowers out from under his arm.

He put the baskets onto the nearest table. "These are beautiful. For me?" she asked, stating the obvious.

It was so nice to see their friendship and relationship develop. A middle-aged man and a middle-aged woman enjoying the innocent flirting and connection normally associated with the young.

"You can stay for afternoon tea if you like - provided you help my brother put up the tree and the decorations," she said.

She learned forward and kissed him on the cheek. This public show of affection caught him by surprise and he flushed again.

"I'd love to," he managed to mumble. Vera led him off to the office, and went in search of a vase.

Before I had time to turn around and get back on with my jobs, the doorbell rang again.

A lady stood before me holding a blue folder. At first, I thought she might have something to do with the advisory team, but then she smiled and I knew she couldn't have been.

"Hello," she said, "It's Kerry. Kerry Gibson. Your new support worker on secondment. You have me for the next twelve weeks I believe."

I had forgotten all about Kerry. Vera had arranged the transfer with a care home in Wigton. Kerry was looking to gain experience elsewhere in a bigger facility.

"Come on in," I said, still trying to take in everything that was going on around me. "Welcome to the madhouse."

I ushered her into our now very crowded reception area. Before shutting the front door, I spotted the tree. It must have been fifteen feet high! Poor Morpeth!

I led Kerry through to the staff room and made her a coffee. She explained that Vera's brother was a coach for Wigton Colts – the rugby team her youngest son played for. They had got chatting at one of the games and one thing led to another.

"Everyone knows everyone else around here - or at least knows someone who does," she laughed.

We chatted for about fifteen minutes, and I felt like I had known her all my life by the end of it. We clicked straight away. She was so giggly and warm. If first impressions count for anything - and I believe they do - she was going to fit right in. I thought it best to tell her a little about our residents and our 'characters'.

It turned out they had their very own Frank over at Wigton. And here I was thinking he was a one off.

Vera asked if I wouldn't mind showing Kerry around the home. She was a little older than me, but not by much. By the time we reached the gardens, I knew all about her and she knew all about me.

"Should we start your training with another coffee before helping to put the tree and the decorations up?" I asked her.

"Sounds perfect to me," she replied.

So, for the rest of that afternoon, Kerry, Doctor Alasdair, Vera, Vera's two brothers and I tried to put up a fifteen-feet tree in a room thirteen feet high from floor to ceiling. Between us, we didn't have a saw to cut down the trunk, so there it stood, bent over at the top feeling rather sorry for itself.

A few residents had gathered around to watch us at work.

"I think it looks nice. A bit...different but I like it," said Beatrice.

"Me too. Well done you lot. Once we get the tinsel and lights on, it will look grand!" added Hilda.

"I agree. I wouldn't imagine there will be a tree like it around here" said Phillipa.

"Or in Morpeth," I said under my breath.

"That looks bloody awful," Frank laughed, walking in through the double doors. "What the hell are you going to put on the top - scaffolding?"

"We'll put you on top," Kerry said, making Vera choke on her tea.

"You will do for me girl" she said, when she stopped coughing.

"And me," laughed Frank. "Nice to see a new face around the place. New blood. And if you are ever at a loose end, I am in room 38."

In the lead up to Christmas it was all hands-on-deck. The Grainger Street decorations looked fabulous around the home, and the bent tree had become something of a welcome novelty for the residents and any visitors to the home.

Kerry settled in straight away as if she had worked with us for years, and Alasdair spent more time in the home than out. His relationship with Vera was blossoming, and so was his understanding of all our beloved clientele.

It also gave him the opportunity to spend a lot more time getting to know Dora and Leonard. He studied their files, their medical history and their behaviours.

Dora was diagnosed with Alzheimer's disease in October 2021, but Alasdair suspected she may have been affected by the disease for much longer. He sat with her and chatted about her loves and likes. He took notes and recorded what she said and how she said it. He noticed behaviours we hadn't.

He found out she had been hiding objects in her room -photos, jewellery, trinkets. He thought it was her way of looking after her most treasured objects. Objects given to her by her late husband or photos of the two of them together. But then she wouldn't remember where she had put them, and then she would panic. Sometimes she wouldn't remember hiding them. She was convinced she had been the victim of a burglary.

Alasdair noted what it was she was hiding and where she was putting them. She was a creature of habit and, nine times out of ten, we could find them again using the information in his notebook. He noticed that she would shake when nervous or keep a picture of her husband in her shoe, presumably to keep him close. Safe.

He listened carefully to her when she was lucid. He listened to what she said, and how she said it.

He would record her and play the conversations back to her when she was confused or needed some clarification. He would put notes around her room - reminders, directions, words of reassurance, reference points.

She was failing - more and more with each day and week that passed - but these little, thoughtful actions helped her cope.

Leonard was struggling too. He knew what was happening to him. The others continued to be supportive, helpful and kind, but he would get so angry with himself for forgetting or for 'losing time'. On occasion, the frustration would then turn to tears. And then he would be embarrassed - ashamed of himself.

Alasdair worked with him too. He was so incredibly patient and observant. He would draw pictures and take photographs. He would record their conversations and play them back to Leonard when he felt calmer. He would explain what was happening to him, and teach him breathing and muscle relaxing techniques to help control his frustration.

He taught him to enjoy the times he was in control, rather than just worry about what was to come. I know this helped Leonard so much. He certainly seemed happier in himself and others noticed it too. He bonded with Kerry and, when she was on shift, he would sit and chat with her for hours. If he lapsed, she would be there when he returned, to continue the conversation as though nothing had happened.

As Alasdair kept saying, "We can't beat the disease. We can't even control it - but we can manage it. We can manage it until the very end. It might try to destroy us, but it won't define us."

I realised once again what was important. Making the most of the quality time we have.

The Dementia was taking chunks of time from Dora and Leonard. This was lost time. But they were still enjoying life and making the most out of the quality time they had. Thanks to Alasdair. Thanks to Kerry.

Despite every obstacle and every worry, I was looking forward to Christmas. We all were. Bent tree an'all!

24

A Wonderful Life

Christmas was always a special time at The Acorns. We really pushed the boat out for the residents. One or two of them would spend Christmas day with their families, but most chose to stay in the home and celebrate with us.

We would have a visit from the local church choir on Christmas Eve, and they would sing a selection of carols and traditional songs.

Neil Tweddle, our chef, would roast chestnuts on an open fire on the patio, and hand out the mulled wine from a vat he brought from home. There would be chocolates and snacks to feast upon, and we would play party games until it was time for the film.

It was tradition in the home to watch 'It's A Wonderful Life', and everyone would cheer when Clarence got his wings. It's a film that always makes me cry happy tears, even though I have seen it about fifty times!

Christmas day itself is always brilliant. We all meet up for breakfast at the usual time, but all the staff dress up as elves. We play all the Christmas classics and sing along over a cup of tea and a bacon sandwich.

Then it is present time! Neil - who is quite a portly chap - dresses up as Father Christmas and comes bearing gifts – sacks and sacks of them!
He lives on his own now, and is grateful to spend all of Christmas day with us.

In some places, the staff have to draw straws as to who will work the Christmas shift, but at The Acorns we fight to be IN work!

The home sets aside an amount of money to cover Christmas lunch and a small gift (no more than £5) for each of the residents, but as staff, we try to do so much more. We work with local businesses and individuals who donate gifts and offer extra money to help make the day special. Many of Peter's 'contacts' donate presents too.

We make sure everyone has a few treats to open on the day, and a lot of thought goes into what we buy. They are always ever so grateful, and they are all so excited - like big children!

After the handing out and opening of the gifts, Neil retires to the kitchen to prepare the meal. One of our local butchers donates the turkeys, veg and stuffing, and our chef always does us proud with a feast fit for a king.

We pull crackers before eating, and everyone wears a daft party hat.

Christmas wouldn't be Christmas without a drink, and the whiskey, sherry and brandy bottles are cracked open and emptied throughout the afternoon.

We respectfully watched the first King's speech and compared him to his mother.

"Too wooden."

"He suits the role, I think."

"Not as good as his mother."

"I think he has aged rather well. Dignified."

"He has been waiting for this opportunity for years."

"I wonder if Camilla has told him what to say?"

"He must be sick to the back teeth of that daughter in law and the ginger one."

In the evening, we have a game of charades in the Keith Chegwin Suite. I'm always useless at it. Doctor Alasdair, on the other hand, was brilliant. He had us all in stitches.

It was lovely to have him join us for the day. His relationship with Vera had really taken off - they were even holding hands at the table. He bought her a lovely, silver necklace and a nice cashmere hat and scarf set. She bought him a bottle of Scottish malt whiskey and some nice pyjamas and slippers. He was so pleased with them; he wore them throughout the day!

We have numerous visitors throughout the day. As usual, my parents joined us in the evening, and I had to endure the embarrassment of everyone telling them, "What a good girl" I am and how "She will go on to make some lucky man very happy in the future."

My parents told them how very proud they were of me.

By 8:30 p.m. we were all worn out. A few went upstairs for an early night, and the rest of us crashed out in front of the TV with more nibbles and snacks. The perfect end to a perfect day.

Alasdair and Vera waved their goodbyes and I settled in for the night shift.

I was joined on the sofa by Dora.

She was holding a glass of sherry in one hand, and a framed picture in the other.

She handed it to me. It was a photograph of her younger self standing side by side with her husband, John. They must have been in their mid-twenties. He was ever so much taller than her

- at least 6 feet tall. He was dressed in a police uniform and looked incredibly smart and proud. Dora had a dark dress on with white buttons from the neck to the waist. They were holding hands.

"I found this yesterday," she said. "It was at the bottom of one of my bags. I must have missed it when I unpacked last year."

I handed the frame back to her, and she looked down at the young faces smiling back up at her.

"He was so handsome. So incredibly handsome. I was ever so proud to call him my husband. We were inseparable, but we never got bored with each other. Never. He made me laugh so much. I was devastated when he passed. Part of me died that day too. I thought I would never find happiness again. I thought that was it. How could I smile again? But coming here, meeting you and all the others, making so many new friends - I feel so honoured to get to know you all. You have made my life worth living again, do you know that?" We sat in silence for a while and watched the tree lights blink on and off.
She picked up the photograph and brushed his face with her index finger.

"I didn't know who it was," she said after a few seconds.

"Who?" I asked.

"John. My husband. When I found the picture in my bag. I didn't recognise the faces. I didn't recognise John. I didn't recognise myself. I left the picture on the bed, and it was only much later in the day, when I looked at it again, did I remember. What is happening to me, Angie?"

I reached over and held her hand.

"Do you remember now?" I asked.

"I do. It was taken in 1966. I remember because it was the year

England won the World Cup. John was on duty, and I was looking after the dogs. One of the other police officers took that picture. He had just bought a new camera and he was testing it out. I remember the day so well. It was a glorious summers day, and John was sweating in that uniform. I think that is what we were laughing about. He told his friend to hurry up so that he could take his blazer off."

She took a sip of her sherry and looked down at the picture again.

"What am I wearing? I look like Queen Victoria!"

"I think you both look very smart," I said. "Little and Large."

"Don't you start," she chuckled. "That is what they used to call us down at the station. The lad who took the picture was a funny lad. Far too fat and unfit to be a police officer. He used to man the desk most of the time. He couldn't catch a cold, never mind a criminal."

She chuckled to herself at the memory, and then looked up at me with a little tear in the corner of her eye.

"I don't want to forget him again, Angie. What is this thing doing to me? I know I am a burden to you all, but I can't help it."

I gave her hand a little reassuring squeeze as the tear rolled down her cheek.

"Look at me," she said, forcing a smile. "A silly old woman with a failing mind. What must you think of me?"

"I think you are bloody brilliant!" I told her. "And we are here for you. Every step of the way. You aren't a burden to me or anyone else here. So what if you forget things now and again. It will happen to us all. Like Doctor Alasdair said, we don't worry about the 'lost time', we make the most of the good times. We face this thing head on - together!"

She smiled at me again and wiped away her tear.

"It is happening more and more, I know. I am not scared of getting old. I am not scared of dying even. I just don't want to be a burden. And I don't want to forget John."

We sat and chatted for a while longer as she finished the rest of her sherry. I helped her up the stairs to her room and made sure she was alright before making my way back down again. I poured myself a whiskey and sat back in the armchair. I felt honoured that Dora had confided in me like that. It made me realise just how important I was to her - to all of them. I looked down and noticed my big red pointed slippers. I was still dressed as an elf.

It had been such a lovely day. Another set of treasured memories created.

I sipped my whiskey and half watched Eric and Ernie perform one of the 1970s Christmas specials on the television.

I must have dozed off. The next thing I remember was the smell of bacon and eggs and the clatter of plates and cutlery coming from the next room. I had slept on the sofa all night!

I looked down and spotted those big red elf slippers again. Someone, at some point in the night, had lifted my head and popped a pillow underneath. They had also covered me with a thick, fleece blanket to keep me warm and snug. I looked around, but there was no one there, but someone had been looking after me too.

My own secret, little angel. My own Clarence.

25

For the Good of the Residents

After the elation of Christmas came the depression of January. Cold weather, dark and dismal evenings and the dreaded visit of the Trust's appointed advisors.

Vera received a message to say they would be arriving at 9:00 a.m., on Thursday 5th January 2023. We were to provide them with coffee, tea and biscuits throughout the day, and a lunch at 12:30 p.m.

We were to clear an office for them for the duration of their visit and ensure there were three chairs in the room. Two for the advisors, and another for the poor victim they were planning to grill and interrogate at any given time of the day.

Vera was told (not asked) to produce reports, files, policies and other paperwork as and when requested.

Needless to say, all the staff were on edge in the days leading up to their visit. We had no idea what they were looking for or what they wanted, and that only served to heighten tension and anxiety. Vera tried to stay positive and upbeat, but she looked like she hadn't slept for days with all the worry.

The two ladies arrived on time. Shirley answered the door and welcomed them in. She received a cursory smile, and then it was down to business. I was carrying some towels to the laundry room, and they glanced over in my direction. Neither of them acknowledged or greeted me. My heart sank and the knot in my stomach tightened. I knew then that I was going to be in for a hard time. They had already made up their mind. They had already decided that I was incompetent.

The morning passed slowly. The staff carried out their duties as normal while Vera danced to their tune, rushing to and from the main office to find any documents they demanded to see. She looked like she had been crying.

I really felt for her.

At lunchtime, the two of them stayed in their little room and Vera and I sat outside on the patio despite the cold and drizzle.

"How did it go this morning?" I asked, not really wanting to know.

"Smiling crocodiles!" she said. "They are so condescending, rude and patronising. They seem to have taken an instant dislike to the place - and me."

Vera was clearly angry, but then that anger turned to tears.

"I don't know what they want. They don't seem to like anything so far. Nothing is good enough. The timetables, the policies, the procedures, the accounts, the record keeping - they even criticised the lunch menu! The skinny one even asked what I was there for. She asked, quite openly, 'So what is your purpose here?'. I couldn't answer. I was lost for words. The two of them bombarded me with questions. It was a double act. They were doing all they could to intimidate me, and it worked. I was...I am, a nervous wreck." She wiped away her tears with her sleeve.

"You are doing a brilliant job. We all are!" I said. "Surely they can see that? The residents are so happy here. There is a waiting list to join us. People are literally knocking on the door to come and stay here. The Acorns has an amazing reputation. I don't know one person who has a bad word to say about the place."

"Well, I know two now. Ms. Buckshaw and her humourless sidekick." I handed her a tissue and moved to sit beside her. We hugged.

"I really don't understand their motives. They are not here to help or support. Not once have they spoken to the residents or made any effort to get to know them. This is all about money, power and ego, not people."

"Are they not coming to speak with them this afternoon?" I asked, rather naively.

"Nope. They are not interested in the residents. This afternoon is all about individual meetings with the staff. Be on your guard. Be strong if you can. Buckshaw is the organ grinder. The other one just sits at her side agreeing with her every word, occasionally throwing in a snipe or a criticism of her own."

"What did they want to see this morning?"

"Everything. I was up and down and back and forth from that office every two minutes. Questions, questions, questions. Everything from the fire drill procedure to how much was spent on tea and coffee for the staff. They wanted to see risk assessments, details of visits and visitors to the home. They asked about the vetting process for anyone who comes in through the front door - even the postman. Every answer I gave, they just shook their heads and whispered to each other, smirking and rolling their eyes. It was horrible. Simply horrible."

"What next?" I asked, half knowing the answer already.

"They want me for the first half an hour of the afternoon, then it is you lot, and at the end of the day, they want to speak with all the staff on duty to present a summary of their findings. Then, after that, who knows?"

I was on pins all afternoon. Sandra was the first to be called in after they had finished with Vera. Then a steady stream of terrified workers expecting the worst. One lady even walked out declaring, "I'm not paid enough for all this crap!" before marching out never to be seen again.

Those not on duty that day were the lucky ones, but their time would come.

At 4:30 p.m. I was called to the office. My anxiety level was through the roof. My throat was dry, I felt like I needed to go to the toilet. I was shaking. I was invited to sit down. I got the false smile, and then it was down to business.

"I see you have worked here for a long time, Andrea."

"Angie," I said, correcting her, then regretting it. I don't know whether they got my name wrong on purpose or if it was a genuine mistake, but by correcting them, I really put their backs up.

"Can you tell us what you actually do here?" the fat controller asked.

I didn't know what to say, but I needn't have worried because she answered for me.

"Because when we were here last, you were doing a jigsaw. We had a tour of the building, and when we returned to the dining room, you were still doing a jigsaw." She gave me that false, crocodile smile.

"I was socialising with the residents," I replied. "It is very much part of my job."

"You aren't here to socialise with the residents," the skinny one said. "You are here to do a job?"

The fat one nodded.

"That is part of the job," I said in my defence.

"You are not here to relax and entertain. You are not here to

229

play games and while away the time. You are here to work! I could have found you fifty other jobs to do in that time. Fifty other jobs to justify your wage."

I looked up at them both. Were they even human?

"We care for our residents. We provide the service of care they need. They trust us. We are their friends and companions."

"You aren't here to be their friend, my dear. You are here to work. That is what you are paid to do. And if you cannot do that, we'll have to find someone who can!"

I couldn't speak. They didn't know me. They didn't know The Acorns and all the people in it. They didn't know or understand the service we provided. They didn't understand the importance of relationships and trust. They weren't bothered about that. They just saw me doing a jigsaw, and that was enough for them to judge my worth.

"You, along with others, will be given a chance to prove that you can actually do the job you are paid to do. You need to read and remember your contractual obligations. At your level, and on your pay scale, you should be flexible and be ready to cover where and when we deem appropriate. Like I said, if you can't or won't, we will find someone else who can. It seems to me that people here have been stealing a wage for far too long."

The skinny one nodded and smirked - smirked not smiled - and made some notes on her pad.

"Our clients deserve the very best, and we are here to ensure they get the very best value for their money. From what we have seen so far, The Acorns is, at best, unsatisfactory and unfit for purpose. Take this as a warning. You need to up your game, young lady. A comprehensive programme for professional development has been developed in line with an exceptional, progressive and robust action plan. Staff training will be given over the next couple of weeks and, unless we see a marked

improvement, action will need to be taken. It is all for the good of the residents.
Remember what we are here for – the good of the residents."

The residents they had yet to meet or speak to.

I walked out of the room in a daze. How dare they? How bloody dare they? Inevitably, as soon as I was out of sight of the office, I burst into tears.

Ralph and Stan were there, playing chess.

"What's up, love?" Ralph said. They both stood up, walked over, and wrapped their arms around me. "Is it Laurel and Hardy that's bothering you?"

I couldn't speak. I hugged them back.

"Let it all out, chicken. Whatever it is, we can sort it out."

I sobbed like a baby in their arms.

"I'm not sure you can," I said. "I'm not sure anybody can."

Before the two women left, Vera asked us to gather in the staff room. It was a tight squeeze. The room was hot and the atmosphere was horrible. Nobody spoke. After ten minutes or so, they came in, clipboards held tightly to their chests.

"Today has not been an easy day for us. I don't imagine it was easy for you either, but it isn't about us or you - it is about those customers out there. Our clients."

I cringed as she spoke. They weren't *clients*!

"Big changes are needed if this place is to provide the level of service required to be successful in this very competitive marketplace. From what I can see, it has been run like a holiday camp for far too long. Please refer back to the brochure and read the stated aims of this business. Are you giving the clients a right to independence? Are you allowing them opportunities to be expressive and creative? Are you respecting their privacy and their right to choose?"

"And that doesn't mean just sitting with them to make a jigsaw," the skinny one said, looking towards the fat one for approval.

"Exactly right. How can you expect the clients to respect you when you show such disregard for them? You need to up your game ladies and gentlemen. I feel I have been sent here for a reason. A mission from above if you like. By all means join me on the journey, but if this path is not for you have the choice to seek employment elsewhere. I may appear harsh, but always remember - this isn't about you. This isn't personal. This is for the clients. Think about what is best for them, not you. I will be in touch very soon, Vera."

And with that, she flashed another one of her false smiles and headed for the door. The skinny one scampered after her. We didn't bother to see them out. We all sat in the staff room for a few minutes, trying to take in what had just happened.

After more crying and a group hug, we made our way back into the reception area. The gang must have been wondering where we all were. We needn't have worried.

We walked into the Keith Chegwin Suite only to be greeted by fifty odd, very serious looking, old people.

It was quite a sight. Ralph was the first to speak.

"We don't know who they were or what they wanted, but I...we... are telling you all this. No one makes our friends cry and gets away with it. No one. Not ever. I asked everyone to come down for this meeting, and I want you to tell us exactly what is going on here. Tell us who they are, and what business they have coming to our home and upsetting our friends."

I burst into tears again. In that moment, I had never felt so appreciated. I looked around at the other staff members, and they were in tears too - even Neil, and he never cries!

"We will sort it out. Whatever it takes, we will sort it. We might be old, but we are a force to be reckoned with."

Frank stood up and walked towards me. I looked up at him. My friendly nemesis. My best enemy. The lovable bane of my life. My adopted grandad. He held open his arms and I fell into them, and let him take my pain away.
I tucked my head into his chest and cried.

Without any sarcasm or quip, he held me close and whispered in my ear.

"Nobody puts my baby in a corner."

After such a horrible day, I felt safe in the bosom of my Acorns family, knowing they would look after me.

26

Sally

The second Wednesday in February 2023, Sally called to say she would be able to come over. It was her first visit for nearly five months. For most of that time, she had been over in New Zealand visiting her sister. She'd decided to have a career break while she was still young and fit enough to hike and explore. I felt a pang of jealousy when she told me, and wondered if I would ever be brave enough to do something similar before I got too old.

I looked up to Sally. She was something of an inspiration for me. She wasn't scared to make changes in her own life if she wasn't happy, and she had a real positive outlook on life. She wasn't particularly well off, but she didn't chase the coin. So long as she could get by and go on holiday now and again, she was content.

She was such a lovely person too. She would do anything for anybody, and I loved it when she visited The Acorns to chat with the old folk.

When she arrived, she had to go through security. That is what we called it now. It wasn't a case of just signing the book in and out. Now, you have to pose for the camera, get your photo taken, then print off an identification badge – a sticker! - which must be worn at all times for the duration of your visit.

There was a form to complete to say who you are visiting, who you work for, and the purpose of your visit.

When Buckshaw visited, she always made sure she checked the CCTV and the timings on the camera and in the book to make sure they are correlated and accurate.

She scrutinised the details and made sure we were accountable for each and every entry. Failure to provide this basic safeguarding check would result in disciplinary action.

'Disciplinary action' were two words she seemed to love more than any others. She had produced a new code of conduct for the staff, and any behaviour she deemed inappropriate would result in a formal written warning. Two formal warnings could (or would) lead to a dismissal. In this code of conduct were twenty-nine bullet points to adhere to such as…

- No swearing or inappropriate language to be used at any time.
- All clients to be addressed as Sir or Madam.
- Staff to wear full uniform, with name badge displayed, at all times.

Buckshaw's 'vision' for The Acorns was to also include a new staff uniform incorporating the new logo, a tree with falling leaves, along with the slogan with the slogan 'Desirable, Independent, Safe, Environment', in other words dise! Even when spelt incorrectly, the connotation of the acronym wasn't lost on us.

Obviously, we reverted back to our normal selves when those two weren't in, but we had to be on our toes when they were for fear of being 'managed out'. Three or four had already left and others would surely follow unless something was done about it.

Sally filled in the forms and wore her badge and just got on with it without a fuss.

Other regular visitors to the home were not so enamoured with the new system. Graeme, our postie, just handed over the letters at the door. He wasn't meant to spend so much time meeting and greeting the residents, and he couldn't risk leaving a paper trail highlighting how long he spent in The Acorns.

The delivery men were the same. They used to come in and play dominoes or cards for half an hour. They stopped coming in for the same reason. We even noticed a reduction in family visits as a result of the new system. Only one or two family members would visit rather than the whole family. It was becoming too time consuming to go through the number of unnecessary protocols that had been introduced, so many of them did not come at all. It was such a shame.

The residents were delighted to see Sally again. They fussed over her and asked her a million and one questions about her trip down under. She was so good with them. She had so much patience, and took a genuine interest in all they had to tell her. As the evening went on, I noticed her sitting in the corner with Dora. The two of them were chatting away, laughing and joking with each other. It was so nice to see.

Laurel and Hardy were not in for the rest of the week, so we were able to relax and enjoy ourselves again.

Alice and Eleanor called me over.

"Are you ok, chicken?" Alice asked.

"I am," I lied.

"Listen, don't you worry yourself about those two. They won't be here for long, trust me. Things will get back to normal, I promise."

"I do hope so," I said, but I wasn't convinced.

"It will be ok. We are hatching a plan," laughed Eleanor.

I had no idea what this plan was or how they thought they could beat the system, but I wasn't going to discourage them.

"When I was a young lass, I worked in a shoe shop in the city centre. It was my first real job, and I was scared of my own shadow back then. The boss knew it and took full advantage of me. She was a bully. The women can be worse than the men when it comes to bullying, believe me," said Alice.

"What did you do?" I asked.

"For a time, I did as I was told and kept my head down - like you are right now. It wasn't the work itself that was the problem, it was that woman. She used to say things to upset me. She would criticise how I looked and what I was wearing. She would send me to work in the back room and tell me she wanted the pretty girls on display in the shop. It really got to me. My dad sorted her out in the end. He was sick of seeing me come home upset, so one day he marched in there and told her where to stick her job. He was a big, dominant man, and she had no answer to him. He told her to pay me until the end of that month, and if she didn't, he would come back and stick a stiletto up her jacksy!" The three of us chuckled.

"Three cheers for your dad!" I said.

"If people think they can bully you and get away with it, they will do, sweetheart. And bullying comes in many forms. At some point, you have to make a stand. In this case, we are standing with you. All of you. There is plenty of fight in this old dog yet let me tell you." We chatted for a while until Sally wandered back over to see me.

"Isn't Dora just wonderful!" she said. "She has so many stories to tell. I could have listened to her all night, but I need to get off. Hubby will be wondering where I have got to. Same time next Wednesday?"

We walked through to reception together. She signed out and waved at the CCTV camera. It was so lovely to have her back.

Over the next few days, the two administrators were in and out. Thankfully for me, they rarely left the office, and as long as you looked busy and didn't stop to talk for long, they left you alone.

I felt sorry for Vera. They seemed to be on her back all the time - delegating more and more jobs and generally making her life a misery. We didn't see much of Alasdair during this time.
The relationship was still going strong, but with the tighter security and accountability, he didn't want Vera to get into trouble. When he did visit, when they weren't in, he carried on monitoring Dora and Leonard, offering tips and advice to help and support them. He suggested a 'Hobbies and Interest' box. I was to make a list of any game or activity they enjoyed and put together a collection for them.

He suggested taking a few minutes each day to play with something in the box, whether it be a card or board game.

He suggested I should ask them to explain the rules and show me how to play.

"Keep the mind active. Encourage them to problem solve and discuss their actions."

He gave me some story packs. Traditional tales and nursery rhymes. He wanted me to mix up the sentences or events in the story and ask them to reorder them. "Problem solving is a high-level skill, and a lot more when you are suffering from Dementia. Make it fun. Tell them what you are doing. Record how long it takes them to complete the task then see if they can beat their time when you repeat the task. Be open and honest with them. It is brain training, and they will benefit from it."

Alasdair was brimming with good ideas. Some worked, some didn't, but he was always looking for new ways to stimulate the brain and battle the disease.

Sally arrived the following Wednesday, bubbling with excitement as usual. She had brought her own box with her. She signed in and went through security.

"Anything to declare?" Kerry asked her as she completed her check in.

"Who are you working with today? What's in the magical, mystery box today?" I asked her.

"I thought I would surprise Dora," she said. "But for now, I would kill for a brew."

We wandered through to the Sir Jimmy Glass Suite, and I went to make the tea while she put her feet up. Within minutes, half a dozen people had gathered around her. She was so popular with the group.

We spent the next couple of hours just chatting and having a laugh. We could relax again. Vera joined us too. We even had a bit of a sing song. The old folk loved to sing. It would come from nowhere. We would be sitting there, talking about something and nothing, and all of a sudden, one of them would pipe up and burst into song. It was usually one from *'the olden days'* as Vera put it.

And again, as soon as one started, they all joined in.

"Oh, I remember that one. Ernie used to sing it to me when I was in the bath."

"Do you remember this one? Him with the teeth sang it."

"I never liked that one. Too bloody maudlin. A song to slit your wrists to."

"He loved himself, didn't he? But what a set of lungs he had?

"She had the voice of an angel. I always wished I could sing like her."

They encouraged each other too.

"Where is Ralph? He can sing that one."

"Sheila could have performed on stage. She has a lovely voice."

"Tommy looked like Sinatra when he was younger. Sings like him too."

Sally, Kerry, Vera and I just let them get on with it. We didn't need the TV or radio on. We had our own live entertainment in the Sir Jimmy Glass Suite.

Later in the evening, when they had exhausted their repertoire, I noticed Sally sidling up to Dora with her box. She knelt down in front of her and took off the lid. I could see her talking away and dipping into the box as she spoke. She had a plastic model of an Alsatian dog and a toy police car. As she talked, she held Dora's hand, but something was wrong. I walked over to them and Sally stood to join me.

"She doesn't remember me. She can't remember talking to me last week," Sally said. "I think I need to save the box for another time."

We both knelt down beside her and held a hand each. She was staring straight ahead. Her cheeks were flushed and her eyes heavy.

"Where am I?" she whispered.

I explained where she was and who we were. I told her all about the home and described her lovely room. I talked about her family and John, her husband. Not a flicker of recognition. She started to cry again.

"I don't know where I am. I don't know you. I'm scared."

We didn't really know what to do or say. All we could do was hold her hand and reassure her. She kept a small picture of John in her handbag, and I reached down to get it for her. She looked down at it and looked back at me shaking her head.

"I don't know."

It really was heart-breaking to see her this way.

Doreen walked over to join us.

"Doctor Deakin recommended music as a stimulus. We have a Glen Miller CD on the side. Shall I put it on?"

She toddled off over to the stereo and found the disc. A few seconds later, the sound of the big band filled the room. Sally looked up at Dora and asked her if she would like to dance. She stood up and led Dora to a space in the corner of the room where there were no chairs. She placed her left hand on the small of her back and held her right hand aloft.

"I'll lead, shall I?" said Sally.

We all watched as the two ladies swayed to the music. As the rhythm quickened, Dora started to move her feet. Sally followed and they made full use of the limited space. Doreen tapped her feet to the beat and others joined in.

As the music slowed towards the end of the track, Dora looked up into Sally's eyes and smiled. She stood on her tiptoes to say something to her. Sally smiled back and gave her a huge squeeze.

They continued to dance the night away - well, until track nine started jumping, and they decided to call it a day.

It was after ten o'clock when Sally signed out. Kerry helped Dora up the stairs and into her bedroom. She was feeling much happier by then.

Sally and I walked to the front door. She had a huge smile on her face.

"Do you know what she said to me when we were dancing? She said, 'John loved Glen Miller.
When we danced, I always had to take the lead with him too.'

She remembered. The music helped."

"That's amazing," I said. "You are amazing! Same time next week?"

"Try stopping me. I'll bring my box!"

I looked down at the signing in book. In the REASONS FOR VISIT section, Sally had written... ***To try and make people happy.***

No doubt we will get into trouble for that, but I didn't care one little bit.

27

Press Ganged

The micromanagement continued throughout February and March.

Buckshaw would walk around the home with a clipboard, making copious notes and tutting. Everyone was on edge. Much to the annoyance of the residents, she had rearranged the chairs in the lounge so that they were facing each other.

Apparently, research proved that this encouraged more social interaction.

A machine for making tea and coffee had been installed in the corner. The staff were told not to make drinks for the residents - they were to do it themselves. It was all part of the drive to make them more independent. Needless to say, when they weren't in the building, we reverted back to normal.

She had brought decorators in to paint the walls a pale blue, as research suggested the colour was calming and helped stimulate positive vibes.

In reality, it made the room feel cold and uninviting. The residents thought the same. Many refused to sit in there anymore, preferring to stay in their own bedrooms.

She seemed to know what was best for them without ever talking to them or getting to know them.

When they were in the building, their presence was a nightmare for the staff, and an annoyance for the residents.

And then the staffing changes started. Chef Neil's hours were cut as Buckshaw believed there was no need for a full-time chef.

Residents were to make their own snacks from now on.

Independence, independence, independence!

Kerry was told she could return to Wigton two weeks early, as she believed we were already overstaffed.

Severely understaffed, more like!

Elaine was told her contract would not be renewed in April, Janice was managed out on health grounds, and a severance agreed. It was horrible. We were all wondering who would be the next victim.

Even the contractor's hours were cut. Window cleaners would be once a quarter rather than once a month. The gardeners were cut from three to two. We were told there would be no money for luxuries. The brand of toilet roll was changed to save a few quid. Part of the outside area was sealed off, and left to overgrow and rot. The place was starting to look a mess, and yet the residential fees continued to rise as quickly as the morale fell.

Enough was enough.

At the start of April, we checked the calendar and were pleased to see that Laurel and Hardy were on a course for the week down in London. We could momentarily relax.

Alice approached me over breakfast.

"Remember I told you we had a plan? Well, it's time to put it into operation. The A Team."

"If you have a problem, and nobody else can help, and if you can find them. Maybe you could hire…The Acorns Team!"

That made me giggle. I wondered just what it was they had in mind! Surely, they hadn't employed the services of a crack commando unit from the Los Angeles underground!

"We have all been talking about this," she said. "All of us. We need to get them out of here. I am not paying over a grand a week to make my own brew, and sit in an ice box. It's time we shared our plans with you."

"I love it when a plan comes together," Eleanor laughed.

"It's a multi-pronged attack. We are going to tackle them from different angles. They won't know what's hit 'em. And if our plan works, we will have them out of here by the end of April - trust me!"

I did trust her. All of them. For the first time in a long time, I felt emboldened.

Unbeknown to the staff, the old folk had been working and planning a strategy behind the scenes. Alice explained that Jack's grandson worked as a reporter for a regional newspaper, and he was happy to come and speak to the residents with a view to running a feature on The Acorns.

"We are all very quotable," she said. "And we have plenty to say."

They had also written to the local M.P., the Trust itself, and a number of charities they were associated with. The power of the pen!

As a staff, we were to do nothing other than our jobs. Although much of the attention would be on us, we were to be seen and not heard. That suited me just fine.

The journalist came to visit the home a couple of days later. Jack reassured me that he was very keen to come, and that he was not being railroaded into it by the A-Team.

Jack was an old military man and, although in his late eighties, he had a sharp mind and a determined streak. He tended to avoid the limelight and the noise, but on this occasion, he was keen to join in.

"Our Andrew is a good un," he said. "He will do us proud. He can't fight for toffee, but you put a pen in his hand or a typewriter in front of him, and you will see his real strength. He's a talented boy."

One thing the home did lack was IT facilities. Yes, in the office we had all the up-to-date computers and systems to help us do the job, but the residents themselves didn't have much. Most of them were happy to keep it that way - a few had mobile phones as a necessity, but it dawned on me that maybe some iPads or a standalone computer in the corner might be a useful addition to the home.

For this mission, they used the only method they were comfortable with - handwritten letters. They had taken photocopies of them before they were posted out (thanks to Graeme), and Alice and Eleanor showed them to me.

They were beautifully written. No grammatical errors or text speak here. They had clearly taken care when drafting. The letters were polite, yet forceful. Genial, yet serious.

They explained the situation (with a hint of exaggeration), and they wanted answers.

The letters were all sent out on Thursday 20th April 2023. An email would have been quicker, but could just as easily have fallen into the Junk Box and been missed altogether. All the letters had been marked PRIVATE AND CONFIDENTIAL with the intention of reaching the intended recipient and not just any old Tom, Dick or Harry in the office.

Alice said we would need to allow at least ten days for any replies before chasing up a response. This was a waiting game and time was against us.

"A person in their eighties doesn't particularly like a ticking clock," she laughed, "but waiting is what we must do to catch the worms."

The first reply didn't take ten days. It came in the form of a telephone call from Mr. Mullholland. Candy answered it. She was in on work experience. A lovely, jolly, kind-hearted girl, with only two brain cells to rub together. She wanted to work in an old folk's home because, in her words, "They just sit around all day watching TV and sleeping."

She wasn't meant to be in the office when Mr. Mullholland called. She was on her way to the photocopier and got lost on the way (they are next door to each other).

When he explained who he was, she hung up on him and came to tell me.

"He said he was a journalist!" she told me in a state of panic.

"And? Why did you hang up?" I asked her.

"My dad said if anyone was an 'ist' they were bad - like a racist or sexist. I think it was one of them dodgy calls."

I explained what a journalist was and, as gently as possible, put her tiny mind at ease. I sent her to collect some tartan paint from the stockroom before giving him a call back.

Mr. Mullholland - Andrew - was a lovely man. Well spoken, calm, polite and supportive. He told me what Jack and the others had already told him, and he asked if he could come to the home later that day to talk to the residents about the state of The Acorns under the new management. As *they* weren't in, it seemed like perfect timing. He reassured me that the focus of the article would be on the residents and not the staff.

He arrived halfway through the six o'clock news which seems appropriate.

I apologised for our secretary, but he just laughed it off.

Everyone knew he was coming along and, after a coffee and a sit down to watch the weather forecast, he was ready to begin.

More and more people entered the room, keen to have their say.

"May I suggest you take your leave for an hour or so?" Alice said. "We don't want to put you in a compromising situation."

I let them get on with it, and didn't even mind when Frank shut the double doors behind me and told me to bugger off.

Mr. Mullholland stayed for most of the evening. I could see him through the glass panels, scribbling notes down on a pad, chatting, nodding and - above all - laughing.

At nine o'clock or so, his grandad, Jack, walked him to the door. I went to greet them both.

"Do you know?" he said, "Before this, I was a teacher for twenty-three years and, for the most part, I loved it before it became more about accountability, and unnecessary paperwork, than children. It feels a little bit like that here, only these people are eighty, not eight. I have enough for my article now. It will be a double page feature, and I reckon I can have it online by Saturday, and in print by Monday if the editor is happy."

"I'm nervous about this," I chuckled, nervously.

"No need for you to be nervous, love. Any comeback will be on us, not the staff." said Jack. "Andrew will look after us. I have every faith in him."

"We aren't Fleet Street," laughed Andrew, "but we do have a bit of clout in the region. It won't go unnoticed." And with that, he was off.

Another reply arrived on Saturday morning. It came in a brown envelope with a stamp on the front showing the crown. It was from our local M.P. - Karen Marshall.

I took it through to Alice who was playing poker with Ralph, Stan and Margaret in the Sir Jimmy Glass Suite. She had a pile of matchsticks in front of her, and was clearly winning.

"How much have you won so far?" I asked her.

"Each matchstick is worth fifty pence," she smiled. "I would guess I have about £100 here to spend in Peter's shop."

"Peter's got a shop?" I asked, incredulously.

"Yeah, and it is better value for money than those high street stores."

I reminded them about our staff agreement (that we didn't agree with). Any gambling had to be reported to the management and stopped with immediate effect. She just laughed.

"Report her!" sighed Ralph. "At this rate I won't have any matchsticks left by lunchtime. I was saving them up for one of those Alexa things. Peter said he could get one for a tenner."

I showed him how much they cost online on my phone.

"Well, I am not paying that much when I can get one off Pete for a fraction of the price."

"But you don't know where he will get it from. You might be an accessory to a crime."

"What are they going to do? I'm too old for prison, and too old for community service!"

He had a point.

"What is that in your hand?" Alice asked.

I handed her the letter.

"Oooh. Thank you. Now you better run along," she said, waving her hand at me. "You don't want to get into any trouble, do you?"

I did as I was told, and walked out of the room.

Glancing back, I noticed them put down their cards and gather around Alice. It was exciting, but incredibly frustrating too.

I kept refreshing my phone on the newspaper's home page, but there was nothing there about The Acorns. I knew the gruesome twosome would be back in on the Monday, and I had no idea what was going on or what they were planning.

Vera and Alasdair popped in after the evening meal. Vera was not on duty, so she was there in an unofficial capacity - a visitor.

They were both on good form - giggling and laughing like a lovestruck, teenage couple. They had been to Chester Zoo for the day, and Alasdair had been his usual charming self. He had bought her a big cuddly gorilla, and even adopted a real one for her. He was a proper softy.

The men mocked and teased him, but he took in on the chin as he always did.

We all sat in the lounge together laughing and joking about nothing in particular. Frank pointed out that Alasdair had an uncanny likeness to the toy gorilla, and he didn't even try to deny it.

"Well, I think they are both cute!" Vera said, defending her new man.

"You must be as blind as a bat then!" laughed Frank.

Suddenly, Eleanor burst into the room holding her mobile phone above her head.

"It's on! It's online. They aren't going to like this," she laughed. "Your Andrew has done us proud."

Jack nodded, calmly. He wasn't one to fuss.

"Read it then, woman" Frank shouted, impatiently.

"Ok, ok. Here goes."

Eleanor pulled her reading glasses down from the top of her head and rested them on the bridge of her nose.

"The headline is, **THE OLD LEFT OUT IN THE COLD.**"

"Oh, I like that," said Alice. He obviously noticed the bloody paint job too."

Eleanor continued to read the rest of the article as we listened intently. I think I had my hand over my mouth for most of it. I looked over at Vera, and she was the same. Alasdair was just smiling and nodding and clapping his hands throughout. The others sat in silence, taking in her every word. When she finished, she lifted her glasses back onto the top of her head.

"Well - what do you make of that?"

Vera and I still had our hands over our mouths. We looked at each other, wide-eyed, unable to take it all in.

"It might be a little different in the print copy on Monday, but not much. This is going to ruffle a few feathers," she laughed, "and this is only the beginning of our plan!"

An hour or so later, I sat in the office and read through the article again. My heart was pounding as I read. All I could think about were the possible consequences. Would they think we were part of it? Probably. Somebody invited them in.

Andrew Mullholland signed and scanned in.

But he was a relative of one of the residents! How were we to know what he was there for? The truth was, the residents had kept the staff at arm's length. We genuinely didn't know what they were up to. It had all been part of their plan.

I read it again.

In 2021, I visited Washington DC for an extended city break. The hotel was out of this world, and far more luxurious than I am used to. My room, a standard double, would not have looked out of place in a palace.

For a start, it was huge. As a solo traveller I wondered how I was going to make the most of the walk-in wardrobe, two chests of drawers and a shelving unit packed with books.

I would have expected an ironing board and a hairdryer, but not a coffee making machine, a fully stocked fridge with complimentary soft drinks, chocolate bars and fruit, a fifty-inch wall-mounted television with a PlayStation attached - and a massage chair.

The bathroom was as big as my flat, and the bed was to die for. Memory foam mattress, electric blanket and marshmallow pillows. I could have spent the whole break in the hotel room! Downstairs they had a spa, gym and a sauna.
There were three restaurants and two lounges. The staff were happy, welcoming and genuine. It was heaven! And all for just £700 for the week.

So, imagine paying double that amount to live in a place where profit is more important than the people. A place where you were little more than a commodity. A place that has been neglected and underfunded for years.

You wouldn't do it, would you?

Well, I know at least fifty people who do, and they are not happy about it.

This place isn't a hotel though, it is a residential home for the elderly. A place where our old folk go to live for the final chapter of their lives.

Welcome to The Acorns.

Seeing the name of the home in the newspaper sent a shiver down my spine. And that was just the opening couple of paragraphs!

He went on to talk about the facilities, and how the place has suffered and fallen into decline over the past few months. The residents gave him all the information he needed to lambast the attitude of the Trust leaders and the behaviour of the administrators sent in to 'manage' the decline. He spelt out, in no uncertain terms, how badly the staff were being treated there as well as the 'helpless' residents.

The blame lies at the door of those holding the purse strings, and not the staff on site who work tirelessly for their minimum wage. These guardian angels deserve better. The policies and protocols in place stifle the staff. They break relationships, not make them. The 'do's and don'ts' lists are designed to build clones and robots. "Have a nice day, can I interest you in one of our new walking sticks…" The only supermarket statement they don't wheel out is, "Can I give you any help with your packing?". And why? Because these octogenarians are the cash cows for the greedy. At £1,400 a week, you can expect to make your own coffee, and sit where you are told. The staff, so integral to the culture and atmosphere of the home, can no longer sit with the residents and complete a jigsaw or play a game of cards. Every minute of their shift has to be accounted for with staff now spending more and more time completing reems of paperwork. There is no time for conversation and pleasantries for risk of a warning or disciplinary action.

The report continued in the same vein. Andrew mentioned the state of the grounds, the cutbacks and the atmosphere. He quoted some of the residents, who didn't hold back with their scathing criticism.

"The staff here are superb," said eighty-six-year-old Alice. "They love us and we love them, but they are placed under so much pressure now, it is impossible for them to manage. This is a home - OUR home. The people who work here are like our grandchildren as well as our full-time carers. That is what we want. Just for it all to go back to what it used to be like."

"This isn't the service I want, need or pay for," said a rather angry and animated Ralph. "Six months ago, The Acorns was the envy of every other residential home in the area with a waiting list to prove it. The Trust management have sucked the life out of it and are sucking the life out of us and their staff too. We demand a review into the operational side of things."

With each quote and every paragraph, it was made abundantly clear where the faults lay, and it wasn't with the staff in the home. In his usual mischievous way, Frank also put the boot in.

"They have no care for privacy and common decency," growled Frank. "On one occasion, they burst into my room during an inspection. I was almost naked. It was so embarrassing and degrading!"

This was a step or two away from the truth but, as part of the whole article, it didn't seem out of place. The article ended with a warning to the Trust.

I thought back to my city break, and that Washington Hotel. It wasn't the fluffy pillows and complimentary chocolates that stay in my memory. It was the people. They cared. They wanted to make my stay as good as it could possibly be.

I was only in that hotel for a few days. The good people at The

Acorns will live out their lives in this home. So, what do they want for their £1,400 a week?

Well, start by turning the clock back six months, let the staff do what they do best, and give the customer the service they deserve.

From The little Acorns the mighty old grow.

When the local newspaper reached the shops on Monday, the local social media sites had already gone into overdrive. The article was having the desired effect. Puppies, kittens, babies and old folk all need to be protected and defended in the public consciousness.

The keyboard warriors were out in force, and a tide of sympathy swept over northern Cumbria.

The hard copy was even more impressive. A large photograph of the sombre-faced residents sat slap bang in the middle of the centre spread. If they were trying to strike a vulnerable pose, they achieved their aim. In the picture, these tough old birds looked crestfallen and weak.

The camera never lies? Don't believe a word of it.

We had yet to find out how the article went down in Trust Towers, but this wasn't the only stomach punch they were about to receive.

On Monday evening, we received a call from our M.P. Karen Marshall.

It was a follow up to the letter she had sent to Alice. She asked if she could call into The Acorns the following morning to speak with the residents. She had read the newspaper article, and was keen to see the state of the place for herself. I ran through to tell Alice. She had her feet in a foot spa, recently purchased from Peter's shop.

"Before you ask," she said, "I know I shouldn't have, but it was only £10. Top of the range! You can't look a gift horse in the mouth."

I explained that I wasn't there to chastise her for receiving stolen goods, but to tell her about the call from our M.P.

"Tomorrow morning?" she asked. "Well, we better hide things like this. We want the place to look as bland as we possibly can. Stan bought one of those X-Box things. Make sure he hides it at the bottom of his wardrobe until she has gone. The last thing we want her to see is him enjoying himself like a bloody teenager."

I asked her what was in the letter.

"She promised us a full investigation. This visit must be part of it. I better brief the troops.

At least she has been true to her word. The newspaper article would have jolted her into action too."

I asked her if I needed to do anything else to prepare for our special visitor.

"Bring out those old damaged chairs from the shed. The ones with the torn leather armrests. Put some mud on the windows and leave a few dirty mugs around the place. Oh, and you might want to move those electric bikes from the hall into the garage."

"What electric bikes?" I asked.

"Peter got a couple for Ken and Frank. They want to keep fit without having to put the effort in."

There was no talking to them! I did as she asked.

The next morning, with the Keith Chegwin Suite purposefully looking a little worse for wear, we braced ourselves for the visit of Mrs. Marshall. We had not heard anything from management, and I was really hoping it would stay that way - at least until the visit was done and dusted.

Karen arrived just before lunch. A smartly dressed lady with shoulder length white hair. She looked far too elegant to be an M.P. We made small talk as I led her through to the lounge to meet Alice and the others.   She was bright and bubbly, but most of all, genuine.

She told me the letter from Alice made her cry. I hadn't read the letter, but I could imagine Alice laid it on thick. Her eyes were everywhere as we walked through reception, down the corridor and into the lounge. They were all in there, looking mournful.

I introduced her to Alice, and played my part in their little planned role play.

"I better get back to the office," I said. "I need to type up a new cleaning rota for next week."

"You sit down, love. This involves you too. And you!" said Alice signalling over to Vera who was, strategically, emptying a bin in the corner of the room.

We joined the group and found a suitably scruffy seat for Mrs. Marshall.

"I read the article in the newspaper, Alice. I wanted to see what it was like for myself."

"Thank you ever so much for taking an interest," said Eleanor. "We weren't expecting you to write never mind visit. We are ever so grateful."

"I work for you," she said. "I will get to the bottom of this and get you some answers."

Over the next hour, she polished off two cups of coffee and listened intently to each and every one of the residents in the room. After a visit to the toilet (in which the toilet roll had been switched to that shiny stuff that was like wiping your backside with tracing paper) she returned a woman on a mission.

"Would you be so kind as to give me a quick tour of the home? This is unacceptable. Simply unacceptable."

Doctor Alasdair stepped up to oblige. He had been briefed too. He knew where to show her and what to point out. It was all very coordinated. You couldn't fail to be impressed.

Before she left, she addressed the room.

"I have worked in schools and factories, offices and shops and I have never seen such a blatant disregard for the customer. Considering the exorbitant fees, I shall be seeking answers from the Trust board with immediate effect."

A tear rolled down her cheek and she let it fall, unashamedly.

"Social injustice is the reason I chose to be an M.P. You have me on your side."

When she left, we watched in silence as she drove away and out of the driveway. A cheer went up in the room, and they high-fived each other and whooped like American cheerleaders.

It was a Bank Holiday on 1st May 2023 - not that a bank holiday meant much to our residents - but it was a special day, because it was the day we got our Acorns back.

When I signed in just before nine a.m. Vera was on the telephone. I was about to walk on to the staffroom to give her some privacy, but she waved to indicate that I could go inside to join her. She was smiling.

I sat opposite her and waited for the call to end. She nodded a lot and said, "Yeah, yes please, of course, I will, thank you, yes please, that would be great, I will, I'll tell them, no problem, I will be there, my pleasure."

When she finally hung up, she was grinning like a Cheshire cat.

"You won't believe this!" Her face was flushed and her hands were shaking.

"What?" I said, laughing. She was bubbling with excitement.

"They won't be back! Laurel and Hardy won't be back. They want me to meet with them tomorrow at head office to discuss a promotion. That was Mandy Hooper on the phone from the Human Resources department!"

"You are joking?" I said seriously. "What did he say?"

"Some rubbish about reassessment and reorganisation of the business. Apparently, the administrators have moved on to oversee a home in Alston. He wants to speak with me about a general management position here!"

"The M.P.? The newspaper?" I asked.

"Who knows? I'm guessing so. Wow. I can't believe it. We have our Acorns back!"

She exhaled loudly and, without any warning, punched the air and screamed.

"Come on," she said, grabbing my hand.

She led me through to the breakfast tables where everyone was chattering away as usual.

"I am so sorry to interrupt your breakfast ladies and gentlemen," she said, still grinning and shaking with excitement. "We have our Acorns back!"

I don't think she could think of anything else to say.

"They have gone!"

Vera and I jumped up and down like schoolgirls, clapping our hands with glee.

I looked over at Alice. She was smiling too. "About bloody time!" And then everyone cheered. I think I hugged and kissed every single one of them. I was buzzing. Vera just collapsed into a seat and started sobbing. It had suddenly all got too much for her.

Doreen and Margaret went over to comfort her.

That adrenaline rush was just amazing.

Eleanor sidled up to me and linked my arm to hers.

"I love it when a plan comes together. Don't you?"

28

Leaving a Legacy

Vera had a successful interview with Sandy. It was never in doubt really seeing as though she was the only candidate. She told us how he showered her with praise for the work she had done to make The Acorns a vibrant and enjoyable place.

The Trust agreed to give her a pay rise, and promised to review the pay progression structure for the rest of the staff. They told her they would also increase the budget to allow her to improve facilities in and around the home. They thanked her for her dedication and years of service, and they urged her to pass on the same message to *her* staff.

Their overall message was to manage the home as she saw fit. So long as the money kept coming in, and the complaints went away, she had free reign to manage as she wished.

Managing as she wished meant managing like she used to. The clock was effectively being turned back six months.

Unfortunately, six months is a long time in an old folk's home, and this good news was tinged with sadness and regret. We lost another long-term resident when Connie passed away.

Connie had suffered from a stroke earlier in the year and she never fully recovered. She was another of the quiet ones, but she had a wicked sense of humour. She could have me in stitches with a quip or observation. Always dead-pan. Always hilarious.

I am sure the strict routines of the previous regime had an impact on her wellbeing. She loved the companionship and the camaraderie of old and, although it was coming back, it came a little too late for her.

We had a small vigil for her in the garden she loved so much. Her death made us all think about what was important, and what we had missed out on the last few months.

Would she have lived longer if nothing had changed? We will never know, but what we do know is, she would have laughed a lot more.

The importance of time again. The time we have should be fun and enjoyable where possible. We should all enjoy each other's company, and cherish our differences and unique qualities.

Connie was unique - like we all are. She stood out *because* of her differences.

At seventy-nine, she was one of the youngest in the home. She had three children - all in their forties. They were very much part of The Acorns family too. They would volunteer to help out whenever we had a party or an event in the home. Losing Connie meant we would lose them over time as well.

The evening of her funeral, we all gathered in the lounge and raised a glass to Connie's memory. Although a regular occurrence, we would never get used to saying goodbye to dear friends and the mood was that of quiet, happy, reflection.

We had received a lovely card and a letter from her son. He thanked us for all we had done for his mother, and made it known just how much she loved her time in The Acorns.

He also gave us a framed picture. It was a sketch of the building itself. The attention to detail was phenomenal. It was signed in the bottom corner - CW 2020.

It turned out Connie Walsh was something of an artist and we had no idea. She was an art teacher in the grammar school, but in her spare time she would sketch and paint and sell her work for considerable sums of money. I even googled her and found a number of her pieces on Google images. She wasn't an arrogant lady. She didn't seek fame. And yet here, under our roof, we had a lady with a considerable talent we knew nothing about.

The picture now hangs proudly on the wall in reception.

This revelation prompted a discussion about life and legacy.

"Connie's life lives on through her artwork," Sheila said. "Those pictures - those sketches - they will be loved and valued for many years after her passing. How many of us can say that about our own contributions?"

"Once I am dust, I am dust. That's it. I don't have a talent like Connie," said May. "I wasn't a bad baker, but I don't think I'll be stealing Mary Berry's limelight anytime soon."

"It doesn't really bother me. What is the point of worrying about a legacy? It doesn't matter much when you are six feet under." Frank mused.

"That may be true, but it is nice to know you achieved something in life. Something that others will enjoy and benefit from once you have gone." said Stephanie.

"When I have gone, the kids will get a few quid between them. I am sure they will enjoy that for a while. I know two of them are already banking on it for a holiday next year. They will be gutted if I am still around." laughed Ralph.

There were a few nods of agreement. Ralph wasn't the only one who felt he was no more than windfall for the next generation.

"Every month I go on is a lump sum my son misses out on," chuckled Wilf. "He is not even coy about it - he tells me straight. When he popped in on Sunday, he told me if I carry on in good health, he will have to reassess which car he is going to buy when I croak!"

I decided to steer the conversation away from family greed and impending death.

"So come on then, tell me about your hidden talents," I said. "What were you good at when you were in your prime?"

"Sex!" shouted Frank. The others groaned and booed him. It lightened the mood and started to get them all thinking.

"I used to be a jockey," said Tony. "I was pretty good too. I made a living from it for a few years, and got a few wins under my belt. Sedgefield was my lucky course - I had half a dozen first place finishes there."

I looked over and tried to imagine him on the back of a horse. He was just over five feet tall and, although he had a little pot belly now, he certainly could have had the right size and stature to be a jockey when he was younger.

"That is brilliant, Tony. What a claim to fame! How did you get into horse riding?" I asked.

"I used to work in the stables as a boy up in Durdar at the racecourse. It wasn't as strict and formal back then like it is now. The trainers were always in and around the place, and one day I just asked for some lessons. I was a cocky little bugger. It turned out I was quite good at it, and it just went from there. I made a few quid, and could easily have gone on to ride at the more illustrious courses for bigger prizes."

"So why didn't you?" I asked.

"I met and married Kath. Her mother didn't approve of gambling, and didn't think what I was doing was a suitable profession if I had any intention of making an honest woman of her daughter. I loved the riding, but I chose Kath above the horses. It was a gamble, but one that paid off."

"So, you could have been a star of the turf and you threw it all away for love?" said Frank.

"I don't know about that, but I have no regrets. It was all for love - and a fear of her mother. I have some photo's somewhere in my wardrobe upstairs. I will hunt them out for you later."

Tony's was the first revelation, but he wasn't to be the last.

"I used to be on the radio. I had my own show," said Sylvia. "I don't suppose any of you will remember, *'For the Record'*? It was the Friday late evening slot on Radio Cumbria. People used to call in with requests and interesting or strange facts about the artists or bands they wanted us to play. Before I made it behind the mic, I used to work as a runner in the studio. I was a confident girl, and I knew the place inside out and back to front. One of the producers told me I had a soothing voice - ideal for radio. It was probably his way of saying I was an ugly bugger, but I wasn't going to look a gift horse in the mouth. I jumped at the chance. At first, I would read the weather reports or the travel updates, but within six months, I had my own show. It was hardly the Radio 1 breakfast slot, but the listening figures were good, and the feedback was excellent."

"I remember that show. Was that you? Well I never! Who would have thought I would be sharing a sofa with a famous DJ?" said May.

"I wouldn't go so far as to say famous, but it was certainly an exciting and different job. Do you want my autograph?" Sylvia chuckled to herself and continued with her knitting.

"So, we have a disc jockey and a normal jockey," I said. "Any more revelations?"

Ralph was the next to speak, "I wasn't a bad footballer, but there just wasn't the money in it back then. I was earning more on the railway than I would have earned as a player. I had a few trials though - and a couple of offers. My old man told me to tell them where to go. He was just thinking of the keep I handed in each week to him and my mother. 'Food before fame' he would say. Do I regret it? I suppose I do a bit."

"Who offered you trials?" asked Ken.

"Carlisle were the first, but they only offered peanuts thinking I would snap up their offer because I was a local lad. Then there was interest from Blackpool, Port Vale and Wolves. They were all asking about me, and all sent scouts to watch me play. The best offer came from Preston North End. I even got to meet Tom Finney. I remember being in awe of the man - what a gentleman he was - but they were only offering a month's trial. I would have had to quit my job and risk the wrath of my old man. I decided to play it safe."

"Anybody else?" I called out. This lot never failed to surprise me.

"I was a bush beater," laughed Colin. "It wasn't so much the job itself, but who I was beating the bushes for."

I had no idea what a bush beater was, but he put me in the picture.

"I used to do a lot of fishing in and around the Scottish Border countryside. I would help out the farmers on their land in return for a chance to fish for salmon or trout in the rivers that ran through their farms. It was my hobby, and the farmers were happy if I helped them out with a few jobs and caught them a nice fish supper. It was easier than applying for licences. In August, the farmers allowed other visitors onto their property - grouse shooters. I used to beat for them. Basically, that meant rustling the bushes and beating the ferns to scare the birds out and get them up into the air."

"Upper class toffs?" Alice scoffed.

"Yeah. And - on occasion - royalty!" added Colin. "Prince Phillip was often up. He loved game shooting. I was his beater on a few occasions. He had a terrible aim, but no one dared tell him. He nearly shot me once or twice. Imagine if your claim to fame was being shot by the Queen's husband!"

"Has anyone else rubbed shoulders with the stars? Can anyone top Tom Finney and Prince Phillip?" I asked.

"I met Sooty and Sweep once in Blackpool," said Doreen. "I had quite a crush on Matthew Corbett. It was on the North Pier."

"I once had a pint in Keswick with Terry Wogan," said Bill.

"I sneezed on Ken Dodd in Leeds. I blame those bloody dusters he used to carry. I was so apologetic. He just laughed it off, bless him."

"I got stuck in a lift with Bob Geldof. He panicked like a little baby."

"I played a charity golf match with Bruce Forsyth. He was bloody useless. He stormed off at the end when his ball went into the river. He bought us all a round of drinks to say sorry afterwards."

"I sold a bra to Denise Welch when I worked in the House of Fraser in Newcastle."

"I had a fight with Melvyn Bragg in Wigton. He called me an idiot if I remember rightly. We went to school together. He went on to be an art critic, TV presenter and author. I went on to be a plumber, so I suppose he was right in the end!"

"I had a one-night stand with Bob Carolgees. Well, it was either him or Mickey Quinn."

"I met Robin Williams in Scunthorpe. Why he was there, God only knows, but he was a decent enough chap. He had a lovely smile. He gave me a boiled sweet."

The stories just kept coming. I was crying with laughter. We all were. By the time we had polished off the last of the sherry and nibbles, we were all exhausted. Connie would have been proud!

I approached Vera a couple of days later with an idea. I loved seeing Connie's sketch in the reception area, and the conversation on the night of her vigil got me thinking.

Could we do something to celebrate the lives of all our residents? Preferably while they are still alive to enjoy them too. She loved the idea, and so did Alasdair, who sat beside her helping her separate a pile of paperclips.

"We could make a book?" Vera suggested. "Perhaps with pictures and information - like a scrapbook."

"Let's think bigger. Something a little out of the box. Leave it with me," Alasdair suggested.

True to his word, he spent the weekend mulling over what we could do, and he came back with a brilliant suggestion. A website!

Not just a website. He suggested we could have a screen in reception, if the budget could stretch to it, and we could have profiles of all the residents displayed on the home page. The screen could be interactive and visitors, staff or residents, could click on a name and their story would appear on the screen.

He said all we would have to do is agree on a format and decide how we wanted to present the information.
As well as the profile pages, we could have tabs to display information about the home as well as other, fun stuff like crazy facts, the history of the building, contact details, a map of the site, a diary of up-and-coming events etc.

He even knew someone who would build the site for us for free.

Vera said there was no better time to ask for money to pay for the equipment with the events of recent weeks, so we decided to go for it.

While we waited for the screen and computer to be bought and installed, we set about typing up the stories and profiles. It was great fun. They all had so much to say.

One of the ladies had a granddaughter who was a professional photographer, and she even bobbed in for an afternoon to take pictures of everyone to go with the profiles. They all looked so handsome and pretty in their finest outfits.

Within a month, the website was up and running and working like a dream. It was a thirty-two-inch screen, and the perfect size. Not too big, but big enough to catch your attention when you walked into the reception.

The residents loved it. The site was constantly updated, and any new resident had their own profile shortly after arriving.

Who would have thought modern technology would have been embraced like this in The Acorns? The website received dozens of daily hits from family and friends, and we even had local businesses sponsoring pages. It would pay for itself by the end of the year!

Well done Alasdair. We now had a permanent record of everything and everyone at the home. We had life stories to go with the photos. We had memories at the touch of a button.

We had a living, breathing website.

Every single one of them now had a footprint - a stamp. A legacy.

29

No Regrets

After the buds had blossomed in spring, and summer began, Dora and Leonard's condition deteriorated. The Alzheimer's was taking more and more control, and their moments of clarity and consciousness were fading away. They still had their moments, where they would share their thoughts and their memories, but they were now few and far between, and it was awful to be on the periphery of this decline.

They were my friends. It hurt to see them suffer like this.

Dora would talk to herself in whispers, often seemingly oblivious to others around her. Most of the time it was just random mumblings.

She would mention food, places or objects, but there wasn't any noticeable reasoning behind these thoughts. She would hold our hands and let us guide her from place to place. She would still sleep well and eat and drink without any problems.

The panic attacks were few and far between, and the upset that once accompanied these frustrations was no longer there. She didn't cry or wail very often anymore. She just sat and talked and mumbled to herself.

Leonard displayed different behaviours, but his own decline was just as pronounced. He would still get angry and frustrated with himself, but he slept much more now. He also ignored his beloved books and newspapers. On occasion, he would still engage in conversations with others, but he would soon drift back into his own little world. There was nothing we could do to reverse the condition or make them better. All we could do was to manage and care as best we could.

Sometime during the first week of July 2023, a lot of us were sitting out on the patio enjoying the first real heatwave of the season. Courtenay had just returned from the local shop with a cardboard box full of ice lollies and choc ices, and was busy sharing them out to anyone who wanted one. She had developed into a beautiful, young lady with a personality to match. The once moody teen was long gone, and she had grown to be a much loved and valuable member of staff.
Alice was incredibly proud of her, and to see their own relationship blossom was lovely.

She now had her own profile on our fledgling website, as did all the other staff. I didn't like my own photograph on there. There was no professional photographer for us - we had to make do with Vera and her smartphone. My face looked blotchy, and it made me appear as though I had a double chin. Maybe I did!

Courtenay looked young and glamorous on her profile. I sometimes wished I could turn back time to when I was younger and thinner. Looking around, I cursed myself for my selfishness. I was surrounded by people who would love to have been my age again. I stopped feeling sorry for myself and had a bite of my ice lolly.

Leonard was sitting inside the conservatory staring out over the garden. Sheila was with him, chatting away, but I don't think he was listening.

I had read through his profile on the website screen the previous day. His granddaughter, Niki, helped us put it together. Apparently, he had been a good darts player in his younger days. He used to play in one of the local city leagues. He represented the Linton Holme Inn on Lindisfarne Street.
The pub seemed to play an important part in his social life, and Niki told me he had so many friends there. She told me about the short time he was in the Navy. He even took part in the Davenport Field Gun Tournament, where a group of naval men assemble canons and drag, carry and reassemble them around a

course. It was an extreme test of physical strength, teamwork and stamina. There was far more to Leonard than lifting a dart or downing a pint of beer. For years, he worked as an HGV driver and club doorman. He was a popular and well-loved man who rarely strayed far from the area he grew up in, but he was very content with his life.

Knowing how much of a socialite he was in his own way, made it all the more difficult to see him in his current state.

The website was proving to be very popular with the residents, but also with their family and friends. Alasdair showed me the amount of unique 'hits' the site was getting.

After two weeks, we had over five hundred views. A little counter in the bottom right-hand corner of the screen kept us up to date. Under the admin settings we could even break this down into more specific groups.

Of the five hundred, over three hundred were from different IP addresses. Alasdair explained that this was likely to be different households or businesses. He said Vera was in the process of setting up a Facebook and Twitter account for The Acorns to encourage more visitors, and to keep families and friends of the home in the loop when we were staging new events or inviting guests in to speak with the residents.

It was all getting a little high tech and modern for me. I may only be in my thirties, but I seem to have morphed into a pensioner having worked here for so long.
To me, social media is an alien concept and, to be honest, I am happy to keep it that way.

My younger friends - mainly old school mates - all have social media accounts and half of them have met their partners through online dating or joined clubs and groups through Facebook or Instagram. That just isn't for me.

I do enjoy playing games on my phone though -mainly jigsaws

or crosswords - but there is one app I use when I am with the residents to help generate debate and discussion. It is called "Would You Rather…". It basically throws up a random question and you have to favour one of the two answers.

There is no right and wrong answer. It is all just a bit of fun.

We decided to have a go that afternoon on the patio as we sucked on our ice lollies. As it was my phone app, I would always be the compere. After voting, I would pick on individuals to explain why they had chosen the answer they did. It was all a bit of fun, and we all had a good laugh.

The first question that popped up on my screen was a bit of a daft one - '**Would you rather have a tail or horns on your head?**'

There were fifteen of us outside that day. I couldn't vote, so we had an even number of participants.

Even though the question was a bit obscure, they still seemed to take it seriously, and challenged each other's way of thinking.

It was a fairly even split - eight voted for horns and six for tails.

"Why a tail, Bob?" I asked.

"So people would know when I was happy without having to speak. It would just wag."

That seemed quite logical.

"And why did you choose horns, Mavis?"

"I've never suited hats."

The questions could be very random. From obscure to philosophical, you never knew what the app was going to throw up next, and that afternoon was no different.

"Would you rather be a cat or a dog?"

"Would you rather live up a tree or underground?"

"Would you rather be the Prime Minister or own a top Premier League football club?"

"Would you rather live in Scotland or Wales?"

"Would you rather be a pianist or a guitarist?"

Needless to say, our lot had an opinion on all of them. Men tended to vote for dogs, women for cats. Carol and Nazreen wouldn't live up a tree because they were scared of heights and felt it would be unsafe anyway as, "We used to have a tree house at home, and my brother fell out of it." That was sixty-five years earlier, but the danger was just as vivid in her mind now as it was then.

Being Prime Minister appealed more than being owner of a top football club. That was the only question where *everyone* voted for the same option. The desire to stamp their own mark on the country was still there despite their age and mobility.

Scotland proved to be more popular than Wales with everything from the language to the condition of the roads given as valid reasons.

Seven voted for pianist and seven for guitarist although they all agreed that everyone should learn to play an instrument - even though most of them couldn't!

The last question - and it was only the last question because it took so bloody long to complete the vote - was also the most thought provoking.

"Would you rather live your life again or come back as someone else?"

After I read out the question, I looked up and waited for a witty response or a smart comment, but there were none. They all sat in silence - lost in their own thoughts. I read the question again, and waited again.

After a while, Eric spoke.

"Now, that is a question. Would I rather go through my time again or come back as someone else? Can that be anybody else? Dead or alive? Historical or famous figures?"

"I'd imagine it could be anyone," I replied.

They all fell silent again.

Eventually, old Jill piped up.

"This is a really hard one, Ang. I have enjoyed my life. I have never really done anything of note, but I have enjoyed it. I got on with my family, I had lots of friends, my husband was a kind and decent man, and nothing bad has ever really happened to me."

"I'd like to be that David Beckham," said Wilf. "He has the looks, he has the money, he has his choice of women and the adulation of millions."

"He chose the wrong spice girl," said Frank. "And it hasn't all been plain sailing for him. He was vilified for getting sent off at the World Cup remember? Folk were after his blood for years. And he was brought up in Essex - who the hell wants that accent?
As for those tattoos! He looks like he's been pinned down by a hundred primary school kids and stencilled to within an inch of his life!"

"But he's rich and has his choice of women!" replied Wilf, repeating his argument.

"You have a good pension from the post office and had three wives. The similarities are striking!" laughed Frank.

Before it descended into a tit-for-tat, I asked if any of them would like to swap their own lives for another.

"Without getting too deep," said Rebecca, getting deep, "You have no idea what might be going on in other people's lives. Even the celebrities, with all their fame and fortune. They will have their own family problems, money worries and illnesses. Unless you have had a really hard time in your own life, you should be very careful what you wish for. I lost my brother when I was fourteen. My dad suffered a heart attack and nearly died when I was in my early twenties. He didn't last much longer after that. They were the real lows in my life. Lows you never get over, but there have been so many highs too. I wouldn't swap my own life for anyone else's."

"Some things you just can't control. Look at old Len. My Jacob used to go out drinking with him. They were great friends." said Bella. "Both of them were like big kids and they didn't have a care in the world. Jacob died in his sleep at the age of seventy-two. Len is still with us - in body if not in mind - but the two of them had such a lovely life. I suppose it all comes down to how much you have enjoyed your time, how you have coped with any obstacles thrown in your way, and also who has shared your life with you. I'm content. I'd rather be me. I wouldn't want to live my life again, but I wouldn't want to live anyone else's either."

"Do you know what eats away at people? Regret." said Ralph. "Regret for things they didn't do rather than the things they did do. They regret marrying the wrong person or staying in the same job. The regret of not travelling or taking risks. We all have them. Some people can dismiss them as part of life's path. They gnaw away at others, festering inside, wishing they had been someone else or somewhere else."

"What do you regret, Ralph?" I asked.

"Not a great deal to be honest. Like I said, I could have chanced my arm at being a professional footballer, but I don't dream of what might have been. I made my decisions at the time and it all worked out fine in the end. I have enjoyed my life."

"You know what annoys me?" said John. "Not making the most of the time we still have to come - not what has already been and gone."

"What do you mean?" I asked again. The result of the vote for this question now seemed irrelevant.

"Well, here we are. A bunch of very old folk. We can't walk far, our bodies are giving up on us - our minds too, and we are sitting here waiting for the big man with the scythe. We ought to be making the most of this time. We might need a bit of help, Ang, but let's go out with a bang. No regrets."

John's Churchillian speech seemed to rouse the others, and they tapped their sticks on the floor or voiced their approval.

"Let's not create anymore regrets. Let's DO, not just wish or hope." he continued. "We should make a bucket list of everything we still want to do, and the places we want to go to - within reason. What do you think, Ang? Could we do that? Would you take it to Vera?"
The others looked at me in anticipation.

"I don't see why not!" I told them. "Get your bucket list together - speak to the others - and I will take it to Vera, and the other staff, and we can see what we can do?" They were all animated again. John had lit a fuse and their enthusiasm and excitement had returned.

I felt very pleased with myself too. Although it was my phone app that started the debate, social interaction once again proved better than social media.

I left them to it after that, and went back inside to do some chores. I was looking forward to receiving their bucket list.

John was right, it wasn't too late to make things happen. It wasn't too late to do something special.

There was still time to live, not regret.

30

The Bucket List

Wednesday 12th July was a wet day. After a fortnight of sunshine, the heavens finally opened and the county was hit by a series of storms, with torrential rain and lightning strikes. One of the churches in Brampton town centre was hit by a bolt, causing a fire and some structural damage to the bell tower.

The rain brought flash floods as the hard ground struggled to swallow the water. Roads were closed and traffic re-routed. First world problems really. No one was hurt, just slightly inconvenienced.

Aside from arriving at work a little late that day, the change in weather didn't really affect me or those inside The Acorns.

"Remember the floods of 2005 and 2015?" said Ronnie. "This is just a puddle in comparison. All my downstairs rooms on Greystone Road were under water. I remember walking down the stairs to get my morning coffee only to be greeted by the television set floating around at the bottom! I stood there like an idiot wondering what to do. All I could think about was finding the remote control. It is amazing what goes through your mind sometimes."

Doreen agreed.

"We were flooded too. We lived on Warwick Road - a few doors down from Brunton Park. The water was nearly six feet deep in the Living Room. Thankfully all of the valuable stuff - photos, family documents and the like - were upstairs. Some folks weren't so lucky. The worst thing was having to live in a hotel for a year while the house was cleaned up and rebuilt."

"You know what was the worst thing for me?" added Tom. "The smell. It was putrid! All that waste and water from the rivers mixed with the sewage and slurry. When the water levels eventually subsided, it was like wading through a farmyard. Once every hundred years they told us - and then it happened again a decade later!"

"Global warming!" I said.

"Messing with the environment is more like it!" said Tom. "Meddling with rivers, habitats and hedges to cater for redevelopments or new housing. That and inadequate flood defences - it was a natural disaster waiting to happen!"

"I lived in Stanwix," laughed Frank. "High up on the hill, looking down on you peasants. I don't know what you are moaning about. The insurance paid out, didn't it? You all got new homes. Twice!"

"If I didn't know you better, Frank Williams, I would have your guts for garters!" laughed BIll.

Changing the subject completely, Betty leaned over and tugged on my sleeve.

"John is looking for you. He has the list. He is in the TV room watching that film about that imbecile in America who can run for miles. Him with the chocolates."

"Forrest Gump?" I said.

"Aye, that's the one. Can't stand it myself. He said for you to go in when you'd overcome the floods, and got your arse back into work." She gave me a cheeky smile and a pat on the bum.

Sure enough, John was sitting in front of the television with Peter and Colin. The film was on, but they weren't really watching it.
Money was changing hands, and they looked up like naughty

little school boys when they realised I had walked into the room.

"I don't care what you are up to or what you are buying," I said, sounding like an old headmistress. "Betty told me you were in here. I believe you have something for me, John?"

He handed me a scroll, held together by an elastic band.

"The bucket list?" I asked, excitedly.

"The bucket list," he replied, grinning. "Have a read, show the boss, and see what you think. We have all added something. We think they are all manageable, but we will need your help and approval."

I promised to go through it with a fine-tooth comb with Vera as soon as she was free to talk. She was on one of those video conference calls with a manager from another home. Apparently, she was training them on good practice. Isn't it is strange how things go full circle? Six months earlier we were considered inadequate for doing exactly what we were doing now, and for what we had always done before!

I sat in the staff room and waited for her to finish up. Other staff on the same shift as me had yet to arrive. Perhaps they had been inconvenienced by the puddle too.

A couple of cleaners were walking around and chatting to the residents, so I knew I would be alright grabbing a few minutes of quiet time.

I decided to have a quick look at the list before sharing it with Vera. I rolled off the elastic band, and opened the scroll like some Roman Emperor ready to address his troops.

It was five pages long and written in the form of a table. I honestly don't think there was one resident at The Acorns who had scruffy handwriting.

Even in blue biro, it was immaculate and beautifully presented.

In column one there was a number, in column two a name, and in the third column there were a couple of sentences noting each person's bucket list choice.

It was so sweet - like a letter to Father Christmas. A wonderful wish list. But it wasn't for Santa - it was for Vera and me. We were the ones entrusted to make their last big dream come true. I felt a weight of responsibility wash over me even before I read the first one. I started crying and laughing at the same time, like a big baby.

I read through the list carefully. I didn't want to miss anyone or anything. I found myself nodding throughout. They were mostly doable, but a few left me open mouthed.

Some would take more organising than others, but I was sure we had it within our capabilities to tick off each and every one of their requests.

At the bottom of the last page, there were two blank rows.

Blank apart from the names - Dora and Leonard.

Underneath the table, someone had written, "D & L to be decided."

That made me cry all over again.

By the time Vera stuck her head around the door, I looked like Alice Cooper. Make up all over the place.

"You are such a softy!" she said. "Come on through to the office and let's have a look at this list."

Half an hour later, Vera looked like me. Eyeliner all over the place and mascara trickling down her cheeks.

Alasdair just happened to walk in and see us in that state. He started to panic, wondering what had happened. He thought there had been a death in the home or something equally tragic! When he found out what we were crying for, he slumped down in one of the chairs and laughed.

"You two will be the death of me!"

We handed him the list to read which gave us time to sort our faces out.

By the time he had finished reading, we were almost back to normal.

"What do you think?" I asked them both.

"I don't foresee any problems there," Alasdair said. "It is what they want after all."

"It will involve a lot of risk assessing, staff cover, transport and insurance worries etc." Vera said.

"You are sounding like a manager now!" he teased.

"But yeah, bugger it. Nothing we can't overcome together. Where there's a will, there's a way! And there is definitely a will."

"You might actually be in a few if you make this happen for them." Alasdair chuckled.

We all agreed to go for it. Vera asked me to arrange a staff and residents meeting in the Keith Chegwin Suite later that day. I was so excited to go and tell them all. Vera stopped me in my tracks before I left the office.

"What do we do about Leonard and Dora?"

"I am sure, between us, we can think of something special for them too," said Alasdair.

And with that, I was off. Scroll in one hand and a handful of tissues in the other.

We all gathered in the lounge that evening. It was a strange atmosphere. There seemed to be a lot of nervous tension in the room.

I think, in their minds at least, they felt they were being a burden. They felt that they were putting us, as staff, into an awkward position.

In a way, they were. Some of the requests would involve bending - or even breaking - the rules, but as a staff, we so wanted to make everyone's wish come true.

All the staff on duty were there in the room and Vera had invited the others to join us. Even though they were not working, nearly everyone showed up. Those that couldn't sent their apologies, but also let it be known that they were right behind the idea. We had a wonderful staff team. A real family.

When we were sure everybody was in and comfortable, Vera walked to the front holding the scroll. The room fell silent.

"We organise trips for you, we entertain you, we feed you and clean for you, and still you want more from us!" she said, holding the scroll in the air.

"Do you realise what you are asking? Do you realise the amount of paperwork this will create? Do you realise the hoops we will have to go through to make this happen? Do you realise we could lose our jobs over this?"

She looked deadly serious for a second, and the residents looked terrified.

Only for a second though.

And then she smiled. A huge grin spread across her face.

"But this isn't any old care home. We don't always go by the book here. This is The Acorns! We make our own rules. We go on days out using Sunderland Football Club's team bus for goodness sake!"

There was a collective sigh of relief and all the smiles returned.

"This is your bucket list and, as a staff, we have all agreed to do what we can to make your dreams come true."

A cheer went up around the room followed by a spontaneous round of applause. It was such a lovely moment of unity.

"Now, this is going to take quite a lot of planning and organising. We can't possibly tick them all off in a week, and we are going to have to prioritise. Some of your requests will be easier to sort than others. Staff will need to be allocated and timetabled."

Vera looked over towards the staff who were lined up against the wall, and then back to the residents.

"My team here - our team - have offered to give up their own time to help. I could not be more proud of them, and I am sure you are too."

Alice stood up and raised her hand.

"Can I just say, on behalf of all of us here, a huge thank you to each and every one of you. You know how much you mean to us. You aren't just employees of this place - you are our family. Three cheers for The Acorns! Hip, hip..."

Everyone shouted the responses and cheered at the end.

"Now get back to whatever you were doing," laughed Vera, "and we will get back to you all very soon." More cheers.

Vera asked if she could speak to all the staff before we dispersed, and we gathered together in the reception area.

There were far too many of us to fit in the staff roo

"Thank you so much for coming, everyone," she began.

"You can see how much it means to them all, and I, we, are determined to tick off every request on that list, one way or another. I will sit down with Ang and Alasdair and try to work out how we are going to do this before getting back to you all. We are going to make a lot of people very happy, you know.

Let's just hope it all goes smoothly. There is a lot at stake here, but I don't need to tell you that. However, if you don't want to be a part of it, just let me know. I don't want to compromise any of you."

Nobody put their hand up. Not one. We had the best team. Acorns United.

31

Risk and Reward

Mavis was the first.

Vera, Alasdair and I had created a timetable and a proposed timeline to enable us to work through the long wish list. It wasn't easy and there was an awful lot to consider.

As well as the paperwork needed for taking people off site, we also needed to factor in the health of the residents, the length of time they would be out the home, which staff were available to accompany them, any transportation needed, family concerns and a million other factors besides. We were guided by the wishes of the residents - if they did not want us to contact immediate family, we didn't.

If they wanted certain shops or products, we had to arrange those too. It was like a military operation, but we got there in the end.

The first five were relatively straightforward and simple - nothing to worry about. We decided that at least two members of staff would accompany each resident.

I wasn't working on the weekend of 19th and 20th August, so I volunteered my services to help make a start on the list. Kerry, who worked with us earlier in the year on secondment, asked if she could join me. We had remained close friends since her time at The Acorns, and I was thrilled to have the chance to spend the weekend with her. She was looking to join us on a permanent basis, and her efforts to help us in our hour of need would not go unnoticed by Vera.

I spoke with her on the phone a few days before the weekend, and told her all about the requests. We were both really excited.

Mavis was ever so excited when we told her she was to be the first one. Her request - or wish - was a simple one. She wanted to walk barefoot on Allonby beach.

We set off early on that Saturday morning. Allonby was about a forty-five-minute drive from Brampton.

The sun was already high in the sky, and it was forecast to be a beautiful day. We talked on the way, and she put her wish into more context.

"I was a young mum. I had three children by the time I was twenty-two. My husband worked hard, but we didn't have a great deal of money. Luckily for us, his friend owned a caravan along the coast - just outside of Allonby - and he used to let us borrow it for a few days each summer. It seems nothing now the way the roads and the cars are, but back then it was a big adventure. The children loved it. The sun always seemed to be shining on us there.

That beach was our special place. My special place. I would sit on the sands and watch them all play. We used to play a little game together. We would walk along the sands and try to collect seaweed in between our toes. Whoever had the most, by the time we reached the sea, would win. It was so silly thinking back, but so lovely too. I want that feeling again. I don't think I will get another chance."

Kerry turned to face her. She pulled out a plastic wand - presumably her daughter's - and waved it in the air.

"You shall go to the beach, my princess!"

We all burst out laughing.

It was a lovely drive over and Mavis told us all about her family.

Her children were now all middle-aged and settled with children of their own. She was ever so proud of them.

When we arrived in Allonby, we parked up near the dunes and Kerry bought us all an ice cream.

"Do you want us to join you on the beach?" I asked.

"No thank you, my love. If you don't mind, I would love to just go for a stroll and lose myself in my memories."

We helped her onto the flat sand and took off her shoes.

"This means the world to me, girls. Thank you ever so much."

And off she went.

We sat on a bench and watched her from a distance. It was so romantic. Her scarf fluttered in the warm breeze as she walked all the way to the water's edge. She left us at 11:00 a.m. and didn't return until after 1:00 p.m.

We handed back her shoes and guided her from the bench. She was clearly exhausted, but exhilarated too.

Kerry had a bottle of water and a towel to wash the sand off her feet and dry them before she slipped her shoes back on.

We walked back to the car and before we all climbed back in, she turned to look back out toward the sea.

"I don't wish to sound sombre or morbid when I say this, because I am not, but this might be the last time I ever see this place. This place that brought me so much joy. I'm ever so grateful to you both - to all the staff - for making this happen. You have made an old lady very happy."

She climbed into the back seat while Kerry and I bawled our eyes out.

Mavis was the first on the bucket list to be ticked off. It was only after she spoke that I realised the enormity of what we were doing. We were making dreams come true.

Tommy was next. His own request was fairly straightforward too. He wanted to stand on top of the Civic Centre in Carlisle - one of the highest buildings in the city. Vera contacted the council offices, and they were very pleasant and accommodating. We arranged to take him over that same Saturday in the evening. One of the site supervisors agreed to meet us there and take us up to the roof. It was ever so exciting, and I think I was just as thrilled as Tommy. Kerry had a fear of heights, and told us she was happy to wait in the car.

"Have you been up before?" I asked him as we pulled up outside.

"No. Never," he said, smiling.

"May I ask why you wanted to do this?"

"I will tell you at the top."

We took the lift up to the top floor and a short flight of stairs took us up to the rooftop. The site manager gave us the safety talk, but seemed to trust us enough to walk around unattended while he smoked a cigarette.

"I used to be a steeplejack," said Tommy. "I loved my job. I loved being up high - chimneys, factories, pylons - you name it. I was fearless when it came to heights. I used to sit up top and eat my sandwiches, just looking out and admiring the views. I was in my own little world. What a sense of freedom. I knew every inch of this city - every road, every park, every business. I can see now how much it has changed. It is so much bigger now - and noisier."

We walked around each side of the building, and Tommy pointed out places of interest, giving me a lesson in local geography and the effects of modernisation.

"Do you know where I was born and brought up?" he said, leaning on the fence and looking down to the ground far below. "Here. On this very spot. The footprint of this huge building was my home."

He smiled, walked over and cupped my face in his hands.

"You have brought me home, Ang. Thank you."

Back at The Acorns, I sat in the staff room with Kerry. "You know what?" Kerry said. "I think I am only just realising the enormity of this bucket list. Not the activities per se, more the emotional impact." I agreed.

Vera came in to join us.

"Two down, and three more to tick off tomorrow!" she said. "I think it is Susan, then Bob, then Edith. Susan asked me to get a big box of chocolates. Will you remember to take them with you? She didn't say why."

I promised I would. We had made a good start, and we were looking forward to what was to come next!

We were all set to go just after breakfast the next day. Susan was looking super smart as she made her way to the front door. She reminded me to put the chocolates in the car.

Our destination was the village of Burgh by Sands, a few miles west of the city. Her request was to visit the house she had lived in most of her life before her husband passed and she relocated to The Acorns.

Unsurprisingly, the house was now occupied by another family, and we had had to ask their permission to visit. Susan worried that we would be a nuisance, and kept apologising, but the family in question could not have been more helpful.
Alasdair had called around to the house a couple of days after we had received the bucket list. He had introduced himself, and explained where he was from and who he represented. The family were delighted to help and play a part in making her wish come true.

Andrew and Stephanie Sproat now lived there with their three children and pet cat, Freddy.

They were very excited to welcome Susan into their home and find out a little more about the history of their house.

It was a beautiful residence just off the main road to the Solway. Susan climbed out of the car and stared up at her old home.

"I am not really sure this is a good idea. What must they think of me? An old busy body poking her nose in a place it isn't wanted. This is their home. I shouldn't be intruding."

We tried to reassure her that the family were looking forward to meeting her, but she was sure she had made a big mistake. That was until Andrew came bounding out the house and down the path. He swung open the gate and waved us in.

"Come in, come in. We have been so looking forward to meeting you, Susan." he gushed.

"I hope you have a good appetite. Steph has made a buffet for us all fit for a King...or Queen!"

He held Susan's hand and guided her up the path towards the back door as Kerry and I followed. By the time we reached the living room, he had charmed her.

"The house is beautiful. A beautiful family home. I am so pleased it has fallen into the hands of people who care. This place meant so much to me."

I handed Andrew the box of chocolates.

"Oooh, my favourites. Thank you so much. No need, no need."

"Just a little something for accommodating me," said Susan.

There was a commotion upstairs then a rumble of footsteps on the stairs as Steph burst into the room. "Forgive me. That bloody cat has brought in another mouse. This one is still alive!"

She looked flustered, and bedraggled.

"So sorry. I have been under the bed trying to drag it out!"

That broke whatever ice there was left to break, and we all laughed at the absurdity of it all.

Andrew was right - Steph had made a mountain of food. Cakes, sandwiches, cheeses and cooked meats all washed down with teas, coffees and cloudy lemonade. It was scrumptious. We couldn't have asked for better hosts. They really made Susan feel at home - again.

"Would you like to look around? The kids are out somewhere so they won't get in your way. I can't vouch for the cleanliness of their rooms, but you are welcome to have a nosey."

"May I? Really? That is ever so kind of you."

Andrew acted as tour guide as Steph and I cleared away the dishes. Kerry had Freddy on her lap and he was going nowhere.

After a look around the upstairs, Andrew helped her downstairs and out into the garden. I watched from the window as the two of them talked animatedly and got along like they had known each other for years.

He led her around to the garage and out of view. By the time we all returned to the comfort of the warm living room, we were ready for another cuppa.

"Did you know?" Andrew began, "That Susan and her husband built our garage!" Susan looked very proud.

"She showed me their initials in the concrete near the doors. I have never noticed them before. Amazing!"

We chatted and talked for over an hour. It was so nice to hear stories from both sides. There was so much love for this house - generations of affection for what was truly a family home.

When it was time to go, Andrew and Steph walked us back to the car to wave us off.

"I have something for you. Hang on." Andrew ran back into the house as we fastened our seatbelts. He rushed back down the path a couple of minutes later with something in his hand. It was a framed picture - a painting of the house.

"Our eldest painted this picture of the house not long after we moved in. We would like you to have it." He handed it through the car window to Susan. "Our house. Your house."

Susan looked down at the picture. "It's beautiful. I couldn't poss.."

"Take it with our pleasure. A reminder. And if you ever want to come and visit the house...or us...again, you are always very welcome."

Steph leaned in through the window and held her hand.

"Thank you for coming. It has been an absolute pleasure meeting you."

Susan didn't say much on the way back. She just kept looking down at the picture in her hand.

It was only when we pulled into the drive at The Acorns did she speak.

Like Tommy and Mavis before her, she could not be more grateful to us for making her wish come true.

We had taken her to a house less than ten miles away for an hour or two, that's all, but to Susan, it was everything.

It was still early in the day when we knocked on Bob's bedroom door. He invited us inside and offered us a seat on his bed while he put his boots on.

Bob was ninety-three, and one of the oldest in the home. He was still fairly sprightly for his age, and rarely asked for help or support from the staff, choosing to be as independent as possible.

"It's a beautiful day, ladies. Do you think I will catch anything?"

It was Bob's wish to go on one last fishing trip on the banks of the river Eden. Apparently, he was a keen fisherman when he was younger, even winning a number of angling awards.

Although still in relatively good health for his age, he needed to use a walking frame to help get around the home, as he was a little unsteady on his feet. He also had the strongest prescription glasses known to man, and wore a hearing aid in each ear.

And yet, there he was, standing in front of us wearing knee length Wellington Boots and waterproof trousers, ready and primed for his afternoon out.

Wayne, one of the delivery men, had offered to come along

with us. His family had a licence to fish in the river at certain times of the year, and he was a keen angler himself.

He had all the equipment, so we didn't need to worry about that.

Everyone we reached out to was keen to help and Wayne was no different. He was rough and ready - a little scary if I am honest. His language could be described as 'industrial' and there were no airs and graces about him.

"Come on old fella, jump in the back seat and get your seatbelt on. God only knows how you are going to get down that river bank to the water. I'll have to catch you in one of these nets if you topple in!" He wasn't quite as polite as that - I'm paraphrasing.

Kerry and I jumped in the car too. I let Kerry sit up front with Wayne.

Wayne was right though - it was a bit of a struggle getting down to the water's edge with Bob. At one point, we thought we had lost him down a pothole, but we managed to steady him and keep moving over the uneven terrain.

Wayne didn't wait for us. He marched on, and by the time we reached the river bank, he had everything set up and ready to start.

We set up a seat for Bob as near to the water's edge as we could. Wayne passed him a junior sized rod and secured the handle to the armrest. Bob was keen to attach the maggots to the hook himself and Wayne, for all his ruggedness, was patient and supportive throughout.

Kerry spread a blanket on the grass nearby, and the two of us lay down to enjoy the sunshine and the peace.
We watched from a safe distance as the two men cast their lines over the water before settling down to wait for a bite, lost

in their own little worlds.

Occasionally, Wayne would check on Bob or pass him a drink or a cigarette, but for the most part, they simply enjoyed their own company.

The afternoon haul wasn't great. They managed just two fish between them. A sorry looking catfish and a young salmon that wouldn't have fed a famished kitten, but that didn't matter. It was the sport - not the prize - that mattered most.

By 5:00 p.m. it was time to pack up and return to the home. Wayne suggested we make a head start to the car while he packed up the equipment. Linking arms, we navigated the uneven ground. The long grass brushed our sunburnt legs, tickling and stinging in equal measure. By the time we reached the car, Wayne was all set to go.

"I'll sleep tonight, girls, that's for sure," Bob said. He reached into his pocket and pulled out a £20 note.

"And that is for you, young man. For your time and effort. You have made this old man very happy."

Wayne refused to take the money, and told him he was a silly old sod.

By the time we got back to The Acorns, Bob was fast asleep. Wayne helped us manoeuvre him into a wheelchair and, within half an hour, he was tucked up in his own bed, minus his waterproof trousers and his Wellington Boots.

Before he left to get on with his own business, Wayne gave me a little Tupperware box.

"Give him these in the morning to remind him of the day."

Inside were two fishing hooks and a fishing float. It was such a kind gesture.

"And this is for you," he said.

He handed me a slip of paper with his mobile number on. That was a kind gesture too, but he wasn't going to hook me.

Kerry and I had one more request to satisfy that Sunday.

Again, it was not a hard one to organise, and it would only take us an hour or two, but it did rely on the goodwill and support of a lot of kind people.

Edith was waiting for us in the Keith Chegwin Suite looking very smart. She was wearing a beautiful navy-blue summer dress with a matching wide-brimmed hat. The dress was complimented with a white lace scarf and a pearl necklace. She could have been mistaken for the Queen. The contrast between her attire and Bob's could not have been more different, but she was not going to a muddy old riverbank, oh no, she was going to the cathedral!

Apparently, when she was just a little girl, Edith used to sing in the cathedral. Her mother had been part of the choir, and she would take Edith along with her.

On the way there, she told us a little bit more about her own experiences.

"We used to walk down for singing practice three evenings a week and be ready to perform during the Sunday services or whenever we were called upon. The cathedral ended up being like a second home to me, I was there that often. Mum loved it and I suppose her enthusiasm rubbed off onto me. As a child, I was mesmerised by the place."

Vera had spoken to the Dean and he, like the others we contacted, had been delighted to help. The choir had agreed to stay back after the Sunday service to sing a few hymns with Edith.

As we drove into the city, she became more and more excited.

"It is over fifty years since I last sang with the choir. It will be over thirty since I was last in the cathedral. I would have liked to have gone for the 900th anniversary celebrations last year, but it was not to be. I had to settle for *Songs of Praise* on television. I hope I don't let them down. It has been such a long time since I sang."

We reassured her that she was under no pressure to perform, but she clearly wanted to shine one last time.

We parked up inside the cathedral grounds and made our way to the side door. Dean Manley was there to greet us.

"Do you know," he said, "We are all thrilled to welcome you back after all this time, Edith. The choir is all waiting for you inside, and our organist is primed and ready to go!"

He was such a gentleman. He led us through the vestibule and the nave then right up the aisle towards the altar where the choir awaited us. It was a stunning sight. The sunlight poured in through the impressive East window, and Edith marvelled at the iconic, 'Angels and Stars' Choir Ceiling.

The singers themselves greeted her like an old friend, and invited her to take a place in the centre of the front row. The Dean had asked us to send a list of her favourite hymns, and she had chosen eight.

I noticed he had also set up a tripod and camera halfway down the aisle.

"Now, I took the liberty of passing on your list to the choir, and they have been practising your favourites in anticipation of your visit. We really hope you enjoy this evening. I have taken the liberty of setting up a camera and, with your permission, I will record the performance and send a copy to you in The Acorns so that you can watch yourself in action so to speak.

299

I am sure the others would like to see you perform too!"

I looked over at Edith. She had a huge smile on her face. He definitely had her blessing.

"I will hand over to Mark to conduct, and I will take my place behind the lens. Edward is up on the organ to give us some musical accompaniment."

Edward waved at us from above, and Mark took up his place a few steps to the left of the choir.

"You have chosen some of our favourites," he said. "Our first hymn will be All Things Bright and Beautiful. Are we ready?"

Everyone nodded, including Kerry and me.

The organist began to play and the choir burst into song a few seconds later. Edith joined in with gusto. She certainly didn't look out of place. At the end of the hymn, those either side of her patted her on the back and shook her hand. She was loving it.

They followed the first one with 'How Great Thou Art' then 'Abide With Me' and 'Amazing Grace' before taking a break for coffee and cake.

Suitably refreshed, they continued with 'Jerusalem', 'Shine Jesus Shine' and 'The Lord's My Shepherd. They finished with a wholehearted rendition of 'He's Got The Whole World In His Hands', and even Kerry and I even joined in.

I sat in the pews after the singing and watched Edith mingle with the choir.
She was having the time of her life. Dean Manley joined me and passed on his email address.

"Send me a quick message and I will get a copy of the video to you in the next couple of days. I am sure it will be wonderful.

They certainly sounded wonderful to me." I agreed. They certainly did.

Edith was buzzing. We even had another sing song in the car on the way back to Brampton.

"I am really looking forward to watching the video," she said. "I couldn't have asked for more. Thank you for such a wonderful evening. I felt like a teenager again."

Back in The Acorns, Kerry and I joined Vera and Alasdair in the office.

"Five ticked off," Vera said. "I think it is fair to say we have five very happy residents." We all agreed. It couldn't have gone better.

"They were the easy ones," laughed Alasdair. "Now the fun begins!"

The list was on the notice board on the wall, and we all looked over at it at the same time.

He was right. The next batch would not be as straight forward, but we promised them all we would do our best to make their wishes come true. It was just that they had some bloody strange wishes!

32

Needle and a Haystack

Alice was next up.

In fact, she was up very early the day of her adventure. She said she couldn't sleep due to all the excitement. This was one I was really worried about, but she didn't seem to be phased in the slightest. She had specifically asked for her granddaughter not to accompany her on her trip, which surprised us greatly as the two of them had been inseparable since Courtenay reached out to her, and then secured a job at The Acorns.

Instead, she asked for Dawn. Dawn was one of our part time cleaners. She lived on Dacre Road in Brampton with her boyfriend Will, her two bull terriers, Simon and Kevin, and her fifteen-year-old son, Ben.

It was pretty obvious why Alice had asked for Dawn to accompany her - she was covered from head to toe in tattoos.

Apart from her face - which itself was covered with piercings of every description - there was barely a square inch of un-inked skin visible. I had never seen her naked, but I am willing to bet her private parts had been exposed to the tattooist at some point too. She had animals, symbols, names, patterns, mythical creatures and teddy bears up and down her legs and arms. On her neck was an upside-down rainbow with a pot of gold on her chest leading to each shoulder. Even her hands and feet hadn't escaped the needle.

Each digit had some kind of individual squiggle or mark. She really was a work of art.

Her appearance didn't frighten the residents - far from it! Her tattoos intrigued them, and she could often be found in the Keith Chegwin Suite showing them off to the masses.

For all her appearance might have shocked some, she was such a kind and gentle soul. Nothing was ever too much trouble for her, and when Alice asked her if she wouldn't mind taking her into the city to get a tattoo of her own, she was bowled over.

When I first read Alice's suggestion on the bucket list, I was quite taken aback. She was in her mid-eighties, and didn't really fit the image. Why would a lady of her age want a tattoo?

"Why not?" was her response. "It won't be the first time I have felt a bit of a prick."

I asked her what she was planning to get, but she wouldn't tell me. It was to be a surprise.

Dawn had arranged to take her to meet Niki who owned the Inkporium located in the Denton Holme area of the city. It was the place she would usually frequent herself whenever she had the urge to 'ink the pink' as she called it.

I watched them leave together. What a contrast, and yet, they got on so well. They were laughing and joking all the way to the car. If Alice was nervous, she wasn't showing it.

While they were away, I turned my attention to some of the others. Four of them had requested the same wish, and it was one that set the health and safety alarm bells ringing like never before. Under normal circumstances, this would simply not be happening - no way. The potential dangers and hazards would have filled fifty risk assessments, not just one.

Four of them - four silly old buggers - wished to climb a mountain in the Lake District! For old times' sake!

I panic when they walk through the garden or up and down the steps. There was so much that could go wrong. This wasn't going to be a stroll in the park - literally! They wanted to climb a mountain!

Uneven paths, potholes, streams, the weather, suitable footwear, fitness levels, getting lost, cramp, medical help etc. etc. It was a mad idea. Crazy. But it is what they wanted, and we promised them. They all said they would sign any disclaimer given to them taking full responsibility for their actions, but we knew only too well that the blame would land squarely at our door should something go wrong.

"Just say we are having a day in the Lakes," laughed Frank.

"And what do I say to the Mountain Rescue team when you are blown off a crevice two thousand feet up? We were just having a little walk near the farm when all of a sudden we lost our way?" Vera exclaimed, a little higher pitched than she planned.

"Say whatever you want. We will take the blame," he replied.

"You will take the blame, but we will get the blame. It is irresponsible. Stupid. Mental. We could all be sacked for this. We could even go to prison!"

"But you promised," Frank said, that mischievous smile back on his face.

And we did. We couldn't back out now.

The how and the where would be decided by Niall McNulty and Catherine Hughes - friends of The Acorns and keen fell walkers. The two of them knew all the residents well, and were often party to their madcap schemes.

Niall helped us source visitors, equipment, transport and days out. He was even known to be part of Peter's crazy schemes.

Nobody really knew who he worked for or what his official job role was, but it worked for us and the residents loved him. We were fairly sure he worked for the council at some point, and that was good enough for Vera.

Catherine was as mad as a box of frogs. She would turn up at The Acorns when she happened to be passing, walking her dog, Ralph.

Ralph wasn't named after our own Ralph, but Frank said he looked a bit like him - short and bedraggled, but happy enough with his lot in life. Four-legged Ralph would just make himself at home and walk around the lounge being petted and mollycoddled.

It was during one such unannounced visit that I told her about the bucket list and our four would-be-mountaineers. Typically, she didn't foresee any problems whatsoever. Not only that, but she said she was happy to help organise it and accompany the gang!

"They will be alright. I'll look after them. They will have a great time. This is so exciting? When is it? Who is going? This is amazing. I can't wait!"

You couldn't help but to be carried away by her enthusiasm, even if she was slightly unhinged. I explained who the hardy souls were. Frank, Eleanor, Wilf and Doreen. The youngest was Wilf. He was seventy-nine. Doreen, at eighty-three was the eldest. I expressed my fears and worries to Catherine once again, but she just laughed it off and told me to 'chill'.

We arranged the walk for Friday 25th August. Niall had sorted a minibus for us all as well as any equipment we needed such as walking sticks and a compass.

He brought along a rucksack full of refreshments and treats for the day. Alasdair was to be the designated driver, and Vera and I joined the party, driven my guilt, worry and anxiety.

Ralph (the dog) sat up front with Catherine and she produced a map to show us the planned route.

"We are going to scale Haystacks," she said. "One of Wainwright's favourites. I think his ashes were scattered up there. Don't worry Frank, your corpse won't be joining him today. It's a slow but steady route to the top. A bit of scrambling here and there, but nothing to worry about. Great views of Buttermere from the summit too. We can get an ice cream from the van when we arrive. I have also booked us into the nearby Bridge Hotel for a bar meal afterwards. I booked a table for nine and a dog, so you better all make it down. They don't like having to rearrange the tables!"

It was a beautiful day again. We had been so lucky with the weather, and this day was no exception.

We were all in good spirits when Alasdair parked up the minibus beside Gatesgarth Farm. Niall looked like a giant tortoise once he had slung his rucksack onto his back. Little Ralph ran ahead, and we made the first few steps of the day towards the footpath to begin our ascent.

To be fair, our magnificent four really looked the part. Frank and Wilf were both wearing shorts, and their sturdy legs certainly looked up for the task ahead. Eleanor and Doreen chattered away without a care in the world.

As is often the way, the first push was the hardest.
By the time we had climbed above the treetops, we were all perspiring and breathing heavily, but we soon got our second wind. It would seem that I had underestimated them. They did not seem to be struggling at all. They were having the time of their lives.

We stopped for a bite to eat at a cluster of rocks about half way up. The views were stunning in every direction, and, again, I promised myself I would get out and about more often.   All this beauty on our doorstep and I waste my days off watching old films or repetitive quiz shows.

After eating we marched on, stopping only briefly so Frank could lie down and have a drink from one of the tarns. It was a real accomplishment to reach the summit - not just for the residents, but for the rest of us too.

"Can you believe it? We've made it!" laughed Eleanor, gazing out over the neighbouring hills.

"I didn't think I would see this again," smiled Wilf. "Paradise, isn't it?"

"Certainly is," agreed Doreen. "I will be stiff tomorrow, but it has been worth it. Every second."

"You can leave me with Wainwright if you like," said Frank. "I can't think of a place I would rather be."

I took lots of photographs for the website and profiles.   There was a great group shot of the four of them cheering with their hands in the air, looking triumphant, Buttermere glistening far below in the background.

I also took a couple of cheeky ones of Alasdair and Vera together.

We sat up there for an hour or so eating Niall's rucksack buffet before making our way back down. There were a couple of slips and stumbles, but nothing to cause alarm - that was until the last stile. Our four octogenarians made it over without any problem, but Vera caught her trousers on a protruding piece of wire, lost her balance and fell on her backside into a muddy puddle to the amusement of the rest of the party.

"Bet you didn't put that on the risk assessment," Frank mocked.

We all had a lovely meal at the Bridge Hotel before returning to The Acorns around 7:00 p.m. Another successful day, and more ticked off on the bucket list.

We all knew we would be a bit stiff and sore the next day, but it was definitely worth it, and we weren't the only ones suffering from our excursions.

Alice was sitting in the Sir Jimmy Glass suite when we hobbled in. She was rubbing her shoulder and chatting away to Dawn and another woman I didn't recognise but, judging by the skin art, I guessed she was the cause of Alice's self-inflicted discomfort. They stopped talking when we walked into the room.

"And how is my brave little soldier?" I asked, trying to offer a sympathetic smile.

"Better than I thought I would be," she said, looking better than I thought she would.

The others sat in the spare seats around her, eager to find out how she had got on.

"This is Niki," said Alice. "Owner of the Inkporium and the cause of my self-inflicted discomfort." She leaned over and gave Niki's hand a squeeze.

"She has been a gem all day. She really put me at ease, and even insisted on coming back here with us to make sure I was alright."

Like Dawn, Niki did not go with convention. Aside from the many tattoos, her pink and orange hair stood out a mile amongst the bald patches and grey perms in the room. She was slim and attractive - clearly someone who took pride in her appearance, but wasn't at all phased by what others thought of her.

As usual, Frank couldn't help himself.

"So, what did you get then? A Zimmer frame with wheels on fire? A skull with a hearing aid on?"

"None of your business, you cantankerous old bugger," she replied. "It isn't for your eyes."

Before the conversation descended into a tit for tat argument, between the two adversaries, I asked Niki if her latest customer had been a good one.

"She was lovely," came the reply. "Tough too. The first is always the hardest. My first was a dolphin on my lower back. Long gone now, but at the time it was a big deal."

"Were you not terrified?" I asked Alice. "I would have been."

"I was a bit, but I couldn't show it. You don't, do you?"

Niki chipped in. "If she was scared, it wasn't obvious. I have had beasts of men under the needle, crying like babies. She was a rock today."

Judging by the way she was positioned; you could tell where her new tattoo was - just at the top of her right arm.

"I added a coat of Dermalize. It acts like a second skin, and allows it to breathe and recover for a few days. It will keep the tattoo clean and free of infection. It also saves having to wear a bandage. By Monday, it should all have settled down. I'll come over again and check it out then, but it already looks fantastic. I can't see you having any problems. Alice, you are now a member of the ink club. You are never too old to join!"

She gave Frank a stare and he shook his head.

"The only needle I want is the flu jab, young lady."

We chatted for a while longer before people started to drift off home or to their rooms. Alice and I were the last to leave.

"Have a couple of paracetamols before sleep to numb the pain," I suggested.

"I might just do that," she replied. "It was exhilarating, you know. I might even have another one! Niki said I had the skin of a fifty-year-old."

"Are you going to show me?" I asked.

"I will, my love, but not just yet. There is someone I need to show it to first."

The next morning, we were all just going about our daily business when Courtenay burst into the office, her eyes puffy and red.

I asked her what was wrong, but she couldn't get her words out. I led her to the staff room and asked her again.

"Nothing is wrong," she sobbed. "Everything is just perfect. She is so perfect. Grandma."

I handed her a box of tissues and waited a few minutes until she was able to compose herself and stop crying.

"Don't be upset with your grandma," I said. "It's what she wanted. It was her wish to get a tattoo. You know how strong willed she is."

"I'm not upset with her. Far from it." Courtenay blew her nose again and pulled a fresh tissue from the box.

"She showed me the tattoo. It was on the top of her back on her right shoulder. It still looks a bit tender, but it is nice and clear. Niki did a wonderful job."

She started crying again.

"So, are you going to tell me? What is it? What does it say?"

"It's a little picture of a cherub," she said. "And underneath, it says, 'Courtenay. My special angel."

She started crying again, and I held her in my arms. One wish. One morning of pain. One gesture. A selfless act that meant the world to someone who would go on living years after she had gone.

These people never cease to amaze me. I held Courtenay and I cried with her. Happy tears. Again.

33

A Sporting Chance

Two more wishes were made reality on the first Saturday in September 2023. One would be witnessed by thousands, the other by just a select few, but both were equally special to the two residents in question.

Peter, accompanied by Alasdair, left The Acorns in a taxi just after 8:30 a.m. en route to Carlisle Racecourse. We were going through something of a heatwave, and that Saturday was right in the middle of it. Even at that early hour, the sun was shining and the temperature was rising.

Ralph's experience would follow on a few hours later in another part of the city.

Peter's choice caused no end of palpitations for us organisers. He wasn't worried, but all the staff were nervous wrecks. It was just not sensible or advisable for an eighty-four-year-old to ride a racehorse at full tilt around a track. How do you write a risk assessment for that never mind seeking suitable insurance cover? Even if we had managed to secure such a policy, it would have been invalid as, like most of Peter's schemes, it was against the rules and probably the law.

Peter loved horse racing, and he loved to have a flutter now and again, but his involvement had always been limited to watching from the side-lines. That said, he did have quite a few contacts in and around the sport. A few years earlier he got to know, and worked with, a few prominent jockeys on the circuit. He even acted as chauffeur for one, taking him from course to course during the racing season. It was through this connection, that the seed of an idea began to sprout.

Peter told his jockey friend about his wish, and asked if it could be made possible. After the initial shock, he not only promised to look into it, but actively encouraged the idea. The 2nd September was then earmarked as a suitable date. There were no race meetings scheduled for that weekend and, aside from a few ground staff and trainers, the place would be all but empty.

Alasdair, who also had a passion for the turf, asked if he could go along with Peter for the experience. Considering he was a doctor, he seemed to have a total disregard for protocol and danger.

"What if he falls off and bangs his head?" Vera asked. "It could be the end of him!"

"It could. But he is eighty-four years old. I am a neurologist. The sheer surge of dopamine due to the excitement and nervous tension can act as a huge motivation for Peter. Something so exciting - despite the obvious dangers - can trigger an enormous amount of pleasurable emotions. These neurotransmitters are also great for memory and motor skills. As a doctor, I should be encouraging, not discouraging him!" he said with a wry smile.

"But it will be my head on the chopping block if he kills himself!" she shouted.

"Why? You don't even know why I am going there, **do you**?" laughed Peter. It was no use arguing with them. They had an answer for everything.

"You go off with Ralph and have a lovely afternoon," said Alasdair. "We will tell you all about it later...providing he doesn't fall off and die!"

"The sooner we finish this bucket list the better," said Vera in a huff. "Now bugger off, you two. We need to sort Ralph out."

Whilst not quite as precarious, Ralph's own wish filled us with worry too. He was even older than Peter, and when we read that he wanted to run out with the Carlisle United football team on matchday, we nearly had a heart attack for him.

What was it with these old people and strenuous exercise? Shouldn't they be slowing down, not speeding up? I hope I have the same energy levels when I reach their age.

Although not one of England's biggest clubs, Carlisle United was a big deal in the city and the county. With no other club within fifty miles, the support base stretched far beyond the city boundaries. It was a real community club and, during the good times, the feel-good factor around the whole area was palpable. Even those with little interest in football understood the importance the club had in the area.

In recent years, good seasons had been few and far between, but in 2023 they were on the crest of a wave following promotion the previous year. Crowds were up, local businesses were keen to sponsor, media attention was all positive and there was a rapport between players and fans that strengthened those community links. Players were often seen in schools, community centres and hospitals handing out free tickets for games or spreading the love. Youngsters around the city were far more likely to be seen wearing the blue of Carlisle United than that of Manchester City or Chelsea.

And not just youngsters. Ralph and Stan were huge United fans, but they hadn't been to a game for years. Ralph even had trials for the club in his youth. They still listened to the games on the radio, but it wasn't the same as being there. We just didn't have the means to take them and look after them due to cost and staffing.

"You want to lead the team out? How on earth do you plan to do that?" Vera asked him.

"As a mascot," he replied.

"The mascots are all children, aren't they?"

"They don't have to be. There isn't a rule to say they have to be children."

"They will think you are potty. You can't go running down that tunnel at your age! What would they think?"

"Well, we won't know unless we ask them, will we?"

I offered to email the club with his hairbrained idea. At least we could show willing and tell him we tried.

I fired off a message to the club's media team expecting nothing more than a courteous rejection letter in reply. How wrong I was. Again!

The next day, I received a reply from Amy Nixon, a member of the club's media team, who thought it was a wonderful idea. She promised to run it by her bosses and get back to me within twenty-four hours.

Sure enough, I received a second email the following morning. Not only were they keen to invite Ralph to take on the role of club mascot on 2nd September 2023 for the match against Bradford City, they also wanted to invite him down as 'Guest of the Day'.

This was a new initiative by the club to reward loyal and dedicated supporters.

Ralph, along with three friends, would be offered a three-course meal before the game, a profile in the matchday programme, a tour of the stadium, free match tickets for the director's box, and a framed photograph with the players.

I was flabbergasted. I printed off the email and showed Vera before taking it to Ralph. He was absolutely bowled over!

"Please accept on my behalf!" he said, excitedly. "Wow. Oh my gosh. What a thrill!" He was like a ten-year-old boy again. He called over to his best friend Stan to tell him the news.

"Will you come with me Stan?" he asked.

Stan didn't need a second invitation. He was as excited as Ralph!

"Will you come too, Ang? And Vera?"

Neither of us were big football supporters, but we suddenly found ourselves as excited as the two old men.

"I'll have to hunt out my dad's old scarf!" Vera said, giggling. "Are you sure you are up for it, Ralph?"

"You try stopping me!" he laughed.

The club couldn't have been any more accommodating. A couple of days later, we received a visit to The Acorns by members of the club's media team along with Club Secretary, Sarah McKnight.

Amy introduced herself, then the others, to Ralph and Stan.

"Today, with your permission, we would like to do an interview for the website and the club's YouTube channel. Just a little bit about you and your connection to Carlisle United. I believe you very nearly played for the first team too?"

Ralph looked at me with mock anger, knowing I had given them the background story before their visit.

"I'll be asking the questions, and Andy will be behind the camera. Just take your time, and don't worry about any mistakes. We can edit it afterwards, and anything you don't like,

316

we can take out. Is that ok?"

Ralph was buzzing. "Ask away. Make sure you get my good side!"

"They haven't got time to do plastic surgery!" called Frank from across the room.

Quite a few of the other residents had gathered behind the camera to watch and offer smiles of encouragement.

It turned out that Ralph was a natural in front of the camera. A consummate professional. He spoke so clearly and vividly that Amy and Andy didn't need to prompt him at all. At the end of the interview, Andy turned to look at the gathered crowd and held his arms out as if to say, "What do you make of that?"

They all started clapping and cheering. He even got a few wolf whistles!

Doreen led Amy and Andy away for a well-earned coffee while Sarah sat down beside Ralph. She thanked him for being such a star before dropping another bomb shell.

"It is a big game on Saturday. We have been running a bit of a ticket promotion as you know and we are expecting a crowd of over twelve thousand. As such, it has generated a bit of national media attention too. Sky Sports have been digging and...well...they heard about you. There has never been an eighty-seven-year-old football league mascot before. You will be the oldest! They want to cover your story on the news channel. If you accept, you won't just be walking out in front of thousands, you will be watched by millions! What do you think about that? Is that ok, or will it all be too much for you?"

For the next couple of minutes, Sarah had to sit and watch as Ralph danced around the room with Stan. Everyone else looked on, wondering just what it was she had said to him.

Eventually, he calmed down and settled back into his seat with a huge grin on his face.

"I take it that's a yes then?" she laughed.

"The nearest thing I have ever had to stardom was when I appeared in the audience on Bullseye in 1984! Damn right it is a yes! Count me in. What do I have to do?"

Word spread like wildfire. Ralph was going to have his ten minutes of fame, and Sky Sports were coming to The Acorns. Their plan was to send a reporter and camera crew to speak with him a few days before the match, then appear again at Brunton Park to film snippets of his big day. The initial interview would be screened on the Thursday and Friday in between other stories and headlines. Ralph fell into the 'fan feel-good' category of news. One of those quirky bulletins to brighten the day of the average viewer in between the nitty gritty of the major headlines and major injury or transfer updates.

Sky had chosen Vicky Gomersall to report on the story, and she had booked herself and the team into The Halston Hotel in the centre of the city. It was all very exciting. Ralph went to meet them for a drink on the Wednesday evening, and they arranged to come to the home for the initial interview early on Thursday. If they thought they were going to have a quiet one-to-one with Ralph, they were very much mistaken.

Ralph might have been the only one in front of the camera, but there were at least fifty people behind it.

He took it all in his stride, and spoke really well about his time as a semi-professional, and how much football had changed over the decades.

Vicky asked him about turning out as a mascot on the Saturday.

"How does it feel to be the Football League's oldest mascot? Are you nervous?"

"I can't wait to get in that changing room and get the boots on!" he answered. "I have waited eighty years to run down that tunnel. It will be a dream come true."

"Do you feel fit and well enough?"

"I am fitter than half of the players I have watched over the years, I can tell you! I've let the manager know that I am ready to play if he needs me."

Throughout Thursday and Friday, we received lots of calls from other media outlets keen to give the story an airing. Everything from local radio stations to national newspapers seemed to have latched on to the story. Some even offered to pay a fee or donate to a charity of Ralph's choosing.

On the day of the game, we were all very excited. Once we had packed off Alasdair and Peter we started to prepare for the day. The Sky Sports News crew planned to meet us before and after the game, and Carlisle United had granted them access all areas during the day. Vicky was a lovely lady, and couldn't do enough for Ralph and the rest of us.

The same could be said for all the staff at the club. Amy met us in the reception area and presented Ralph with his full kit for the day. First team player, Owen Moxen, had donated a pair of his boots to Ralph. They were a size too big, but that didn't bother Ralph. He was grateful and humbled by everyone's generosity and hospitality.

Amy led us through to the offices, and introduced us to the staff. You would think the King himself had just walked in such was the greeting he received.

While it was still relatively quiet, we were taken on a stadium tour and we all got to sit in the manager's seat, and a walk onto the hallowed turf.

Stan and Ralph were like kids in a sweet shop. We were then taken to Foxy's restaurant for the pre match meal.

Vera, Stan and I tucked into a sumptuous meal while Ralph made do with soup and a roll. He didn't want to risk getting a stitch before the big event.

At 1:30 p.m., as the crowds began to file in, Amy came to collect Ralph and the rest of us made our way to the director's bar. She promised to look after him.

We settled into our seats about twenty minutes before kick-off and spotted Ralph out on the pitch in full kit chatting to the players. He passed balls across the pitch like a man half his age. He hadn't lost his touch!

As kick off approached, the large crowd geared up for the arrival of the teams. We watched as the cameras jostled for a place around the tunnel area.

Long standing Club Chairman, Andrew Jenkins, tapped me on the shoulder and said,

"Those cameras are there for the mascot, not the players. He is even older than I am!"

Sure enough, when the music started and the crowd roared to greet the team's arrival, Ralph was first out of the tunnel with a ball in his hand.

The journalists had their money shot. We could see Vicky talking into the camera as the players darted onto the pitch to limber up. They didn't need to wait for Ralph - he darted on with them.

He received a fabulous welcome from the masses behind the goal in the Warwick Road End, and took great pleasure in smashing a ball low into the net beyond the reach of Tomas Holy, the team's giant goalkeeper.
The crowd roared and chanted Ralph's name, and he responded

with a wave and a bow.

As is the custom for all mascots, Ralph was taken to the centre circle by the captain, Morgan Feeney, for photographs and handshakes with the referee. The Bradford City mascot - a little ginger haired lad no more than six years old - couldn't understand why his opposite number looked older than Methuselah.

 The whistle then blew, and the players made their way into position for the start of the game. The two mascots jogged off the pitch to rapturous applause. I felt ever so proud of him. Vera was crying - Stan too!

About fifteen minutes into the game, and after a quick change, Ralph joined us in the director's box. He was glowing. Everyone patted him on the back, and fans leaned over the barrier to congratulate him on his achievement. You would have thought David Beckham had just walked in!

To round off a wonderful afternoon, the team topped it off with a resounding three-nil victory.

In the media room, Ralph joined elated manager, Paul Simpson, for post-match interviews.

"I'll keep mine brief," Simpson told him. "It is you they want to listen to, not me."

By the time we left Brunton Park and headed back towards Brampton, the crowds had long since dispersed and the roads were quiet.

"Have you had a chance to catch your breath?" I asked Ralph.

"I have had the most magical day." And with that, it all got too much for him and he broke down in tears. Everything seemed to catch up with him in that moment, and Stan and I gave him a monster hug.

"You were brilliant my friend. Just brilliant. I'm proud of you," said Stan.

"We all are," added Vera.

By the time we arrived back at The Acorns, he had regained his composure and was ready to greet his adoring fans who were all eagerly awaiting his return in the Keith Chegwin Suite. They cheered as he walked into the room.

Vera handed him a carrier bag. "A gift from the club," she said.

In it was the full strip he wore, and the boots given to him by Owen Moxen - who just happened to be one of the goal scorers that day.

"Amy said she would send us a selection of photographs from the day for you to keep."

He started crying again, but this time he didn't even try to hide it.

It was after 7:00 p.m. when we arrived back at The Acorns, but there was still one - or should I say two - noticeable absentees. Peter, and his 'helper' Alasdair, were nowhere to be seen. Vera tried to call him on his mobile, but the call went straight to voicemail.

"What if something has happened to them?" she said, starting to panic.

"Don't worry," I said, trying to reassure her, "Alasdair would have called you."

"What if something has happened to him too?"

In our job - like many in the caring profession - the first instinct is to panic. Reason and composure come well down the line.

By 7:45 p.m., we were all set to call the police, the fire brigade and the air ambulance, just as the door clicked open and our two missing men walked in, looking a little worse for wear. I noticed a taxi disappear out of the front gate.

"We decided to leave the car. We've had a drink," said Alasdair, stating the obvious.

They were both a little tipsy, but in good spirits.

"I take it it went well then?" I asked. "Have you had a lovely day?"

Peter slumped into the nearest empty armchair.

"The best. I won't be able to walk for a week now though."

"Go get them a strong coffee, Ang. This we have got to hear!" said Vera, plonking herself next to Peter. Sheepishly, Alasdair joined her.

By the time I returned with the brews, they were ready to tell their tale.

"We met Conor up at the course. He had the key for the main stable. There wasn't another soul around apart from some dippy farm hand who let us in. He left us alone after that. There were five or six other horses in the stable, but Conor introduced me to 'Mr. Lucky'. He was nine years old and a little past his prime. Conor said he had a passive nature, and wouldn't mind an ageing amateur on his back."

Alasdair chuckled away to himself as Peter carried on with his story.

"Anyway, he led Mr. Lucky out onto the parade ring and we followed on. He was a beauty. Jet black and elegant - calm as you like. Conor climbed up into the saddle and pulled back ever so slightly on the reins. Mr. Lucky started to walk forward and then around the oval. He pulled a little tighter, and the horse started to trot slowly around. Despite being such a strong and imposing beast, the jockey had full control. He explained what I had to do and how to do it. He showed me how to slow down and how to speed up. He taught me how to keep my balance and how to position my body for maximum comfort. It all seemed so simple."

"It wasn't though, was it?" laughed Alasdair.

"You don't realise just how big those buggers are. You got that step ladder, and helped me get my leg over. That hasn't happened for a few years. It felt like I was sitting on top of a giraffe. I could barely see the floor. Conor held the reins and walked us around the parade ring as I held on for dear life. Mr. Lucky must have wondered what the hell was on his back!"

"You should have seen his face," chuckled Alasdair. "Totally out of his comfort zone. And you shouldn't have lied to him."

"Lied to him? What do you mean?" asked Vera.

"After five minutes, the dozy old sod told him he was ready to go out onto the course."

"Well, I didn't want him to think I was some kind of wimp. I couldn't walk around the yard all day," said Peter.

"Did he just take your word for it?" I laughed.

"Yes, he did. Just like that. He said he had a call to make, and if I was good to go, he would lead me to the starting line."

By this time, Alasdair was wiping away a tear, desperately trying hard not to break down with laughter.

"He gave me full control of the rein, slapped its arse and off it went!" said Peter.

By this time, we were all giggling. I was trying to picture the scene.

"He just bloody walked away back to the stables to get his jacket. I was too scared to speak or look around at this point. Mr. Lucky started trotting and then galloping. I was bouncing up and down like a pea on a drum. My feet were in the stirrups, thank God, but my arse was hitting that saddle with every bound."

We were in stitches.

"I haven't felt pain like that since I had the cane at school. And then came the first bend…"

"You should have seen him," howled Alasdair, "He looked absolutely terrified. By the time he reached the third bend, he was hanging off its side!"

"Where was Conor?" Vera asked, struggling to get her words out.

"He went for a coffee!" screamed Alasdair.

That was enough - we were doubled over with laughter. Even those out of earshot in the room were laughing just watching us. Peter tried to look serious, but he couldn't help himself.

"I managed to get my hands under the straps of the saddle for a better grip. For some reason, I thought the thing would slow down and stop as we approached the winning post, but it just kept on going…"

"Stop it, my stomach's killing me!" Alasdair shouted. His face was bright red and his eyes filled with tears.

"What did you do?" I asked, gasping for breath.

"What the hell could I do?" said Peter. "I just had to hang on and wait for it to tire itself out."

"Four laps later!" Alasdair howled, almost lying on the floor by this point.

"Eventually, it came to a stop. I didn't need any help getting off - I was already close enough to the ground. I let my foot slip out of the stirrup, and then let go of the rein. I fell down onto the soft grass. It didn't hurt. Only my pride. I have never been so happy to get back onto solid ground. Alasdair ran over to make sure I was alright. No sign of Conor."

Alasdair could still barely get his words out, but he managed to continue the story.

"We hobbled back up to the stables and checked for cuts and bruises, but he was ok. After a while, Conor returned and asked how it went. Peter told him he had had the ride of his life - which was the truth! He then asked where Mr. Lucky was. Well, we didn't know. We had left him on the course. Conor started to panic and shot off to look for him, but he was nowhere to be seen. He ran up into the grandstand for an elevated view, but still no sign of him. And then he noticed..."

Alasdair started laughing again.

"Then he noticed that the stable boy fella had left the gate open to bring his tractor in. Mr. Lucky had only gone and bolted down the road towards town."

"Oh my God!" said Vera, her hand over her mouth. "The horse is alright, isn't it?"

"He is now," said Peter. "It is bloody lucky though that's for sure. We had to call the police - and a vet. Conor was livid!"

"Where did you find it?" Vera asked.

"In a pub car park about two miles from the racecourse!" said Alasdair.

"Praise the Lord for that. Was it ok?"

"Compared to Conor, it was fine," smiled Peter. "That is why we are late. We stayed in the pub while the vet took Mr. Lucky and Conor back to the stables in a horsebox. We thought we had better give him some space to cool off."

Vera smiled at him. "Are you satisfied now then? Can we tick that one off now or do you want to have another go?"

"I think my jockeying days are over. I will stick to the betting shops now."

That day, the city witnessed two great sporting occasions. One in front of twelve thousand paying customers, and in the glare of the national media.

The other in front of a doctor, a trusting jockey, an irresponsible farmhand, and half a dozen unsuspecting customers at the St. Nicholas Arms public house on London Road.

34

Out and About

Throughout September, we set about completing the bucket list. We still had over thirty to go, and many of them involved days out of the county.

Again, Niall sorted out the use of the minibus at no cost to The Acorns, and Peter knew a farmer who was happy to provide us with a few gallons of red diesel at a fraction of the cost of the fuel at the filling stations. It wasn't until much later that I found out it was highly illegal to use red diesel on public roads unless you have special permission to do so - which Peter clearly hadn't!

Thankfully, we didn't get caught.

Again, we had to plan the excursions around staff availability, but as usual, everyone bent over backwards to make it happen. We looked at locations and timings, and tried our very best to use the minibus effectively.

We had a day trip to the north east to tick three more off the bucket list. Colin wanted to visit the place where the ship building yards used to stand on the River Wear where he worked as a teen in Sunderland.

Edna wanted to see the puffins at Marsden Rock, near South Shields, one last time - the place she met her husband.

Bill asked if it could be arranged for him to see and ring, the bells in Durham Cathedral. He used to study bells as a youngster. A true campanologist. Yet again, the staff there were delighted to help. The three returned to The Acorns having had a truly wonderful day out.

The mini bus spent a day in Blackpool. Courtney and Phillipa accompanied Philip, Dennis, Jackie and Eileen on the roller coasters at the pleasure beach and then guided them up to the top of the tower. These thrill seekers just wanted to experience that adrenaline rush one more time. Three of the four had known heart conditions listed on their medical records, but they didn't declare this to the young Pleasure Beach employees who strapped them into their seats and sent them on their way, hurtling along rails at terrifying speeds or flying upside down with their stomachs in their mouths! They all returned in one piece with smiles as wide as the Golden Mile.

Courtenay told us they were all incredibly brave, and no white-knuckle ride got the better of them.

And then there was the trip to Dumfries. We took the car for that one. Cameron wanted to visit the Robert Burns house and museum. Apparently, when he was at school, he used to learn all of Burns' poems by heart, then perform them in front of the great man's town centre statue, hoping to earn a few coins at the same time. At one point, he was as popular in the town as the poet himself!

He was over the moon to find out that he even had a mention on one of the museum's display boards. He'd forgotten all about the newspaper article. The headline - *Local Lad's Cup of Kindness* - told the story of how a young Cameron had wooed tourists and locals alike with his renditions of Burns' poetry.

The residents were learning more and more about themselves the older they became!

The mini bus had a trip to North Yorkshire too. Flora and Ella wished to travel from Pickering to Whitby on an old steam train. It was a route they had travelled on many occasions in the past, and they wanted to experience it again one last time.

The company was first class throughout the day.

We secured tickets for a meal on the Pullman Dining Train, and the driver even invited the ladies onto the footplate between stations. They had the time of their lives.

The furthest trip out for the minibus was to the capital. We booked a hotel for the night near Watford and travelled into the city on The Tube. I volunteered to join them along with Kerry. I wasn't going to miss out on a trip to the theatre!

Norma, Frederick, Jane and Archie all chose to see a show. We booked tickets for 'Les Miserables' at the Sondheim Theatre on Shaftesbury Avenue, but we allowed plenty of time to explore Covent Garden, Leicester Square and Soho before the performance.

They were all surprised at how much the area had changed since they were younger.

Before the show, we stopped for a drink at the Golden Lion, on Romilly Street. It was a small pub, but homely with a pleasant and friendly atmosphere. A group of kind Goths even offered up their seats and table for our gang. Archie bought them all a drink as a thank you.

"Over five pounds a pint!" he said, returning from the bar, making us all laugh at his innocence

"That's about the norm now," I told him. "It isn't much cheaper back home."

"Ah well. You can't take it with you, can you?" And with that, he downed his whiskey and went back to the bar for another. The Goths were suitably impressed.

The show was breath-taking and everyone had a great time. I wasn't sure I would like it at first, but it was wonderful. So emotive. We were all on our feet, singing and dancing at the end.

After the show, we made our way back to Piccadilly Circus and onto the busy Tube. Revellers were singing and dancing, ready for the night ahead, but we were all shattered and desperate for our beds. It had been a lovely day yet again. When the train pulled up at Watford's station, the train carriage was all but empty.

"That might very well be the last show we ever get to see. Maybe our last trip to the capital," said Jane. "If it is, I just want to thank you both for bringing us down to London. We have all had such a wonderful time."

Her kind words got me thinking again. Sadly, it might very well be their last time. I didn't want it to be mine. Another reminder that life is for living and we need to make the most of each and every day.

It was a long drive home the following day, but we enjoyed every minute - singing songs and telling daft stories or jokes.

Jane even suggested she might become a goth. "You are never too old to try something new, and I always suited black."

We didn't need to use the minibus to make Carol's dream come true - we needed a motorbike!

Carol had moved up from Chatham in Kent when she was only sixteen. She took up a job as a live-in nanny near Manchester. It was a brave decision to leave behind her family home at such a young age, but she never looked back. She met Brian - her husband to be - shortly after moving north. Brian was almost a decade older than her, but the age gap didn't matter a jot as they lived to have a long and happy marriage together. Carol and Brian had two children - Cheryl and Samantha. Both ladies were regular visitors to The Acorns, and we have got to know them very well.

For her bucket list wish, Carol asked if she could have a ride on a motorbike. She explained that, as a young couple, Brian and her used to travel everywhere on one. The bike was their 'freedom vehicle'! When Cheryl was born, they even added a sidecar to cater for the family needs. They were certainly different times then.

At eighty-two years old, it was another wish that laughed in the face of health and safety regulations, but it was what she wanted to do!

During one of their visits to the home, I told the two daughters about the bucket list and their mother's crazy request.

"Once she has something in her head, there will be no talking her round." Samantha told me. She didn't seem shocked at all. Neither was Cheryl.

"If that is what she wants, we will see what we can do."

A couple of days later, Samantha called us to say her husband, Andrew, was willing to take her out on the back of his friend's bike - a Kawasaki Z650. Apparently, he had a few motorbikes, but this one had a larger seat suitable for a passenger. It was all just too surreal.

It was the Wednesday of the following week when he roared through the gates and up the drive. Carol was waiting in the reception area wearing borrowed leathers, looking like a geriatric Cat Woman.

Was she scared? Was she heck! We put on her helmet and helped her on to the back, and she wrapped her arms around her son-in-law's waist.

"Like the old times eh!" he shouted back over the roar of the engine.

Before I had a chance to tell them to take care and go slow, they were off. They turned left towards the Alston Road, and within a couple of seconds they were out of sight.

They must have been out for well over an hour. I was just so relieved to see her still clinging on when the bike turned back into the driveway and came to a stop. I rushed out and helped her off the back, gently pulling off her helmet. Her hair was all over the place, and her cheeks were flushed pink.

Andrew lifted up his visor and grinned. "We got to over seventy-five miles an hour on one stretch, didn't we? This thing can't half travel! It's a beast on the bends. I thought you were going to come off at one point."

I closed my eyes and tried to imagine the scene.

"Thank God you are back safe and sound, Carol. I have been worried sick."

"No need to worry," she gushed. "That was the most exhilarating experience I think I have ever had. I have never experienced speed and power like it. Our old bike would be lucky to get over fifty!"

She thanked her son-in-law for his time. He pulled his visor down again, started the engine and zoomed off, waving as he turned the corner. What a family!

I helped her inside and into the lounge.

"Weren't you scared?" I asked. "Did you not find it difficult?"

She looked at me and smiled. "You only live once, Ang. I live for fun and excitement and that was right up there with some of the best things I have ever experienced.

Thank you so much. Was it difficult? Nah. Do you know what the hardest thing was?"

I leaned in. "No, tell me."

"Getting these bloody leathers on and off. Give me a hand will you."

I held her hand and led her up to her bedroom to get this old biker back into her nightie and dressing gown.

There were a few others on the bucket list that we could tick off without having to travel too far, but we had to call on the help and goodwill of local businesses and experts in their field.

One such establishment was 'Quirky Workshops', located five miles west of Penrith. The establishment - a seventeenth century farmhouse in the village of Greystoke - offered an abundance of workshops, courses and craft activities to suit any creative taste, from painting and printing to cookery to cobbling. They also offered workshop sessions in pottery, which is exactly what we were looking for.

Norma suffered terribly from arthritis. Her poor fingers were curled and twisted and she was often in horrendous pain. She struggled to hold her tea cup or use her knife and fork without help, and yet, her bucket list wish was to attend pottery classes.

I emailed a number of places in the area, but Quirky Workshops really drew me in. The place was a hidden gem - a hive of activity slightly off the beaten track - known by those in the know, but still rustic and private enough to fend off unwanted commercialism.

Despite its rural location, the business was thriving. I spoke to the lovely Annie on the phone and she, in turn, passed me onto their pottery guru, Bob Park.

I explained what we were doing and why. I also told him about Norma's condition and her struggles - none of which seemed to worry him.

"We will work with her. At her pace. At her level. Has she ever tried pottery before?"

I didn't know. In all the rush and commotion, I hadn't asked her. I promised to call him back when I had spoken to Norma.

She was sitting up in her room listening to the radio when I barged in, disturbing her peace and quiet. She didn't mind. Norma was such a calm old soul. Nothing seemed to worry or upset her. She never complained about the pain she was in or asked for any help or support unless necessary. Even on her bucket list request she had written *'if you don't mind'* at the end.

I asked her if she had ever tried pottery in the past.

"We used to live out in the sticks - next to a farmhouse. The farmer's wife had her own pottery wheel and my sister and I were fascinated by it. We would watch her at work and then, one day, she asked if we would like to have a go. At first, I found it incredibly difficult and messy. She used to laugh at us but, with practice, I started to get the hang of it. I got to make bowls and plates, mugs and jugs. It was great fun.

I just thought, maybe, it would be lovely to have another go!"

She looked down at her hands and smiled. "If I can anyway."

I told her I had a place in mind and that, hopefully, we could set up a session or two. She was ever so excited. I spoke to Bob again the next day, and explained the situation.

"Get her over here and we will see what we can do. Despite the arthritis, she already has a grounding. The techniques will soon come back to her, I'm sure."

We set up a tutorial for the following week. My dad drove Norma and me to Greystoke and left us to potter, while he went off to potter around Penrith for the afternoon.

Bob welcomed us both inside and introduced us to other like-minded amateurs.

He explained that we would be firing pottery in the Japanese Raku style. He told us that Raku firing was one of the most dramatic and exciting ways to fire pottery. Developed in the sixteenth century, the pieces are glazed with copper-based glazes, dried and put directly into a hot kiln outside for half an hour at a temperature of approximately one thousand degrees Celsius. They would then be put into a reduction chamber, which was basically a nest of sawdust covered with a metal lid.

These temperature changes helped produce pieces unique in style and colour. Indeed, no two pieces are ever the same. Raku literally translates into 'Happiness in the accident'. He showed us some completed pieces. They were ever so beautiful. So many striking colours and intricate designs.

Norma was reluctant to hold them in case she dropped them. Bob insisted she did so in order to feel how smooth and polished they were.

Despite her condition, she clearly knew what she was doing at the wheel - unlike me. My effort to make a bowl looked more like something a dog would leave behind on a field. After a few attempts, I got there in the end. Once dried out and fired, it would have been just about possible to eat soup from my bowl without spilling any.

Norma, on the other hand, produced something far superior to mine. She was very modest, claiming it was no good, but even Bob was impressed by her first effort. We moved on to other, more intricate designs over three different sessions, and Norma absolutely loved it.

At the end of it all, we returned to The Acorns with a cardboard box full of our efforts. The glaze and colours truly did look stunning. Bob even presented Norma with one of his own designs - a vase for her window ledge. I bought her some flowers to go in it. Despite her obvious disability, she had produced pottery to be proud of once again. She was ever so pleased with her efforts. The arthritis wasn't going to beat her!

Another creative person in our group was Ann. Her long-time hobby - while her husband was out at work - was to design and make handmade greetings cards and scrapbooks for all occasions.

Ann never ventured far from home, but her ambitions stretched way beyond the town in which she spent most of her life. She told me she watched the *Dragon's Den* programme religiously, and felt she had the knowhow and the quality of product capable of selling big and making lots of money.

She always had a dream of pitching her ideas to the 'Dragons' (a collection of very wealthy individuals looking to invest in the next great idea).

Ann's hook was to offer a collection of desirable and personalised craft products that would appeal to men looking for a quick, romantic gift for their partner. She planned to call the business, **ForgetHerNot**.

Alas, her dream of appearing on the show proved to be just that - a dream - but her bucket list wish showed us that the creative fires within her hadn't died out yet!

Ann still had boxes and boxes of her designs and templates stored in her daughter's attic, and she wanted to do something with them, but had no idea what. Our accountant, Emma, suggested she set up a shop online. "There are some great websites. All you have to do is set up your own shop, upload your ideas or templates and start selling. You set up your business name, design your own logo, add a few images, and off you go. You even set the price!

People are always searching for new gift ideas. Once your business starts getting a few hits and sales, I am sure it will take off!"

Emma promised to work with Ann, and help her set up a business based on her own ideas and products. Within a few days, **ForgetHerNot** was no longer just an idea and a set of products in an attic - it was a real business. A few of us bought one or two of her listings just to get some traffic on there, but then we started to see some *'stranger sales'*.

After the first month, she had made £45.26 after paying the administration fees. In the second month, it had more than doubled, and within four months the bank account balance had topped a thousand pounds!

Who needed a dragon?

Not only did Ann prove she could be a successful businesswoman, she also proved just what a loving and caring mother she was. She insisted Emma set up an account for the profits to be transferred into each month. The monies earned were to be shared equally between her two children - a rainy day bonus fund for them, should they ever find themselves in financial difficulty.

Ann passed away about six months after setting up her business, but her legacy lived on. The money kept coming in, and her business went from strength to strength.

ForgetHerNot might have been aimed at men looking for last minute inspiration, but it was also a suitable name for the founder. Gone, but never ever forgotten.

Ann's wish came true and the consequences of her actions would live on long after her passing. Yet another beautiful reminder of just how special our residents were.

Throughout August, September and October, we worked our way through the list. Not all the wishes were extravagant or exciting. To many people, a lot of them would be considered mundane or boring - hard work even - but to each and every one of our residents, the wishes had their own special importance. As a staff, we all mucked in to help in any we could.

Kath wanted to organise a litter pick along the riverside path she used to walk along with her dog. After a call to help on our new Facebook group, we ended up with over fifty volunteers including the local Vicar, and a rock group from Haltwhistle.

The amount of rubbish collected that day was enough to fill two skips! That venture also received some local press coverage, and it even inspired a group of local teens to set up their own clean up group to help preserve wildlife and protect the local environment.

Flora's wish was simply to visit the graves of her parents in a small cemetery beside Rosley village church. That was a simple enough task in itself, but when we visited and noticed how weatherworn and overgrown the place had become, we were all determined to restore it back to its former glory.

We were like the Groundforce team! Over a period of about a month, we had cleared away the weeds and waste, planted new shrubs and trees, mowed the lawns and straightened the headstones. Local stonemason, Ian Lowes, even offered to re-carve the names and messages onto the sandstone slabs for no charge.

They looked immaculate when he had finished. Flora was so grateful. The whole cemetery looked beautiful and peaceful once again.

"Your parents would be ever so proud of you!" Vera told her.

She gushed like a young girl again. "That is all I ever wanted," she said.

Really, it was fun going through each and every challenge on the list. We played crazy golf, visited a shooting range, helped out at the RSPCA centre, acted out a scene with a local theatre group, judged a boxing match, visited an observatory to study the stars, attended yoga, judo and mandarin classes, and scaled a climbing wall. Not one individual, expert or organisation charged us for their time or effort. It was absolutely wonderful.

The bucket list chart on the office wall was covered in notes, squiggles and scrawls. More importantly, it was also covered in ticks. We had worked our way through the list and completed every single one on there. It was an incredible achievement, and one we were all so proud of. The residents were all incredibly grateful, and the bonds between us all could not have been stronger.
Completing that list was such a triumph for everyone concerned.

And yet our mission was not quite complete. Two wishes and activities were not on the list.

Two wishes had yet to be added - Leonard and Dora.

They were no longer able to express what they wanted.
We could only try and imagine what their wish would be.

So that is what we did. They were not going to be left out.

35

Community Trust

Leonard was watching television with Alasdair when his daughter Niki arrived.

We had invited her along to discuss the bucket list to see if we could find a suitable 'wish' for her dad. It wasn't going to be easy.

It was heart-breaking to see Leonard in this state. For most of his life, he had been a strong, reliable and independent man. The Alzheimer's had taken a strong hold now, and his deterioration had been rapid throughout Spring and into Summer.

Now, he rarely spoke or communicated. He ate very little, and had lost around two stone in weight over the previous couple of months. He could still walk around unaided, find his own space or wander around the gardens enjoying the summer sun, but we had to stay vigilant in case of a panic attack or a fall.

Occasionally, he would show a glimmer of his old self - a smile or a wink - but these instances were now few and far between.

Alasdair was talking away to him. The two were watching a nature programme together. Something about bird migration. I don't think either of them had a particular interest in the subject, but it was nice to see them relaxed and stress free.

Niki joined Vera and me in the office and we chewed the fat for a while before moving on to the topic in hand.

"What do you think he would still like to do? What would he enjoy, even now?" asked Vera.

"Do you know, I am not really sure. He is my dad and I love him to bits, but he was never what you would call adventurous. He tended to stay local with his friends. The world was his oyster, but he would rather have a bag of fish and chips and stay in watching television with the family, or go down to the pub with his friends."

Niki pondered some more, trying to drag up memories of her dad from when she was younger.

"He had his time in the Navy, and he loved driving the trucks up and down the country, but he was always a homebird. I know it doesn't sound very exciting."

I got thinking about my own life again. I loved my life, but there were parallels with Leonard. I hadn't travelled very far, I loved spending time in the company of my family and friends, I didn't have wild or crazy ambitions to conquer the world - or anything else for that matter. I was a homebird too. I then tried to ponder what my own wish would be, and I struggled to think of anything beyond the realms of my family and local area.

Perhaps we didn't need to.

"Considering how your dad is right now," I said, "Perhaps we ought to think closer to home. The illness is destroying the memories - the links in his brain. The strongest links will still be the ones he holds most dear, surely?"

Niki looked across at me and smiled.

"Why don't we give him a night in the pub again?"

It didn't seem like an exciting adventure, but it made sense.

"I will speak to the landlord in his favourite pub. Dad loved his darts and snooker and pool. He loved playing cards and dominos. Maybe we can have a big games night for all the locals and invite all his old friends. I'm sure they will be up for it - any excuse for a good drink and a chance to fill the place up for the night. As awful as it is to say, it will also be a chance for them all to say their goodbyes to dad. So many people ask about him. It would be lovely to take him back to the place that brought him so many good memories over the years."

So that was that. We left it in Niki's capable hands to organise.

Before she left, she nipped into the television room to join Leonard and Alasdair. Vera and I watched from a distance as she bent over to kiss him on the top of the head - her dad that is, not Alasdair.

The three of them sat together for a while watching the birds fly south. Niki held his hand in hers and stroked his arm.

It was such a tender, loving moment.

We didn't have to fly anywhere to make Leonard's wish come true. The Linton Holme Inn on Lindisfarne Street was no palace or palladium. It was a local pub, hidden away amongst crowded terraced streets and cobbled roads, but it was a special place for Leonard and that was all that mattered to us.

When Niki left, she promised to contact us again once she had spoken to the landlord of the pub and a few of his old friends.

Leonard may have been oblivious to the plans going on around him, but the others soon latched on, and the thought of a night in the pub appealed to a few of them.

"It is only right that we go along to help Lennie on his big night," said Frank. "We can help look after him...and have a few beers at the same time."

"Your doctor advised against drinking too much alcohol, young man!" Vera scalded.

"My doctor didn't specify what 'too much' was. A pint of two won't hurt. And a few chasers."

"On your head be it," she said, knowing that trying to talk him out of it was a waste of air and energy.

Frank told Ralph, Ralph told Peter, Peter told Alice, and before long the whole bloody home knew.

"We are going to need to borrow that minibus again!" Frank told me.

I tutted, but secretly I was delighted. I wasn't going to miss out on a few drinks either.

Of course, we told Leonard all about it. We explained that we were going to visit his favourite pub, and have a wonderful night with old friends, but there was no flicker of understanding or recognition on his face. Just the blank stare. I just hoped that somewhere inside that brain, he could process a little of what was being said.

Later in the day, I sat in the office with Alasdair. He had been reading the newspapers and looking online. It appeared that researchers and scientists had made a momentous breakthrough in the development of a drug designed to slow the destruction of the brain in Alzhiemer's.

Alasdair explained that Lacanemab, has been designed to attack the *beta amyloid* that builds up in the brain of people who are suffering from the disease. The beta amyloid is a type of sticky goo that develops around the neuron's and prevents links being formed. It also damages established links, hence the memory loss.

Current prescribed drugs only help manage the symptoms, but this could actually be preventative. It said the new drug was considered revolutionary by some, but it was very much in the development stage.

This revolution had arrived too late for Leonard and Dora, but for future generations there was at least some hope.

Alasdair was very excited by the news.

"It never ceases to amaze me just what goes on in these laboratories. Scientific research shapes the future. To see how much progress has been made in cancer treatment, HIV, and now Dementia, is just staggering. I take my hat off to these people. Just imagine, if this works, and they work out how to identify early signs of Alzheimer's, we could be witnessing the beginning of the end of this disease!"

It was a sobering thought and one to lift the spirits, but in the here and now, all we could do was support the people who were suffering.

Niki called us that evening. She had spoken to the landlord of the Linton and he was only too happy to help and get involved. He even invited us to the bar to help plan the night. Naturally, I volunteered to be the representative from The Acorns for this planning committee. Niki said she would sort out a get together in the week. She had also spoken to a few relatives and old friends who were equally keen to get involved. The big night was starting to take shape.

Neil, our chef, volunteered to provide a buffet for the night, Brampton Paul (Paul from Brampton) offered to put on a quiz and a karaoke, and Niall said he would sort out the minibus.

It was a twenty-two-seater, and all twenty-two seats had been booked up before we had even set a date!

Niki and I met Dave on the following Wednesday evening in the pub. The heavens opened on the drive over, and the rain was still battering down when we parked up. Neither of us had bothered to bring an umbrella, and by the time we had made the dash from the car to the pub entrance wearing our inappropriate heels, we were already dripping wet.

Dave was behind the bar when we walked in and he greeted us with a hearty laugh. He tossed a couple of tea towels our way, shaking his head and chuckling.

"Welcome to the Lint!" he said, as he guided us to a table near the fire. We were in the last throes of summer, but the temperature was definitely dropping and we were grateful for the heat.

Niki explained what we were doing and why.

"In that case," said Dave, "we need to make it a night he won't forget, so to speak. You tell me what you need at this end, and I will do what I can. The pub will be yours for the night."

We checked the calendar and settled on Saturday 16th September. That would give us time to get everything sorted.

"I want it to be like the old days for dad. Everyone having a great time together - young and old. I will invite a lot of old faces, but I want the locals and the young ones to join us too. We will provide the food and entertainment, but can I ask you to open up the pool table, the dart board, the card table and the dominos. Maximum fun and stimulation. Even if he doesn't join in, I want him to see, hear and feel everything. This was his special place. It still is."

Dave was on the same page.

"No problem, love. It has been a bit quiet here of late. We need a night like this to liven everyone up and show them the importance of their local boozer."

We left the Linton dry and energised. We had a date; we had the venue of our choice and we had a mountain of goodwill. The 16th September couldn't come quickly enough.

Everything seemed to fall into place. Niki kept in touch and she had made an incredible effort hunting down, contacting and inviting Leonard's old friends.

"Dad's old friend, Jeff, is coming," she told me. "And Syd Creighton, Big H, Black Pete, Judy, the Gibson brothers, Father Angus, Big Pig and Blinker."

It sounded like the line up for a poor man's version of Britain's Got Talent.

"The rugby lads are all coming - and the bikers. Don't worry, they don't clash. They get along just nicely, so long as they stay in their own corners of the pub," she chuckled.

I told her we had a full minibus and two full cars. The place was going to be packed out!

On the morning of the big night, Brampton Paul and Neil went along to set up the food, the karaoke and quiz tables. Dave had set aside one of the alcoves.

Niki had also found dozens of old photographs of her dad and his friends - most of them taken inside the pub. These were to be pinned up on the notice board near the entrance. Yet more reminders for Leonard of the past and his good old days.

While all this was going on, we were back at The Acorns helping our revellers decide what they were going to wear for the night.

"I'm not wearing my suit. It is meant to be a fun night out, not a funeral!" said Frank. "I'm the life and soul. I should still get into my checked, light blue shirt."

"Life and soul? Who does he think he is, Tommy Cooper?" laughed Alice.

"Alice Cooper is more like it!" Doris chipped in.

"And are you going out in that green dress?" Frank fought back. "You look like a bloody Christmas tree."

Although cutting, there was no malice in the insults, and they all just laughed it off. I felt like I was a teacher on playground duty half the time.

To be fair, they all scrubbed up well and looked very smart by the time the minibus arrived to take us to the Linton Tavern.

Bella watched from the door as we all boarded the bus. She was one of the management team, but only worked part time now as she had a young family to take care of. She offered to do this extra shift for Leonard. He was one of her favourites.

Kerry and I travelled on the bus, and one or two of the other staff followed on in the cars.

We pulled up outside the pub just before 7:30 p.m. It was still fairly light outside, but the music was already playing and the multi coloured disco lights illuminated the street. Niki was stood at the door to greet us. Leonard was sitting at the back of the bus with Doreen and he was one of the last to get off. Kerry helped him down the stairs. He stopped and stared up at the building in front of him - a building he had frequented hundreds of times before, and yet, he gave no indication that he recognised the place.

The others filed through the front door to join the throng inside. Niki linked arms with her dad. "Shall we go in ?" she said to him. He allowed himself to be led, and we followed on.

Dave had reserved a table for the main guest under the windows. From here, he had a good, clear view of the whole pub and its customers. A few people waved or called over to Leonard, raising a glass to him as they did so. Again, he just sat and stared.

Unperturbed, Niki sat with him and held his hand. She pointed at individuals around the bar and gave her dad a reminder of who they were and how he knew them.

Still nothing.

Dave brought over a pint of mixed for him - a decent froth on it, just how he used to like it. It sat in front of him, untouched, on the table while he stared around at all the commotion in front of him.

The rugby players played darts and the bikers played pool.

Neil unveiled the buffet and people tucked in while listening to some of the locals attempt to mimic Elton John and Michael Jackson on the karaoke.

Leonard watched on.

I looked over at Niki. She looked crestfallen. She so wanted to please her dad - to give him that one last night of enjoyment, but he seemed lost in his own little world. The music, the singing, the dancing, the laughter - it was no more than a sideshow now. A parallel universe for him. Memories lost.

And then...

Leonard's old pal, Jeff, came over to sit opposite him and Niki. On the table, he plonked a pack of cards.

"Fancy a game, pal? For old times' sake?"

For the first time that evening, Leonard smiled. Not a big smile or a grin, but a smile nonetheless.

"I'll shuffle," said Jeff, picking up the pack. "Let's start with something simple. Snap?"

He gave Niki a wink and started to deal for the three of them. Leonard leaned forward to collect his share of the cards. It was such a simple gesture, but it meant the world to Niki. She squeezed her dad's hand and beamed like she had won the lottery.

She turned her card. Jeff did the same...then Leonard followed suit. They continued the rounds until there were no cards left. No matching pairs that time - or a second time. It didn't matter. Leonard was there. He knew what he was doing.

And then we noticed something else. He had taken a drink from his pint. A third of the ale had disappeared from inside the glass, and he had froth on his upper lip.

To us, this was monumental - as monumental as the super drug Alasdair has talked about earlier.

Niki took some of the photographs off the wall and placed them in front of him.

He stared down at them and smiled again. We watched as he moved them around the table. He stopped at one. It was a picture of the beer garden. A summer's day taken decades earlier. I didn't recognise any of the faces in the picture. Half of them were blurred or the people in question had their back to the camera. Niki watched her dad stare at the photo for what seemed like an age.

Then he put his index finger on one of the figures in the photo. It was a young girl. She had short hair and was wearing a sleeveless, black top. He was smiling again.

Niki looked up at me, tears streaming down her face.

"That's me!" she said. "That's me under his finger."

And that was it. I started crying, Jeff started crying and everyone else watching burst into tears too - except Leonard.

He just looked down, stared and smiled. He knew.

He remembered.

The rest of the evening was a ball. The quiz went down a treat. The bikers won by a country mile, but everyone enjoyed it.

Frank was convinced Tik Tok was a clock in Beijing and argued the point well into the night. We played dominoes, bridge and charades. Ralph and Stan beat the rugby lot in a pool competition, and Doreen nearly took the barmaid's eye out playing darts.

And through it all, Leonard drank his pint, watched on and smiled.

The minibus and the cars came to collect us just before the bell chimed for last orders. We were back in The Acorns just before midnight.

Niki helped her dad up to his room, and into bed. He was fast asleep before she left.

"He remembered me," she said, before bursting into tears again.

"The strongest memories are those with the strongest links!" Alasdair said to her. He didn't need to say any more than that.

It had been yet another amazing night - another wish fulfilled.

Niki left The Acorns on top of the world as Leonard slept soundly upstairs.

Alzheimer's hadn't beaten him yet.

36

One Last Waltz

And then there was Dora.

One more wish to go to complete the bucket list for the residents of The Acorns.

As with Leonard, we decided to consult with the family to see if we could think of something – anything - that she might enjoy and appreciate.

It was no easy task. Like Leonard, Dora's condition had considerably worsened throughout 2023. She was still mobile, but she needed to be supervised whenever she decided to go for a walk. She would often sit near the conservatory window, looking out at the garden for hours. Occasionally she would cry and wail for no known reason, but in the main, she remained silent.

We made her as comfortable and as safe as possible - she wasn't in any obvious pain, and yet the tears would flow and she would be inconsolable when they did. We couldn't possibly comprehend how she was feeling or what was causing these moments of upset and anxiety. All we could do was be there for her.

In all the time she was with us, she'd never had a great appetite. At mealtimes, she would pick at her food, taking small bites or nibbles before leaving the majority on the plate. We made sure she had regular snacks throughout the day just to keep her energy levels up.

She talked to herself in whispers. A lot of the time, it was hard to decipher what she was actually saying. She would mumble or stutter. Sometimes I would hear the name of a family member or a friend, but most of the time she just made comments or gave herself simple reminders. "Time to drink", "I need to read", "What time is bedtime?", "Don't sit on that seat, it is very uncomfortable", "Rose likes milk chocolates. They are her favourites".

Most of the time, she was lost in her own world, but occasionally, like Leonard, she let us know she was still with us. Sometimes she would refer to us by our first names. This was massive, as it showed she still had an awareness of where she was and who she was with.

She would mention things that had happened earlier in the day or week. "The new rose bush looks grand", "The woodpecker is back in the garden, I see", "Shirley looks lovely today. Has she had her hair done?"

Alasdair was so proud of her. He said she was fighting it. She was small and frail, but defiant too. She was holding on to her own life - her own sanity - determined to hold the Dementia at bay as much as she could until it finally consumed her. He said the techniques we had used had worked and were still working.

Surrounding her with reminders from her happy past - photos, films, audio recordings etc. We told her the same stories over and over. We gave her ornaments and trinkets to remind her of happier times. They all helped her keep a hold of her memories.

Distant they may be, but they were still there.

Dora's daughter and granddaughter came up to visit in late September to throw some ideas down on paper. Someone suggested a visit to the RSPCA to see the dogs and cats, but we felt the noise and distress of the animals in their cages might frighten her.

Vera wondered if it would be a good idea to plot a route map of where she used to walk with her husband, but neither Amanda nor Joanne knew where to start on that one.

A tour of the police station was mentioned and then dismissed. Today's modern building was a far cry from the homely station she once knew and loved.

She had been a lady of simple pleasures. John was her life and her world. Yes, she had travelled a little. She loved Scotland. Growing up, she had caravan holidays in Oban, Fort William and Aviemore. I suggested a trip up to the mountains there, but Amanda didn't feel she would get anything from it. Again, it was the people rather than the place that made it so special for her.

We struggled to decide on anything that would tick the box, and the ladies left us that afternoon no further forward than when they arrived. This Dora was no great explorer. For most of her life, she had lived and stayed local. She had married young and settled into a happy, simple life. If she had any remaining ambitions and dreams, the Dementia locked them away in its dungeons. She was a prisoner to the disease and we had no idea how to free her.

And then something happened - or someone.

I don't really believe in fate or fortune, but a phone call from an unexpected source triggered a eureka moment.

Eli, from the Glasgow University Ballroom and Latin Dancing Society, got in touch asking if we would be interested in supporting Bas and Jennifer. The two dancers had made it to the National Ballroom Dancing Finals which were being held at King George's Hall in Blackburn, Lancashire.

After our wonderfully successful trip up to Glasgow, she wondered if we would be interested in taking a contingent down to support the pair. She said she could get us up to ten tickets if we were keen to go. It seemed like an opportunity too good to turn down. We jumped at the chance.

Vera telephoned Joanne, and she thought it would be a fantastic experience for her grandma. She loved ballroom dancing, and had really enjoyed the trip to Glasgow. If nothing else, it would be a chance to see professional dancers in full flow.

The finals were scheduled for the evening of Saturday 4th November - the day before Bonfire Night.

Rather cheekily, I asked Niall if we could borrow the minibus once again, and as usual, he was delighted to help out. "The wheels are all yours," he said. "I'm happy to be your chauffeur once again."

He asked if it would be ok to bring his wife Katy along. She loved Strictly Come Dancing on TV and as tickets for the show are almost impossible to source, this would be the next best thing.

Katy was another lady who had helped us out countless times over the years for no recompense. Like Niall, she had given up evenings and weekends to help and support the old people, and the least we could do for her was book her a place on the bus.

So, with Mr. and Mrs. McNulty on board, we still had eight tickets. Dora, obviously, would be taking one. Vera, Alasdair and myself would take another three, and Amanda and Joanne would be coming along too. That left us with two more tickets.

We knew so many of the residents would be keen to go, but we approached her two closest friends, Doreen and Alice, to see if they would like to come too. They were delighted, and the others understood, which was a huge weight off our minds as we didn't want to offend or leave anyone out.

"I had a girlfriend from Blackburn once," Frank told me. "A big fat thing she was.

A forklift truck driver in the Post Office warehouse. I used to work across the North West offices for a while."

Ignoring his sexism and insults, I was intrigued. I asked him about her, then, as usual, wished I hadn't.

"She made a beeline for me. I was a handsome young man then. She was a few years older - and a few stone heavier - than me. In for a penny, in for pound as they say. Well, over two hundred pounds I'd guess!" he laughed.

"Not exactly love!" I said, getting cross with him. "What happened?"

"She had a heart attack during sex. I must have been too much for her. I didn't realise until after the event. I thought she was just having fun. The ambulance driver wasn't happy with me, I can tell you!"

"She was ok though, wasn't she?" I pushed.

"She was fine. I wasn't though - it quite shook me up. Needless to say, I pulled the plug on that particular job. I haven't been to Blackburn since, and I don't intend to start now, even if you had a hundred free tickets!"

Throughout October, we kept in touch with Eli, and she even came down to visit us at The Acorns to hand over the tickets. It was such a lovely gesture, and everyone was so pleased to see her again. A few of them even got up to dance with her in the Keith Chegwin Suite.

She told us about the competition, and how well they had performed to get to the finals.

Nationwide, it started with two hundred couples. There were various regional heats, and Bas and Jennifer had triumphed in the West of Scotland section before beating couples from Aberdeen, Largs and Dundee to make it to the final stages. In Blackburn, there would be seven couples from all over the UK competing for the National Ballroom Dancing Winners of 2023. Each couple would have three independent dance routines to perform before the last dance, when everyone would be invited to the floor at the same time.

The compere for the evening would be none other than Julie Hill – a two times winner with her husband, Andrew. Eli told us that Julie was a goddess in ballroom dancing circles, and to have her leading the proceedings was quite a coup.

The concert hall itself was a fine venue to be hosting such a prestigious competition. It opened in 1921, eight years in the making, after the advent of World War I delayed its construction. Always a grand structure, the Grade II listed building was extensively renovated in 1994, ready to host some of the biggest names in music and entertainment.

With the main floor used for the dancing, the capacity was restricted to just over one thousand spectators in the upper and lower tiers - still more than enough to generate a rousing and exciting atmosphere.

Other than Cannon and Ball on Blackpool's North Pier, I had never been to a live show before. I felt honoured to be included in the lucky ten.

As the day itself approached, we ironed out the finer details for the trip - times, collection and drop off points, evening meals and snacks, route plans etc.

Amanda and Joanne told Dora all about the up-and-coming adventure. How much she took on board, we don't know, but they made sure she heard everything about the trip and was kept in the loop throughout.

Alasdair continued to work with her throughout the day to keep her mind stimulated and active. He would use small jigsaw puzzles, stress relief toys and music.

Occasionally she would respond by joining in, playing or just smiling. He said that it was all still progress.

She was still there. Still fighting it.

Vera bought her a new dress for the occasion - a twist waist, pleated hem, burgundy number. Amanda helped her try it on when it arrived. She looked simply stunning. Doreen presented her with a white, silk shawl. It complimented the dress perfectly.   She was going to be our star of the show.

On Saturday 4th November at 2.00 p.m. we set off to Lancashire dressed up to the nines and feeling fantastic. Even Alasdair and Niall scrubbed up well in their suits.

We looked like we were heading for a day at Ascot, not Blackburn.

Katy looked like royalty in her deep purple, chiffon and lace dress and matching cocktail hat with flower mesh ribbon and feathers.

She didn't escape Frank's gaze.

"If I were thirty years younger…"

"If you were thirty years younger, she would be a teenager, you pervert!" shouted Alice, defending her travel companion.

They all just laughed. As usual.

The journey down was straightforward enough. We stopped at Westmorland Services for a coffee and a scone. We received a few admiring glances and wolf whistles from a party of rugby players coming out of the toilets.

"Don't you worry ladies, I will defend your honour!" said Alasdair, running into the cafe before us like the coward he was.

The traffic slowed us up a little near Preston, but we pulled up at a car park around the corner from King George's Hall just after 5 p.m.

Shops were starting to shut and people were making their way home for the day. We decided to go to a bar for a drink across the road. It was a rough and ready establishment - not one used to welcoming a glamorous party like ours, but the staff were hospitable and friendly.

Dora allowed herself to be led throughout the day. She didn't show any signs of anxiety or upset despite the unfamiliar settings. Holding hands with her two favourite ladies put her at ease.

At half past six, we decided to finish our drinks and make our way over the road and inside the hall. By this time, the working folk and the shoppers had all gone home, but the area was still busy with other concert goers making their way towards the hall.

We walked up the stairs and into the reception area to show our tickets. Eli was there with others from the Glasgow Ballroom club. She told us we had some great seats beside them on the lower tier around the perimeter of the dance floor.

There was a lot of excited chatter on the way through to the seats. Eli was convinced Bas and Jennifer had as good a chance as anyone of winning the competition.

She was right about the seats – we were right on the front row to the left of the stage. What a view!

The upper tier was already packed and around the venue there was hardly a spare seat. The judge's table was on the stage and three seats sat unoccupied, awaiting their arrival. Below them was the band, calmly playing away, almost unnoticed as the crowd shuffled in.

I sat in between Vera and Joanne. Dora was two seats up from me, flanked by her daughter and granddaughter. Her eyes were everywhere. She seemed to be marvelling at the splendor of the place with all the people milling around in their finery.

Just after 7:00 p.m., as the last of the spectators took their seats, the main lights dimmed and a powerful spotlight illuminated the centre of the dance floor. Over the speaker system, we were introduced to Julie Hill.

 The band struck up, this time with more gusto and verve, as Mrs. Hill made her way onto the floor and under the spotlight to rapturous applause. She smiled and waved at the audience, and waited for them all to settle down. It was clear that the hall was full of fans and ballroom dance enthusiasts.
I felt a bit of a fraud, but it was a wonderful pleasure to actually be there.

Julie began.

"May I start by saying just how delighted I am to be here tonight."

More applause.

"I am afraid you will have to be content with just me for the evening. Andrew has the far less daunting challenge of babysitting the children tonight and, as they are both fully grown adults, I think he had the easier task!

It may surprise you to know that I am a shy and retiring lady. I am not one for the limelight - she says, standing under this spotlight in front of over a thousand people - but it is true. I had terrible butterflies in my stomach before I walked out to greet you, but something transformative happens to me once I set foot on the dance floor. I seem to grow in confidence. I feel twenty-five again! I relish the intensity of competition, and the warmth of a crowd. There is no feeling like it!"

The crowd rose to their feet and clapped and cheered.

"I'm a teaching assistant now, and that's what you call a challenging crowd!" Julie laughed.

I looked down the line at our representatives. Dora was staring at Julie, her hands clasped together. She seemed to be concentrating on her every word and movement.

"But that is enough about me for now," Julie said, smiling. "You haven't come here tonight to listen to an ageing light from the past, you are here to marvel at the stars of the present and the future, and what a show we have for you tonight. We have seven extraordinarily talented couples who will take to this very floor to entertain and amaze. Sadly, as is always the case, we can only have one winning pair and, making the difficult decisions tonight will be our panel of expert judges. Allow me to introduce you to them."

Julie invited the three onto the floor to share the adulation from the crowd. First, there was William Edgar. A suave, handsome man – a bit of mature eye candy for the ladies, Apparently, he had trained some of the best names in the business - all of whom meant nothing to me.

Sheila Templeton was next up. She grabbed the microphone from Julie, and wound the crowd up some more. Apparently, she was also a national champion way back in 1982 with her husband Norman.

The third judge cut a more reserved figure. She stood half in and half out of the spotlight before Sheila pulled her in closer. Julie introduced her as Joanne Clifford.

The crowd all rose to their feet yet again and cheered enthusiastically. I looked down the line. Doreen and Alice caught my eye and shrugged.

Eli walked down the line and crouched behind me.

"I can tell you aren't as starstruck as the majority of the crowd!" she laughed.

Again, I apologised for my ignorance, but she told me not to be so daft.

"Joanne Clifford is the ballroom guru. She is currently Chief Executive of the Ballroom Dancing Institute. If it wasn't for her passion and drive, our funding would be almost non-existent, and we wouldn't all be here today. When she was younger, she even had a hand in Torvill and Dean's Olympic gold medal win in 1984 at the Sarajevo Winter Games. It was said, she suggested they dance to the Bolero to suit their style. They had to be graceful on the dance floor before they could be graceful on the ice. She didn't take any credit for it though. She hid from the spotlight - just like she is doing now."

The judges made their way to the seats on the stage and, all of a sudden, the lights came on. The band struck up again and Julie introduced each couple. She spoke a little about who they were, which club they represented, and where they were from.

There was another Scottish lady in the group, but she was representing Sussex along with her husband, Johnny, who hailed from that area.

Julie told a few stories about each of the contestants. Apparently, Johnny's dancing career very nearly reached a premature end when he was showing off in front of the children on the trampoline. He had catapulted himself into a nearby bush, but it was more damage to pride than body on that occasion. His wife, Leigh, also had a relationship with a hedge after a horse bucked and tossed her off mid ride.

The couple from Norfolk had, at one time, got stuck in quicksand off the coast at Cromer and had to be rescued by lifeguards.

The pair from Wales once had their identities stolen, and when the local police descended on their house with police dogs in tow, they were convinced they were about to uncover the largest drugs haul Bangor had ever seen!

Even Julie had her own tale to tell. On one family holiday in Menorca, she paid a visit to the toilet while the family collected the luggage. The door handle broke off while she was inside, and she was trapped. As a claustrophobic, it was hell on earth, but the family were less than sympathetic. It took numerous maintenance men to free her, by which time she was pouring with sweat and having a nervous breakdown!

I think this was all designed to put the contestants at ease, and the stories certainly brought a bit of levity at the start of the evening.

After the tales and introductions, the couples walked to their designated seats, and awaited instruction.

Bas and Jennifer were the last out of the traps - couple number seven. They looked ever so dapper. Bas wore a pin-striped waistcoat and trousers, and a sharp, whiter than white shirt which matched his teeth. His cufflinks and silver buttons glistened in the lights. He looked incredibly handsome, but he was happy to be upstaged by his partner, Jennifer. She wore a knee length, royal blue, spandex number with a tight, white belt shaping her figure to perfection. I was in awe and riddled with jealousy. I looked at Vera and she breathed in to hide her stomach, then burst out laughing.

When they were all lined up together, Julie introduced the first dance - The Tango.

Apparently, each couple had chosen their own pieces of music to accompany their dances.

Each Tango lasted two to three minutes. The levels of concentration must have been huge so as not to put a foot wrong. The judges watched on intently. To my untrained eye, each dance looked simply perfect, but I noticed the judges shake their heads on occasion or look down to scribble something on their notepads.

The second dance, The Samba, raised the bar again. The music was more upbeat, the pace faster - more scope for fault. Each couple performed admirably again, and we, as a group, urged on Bas and Jennifer. They were doing Glasgow proud!

The third dance was The Waltz. Eli told us it would all come down to this one.

The final dance - the whole group one - was little more than a novelty for old fashioned watchers who liked to see the dance floor full. There was still a lot of skill involved, and nobody wanted to stand out in the wrong way by bumping into others or stepping out of line, but the judges would be deciding on the winner after The Waltz.

At the end of the dancing, all the couples received a huge and well-deserved standing ovation. They acknowledged the crowd and went back to sit in their seats to await the result.

In third place was the couple from Cornwall - Bobby and Dorothy. From the smiles on their faces, you got the impression they were happy with their final position. They collected their medals and a £250 voucher from Julie.

"In second place..." Julie began. We all held our breath. "Second place goes to Bas and Jennifer from Glasgow."

We exhaled.

It only took a second or two to get over the disappointment, and we all stood to cheer them onto the dance floor to collect their medals and prize money.

£1,000 was better than a kick in the teeth!

Sussexes finest, Leigh and Johnny, picked up the prize as national champions. Julie said the scores had been very close and the standard exceptionally high. It was hard to disagree.

The winners walked away with gold medals and a cheque for £5,000.

"He can get a new trampoline with some of that money!" laughed Katy.

It had been a truly memorable night for all involved. The band played on as the crowds started to file out. The judges, and Julie, retired to their changing rooms backstage, and the competitors joined their friends, family and fellow club members.

We all walked over to congratulate Bas and Jennifer. They were exhausted.

The physical and mental strain showed and the two of them slumped into a couple of chairs nearby - tired but happy.

The place emptied quite quickly, and we were one of the last parties in the room. The side lights were still on, and the huge spotlight continued to shine down on the centre of the dance floor where Julie had stood last.

But now there was another figure under the light.

Dora had shuffled away from Amanda and Joanne as they chatted, and she stood right in the centre of the floor, swaying from side to side to the rhythm of the band.

Alasdair spotted her too and dashed over to the band to encourage them to keep playing.

I was the nearest one to her and, instinctively, I walked over to join her. I held out my right hand and she held it with her left. I was a few inches taller than her, but not enough to make it awkward or uncomfortable.
I felt her right hand cup the small of my back, and we moved

from side to side. I held her in the same way.

All the others were watching now, including the contingent from Glasgow.

We started The Waltz Box Step - the moves we had been taught on our day up to Scotland. I was amazed I still remembered them. Forward, side, close, back, side, close. One, two, three, one two three.

It sounds so simple but I felt like I was all over the place. Dora wasn't though. She guided me, and we soon found our rhythm.

One, two, three.

"Follow me, John," she whispered.

One, two, three.

"The dogs are fine. All fed and happy."

One, two, three.

"I'm ok aren't I john? I haven't let you down, have I?"

One, two, three.

I didn't know what to say or what to do. I was in shock. Alasdair nodded and encouraged me on.

One, two, three.

"You haven't let anyone down," I said. "You are amazing!"

One, two, three.

She smiled.

"I do love you, John. With all my heart."

One, two, three.

"And I love you too. You are the best wife a man could have."

One, two, three.

She smiled again, and gripped my waist a little tighter.

"You are my world."

One, two, three.

The tears poured down my face, and I looked over to the others for support. They were all crying too. Katy desperately tried to stop her mascara from blotching, but it was too little, too late.

One, two, three.

Alasdair shook his head in wonder. Doreen and Alice linked arms and shared tissues.

One, two, three.

Amanda and Joanne watched on from the side - dumbstruck.

When the music stopped and the spotlight went off, we stopped dancing. Dora stood looking up at the ceiling. The moment had passed.

Her girls rushed forward to hug her, and guide her back to the side chairs.

Vera ran over and hugged me.

"No more now," she sobbed. "We have completed the list. Everyone ticked off. We did it. We all made it happen."

I hugged her back and didn't want to let go.

"We did it. She did it."

It was a moment I will never, ever forget.

Life, love and loss all there in one precious moment.

We made our way back to the minibus before setting off back north. The older ones slept most of the way back. Like babies.

It had been such a wonderful night.

37

A New Chapter

Leonard passed away on the 9th January 2024 - Dora just over a fortnight later.

They had spent the last few weeks of their lives in the Eden Valley Hospice. Both died peacefully in their sleep. For that, we couldn't ask anymore.

We were used to residents coming and going, but in many ways, their passing marked the end of an eventful chapter for The Acorns.

With every end, there was a new beginning, and it was not long before a new batch of residents filled the vacant slots. There were some characters among them too.

Celia hailed from Jamaica. She was a larger-than-life character with a booming, infectious laugh. Her son was a doctor at the hospital in Carlisle, and he adored his mother. He would visit the home regularly, and was always on hand if we needed any help, advice or support.

Then there was Toby who was a master story and joke teller. When he joined us, he was eighty-nine, but acted like he was still a teen. He was a breath of fresh air.

We welcomed new staff too. Young Elsa joined us straight from college. She struck up a great friendship with Courtenay, and the two of them were adored by the residents.

Alasdair and Vera got engaged in the Spring. He proposed right in the middle of the Keith Chegwin Suite just after the evening meal. We were all so pleased for them both.

Things were changing, but they were still good. I loved working at The Acorns. I know I could have worked elsewhere for more money and promotion opportunities, but I didn't want to leave. Ever. This was not just my workplace - it was my second home.

And yet some things never change. Frank. A few months older, but no wiser. He sat beside me outside on the new patio chairs one day in April. I waited for him to speak.

"Is it just me, or are you starting to get a double chin?"

I didn't rise to it.

I watched him put on his sunglasses and stretch out on the lounger, biding my time.

"Liquorice toffee?" I said, holding out the bag. "I do love these."

"I knew it was you who stole mine, you little bugger!" he laughed.

I sat back in my chair and smiled. He wasn't going to get the better of me.

I looked around the garden at the flowers and trees. I could hear the insects and the birds. I could hear laughter and chatter. People were wandering around, going about their business.

Life. Everywhere.

I popped a toffee in my mouth, and closed my eyes.

When I am old and close to my end, I want to be here. I want to be a resident at The Acorns.

My home.

ONE LAST WALTZ

Acknowledgements

Writing the acknowledgements page is never easy, as I am always terrified that I will forget to thank someone who has helped me stumble over the finish line.
I suppose that is why I like to include so many people I know and love within the story itself. It is my way of thanking them for being so supportive throughout the whole process. A way to show people that they are in my thoughts and that they are very much appreciated.

Finding my mistakes is an arduous task for those willing to give up their time to do so. For that, I would like to thank Emma, Gillian and Jacquii.
Jacquii's technical support has also been invaluable. Without her expertise, the text would probably be all over the place and the cover picture upside down!

I would like to thank all the shops and businesses mentioned for giving me permission to include them within the story. Their help, support and advice has been invaluable.

One Last Waltz is a story about the importance of life.
Along the bumpy road from the cradle to the grave, we all experience highs and lows - good times and bad.
We love, we live, we grieve, we celebrate, we laugh and we cry.

During the research for this book, I have gone through all those emotions, and a dozen more besides.

Talking to people about their own lives has been a pleasure and a privilege. To be allowed to share someone's memories (and include them as part of the story) has been an honour, and I hope I have done justice to each and every one of you.

The Acorns is a fictional home. I am aware that not all
establishments housing the elderly are like The Acorns
- conditions and facilities vary from place to place – but
maybe they should strive to be.
It is certainly a place I would like to go to end my days.

Finally, I would like to mention The Alzheimer's Society.
I have agreed to donate 20% of any royalties earned from this
book to this charity.

Treasure the people who mean the world to you. We are all
just here for a short amount of time.
What would be on your bucket list?

PS

Printed in Great Britain
by Amazon

32126396R00215